Praise for #1 *New York Times* bestselling author

NORA ROBERTS

"The publishing world might be hard-pressed to find an author with a more diverse style or fertile imagination than Roberts."
—*Publishers Weekly*

"Roberts is indeed a word artist, painting her story and her characters with vitality and verve."
—*Los Angeles Daily News*

"You can't bottle wish fulfillment, but Nora Roberts certainly knows how to put it on the page."
—*New York Times*

"Roberts...is at the top of her game."
—*People* magazine

"Roberts has a warm feel for her characters and an eye for the evocative detail."
—*Chicago Tribune*

"Roberts' bestselling novels are some of the best in the romance genre. They are thoughtfully plotted, well-written stories featuring fascinating characters."
—*USA TODAY*

Dear Reader,

When love is on the line, what *won't* you do? That is what these two couples have to ask themselves in these classic romances from beloved author Nora Roberts. Their journeys to each other will keep you turning the pages!

She was known as the ice princess. He could set hearts ablaze with a single glance. When old flames Asher Wolfe and Ty Starbuck reunite after years apart, they find that *Opposites Attract* once again. Yet while their chemistry is undeniable, secrets from their past threaten to tear them apart. Can they set aside old hurts and misunderstandings and start a new life—before it's too late?

When two rival journalists pursuing the story of their careers are forced to be *Partners,* things are sure to get intense—in more ways than one! While investigating a New Orleans murder case, the spark of attraction between Lauren Armand and Matthew Bates is fanned to a blaze. Add to this the killer who's on their trail, and the heat is *definitely* on, as Lauren and Matthew risk everything for life and love.

We hope these stories encourage you to go the distance in your own lives when hearts are at stake and you're *Playing for Keeps!*

The Editors
Silhouette Books

NORA ROBERTS

Playing for Keeps

Silhouette® Books ™
Published by Silhouette Books
America's Publisher of Contemporary Romance

SILHOUETTE BOOKS

PLAYING FOR KEEPS

ISBN-13: 978-0-373-28166-4

This edition published by arrangement with Harlequin Books S.A.

For questions and comments about the quality of this book, please contact us at CustomerService@Harlequin.com.

Visit Silhouette Books at www.Harlequin.com

Printed in U.S.A.

CONTENTS

Also available from Silhouette Books and Harlequin Books by

NORA ROBERTS

THE MACGREGOR GROOMS
Three bachelors find true love...
when they aren't even looking!

MYSTERIOUS
Things aren't always as they seem...
when it comes to matters of the heart

A DAY AWAY
Sometimes love is just around the bend...

FIRST IMPRESSIONS
Indulge in the warmth and sweetness of true love!

GOLDEN SHORES
Could the one thing you've been searching
for be right before your eyes?

CAPTIVATED & ENTRANCED
Two classic tales about the truest magic of all...*love*

And coming soon,
CHARMED & ENCHANTED

Be sure to look for more Nora Roberts titles
in your local stores, or contact our
Harlequin Reader Service Center,
U.S.A.: 3010 Walden Avenue
P.O. Box 1325, Buffalo, NY 14269
Canada: P.O. Box 609, Fort Erie, Ontario L2A 5X3
Visit Silhouette Books at www.Harlequin.com

OPPOSITES ATTRACT

For Joan Schulhafer,
leader of tours, handler of details and good friend

Chapter 1

"Advantage, Starbuck."

Isn't it always? Asher mused. For a moment the large arena held that humming silence peculiar to indoor sports events. There was an aroma of roasted peanuts and sweat. The overhead lights heated the scent somewhat pleasantly while the crush of bodies added enforced camaraderie. A small child sent up a babbling complaint and was hushed.

Seated several rows back at mid-court, Asher Wolfe watched Ty Starbuck—tennis master, Gypsy, eternal boy of summer and former lover. She thought again, as she had several times during more than two hours of play, that he'd changed. Just how wasn't yet completely clear. More than three years had passed since she'd seen him in the flesh. But he hadn't aged, or thickened, or lost any of his characteristic verve.

Rarely over the years had she watched a televised match—it was too painful. Too many faces were familiar, with his the most strictly avoided. If Asher had chanced to come across a write-up or picture of him in the sports pages or in a gossip column, she had immediately put it aside. Ty Starbuck was out of her life. Her decision. Asher was a very decisive woman.

Even her decision to come to the U.S. Indoor Tennis Championship had been a cool-headed one. Before making this trip, she had carefully weighed the pros and cons. In the end logic had won. She was getting back into the game herself. On the circuit, meetings with Ty would be unavoidable. She would see him now, letting the press, her colleagues and fans see clearly that there was nothing left of what had been three years before. Ty would see too, and, she hoped fervently, so would she.

Ty stood behind the baseline, preparing to serve. His stance was the same, she mused, as was his sizzling concentration. He tossed the ball up, coming back and over with the wicked left-handed serve that had become synonymous with his name, a Starbuck.

Asher heard the explosion of his breath that forced the power into it. She held her own. A lesser player than the Frenchman, Grimalier, would never have gotten a racket on the ball. His return was quick—force meeting force—and the rally began.

The crowd grew noisier as the ball smashed and thudded. Echoes bounced crazily. There were cries of encouragement, shouts of appreciation for the prowess of the two players. Ty's basic entertainment value hadn't decreased since Asher had been out of the game. Fans adored or detested him, but they never, never ignored him. Nor could she, though she was no longer certain which category she fell into. Every muscle of his body was familiar to her, every move, every expression. Her feelings were a confused jumble of respect, admiration and longing, which swirled to reach a vortex of pain, sharply remembered. Still, she was caught up in him again. Ty Starbuck demanded every last emotion and didn't really give a damn if it was love or hate.

Both men moved quickly, their eyes riveted on the small white sphere. Backhand, forehand, drop shot. Sweat poured down unheeded. Both the game and the fans demanded it. A tennis buff wanted to see the effort, the strain, wanted to hear the grunts and whistling breaths, wanted to smell the sweat. Despite her determination to remain dispassionate, Asher found herself watching Ty with the undiluted admiration she'd held for him for more than ten years.

He played with nonchalant flash—contradictory terms, but there it was. Strength, agility, form—he had them all. He had a long, limber body, seemingly elastic until the muscles flowed and bunched. His six-two height gave him an advantage of reach, and he could twist and turn on a dime. He played like a fencer—Asher had always thought a swashbuckler. Graceful sweeps, lunges, parries, with an almost demonic glint in his dusk-gray eyes. His face was that of the adventurer—narrow, rakish, with a hint of strong bone vying with an oddly tender mouth. As always, his hair was a bit too long, flowing wild and black around a white sweatband.

He was a set up, and held advantage, but he played as though his life depended on this one point. That hadn't changed, Asher thought, as her heart pounded at double time. She was as involved in the match as if she were the one with the racket in her hand and the sweat rolling over her skin. Her palms were slick, her own muscles tight. Tennis involved its onlookers. Starbuck absorbed them. That hadn't changed either.

Ty smashed the ball crosscourt at the sideline. It careened away even as the Frenchman dove toward it. Asher sucked in her breath at the speed and placement of the ball.

"Wide," the line judge said dispassionately. A loud complaint poured out of the crowd. Asher fixed her eyes on Ty and waited for the explosion.

He stood, breathing hard from the punishing rally, his eyes fixed on the judge. The crowd continued to roar disapproval as deuce was called. Slowly, his eyes still on the judge, Ty swiped his wristband over his brow. His face was inscrutable but for his eyes, and his eyes spoke volumes. The crowd quieted to a murmur of speculation. Asher bit hard on her bottom lip. Ty walked back to the baseline without having uttered a sound.

This was the change, Asher realized with a jolt. Control. Her breath came out slowly as the tension in her shoulders diminished. In years past, Ty Starbuck would have hurled abuse—and an occasional racket—snarled, implored the crowd for support or berated them. Now he walked silently across the service court with temper smoldering in his eyes. But he held it in check. This was something new.

Behind the baseline Ty took his time, took his stance, then cracked an ace, like a bullet from a gun. The crowd screamed for him. With a quiet, insolent patience he waited while the scoring was announced. Again, he held advantage. Knowing him, and others like him, Asher was aware that his mind was occupied with his next move. The ace was already a memory, to be taken out and savored later. He still had a game to win.

The Frenchman connected with the next serve with a blazing forehand smash. The volley was sweating, furious and blatantly male. It was all speed and fire, two pirates blasting at each other across a sea of hardwood. There was the sound of the ball hitting the heart of the racket, the skid of rubber soles on wood, the grunts of the competitors as they drew out more force, all drowned beneath the echoes of cheers. The crowd was on its feet. Asher was on hers without even being aware of it. Neither man gave quarter as the seconds jumped to a minute, and a minute to more.

With a swing of the wrist the Frenchman returned a nearly impossible lob that drove him behind the baseline. The ball landed deep in the right court. With a forceful backhand Ty sent the ball low and away from his opponent, ending the two-and-a-half-hour match, three sets to one.

Starbuck was the U.S. Indoor Tennis champion, and the crowd's hero.

Asher let the enthusiasm pour around her as Ty walked to the net for the traditional handshake. The match had affected her more than she'd anticipated, but she passed this off as professional admiration. Now she allowed herself to wonder what his reaction would be when he saw her again.

Had she hurt him? His heart? His pride? The pride, she mused. That she could believe. The heart was a different matter. He would be angry, she concluded. She would be cool. Asher knew how to maintain a cool exterior as well as she knew how to smash an overhead lob. She'd learned it all as a child. When they met, she would simply deploy his temper. She had been preparing for the first encounter almost as religiously as she had been preparing to pick up her profession again. Asher was going to win at both. After he had finished with the showers and the press, she would make it a point to seek him out. To congratulate him—and to present the next test. It was much wiser for her to make the first move, for her to be the one prepared. Confident, she watched Ty exchange words with Grimalier at the net.

Then Ty turned his head very slowly, very deliberately. With no searching through the crowd, no hesitation, his eyes locked on hers. The strength of the contact had her drawing in a sharp, unwilling breath. His eyes held, no wavering. Her mouth went dry. Then he smiled, an unpleasant, direct challenge. Asher met it, more from shock than temerity as the crowd bellowed his name. *Starbuck* echoed from the walls like a litany. Ten seconds—fifteen—he neither blinked nor moved. For a man of action he had an uncanny ability for stillness. Boring into hers, his eyes made the distance between them vanish. The smile remained fixed. Just as Asher's palms began to sweat, he turned a full circle for the crowd, his racket above his head like a lance. They adored him.

He'd known, Asher thought furiously as people swarmed around her. He had known all along that she was there. Her anger wasn't the hot, logical result of being outmaneuvered, but small, silver slices of cold fury. Ty had let her know in ten seconds, without words, that the game was still on. And he always won.

Not this time though, she told herself. She had changed too. But she stood where she was, rooted, staring out at the now empty court. Her thoughts were whirling with memories, emotions, remembered sensations. People brushed by her, already debating the match.

She was a tall, reed-slim figure tanned gold from hours in the sun. Her hair was short, sculptured and misty-blond. The style flattered, while remaining practical for her profession. Over three years of retirement, Asher hadn't altered it. Her face seemed more suited to the glossy pages of a fashion magazine than the heat and frenzy of a tennis court. A weekender, one might think, looking at her elegant cheekbones in an oval face. Not a pro. The nose was small and straight above a delicately molded mouth she rarely thought to tint. Makeup on the courts was a waste of time, as sweat would wash it away. Her eyes were large and round, a shade of blue that hinted at violet. One of her few concessions to vanity was to darken the thick pale lashes that surrounded them. While other women competitors added jewelry or ribbons and bows to the court dress, Asher had never thought of it. Even off the court her attire leaned toward the simple and muted.

An enterprising reporter had dubbed her "The Face" when she had been eighteen. She'd been nearly twenty-three when she had retired from professional play, but the name had stuck. Hers was a face of great beauty and rigid control. On court, not a flicker of expression gave her opponent or the crowd a hint of what she was thinking or feeling. One of her greatest defenses in the game was her ability to remain unruffled under stress. The standard seeped into her personal life.

Asher had lived and breathed tennis for so long that the line of demarcation between woman and athlete was smudged. The hard, unbendable rule, imposed by her father, was ingrained into her—privacy, first and last. Only one person had ever been able to cross the boundary. Asher was determined he would not do so again.

As she stood staring down at the empty court, her face told nothing of her anger or turmoil—or the pain she hadn't been prepared for. It was calm and aloof. Her concentration was so deep that the leader of the small packet of people that approached her had to speak her name twice to get her attention.

She'd been recognized, she discovered. Though Asher had known it was inevitable, it still gave her a twist of pleasure to sign the papers and programs thrust at her. She hadn't been forgotten.

The questions were easy to parry, even when they skirted close to her relationship with Ty. A smile and double-talk worked well with fans. Asher wasn't naïve enough to think it would work with reporters. That, she hoped, was for another day.

As she signed, and edged her way back, Asher spotted a few colleagues—an old foe, a former doubles partner, a smattering of faces from the past. Her eyes met Chuck Prince's. Ty's closest friend was an affable player with a wrist of steel and beautiful footwork. Though the silent exchange was brief, even friendly, Asher saw the question in his eyes before she gave her attention to the next fan.

The word's out, she thought almost grimly as she smiled at a teenage tennis buff. Asher Wolfe's picking up her racket again. And they'd wonder, and eventually ask, if she was picking up Ty Starbuck too.

"Asher!" Chuck moved to her with the same bouncy stride he used to cross a court. In his typical outgoing style he seized her by the shoulders and kissed her full on the mouth. "Hey, you look terrific!"

With a laugh Asher drew back the breath his greeting had stolen from her. "So do you." It was inevitably true. Chuck was average in almost every way—height, build, coloring. But his inner spark added appeal and a puckish sort of sexuality. He'd never hesitated to exploit it—good-naturedly.

"No one knew you were coming," Chuck complained, easing her gently through the thinning crowd. "I didn't know you were here until..." His voice trailed off so that Asher knew he referred to the ten seconds of potent contact with Ty. "Until after the match," he finished. He gave her shoulder a quick squeeze. "Why didn't you give someone a call?"

"I wasn't entirely sure I'd make it." Asher allowed herself to be negotiated to a clear spot in a rear hallway. "Then I thought I'd just melt into the crowd. It didn't seem fair to disrupt the match with any the-prodigal-returns business."

"It was a hell of a match." The flash of teeth gleamed with enthusiasm. "I don't know if I've ever seen Ty play better than he did in the last set. Three aces."

"He always had a deadly serve," Asher murmured.

"Have you seen him?"

From anyone else the blunt question would have earned a cold stare. Chuck earned a quick grimace. "No. I will, of course, but I didn't want to distract him before the match." Asher linked her fingers—an old nervous habit. "I didn't realize he knew I was here."

Distract Starbuck, she thought with an inner laugh. No one and nothing distracted him once he picked up his game racket.

"He went crazy when you left."

Chuck's quiet statement brought her back. Deliberately she unlaced her fingers. "I'm sure he recovered quickly." Because the retort was sharper than she had intended, Asher shook her head as if to take back the words. "How have you been? I saw an ad with you touting the virtues of a new line of tennis shoes."

"How'd I look?"

"Sincere," she told him with a quick grin. "I nearly went out and bought a pair."

He sighed. "I was shooting for macho."

As the tension seeped out of her, Asher laughed. "With that face?" She cupped his chin with her hand and moved it from side to side. "It's a face a mother could trust—foolishly," she added.

"Shh!" He glanced around in mock alarm. "Not so loud, my reputation."

"Your reputation suffered a few dents in Sydney," she recalled. "What was that—three seasons ago? The stripper."

"Exotic dancer," Chuck corrected righteously. "It was merely an exchange of cultures."

"You did look kind of cute wearing those feathers." With another laugh she kissed his cheek. "Fuchsia becomes you."

"We all missed you, Asher." He patted her slim, strong shoulder.

The humor fled from her eyes. "Oh, Chuck, I missed you. Everyone, all of it. I don't think I realized just how much until I walked in here today." Asher looked into space at her own thoughts, her own memories. "Three years," she said softly.

"Now you're back."

Her eyes drifted to his. "Now I'm back," she agreed. "Or will be in two weeks."

"The Foro Italico."

Asher gave him a brief smile that was more determination than joy. "I've never won on that damn Italian clay. I'm going to this time."

"It was your pacing."

The voice from behind her had Asher's shoulders stiffening. As she faced Chuck her eyes showed only the merest flicker of some secret emotion before they calmed. When she turned to Ty he saw first that his memory of her beauty hadn't been exaggerated with time, and second that her layer of control was as tough as ever.

"So you always told me," she said calmly. The jolt was over, she reasoned, with the shock of eye contact in the auditorium. But her stomach muscles tightened. "You played beautifully, Ty...after the first set."

They were no more than a foot apart now. Neither could find any changes in the other. Three years, it seemed, was barely any time at all. It occurred to Asher abruptly that twenty years wouldn't have mattered. Her heart would still thud, her blood would still swim. For him. It had always, would always be for him. Quickly she pushed those thoughts aside. If she were to remain calm under his gaze, she couldn't afford to remember.

The press were still tossing questions at him, and now at her as well. They began to crowd in, nudging Asher closer to Ty. Without a word he took her arm and drew her through the door at his side. That it happened to be a woman's rest room didn't faze him as he turned the lock. He faced her, leaning lazily back against the door while Asher stood straight and tense.

As he had thirty minutes before, Ty took his time studying her. His eyes weren't calm, they rarely were, but the emotion in them was impossible to decipher. Even in his relaxed stance there was a sense of force, a storm brewing. Asher met his gaze levelly, as he expected. And she moved him. Her power of serenity always moved him. He could have strangled her for it.

"You haven't changed, Asher."

"You're wrong." Why could she no longer breathe easily or control the furious pace of her heart?

"Am I?" His brows disappeared under his tousled hair for a moment. "We'll see."

He was a very physical man. When he spoke, he gestured. When he held a conversation, he touched. Asher could remember the brush of his hand—on her arm, her hair, her shoulder. It had been his casualness that had drawn her to him. And had driven her away. Now, as they stood close, she was surprised that Ty did not touch her in any way. He simply watched and studied her.

"I noticed a change," she countered. "You didn't argue with the referees or shout at the line judge. Not once." Her lips curved slightly. "Not even after a bad call."

He gave her a lightly quizzical smile. "I turned over that leaf some time ago."

"Really?" She was uncomfortable now, but merely moved her shoulders. "I haven't been keeping up."

"Total amputation, Asher?" he asked softly.

"Yes." She would have turned away, but there was nowhere to go. Over the line of sinks to her left the mirrors tossed back her reflection…and his. Deliberately she shifted so that her back was to them. "Yes," she repeated, "it's the cleanest way."

"And now?"

"I'm going to play again," Asher responded simply. His scent was reaching out for her, that familiar, somehow heady fragrance that was sweat and victory and sex all tangled together. Beneath the placid expression her thoughts shot off in a tangent.

Nights, afternoons, rainy mornings. He'd shown her everything a man and woman could be together, opened doors she had never realized existed. He had knocked down every guard until he had found her.

Oh God, dear God, she thought frantically. Don't let him touch me now. Asher linked her fingers together. Though his eyes never left hers, Ty noted the gesture. And recognized it. He smiled.

"In Rome?"

Asher controlled the urge to swallow. "In Rome," she agreed. "To start. I'll go in unseeded. It has been three years."

"How's your backhand?"

"Good." Automatically she lifted her chin. "Better than ever."

Very deliberately Ty circled her arm with his fingers. Asher's palms became damp. "It was always a surprise," he commented, "the power in that slender arm. Still lifting weights?"

"Yes."

His fingers slid down until they circled the inside of her elbow. It gave him bitter pleasure to feel the tiny pulse jump erratically. "So," he murmured softly, "Lady Wickerton graces the courts again."

"Ms. Wolfe," Asher corrected him stiffly. "I've taken my maiden name back."

His glance touched on her ringless hands. "The divorce is final?"

"Quite final. Three months ago."

"Pity." His eyes had darkened with anger when he lifted them back to hers. "A title suits you so well. I imagine you fit into an English manor as easily as a piece of Wedgwood. Drawing rooms and butlers," he murmured, then scanned her face as if he would memorize it all over again. "You have the looks for them."

"The reporters are waiting for you." Asher made a move to her left in an attempt to brush by him. Ty's fingers clamped down.

"Why, Asher?" He'd promised himself if he ever saw her again, he wouldn't ask. It was a matter of pride. But pride was overwhelmed by temper as the question whipped out, stinging them both. "Why did you leave that way? Why did you run off and marry that damn English jerk without a word to me?"

She didn't wince at the pressure of his fingers, nor did she make any attempt to pull away. "That's my business."

"*Your* business?" The words were hardly out of her mouth before he grabbed both her arms. "*Your* business? We'd been together for months, the whole damn circuit that year. One night you're in my bed, and the next thing I know you've run off with some English lord." His control slipped another notch as he shook her. "I had to find out from my sister. You didn't even have the decency to dump me in person."

"Decency?" she tossed back. "I won't discuss decency with you, Ty." She swallowed the words, the accusations she'd promised herself never to utter. "I made my choice," she said levelly, "I don't have to justify it to you."

"We were lovers," he reminded her tightly. "We lived together for nearly six months."

"I wasn't the first woman in your bed."

"You knew that right from the start."

"Yes, I knew." She fought the urge to beat at him with the hopeless rage that was building inside her. "I made my choice then, just as I made one later. Now, let me go."

Her cool, cultured control had always fascinated and infuriated him. Ty knew her, better than anyone, even her own father—certainly better than her ex-husband. Inside, she was jelly, shuddering convulsively, but outwardly she was composed and lightly disdainful. Ty wanted to shake her until she rattled. More, much more, he wanted to taste her again—obliterate three years with one long greedy kiss. Desire and fury hammered at him. He knew that if he gave in to either, he'd never be able to stop. The wound was still raw.

"We're not finished, Asher." But his grip relaxed. "You still owe me."

"No." Defensive, outraged, she jerked free. "No, I don't owe you anything."

"Three years," he answered, and smiled. The smile was the same biting challenge as before. "You owe me three years, and by God, you're going to pay."

He unlocked the door and opened it, stepping back so that Asher had no choice but to meet the huddle of reporters head-on.

"Asher, how does it feel to be back in the States?"

"It's good to be home."

"What about the rumors that you're going to play professionally again?"

"I intend to play professionally beginning with the opening of the European circuit in Rome."

More questions, more answers. The harsh glare of a flash causing light to dance in front of her eyes. The press always terrified her. She could remember her father's constant instructions: Don't say any more than absolutely necessary. Don't let them see what you're feeling. They'll devour you.

Churning inside, Asher faced the pack of avid reporters with apparent ease. Her voice was quiet and assured. Her fingers were locked tightly together. With a smile she glanced quickly down the hall, searching for an escape route. Ty leaned negligently against the wall and gave her no assistance.

"Will your father be in Rome to watch you play?"

"Possibly." An ache, a sadness, carefully concealed.

"Did you divorce Lord Wickerton so you could play again?"

"My divorce has nothing to do with my profession." A half-truth, a lingering anger, smoothly disguised.

"Are you nervous about facing young rackets like Kingston and old foes like Martinelli?"

"I'm looking forward to it." A terror, a well of doubt, easily masked.

"Will you and Starbuck pair up again?"

Fury, briefly exposed.

"Starbuck's a singles player," she managed after a moment.

"You guys'll have to keep your eyes open to see if that changes." With his own brand of nonchalance, Ty slipped an arm around Asher's rigid shoulders. "There's no telling what might happen, is there, Asher?"

Her answer was an icy smile. "You've always been more unpredictable than I have, Ty."

He met the smile with one of his own. "Have I?" Leaning down, he brushed her lips lightly. Flashbulbs popped in a blaze of excitement. Even as their lips met, so did their eyes. Hers were twin slits of fury, his grimly laughing and ripe with purpose. Lazily he straightened. "The Face and I have some catching up to do."

"In Rome?" a reporter cracked.

Ty grinned and quite deliberately drew Asher closer. "That's where it started."

Chapter 2

Rome. The Colosseum. The Trevi fountain. The Vatican. Ancient history, tragedy and triumphs. Gladiators and competition. In the Foro Italico the steaming Italian sun beat down on the modern-day competitors just as it had on those of the Empire. To play in this arena was a theatrical experience. It was sun and space. There were lush umbrella pines and massive statues to set the forum apart from any other on the circuit. Beyond the stadium, wooded hills rose from the Tiber. Within its hedge trimmings, ten thousand people could chant, shout and whistle. Italian tennis fans were an emotional, enthusiastic and blatantly patriotic lot. Asher hadn't forgotten.

Nor had she forgotten that the Foro Italico had been the setting for the two biggest revelations in her life: her consuming love for tennis, her overwhelming love for Ty Starbuck.

She had been seven the first time she had watched her father win the Italian championship in the famed *campo central.* Of course she had seen him play before. One of her earliest memories was of watching her tall, tanned father dash around a court in blazing white. Jim Wolfe had been a champion before Asher had been born, and a force to be reckoned with long after.

Her own lessons had begun at the age of three. With her shortened racket she had hit balls to some of the greatest players of her father's generation. Her looks and her poise had made her a pet among the athletes. She grew up finding nothing unusual about seeing her picture in the paper or bouncing on the knee of a Davis Cup champion. Tennis and travel ruled her world. She had napped in the rear of limousines and walked across the pampered grass of Wimbledon. She had curtsied to heads of state and had her cheek pinched by a president. Before she began attending school she had already crossed the Atlantic a half dozen times.

But it had been in Rome, a year after the death of her mother, that Asher Wolfe had found a life's love and ambition.

Her father had still been wet and glowing from his victory, his white shorts splattered with the red dust of the court, when she had told him she would play in the *campo central* one day. And win.

Perhaps it had been a father's indulgence for his only child, or his ambition. Or perhaps it had been the quietly firm determination he saw in seven-year-old eyes. But Asher's journey had begun that day, with her father as her guide and her mentor.

Fourteen years later, after her own defeat in the semi-finals, Asher had watched Starbuck's victory.

There had been nothing similar in the style of her father and the style of the new champion. Jim Wolfe had played a meticulous game—cold control with the accent on form. Starbuck played like a fireball—all emotion and muscle. Often, Asher had speculated on what the results would be if the two men were to meet across a net. Where her father brought her pride, Ty brought her excitement. Watching him, she could understand the sense of sexuality onlookers experienced during a bullfight. Indeed, there was a thirst for blood in his style that both alarmed and fascinated.

Ty had pursued her doggedly for months, but she had held him off. His reputation with women, his temper, his flamboyance and nonconformity had both attracted and repulsed her. Though the attraction was strong, and her heart was already lost, Asher had sensibly listened to her head. Until that day in May.

He'd been like a god, a powerful, mythological warrior with a strength and power that even the biased Italian crowd couldn't resist. Some cheered him, some cheerfully cursed him. He'd given them the sweat they had come to see. And the show.

Ty had taken the championship in seven frenzied sets. That night Asher had given him both her innocence and her love. For the first time in her life she had allowed her heart complete freedom. Like a blossom kept in the sheltered, controlled climate of a hothouse, she took to the sun and storm wildly. Days were steamier and more passionate—nights both turbulent and tender. Then the season had ended.

Now, as Asher practiced in the early morning lull on court five, the memories stirred, sweet and bitter as old wine. Fast rides on back roads, hot beaches, dim hotel rooms, foolish laughter, crazy loving. Betrayal.

"If you dream like that this afternoon, Kingston's going to wipe you out of the quarter-finals."

At the admonishment, Asher snapped back. "Sorry."

"You should be, when an old lady drags herself out of bed at six to hit to you."

Asher laughed. At thirty-three, Madge Haverbeck was still a force to be reckoned with across a net. Small and stocky, with flyaway brown hair and comfortably attractive features, she looked like an ad for home-baked cookies. She was, in fact, a world-class player with two Wimbledon championships, a decade of other victories that included the Wightman Cup and a wicked forehand smash. For two years Asher had been her doubles partner to their mutual satisfaction and success. Her husband was a sociology professor at Yale whom Madge affectionately termed "The Dean."

"Maybe you should sit down and have a nice cup of tea," Asher suggested while tucking her tongue in her cheek. "This game's rough on middle-aged matrons."

After saying something short and rude, Madge sent a bullet over the net. Light and agile, Asher sprang after it. Her concentration focused. Her muscles went to work. In the drowsy morning hum the ball thudded on clay and twanged off strings. Madge wasn't a woman to consider a practice workout incidental. She hustled over the court, driving Asher back to the baseline, luring her to the net, hammering at her by mixing her shots while Asher concentrated on adjusting her pace to the slow, frustrating clay.

For a fast, aggressive player, the surface could be deadly. It took strength and endurance rather than speed. Asher thanked the endless hours of weight lifting as she swung the racket again and again. The muscles in the slender arm were firm.

After watching one of Asher's returns scream past, Madge shifted her racket to her left hand. "You're pretty sharp for three years off, Face."

Asher filled her lungs with air. "I've kept my hand in."

Though Madge wondered avidly about Asher's marriage and years of self-imposed retirement, she knew her former partner too well to question. "Kingston hates to play the net. It's her biggest weakness."

"I know." Asher slipped the spare ball in her pocket. "I've studied her. Today she's going to play my game."

"She's better on clay than grass."

It was a roundabout way of reminding Asher of her own weakness. She gave Madge one of her rare, open smiles. "It won't matter. Next week I'm playing center court."

Slipping on a warm-up jacket, Madge gave a hoot of laughter. "Haven't changed much, have you?"

"Bits and pieces." Asher dabbed at sweat with her wristband. "What about you? How're you going to play Fortini?"

"My dear." Madge fluffed at her hair. "I'll simply overpower her."

Asher snorted as they strolled off the court. "You haven't changed either."

"If you'd told me you were coming back," Madge put in, "we'd be playing doubles. Fisher's good, and I like her, but..."

"I couldn't make the decision until I was sure I wouldn't make a fool of myself." Slowly Asher flexed her racket arm. "Three years, Madge. I ache." She sighed with the admission. "I don't remember if I ached like this before."

"We can trade legs any time you say, Face."

Remembering, Asher turned with a look of concern. "How's the knee?"

"Better since the surgery last year." Madge shrugged. "I can still forecast rain though. Here's to a sunny season."

"I'm sorry I wasn't there for you."

Madge hooked her arm through Asher's in easy comradeship. "Naturally I expected you to travel six thousand miles to hold my hand."

"I would have if…" Asher trailed off, remembering the state of her marriage at the time of Madge's surgery.

Recognizing guilt, Madge gave Asher a friendly nudge with her elbow. "It wasn't as big a deal as the press made out. Of course," she added with a grin, "I milked it for a lot of sympathy. The Dean brought me breakfast in bed for two months. Bless his heart."

"Then you came back and demolished Rayski in New York."

"Yeah." Madge laughed with pleasure. "I enjoyed that."

Asher let her gaze wander over the serene arena, quiet but for the thud of balls and hum of bees. "I have to win this one, Madge. I need it. There's so much to prove."

"To whom?"

"Myself first." Asher moved her shoulders restlessly, shifting her bag to her left hand. "And a few others."

"Starbuck? No, don't answer," Madge continued,

seeing Asher's expression out of the corner of her eye. "It just sort of slipped out."

"What was between Ty and me was finished three years ago," Asher stated, deliberately relaxing her muscles.

"Too bad." Madge weathered Asher's glare easily. "I like him."

"Why?"

Stopping, Madge met the direct look. "He's one of the most alive people I know. Ever since he learned to control his temper, he brings so such emotion to the courts. It's good for the game. You don't have a stale tournament when Starbuck's around. He also brings that same emotion into his friendships."

"Yes," Asher agreed. "It can be overwhelming."

"I didn't say he was easy," Madge countered. "I said I liked him. He is exactly who he is. There isn't a lot of phony business to cut through to get to Starbuck." Madge squinted up at the sun. "I suppose some of it comes from the fact that we turned pro the same year, did our first circuit together. Anyway, I've watched him grow from a cocky kid with a smart mouth to a cocky man who manages to keep that wicked temper just under the surface."

"You like him for his temper?"

"Partly." The mild, homey-looking woman smiled. "Starbuck's just plain strung right, Asher. He's not a man you can be ambivalent about. You're either for him or against him."

It was as much inquiry as statement. Saying nothing, Asher began to walk again. Ambivalence had never entered into her feeling for Ty.

On his way home from his own practice court Ty

watched them. More accurately he watched Asher. While she remained unaware of him, he could take in every detail. The morning sun glinted down on her hair. Her shoulders were strong and slender, her gait long, leggy and confident. He was grateful he could study her now with some dispassion.

When he had looked out and had seen her in the stands two weeks before, it had been like catching a fast ball with his stomach. Shimmering waves of pain, shock, anger, one sensation had raced after the other. He had blown the first set.

Then he had done more than pull himself together. He had used the emotions against his opponent. The Frenchman hadn't had a chance against Ty's skill combined with three years of pent-up fury. Always, he played his best under pressure and stress. It fed him. With Asher in the audience the match had become a matter of life and death. When she had left him she'd stolen something from him. Somehow, the victory had helped him regain a portion of it.

Damn her that she could still get to him. Ty's thoughts darkened as the distance between them decreased. Just looking at her made him want.

He had wanted her when she had been seventeen. The sharp, sudden desire for a teenager had astonished the then twenty-three-year-old Ty. He had kept a careful distance from her all that season. But he hadn't stopped wanting her. He had done his best to burn the desire out by romancing women he considered more his style—flamboyant, reckless, knowledgeable.

When Asher had turned twenty-one Ty had abandoned common sense and had begun a determined, almost obsessive pursuit. The more she had evaded him, the firmer she refused, the stronger his desire had grown. Even the victory, tasted first in Rome, hadn't lessened his need.

His life, which previously had had one focus, then had realigned with two dominating forces. Tennis and Asher. At the time he wouldn't have said he loved tennis, but simply that it was what and who he was. He wouldn't have said he loved Asher, but merely that he couldn't live without her.

Yet he had had to—when she'd left him to take another man's name. A title and a feather bed, Ty thought grimly. He was determined to make Asher Wolfe pay for bringing him a pain he had never expected to feel.

By turning left and altering his pace Ty cut across her path, apparently by chance. "Hi, Madge." He gave the brunette a quick grin, flicking his finger down her arm before turning his attention fully to Asher.

"Hiya, Starbuck." Madge glanced from the man to the woman and decided she wasn't needed. "Hey, I'm late," she said by way of explanation, then trotted off. Neither Asher nor Ty commented.

From somewhere in the surrounding trees Asher heard the high clear call of a bird. Nearer at hand was the slumberous buzz of bees and dull thud of balls. On court three, someone cursed fluently. But Asher was conscious only of Ty beside her.

"Just like old times," he murmured, then grinned at her expression. "You and Madge," he added.

Asher struggled not to be affected. The setting had too many memories. "She hit to me this morning. I hope I don't have to face her in the tournament."

"You go against Kingston today."

"Yes."

He took a step closer. In her mind's eye Asher saw the hedge beside her. With Ty directly in her path, dignified retreat was impossible. For all her delicacy of looks, Asher didn't run from a battle. She linked her fingers, then dragged them apart, annoyed.

"And you play Devereux."

His acknowledgment was a nod. "Is your father coming?"

"No." The answer was flat and brief. Ty had never been one to be put off by a subtle warning.

"Why?"

"He's busy." She started to move by him, but succeeded only in closing the rest of the distance between them. Maneuvering was one of the best aspects of Ty's game.

"I've never known him to miss one of your major tournaments." In an old habit he couldn't resist nor she prevent, he reached for her hair. "You were always his first order of business."

"Things change," she responded stiffly. "People change."

"So it seems." His grin was sharp and cocky. "Will your husband be here?"

"Ex-husband." Asher tossed her head to dislodge his hand. "And no."

"Funny, as I recall he was very fond of tennis." Casually he set down his bag. "Has that changed too?"

"I need to shower." Asher had drawn nearly alongside of him before Ty stopped her. His hand slipped to her waist too quickly and too easily.

"How about a quick set for old times' sake?"

His eyes were intense—that oddly compelling color that was half night and half day. Asher remembered how they seemed to darken from the pupils out when he was aroused. The hand at her waist was wide-palmed and long-fingered—a concert pianist's hand, but it was rough and worked. The strength in it would have satisfied a prizefighter.

"I don't have time." Asher pushed to free herself and connected with the rock-hard muscles of his forearm. She pulled her fingers back as though she'd been burned.

"Afraid?" There was mockery and a light threat with the overtones of sex. Her blood heated to the force she had never been able to fully resist.

"I've never been afraid of you." And it was true enough. She had been fascinated.

"No?" He spread his fingers, drawing her an inch closer. "Fear's one of the popular reasons for running away."

"I didn't run," she corrected him. "I left." *Before you did,* she added silently. For once, she had outmaneuvered him.

"You still have some questions to answer, Asher." His arm slid around her before she could step back. "I've waited a long time for the answers."

"You'll go on waiting."

"For some," he murmured in agreement. "But I'll have the answer to one now."

She saw it coming and did nothing. Later she would curse herself for her passivity. But when he lowered his mouth to hers, she met it without resistance. Time melted away.

He had kissed her like this the first time—slowly, thoroughly, gently. It was another part of the enigma that a man so full of energy and turbulence could show such sensitivity. His mouth was exactly as Asher remembered. Warm, soft, full. Perhaps she had been lost the first time he had kissed her—drawn to the fury—captured by the tenderness. Even when he brought her closer, deepening the kiss with a low-throated groan, the sweetness never diminished.

As a lover he excelled because beneath the brash exterior was an underlying and deep-rooted respect for femininity. He enjoyed the softness, tastes and textures of women, and instinctively sought to bring them pleasure in lovemaking. As an inherent loner, it was another contradiction that Ty saw a lover as a partner, never a means to an end. Asher had sensed this from the first touch so many years ago. Now she let herself drown in the kiss with one final coherent thought. It had been so long.

Her arm, which should have pushed him away, curved up his back instead until her hand reached his shoulders. Her fingers grasped at him. Unhesitatingly she pressed her body to his. He was the one man who could touch off the passion she had so carefully locked inside. The only man who had ever reached her core and gained true intimacy—the meeting of minds as well as of bodies. Starved for the glimpses of joy she remembered, Asher clung while her mouth moved avidly on his. Her greed for more drove away all her reserve, and all her promises.

Oh, to be loved again, truly loved, with none of the emptiness that had haunted her life for too long! To give herself, to take, to know the pure, searing joy of belonging! The thoughts danced in her mind like dreams suddenly remembered. With a moan, a sigh, she pressed against him, hungry for what had been.

The purpose of the kiss had been to punish, but he'd forgotten. The hot-blooded passion that could spring from the cool, contained woman had forced all else from his mind but need. He needed her, still needed her, and was infuriated. If they had been alone, he would have taken her and then faced the consequences. His impulses were still difficult to control. But they weren't alone. Some small part of his mind clung to reality even while his body pulsed. She was soft and eager. Everything he had ever wanted. All he had done without. Ty discovered he had gotten more answers than he'd bargained for.

Drawing her away, he took his time studying her face. Who could resist the dangerous power of a hurricane? The wicked, primitive rumblings of a volcano? She stared at him, teetering between sanity and desire.

Her eyes were huge and aware, her lips parted breathlessly. It was a look he remembered. Long nights in her bed, hurried afternoons or lazy mornings, she would look at him so just before loving. Hot and insistent, desire spread, then closed like a fist in his stomach. He stepped back so that they were no longer touching.

"Some things change," he remarked. "And some things don't," he added before turning to walk away.

There was time for deep breathing before Asher took her position for the first serve. It wasn't the thousand pairs of eyes watching around the court that had her nerves jumping. It was one pair, dark brown and intense, seventy-eight feet away. Stacie Kingston, age twenty, hottest newcomer to the game in two years. She had energy, force and drive, along with a fierce will to win. Asher recognized her very well. The red clay spread out before her, waiting.

Because she knew the importance of mastering the skittish nerves and flood of doubts, she continued to take long, deep breaths. Squeezing the small white ball, Asher discovered the true meaning of trial by fire. If she won, here where she had never won before, three years after she had last lifted a racket professionally, she would have passed the test. Rome, it seemed, would always be her turning point.

Because it was the only way, she blocked out the past, blocked out tomorrow and focused wholly on the contest. Tossing the ball up, she watched the ascent, then struck home. Her breath came out in a hiss of effort.

Kingston played a strong, offensive game. A studied, meticulous player, she understood and used the personality of clay to her advantage, forcing Asher to the baseline again and again. Asher found the dirt frustrating. It cut down on her speed. She was hurrying, defending herself. The awareness of this only made her rush more. The ball eluded her, bouncing high over her head when she raced to the net, dropping lazily into the forecourt when she hugged the baseline. Unnerved by her own demons, she double-faulted. Kingston won the first game, breaking Asher's serve and allowing her only one point.

The crowd was vocal, the sun ferocious. The air was thick with humidity. From the other side of the hedge Asher could hear the games and laughter of schoolchildren. She wanted to throw aside her racket and walk off the court. It was a mistake, a mistake, her mind repeated, to have come back. Why had she subjected herself to this again? To the effort and pain and humiliation?

Her face was utterly passive, showing none of the turmoil. Gripping the racket tightly, she fought off the weakness. She had played badly, she knew, because she had permitted Kingston to set the pace. It had taken Asher less than six minutes from first service to defeat. Her skin wasn't even damp. She hadn't come back to give up after one game, nor had she come back to be humiliated. The stands were thick with people watching, waiting. She had only herself.

Flicking a hand at the short skirt of her tennis dress, she walked back to the baseline. Crouched, she shifted her weight to the balls of her feet. Anger with herself was forced back. Fear was conquered. A cool head was one of her greatest weapons, and one she hadn't used in the first game. This time, she was determined. This time, the game would be played her way.

She returned the serve with a drop shot over the net that caught Kingston off balance. The crowd roared its approval as the ball boy scurried across the court to scoop up the dead ball.

Love-fifteen. Asher translated the scoring in her head with grim satisfaction. Fear had cost her the first game. Now, in her own precise way, she was out for blood. Kingston became more symbol than opponent.

Asher continued to draw her opponent into the net, inciting fierce volleys that brought the crowd to its feet. The roar and babble of languages did not register with her. She saw only the ball, heard only the effortful breathing that was hers. She ended that volley with a neatly placed ball that smacked clean at the edge of the baseline.

Something stirred in her—the hot, bubbling juice of victory. Asher tasted it, reveled in it as she walked coolly back to position. Her face was wet now, so she brushed her wristband over her brow before she cupped the two service balls in her hand. Only the beginning, she told herself. Each game was its own beginning.

By the end of the first set the court surface was zigzagged with skid marks. Red dust streaked the snowy material of her dress and marked her shoes. Sweat rolled down her sides after thirty-two minutes of ferocious play. But she'd taken the first set six-three.

Adrenaline was pumping madly, though Asher looked no more flustered than a woman about to hostess a dinner party. The competitive drives she had buried were in complete control. Part of her sensed Starbuck was watching. She no longer cared. At that moment Asher felt that if she had faced him across the net, she could have beaten him handily. When Kingston returned her serve deep, Asher met it with a topspin backhand that brushed the top of the net. Charging after the ball, she met the next return with a powerful lob.

The sportswriters would say that it was at that moment, when the two women were eye to eye, that Asher won the match. They remained that way for seconds only, without words, but communication had been made. From then Asher dominated, forcing Kingston into a defensive game. She set a merciless pace. When she lost a point she came back to take two. The aggressiveness was back, the cold-blooded warfare the sportswriters remembered with pleasure from her early years on the court.

Where Starbuck was fire and flash, she was ice and control. Never once during a professional match had

Asher lost her iron grip on her temper. It had once been a game among the sportswriters—waiting for The Face to cut loose.

Only twice during the match did she come close to giving them satisfaction, once on a bad call and once on her own poor judgment of a shot. Both times she stared down at her racket until the urge to stomp and swear had passed. When she had again taken her position, there had been nothing but cool determination in her eyes.

She took the match six-three, six-one, six-two in an hour and forty-nine minutes. Twice she had held Kingston's service to love. Three times she had served aces—something Kingston with her touted superserve had been unable to accomplish. Asher Wolfe would go on to the semi-finals. She had made her comeback.

Madge dropped a towel over Asher's shoulders as she collapsed on her chair. "Good God, you were terrific! You destroyed her." Asher said nothing, covering her face with the towel a moment to absorb sweat. "I swear, you're better than you were before."

"She wanted to win," Asher murmured, letting the towel drop limply again. "I *had* to win."

"It showed," Madge agreed, giving her shoulder a quick rub. "Nobody'd believe you haven't played pro in three years. I hardly believe it myself."

Slowly Asher lifted her face to her old partner. "I'm not in shape yet, Madge," she said beneath the din of the still-cheering crowd. "My calves are knotted. I don't even know if I can stand up again."

Madge skimmed a critical glance over Asher's features. She couldn't detect a flicker of pain. Bending, she scooped up Asher's warm-up jacket, then draped it over Asher's shoulders. "I'll help you to the showers. I don't play for a half hour. You just need a few minutes on the massage table."

Exhausted, hurting, Asher started to agree, then spotted Ty watching her. His grin might have been acknowledgment of her victory. But he knew her, Asher reflected, knew her inside as no one else did.

"No thanks, I'll manage." Effortfully she rose to zip the cover around her racket. "I'll see you after you beat Fortini."

"Asher—"

"No, really, I'm fine now." Head high, muscles screaming, she walked toward the tunnel that led to the locker rooms.

Alone in the steam of the showers, Asher let herself empty, weeping bitterly for no reason she could name.

Chapter 3

It was the night after her victory in the semi-finals that Asher confronted Ty again. She had kept herself to a rigorous schedule of practice, exercise, press, and play. Her pacing purposely left her little time for recreation. Practice was a religion. Morning hours were spent in the peaceful tree-shaded court five, grooving in, polishing her footwork, honing her reflexes.

Exercise was a law. Push-ups and weight lifting, stretching and hardening the muscles. Good press was more than a balm for the ego. Press was important to the game as a whole as well as the individual player. And the press loved a winner.

Play was what the athlete lived for. Pure competition—the testing of the skills of the body, the use of the skills of the mind. The best played as the best dancers danced—for the love of it. During the days of her second debut, Asher rediscovered love.

In her one brief morning meeting with Ty she had rediscovered passion. Only her fierce concentration on her profession kept her from dwelling on a need that had never died. Rome was a city for lovers—it had been once for her. Asher knew that this time she must think of it only as a city for competition if she was to survive the first hurdle of regaining her identity. Lady Wickerton was a woman she hardly recognized. She had nearly lost Asher Wolfe trying to fit an image. How could she recapture herself if she once again became Starbuck's lady?

In a small club in the Via Sistina where the music was loud and the wine was abundant, Asher sat at a table crowded with bodies. Elbows nudged as glasses were reached for. Liquor spilled and was cheerfully cursed. In the second and final week of the Italian Open, the tension grew, but the pace mercifully slowed.

Rome was noise, fruit stands, traffic, outdoor cafés. Rome was serenity, cathedrals, antiquity. For the athletes it was days of grueling competition and nights of celebration or commiseration. The next match was a persistent shadow over the thoughts of the winners and the losers. As the music blared and the drinks were poured, they discussed every serve, every smash and error and every bad call. Rome was blissfully indolent over its reputation for bad calls.

"Long!" A dark, lanky Australian brooded into his wine. "That ball was inside by two inches. Two bloody inches."

"You won the game, Michael," Madge reminded him

philosophically. "And in the second game of the fifth set, you had a wide ball that wasn't called."

The Australian grinned and shrugged. "It was only a little wide." He brought his thumb and forefinger close together at the good-natured razzing of his peers. "What about this one?" His gesture was necessarily shortened by the close quarters as he lifted a drink toward Asher. "She beats an Italian in the Foro Italico, and the crowd still cheers her."

"Breeding," Asher returned with a mild smile. "The fans always recognize good breeding."

Michael snorted before he swallowed the heavy red wine. "Since when does a bloody steamroller need breeding?" he countered. "You flattened her." To emphasize his point he slammed a palm down on the table and ground it in.

"Yeah." Her smile widened in reminiscent pleasure. "I did, didn't I?" She sipped her dry, cool wine. The match had been longer and more demanding than her first with Kingston, but her body had rebelled a bit less afterward. Asher considered it a double victory.

"Tia Conway will go for your jugular," he said pleasantly, then called to his countrywoman at a nearby table. "Hey, Tia, you gonna beat this nasty American?"

A dark, compact woman with striking black eyes glanced over. The two women measured each other slowly before Tia lifted her glass in salute. Asher responded in kind before the group fell back to its individual conversations. With the music at high volume, they shouted to be heard, but words carried only a foot.

"A nice woman," Michael began, "off the court. On it, she's a devil. Off, she grows petunias and rosemary. Her husband sells swimming pools."

Madge chuckled. "You make that sound like a misdemeanor."

"I bought one," he said ruefully, then looked back at Asher. She was listening with half an ear to the differing opinions on either side of her of a match by two players. "Still, if I played mixed doubles, I'd want Face for a partner." Asher acknowledged this with a curious lift of a brow. "Tia plays like a demon, but you have better court sense. And," he added as he downed more wine, "better legs."

For this Madge punched him in the shoulder. "What about me?"

"You have perhaps the best court sense of any female world-class player," Michael decided slowly. "But," he continued as Madge accepted her due with a regal nod, "you have legs like a shotputter."

A roar of laughter rose up over Madge's indignation. Asher leaned back in her chair, enjoying the loosening freedom of mirth as Madge challenged Michael to show his own and be judged. At that moment Asher's eyes locked with Ty's. Her laughter died unnoticed by her companions.

He'd come in late and alone. His hair was unruly, as though he had ridden in a fast car with the top down. Even completely relaxed, dressed in jeans, his hands in his pockets, some aura of excitement swirled around him. In the dim light his face was shadowed, all hollows and planes, with his eyes dark and knowing. No woman could be immune to him. A former lover was helpless not to remember what magic his mouth could perform.

Asher sat still as a stone—marble, pale and elegant in the rowdy, smoke-curtained bar. She couldn't forget any more than she could stop wanting. All she could do was refuse, as she had three years before.

Without taking his eyes from hers Ty crossed the room, skirted crowded tables. He had Asher by the arm, drawing her to her feet before the rest of the group had greeted him.

"We'll dance." It was a command formed in the most casual tones. As on court, Asher's decision had to be made in a tenth of a second. To refuse would have incited speculative gossip. To agree meant she had her own demons to deal with.

"I'd love to," she said coolly, and went with him.

The band played a slow ballad at ear-splitting volume. The vocalist was flat, and tried to make up for it by being loud. Someone knocked a glass off a table with a splintering crash. There was a pungent scent of spilled wine. A bricklayer argued with a Mexican tennis champion on the proper way to handle a topspin lob. Someone was smoking a pipe filled with richly sweet cherry tobacco. The floorboards were slightly warped.

Ty gathered her into his arms as though she had never been away. "The last time we were here," he murmured in her ear, "we sat at that corner table and drank a bottle of Valpolicella."

"I remember."

"You wore the same perfume you're wearing now." His lips grazed her temple as he drew her closer. Asher felt the bones in her legs liquefy, the muscles in her thighs loosen. "Like sun-warmed petals." Her heartbeat was a light, uncertain flutter against his. "Do you remember what we did afterward?"

"We walked."

The two hoarsely spoken words seemed to shiver

along his skin. It was impossible to keep his mouth from seeking small tastes of her. "Until sunrise." His breath feathered intimately at her ear. "The city was all rose and gold, and I wanted you so badly, I nearly exploded. You wouldn't let me love you then."

"I don't want to go back." Asher tried to push away, but his arms kept her pressed tight against him. It seemed every line of his body knew every curve of hers.

"Why? Because you might remember how good we were together?"

"Ty, stop it." She jerked her head back—a mistake as his lips cruised lazily over hers.

"We'll be together again, Asher." He spoke quietly. The words seemed to sear into the tender flesh of her lips. "Even if it's only once…for old times' sake."

"It's over, Ty." The claim was a whisper, the whisper unsteady.

"Is it?" His eyes darkened as he pressed her against him almost painfully. "Remember, Asher, I know you, inside out. Did your husband ever find out who you really are? Did he know how to make you laugh? How," he added in a low murmur, "to make you moan?"

She stiffened. The music whirled around them, fast now with an insistent bass beat. Ty held her firmly against him, barely swaying at all. "I won't discuss my marriage with you."

"I damn well don't want to know about your *marriage.*" He said the word as if it were an obscenity as his fingers dug into the small of her back. Fury was taking over though he'd sworn he wouldn't let it. He could still get to her. Yes, yes, that was a fact, he knew, but no more than she could still get to him. "Why did you come back?" he demanded. "Why the hell did you come back?"

"To play tennis." Her fingers tightened on his shoulder. "To win." Anger was growing in her as well. It appeared he was the only man who could make her forget herself enough to relinquish control. "I have every right to be here, every right to do what I was trained to do. I don't owe you explanations."

"You owe me a hell of a lot more." It gave him a certain grim satisfaction to see the fury in her eyes. He wanted to push. Wanted to see her anger. "You're going to pay for the three years you played lady of the manor."

"You don't know anything about it." Her breath came short and fast. Her eyes were nearly cobalt. "I paid, Starbuck, I paid more than you can imagine. Now I've finished, do you understand?" To his surprise, her voice broke on a sob. Quickly she shook her head and fought back tears. "I've finished paying for my mistakes."

"What mistakes?" he demanded. Frustrated, he took her by the shoulders. "What mistakes, Asher?"

"You." She drew in her breath sharply, as if stepping back from a steep edge. "Oh, God, you."

Turning, she fought her way through the swarm of enthusiastic dancers. Even as she sprang out into the sultry night Ty whirled her around. "Let me go!" She struck out blindly, but he grabbed her wrist.

"You're not going to walk out on me again." His voice was dangerously low. "Not ever again."

"Did it hurt your pride, Ty?" Emotion erupted from her, blazing as it could only from one who constantly denied it. "Did it hurt your ego that a woman could turn her back on you and choose someone else?"

Pain ripped through him and took over. "I never had

your kind of pride, Asher." He dragged her against him, needing to prove he had some kind of power over her, even if it was only physical. "The kind you wear so that no one can see you're human. Did you run because I knew you? Because in bed I could make you forget to be the perfect lady?"

"I left because I didn't want you!" Completely unstrung, she shouted, pounding with her free hand. "I didn't want—"

He cut her off with a furious kiss. Their tempers soared with vivid passion. Anger sizzled in two pairs of lips that clung because they were helpless to do otherwise. There was never any choice when they were together. It had been so almost from the first, and the years had changed nothing. She could resist him, resist herself, for only so long. The outcome was inevitable.

Suddenly greedy, Asher pressed against him. Here was the sound and the speed. Here was the storm. Here was home. His hair was thick and soft between her questing fingers, his body rock-hard against the firmness of hers. His scent was his "off-court" fragrance—something sharp and bracing that she'd always liked.

The first taste was never enough to satisfy her, so she probed deeper into his mouth, tongue demanding, teeth nipping in the way he himself had taught her. A loud crash of brass from the band rattled the windows behind them. Asher heard only Ty's moan of quiet desperation. Between the shadows and the moonlight they clung, passion building, old needs merging with new.

Her breath trembled into the night as he took a crazed journey of her face. His hands slid up until his thumbs hooked gently under her chin. It was a familiar habit, one of his more disarming. Asher whispered his name half in plea, half in acceptance before his mouth found hers again. He drew her into him, slowly, inevitably, while his fingers skimmed along her cheekbones. The more tempestuous the kiss, the more tender his touch. Asher fretted for the strong, sure stroke of his hands on her body.

Full circle, she thought dizzily. She had come full circle. But if once before in Rome she had been frightened when his kisses had drained and exhilarated her, now she was terrified.

"Please, Ty." Asher turned her head until her brow rested on his shoulder. "Please, don't do this."

"I didn't do it alone," he muttered.

Slowly she lifted her head. "I know."

It was the vulnerability in her eyes that kept him from dragging her back to him. Just as it had been her vulnerability all those years before that had prevented him taking her. He had waited for her to come to him. The same would hold true this time, he realized. Cursing potently under his breath, Ty released her.

"You've always known how to hold me off, haven't you, Asher?"

Knowing the danger had passed, she let out an unsteady breath. "Self-preservation."

Ty gave an unexpected laugh as his hands dove for his pockets. "It might have been easier if you'd managed to get fat and ugly over the last three years. I wanted to think you had."

A hint of a smile played on her mouth. So his moods could change, she thought, just as quickly as ever. "Should I apologize for not accommodating you?"

"Probably wouldn't have made any difference if you had." His eyes met hers again, then roamed her face.

"Just looking at you—it still takes my breath away." His hands itched to touch. He balled them into fists inside his pockets. "You haven't even changed your hair."

This time the smile bloomed. "Neither have you. You still need a trim."

He grinned. "You were always conservative."

"You were always unconventional."

He gave a low appreciative laugh, one she hadn't heard in much too long. "You've mellowed," he decided. "You used to say radical."

"*You've* mellowed," Asher corrected him. "It used to be true."

With a shrug he glanced off into the night. "I used to be twenty."

"Age, Starbuck?" Sensing a disturbance, Asher automatically sought to soothe it.

"Inevitably." He brought his eyes back to hers. "It's a young game."

"Ready for your rocking chair?" Asher laughed, forgetting caution as she reached up to touch his cheek. Though she snatched her hand away instantly, his eyes had darkened. "I—" She searched for a way to ease the fresh tension. "You didn't seem to have any problem smashing Bigelow in the semi-finals. He's what, twenty-four?"

"It went to seven sets." His hand came out of his pocket. Casually he ran the back of it up her throat.

"You like it best that way."

He felt her swallow quickly, nervously, though her eyes remained level. "Come back with me, Asher," he murmured. "Come with me now." It cost him to ask, but only he was aware of how much.

"I can't."

"Won't," he countered.

From down the street came a high-pitched stream of Italian followed by a bellow of laughter. Inside the club the band murdered a popular American tune. She could smell the heat-soaked fragrance of the window-box geraniums above their heads. And she could remember, remember too well, the sweetness that could be hers if she crossed the line. And the pain.

"Ty." Asher hesitated, then reached up to grasp the hand that lingered at her throat. "A truce, please. For our mutual benefit," she added when his fingers interlaced possessively with hers. "With us both going into the finals, we don't need this kind of tension right now."

"Save it for later?" He brought her reluctant hand to his lips, watching her over it. "Then we pick this up in Paris."

"I didn't mean—"

"We deal now or later, Face, but we deal." He grinned again, tasting challenge, tasting victory. "Take it or leave it."

"You're just as infuriating as ever."

"Yeah." The grin only widened. "That's what keeps me number one."

On an exasperated laugh, Asher let her hand relax in his. "Truce, Starbuck?"

He let his thumb glide back and forth over her knuckles. "Agreed, on one condition." Sensing her withdrawal, he continued. "One question, Asher. Answer one question."

She tried to wrest her hand away and failed. "What question?" she demanded impatiently.

"Were you happy?"

She became very still as quick flashes of the past raced through her head. "You have no right—"

"I have every right," he interrupted. "I'm going to know that, Asher. The truth."

She stared at him, wanting to pit her will against his. Abruptly she found she had no energy for it. "No," she said wearily. "No."

He should have felt triumph, and instead felt misery. Releasing her hand, he stared out at the street. "I'll get you a cab."

"No. No, I'll walk. I want to walk."

Ty watched her move into the flood of a streetlight and back into the dark. Then she was a shadow, disappearing.

The streets were far from empty. Traffic whizzed by at the pace that seemed the pride of European cities. Small, fast cars and daredevil taxis. People scattered on the sidewalks, rushing toward some oasis of nightlife. Still, Ty thought he could hear the echo of his own footsteps.

Perhaps it was because so many feet had walked the Roman streets for so many centuries. Ty didn't care much for history or tradition. Tennis history perhaps—Gonzales, Gibson, Perry, these names meant more to him than Caesar, Cicero or Caligula. He rarely thought of his own past, much less of antiquity. Ty was a man who focused on the present. Until Asher had come back into his life, he had thought little about tomorrow.

In his youth he had concentrated fiercely on the future, and what he would do if… Now that he had done it, Ty had come to savor each day at a time. Still, the future was closing in on him, and the past was never far behind.

At ten he had been a hustler. Skinny and streetwise, he had talked his way out of trouble when it was possible, and slugged his way out when it wasn't. Growing up in the tough South Side of Chicago, Ty had been introduced to the seamier side of life early. He'd tasted his first beer when he should have been studying rudimentary math. What had saved him from succumbing to the streets was his dislike and distrust of organized groups. Gangs had held no appeal for Ty. He had no desire to lead or to follow. Still, he might have chosen a less honorable road had it not been for his unquestioning love for his family.

His mother, a quiet, determined woman who worked nights cleaning office buildings, was precious to him. His sister, four years his junior, was his pride and self-assumed responsibility. There was no father, and even the memory of him had faded before Ty reached mid-childhood. Always, he had considered himself the head of the family, with all the duties and rights that it entailed. No one corrected him. It was for his family that he studied and kept on the right side of the law—though he brushed the line occasionally. It was for them that he promised himself, when he was still too young to realize the full extent of his vow, to succeed. One day he would move them out, buy them a house, bring his mother up off her knees. The picture of how hadn't been clear, only the final result. The answer had been a ball and racket.

Ada Starbuck had given her son a cheap, nylon-stringed racket for his tenth birthday. The gift had been an impulse. She had been determined to give the boy something other than the necessary socks and underwear. The racket, such as it was, had been a gesture of hope. She could see too many of her neighbors' children fall into packs. Ty, she knew, was different. A loner. With the racket he could entertain himself. A baseball or football required someone to catch or pass. Now Ty could use a concrete wall as his partner. And so he did—at first for lack of something better to do. In the alley between apartment buildings he would smash the ball against a wall scrawled with spray paint. DIDI LOVES FRANK and other less romantic statements littered his playing field.

He enjoyed setting his own rhythm, enjoyed the steady thud, thump, smash he could make. When he became bored with the wall, he began haunting the neighborhood playground courts. There, he could watch teenagers or middle-aged weekenders scramble around the courts. He hustled pennies retrieving balls. Deciding he could do better than the people he watched, Ty badgered an older boy into a game.

His first experience on a court was a revelation. A human forced you to run, sent balls over your head or lined them at you with a speed a stationary wall couldn't match. Though he lost handily, Ty had discovered the challenge of competition. And the thirst to win.

He continued to haunt the courts, paying more attention to details. He began to select the players who took the game seriously. Possessing quite a bit of charm even at that age, Ty talked himself into more games. If someone took the time to teach, he listened and adjusted the advice to suit his own style. And he was developing a style. It was rough and untutored, with the flash the sportwriters would later rave about just a spark. His serve was a far cry from a grown Starbuck's, but it was strong and uncannily accurate. He was still awkward, as growing boys are, but his speed was excellent. More than anything else, his fierce desire to win had his game progressing.

When the cheap racket simply disintegrated under constant use, Ada raided the household budget and bought Ty another. Of the hundreds of rackets he had used in his career, some costing more than his mother had made in a week, Ty had never forgotten that first one. He had kept it, initially from childhood sentiment, then as a symbol.

He carved out a name for himself in the neighborhood. By the time he was thirteen it was a rare thing for anyone, child or adult, to beat Ty Starbuck on the courts. He knew his game. He had read everything he could get his hands on—tennis as a sport, its history, its great players. When his contemporaries were immersed in the progress of the White Sox or the Cubs, Ty watched the Wimbledon matches on the flickering black-and-white TV in his apartment. He had already made up his mind to be there one day. And to win. Again, it was Ada who helped the hand of fate.

One of the offices she cleaned belonged to Martin Derick, a lawyer and tennis enthusiast who patronized a local country club. He was an offhandedly friendly man whose late hours brought him in contact with the woman who scrubbed the hall outside his door. He called her Mrs. Starbuck because her dignity demanded it, and would exchange a word of greeting on his way in or out. Ada was careful to mention her son and his tennis abilities often enough to intrigue and not often enough to bore. Ty had come by his shrewdness naturally.

When Martin casually mentioned he would be interested in seeing the boy play, Ada told him there was an informal tournament set for that Saturday. Then she hurriedly arranged one. Whether curiosity or interest prompted Martin to drive to the battered South Side court, the results were exactly as Ada hoped.

Ty's style was still rough, but it was aggressive. His temper added to the spark, and his speed was phenomenal. At the end of a set, Martin was leaning against the chain-link fence. At the end of the match, he was openly cheering. Two hours on the manicured courts of his club had never brought him quite this degree of excitement. Ideas humming in his brain, he walked over to the sweaty, gangly teenager.

"You want to play tennis, kid?"

Ty spun the racket as he eyed the lawyer's pricey suit. "You ain't dressed for it." He gave the smooth leather shoes a mild sneer.

Martin caught the insolent grin, but focused on the intensity of the boy's eyes. Some instinct told him they were champion's eyes. The ideas solidified into a goal. "You want to play for pay?"

Ty kept spinning the racket, wary of a hustle, but the question had his pulse leaping. "Yeah. So?"

This time Martin smiled at the deliberate rudeness. He was going to like this kid, God knew why. "So, you need lessons and a decent court." He glanced at Ty's worn racket. "And equipment. What kind of power can you get out of plastic strings?"

Defensive, Ty tossed up a ball and smashed it into the opposing service court.

"Not bad," Martin decided mildly. "You'd do better with sheep gut."

"Tell me something I don't know."

Martin drew out a pack of cigarettes and offered one to Ty. He refused with a shake of his head. Taking his time, Martin lit one, then took a long drag.

"Those things'll mess up your lungs," Ty stated idly.

"Tell me something I don't know," the lawyer countered. "Think you can play on grass?"

Ty answered with a quick, crude expletive, then sliced another ball over the net.

"Pretty sure of yourself."

"I'm going to play Wimbledon," Ty told him matter-of-factly. "And I'm going to win."

Martin didn't smile, but reached into his pocket. He held out a discreet, expensively printed business card. "Call me Monday," he said simply, and walked away.

Ty had a patron.

The marriage wasn't made in heaven. Over the next seven years there were bitter arguments, bursts of temper and dashes of love. Ty worked hard because he understood that work and discipline were the means to the end. He remained in school and studied only because his mother and Martin had a conspiracy against him. Unless he completed high school with decent grades, the patronage would be removed. As to the patronage itself, Ty accepted it only because his needs demanded it. But he was never comfortable with it. The lessons polished his craft. Good equipment tightened his game. He played on manicured grass, well-tended clay and wood, learning the idiosyncrasies of each surface.

Every morning before school he practiced. Afternoons and weekends were dedicated to tennis. Summers, he worked part-time in the pro shop at Martin's club, then used the courts to hone his skill. By the time he was sixteen the club's tennis pro could beat him only if Ty had an off day.

His temper was accepted. It was a game of histrionics. Women found a certain appeal in his lawlessness. Ty learned of female pleasures young, and molded his talent there as carefully as he did his game.

The only break in his routine came when he injured his hand coming to the defense of his sister. Ty considered the two-week enforced vacation worth it, as the boy Jess had been struggling with had a broken nose.

He traveled to his first tournament unknown and unseeded. In a lengthy, gritty match heralded in the sports pages, he found his first professional victory. When he lost, Ty was rude, argumentative and brooding. When he won, he was precisely the same. The press tolerated him because he was young, brilliant and colorful. His rise from obscurity was appreciated in a world where champions were bred in the affluent, select atmosphere of country clubs.

Before his nineteenth birthday Ty put a down payment on a three-bedroom house in a Chicago suburb. He moved his family out. When he was twenty he won his first Wimbledon title. The dream was realized, but his intensity never slackened.

Now, walking along the dark streets of Rome, he thought of his roots. Asher made him think of them, perhaps because hers were so markedly different. There had been no back alleys or street gangs in her life. Her childhood had been sheltered, privileged and rich. With James Wolfe as a father, her introduction to tennis had come much earlier and much easier than Ty's. At four she had a custom-made racket and had hit balls on her father's private courts. Her mother had hired maids to scrub floors, not been hired out to scrub them.

At times Ty wondered if it was that very difference that had attracted him to her. Then he would remember the way she felt in his arms. Backgrounds were blown to hell. Yet there was something about her reserve that had drawn him. That and the passion he had sensed lay beneath.

The challenge. Yes, Ty admitted with a frown, he was a man who couldn't resist a challenge. Something about the cool, distant Asher Wolfe had stirred his blood even when she had been little more than a child. He'd waited for her to grow up. And to thaw out, he reminded himself ruefully. Turning a corner without direction, Ty found himself approaching one of Rome's many fountains. The water twinkled with light gaiety while he watched, wishing his blood were as cool.

God, how he wanted her still. The need grated against pride, infuriating and arousing him. He would have taken her back that night even knowing she had been another man's wife, shared another man's bed. It would have been less difficult to have thought about her with many lovers than with one husband—that damn titled Englishman whose arms she had run to straight from his own. *Why?* The question pounded at him.

How many times in those first few months had he relived their last few days together, looking for the key? Then he'd layered over the hurt and the fury. The wound had healed jaggedly, then callused. Ty had gone on because he was a survivor. He'd survived poverty, and the streets, and the odds. With an unsteady laugh he raked a hand through his thick mop of hair. But had he really survived Asher?

He knew he had taken more than one woman to bed because her hair was nearly the same shade, her voice nearly the same tone. Nearly, always nearly. Now, when he had all but convinced himself that what he remembered was an illusion, she was back. And free. Again, Ty laughed. Her divorce meant nothing to him. If she had still been legally tied to another man, it would have made no difference. He would still have taken her.

This time, he determined, he'd call the shots. He was out of patience. He would have her again, until he decided to walk away. Challenge, strategy, action. It was a course he had followed for half his life. Taking out a coin, he flipped it insolently into the rippling waters of a fountain, as if daring luck to evade him. It drifted down slowly until it nestled with a hundred other wishes.

His eyes skimmed the streets until he found the neon lights of a tiny bar. He wanted a drink.

Chapter 4

Asher had time to savor her title as Italian Women's Champion on the flight between Rome and Paris. After the match she had been too exhausted from nearly two hours of unrelenting competition to react. She could remember Madge hugging her, the crowd cheering for her. She could remember the glare of flashbulbs in her face and the barrage of questions she had forced herself to answer before she all but collapsed on the massage table. Then the celebrations had run together in a blur of color and sound, interviews and champagne. Too many faces and handshakes and hugs. Too many reporters. Now, as the plane leveled, reaction set in. She'd done it.

For all of her professional career, the Italian clay had beaten her. Now—now her comeback was viable. She had proven herself. Every hour of strain, every moment of physical pain during the last six months of training had been worth it. At last Asher could rid herself of all the lingering doubts that she had made the right decision.

Though there had been no doubts about her choice to leave Eric, she mused, feeling little emotion at the dissolution of her marriage—a marriage, Asher remembered, that had been no more than a polite play after the first two months. If she had ever made a truly unforgivable mistake, it had been in marrying Lord Eric Wickerton.

All the wrong reasons, Asher reflected as she leaned back in her seat with her eyes closed. Even with her bitter thoughts of Eric, she could never remove the feeling of responsibility for taking the step that had legally bound them. He had known she hadn't loved him. It hadn't mattered to him. She had known he wanted her to fit the title of Lady. She hadn't cared. At the time the need to escape had been too overpowering. Asher had given Eric what he had wanted—a groomed, attractive wife and hostess. She had thought he would give her what she needed in return. Love and understanding. The reality had been much, much different, and almost as painful as what she had sought to escape. Arguments were more difficult, she had discovered, when two people had no mutual ground. And when one felt the other had sinned…

She wouldn't think of it, wouldn't think of the time in her life that had brought such pain and disillusionment. Instead, she would think of victory.

Michael had been right in his assessment of Tia on the court. She was a small, vibrant demon who played hard and never seemed to tire. Her skill was in picking holes in her opponent's game, then ruthlessly exploiting them. On court she wore gold—a thin chain around her neck, swinging hoops at her ears and a thick clip to tame her raven hair. Her dress was pastel and frilled. She played like an enraged tigress. Both women had run miles during the match, taking it to a full five sets. The last one had consisted of ten long, volatile games with the lead shooting back and forth as quickly as the ball. Never had it been more true that the match wasn't over until it was over.

And when it was over, both women had limped off the court, sweaty, aching and exhausted. But Asher had limped off with a title. Nothing else mattered.

Looking back at it, Asher found herself pleased that the match had been hard won. She wanted something the press would chatter about, something they would remember for more than a day or two. It was always news when an unseeded player won a world title—even considering Asher's record. As it was, her past only made her hotter copy. She needed that now to help keep the momentum going.

With Italy behind her, Paris was next. The first leg of the Grand Slam. She had won there before, on clay, the year she had been Starbuck's lady. As she had with Eric, Asher tried to block Ty out of her mind. Characteristically he wasn't cooperative.

We pick this up in Paris.

The words echoed softly in her head, part threat, part promise. Asher knew him too well to believe either was idle. She would have to deal with him when the time came. But she wasn't naïve or innocent any longer. Life had taught her there weren't any easy answers or fairy-tale endings. She'd lost too much to believe happy-ever-after waited at the end of every love affair—as she had once believed it had waited for her and Ty. They were no longer the prince and princess of the courts, but older, and, Asher fervently hoped, wiser.

She was certain he would seek to soothe his ego by trying to win her again—her body if not her heart. Remembering the verve and depth of his lovemaking, Asher knew it wouldn't be easy to resist him. If she could have done so without risking her emotions, Asher would have given Ty what he wanted. For three colorless years she had endured without the passion he had brought to her life. For three empty years she had wondered and wanted and denied.

But her emotions weren't safe. On a sigh, Asher allowed herself to feel. She still cared. Not a woman to lie to herself, Asher admitted she loved Ty, had never once stopped loving him. It had never been over for her, and deep within she carried the memory of that love. It brought guilt.

What if he had known? she thought with the familiar stir of panic. How could she have told him? Asher opened her eyes and stared blindly through the sunlight. It was as harsh and unforgiving as the emotions that raged through her. Would he have believed? Would he have accepted? Before the questions were fully formed, Asher shook her head in denial. He could never know that she had unwittingly married another man while she carried Ty's child. Or that through her own grief and despair she had lost that precious reminder of her love for him.

Closing her eyes, Asher willed herself to sleep. Paris was much too close.

* * *

"Ty! Ty!"

Pausing in the act of zipping the cover on his racket, Ty turned. Pleasure shot into his eyes. In a quick move he dropped his racket and grabbed the woman who had run to him. Holding her up, he whirled her in three dizzying circles before he crushed her against him. Her laughter bounced off the air in breathless gasps.

"You're breaking me!" she cried, but hugged him tighter.

Ty cut off her protest with a resounding kiss, then held her at arm's length. She was a small woman, nearly a foot shorter than he, nicely rounded without being plump. Her gray-green eyes were sparkling, her generous mouth curved in a dazzling smile. She was a beauty, he thought—had always been a beauty. Love surrounded him. He tousled her hair, dark as his own, but cut in a loose swinging style that brushed her shoulders. "Jess, what are you doing here?"

Grinning, she gave his ear a sisterly tug. "Being mauled by the world's top tennis player."

Ty slipped an arm around her shoulders, only then noticing the man who stood back watching them. "Mac." Keeping his arm around Jess, Ty extended a hand.

"Ty, how are you?"

"Fine. Just fine."

Mac accepted the handshake and careful greeting with light amusement. He knew how Ty felt about his little sister—the little sister who was now twenty-seven and the mother of his child. When he had married Jess, over two years before, Mac had understood that there was a bond between brother and sister that would not be severed. An only child, he both respected and envied it. Two years of being in-laws had lessened Ty's caution with him but hadn't alleviated it. Of course, Mac mused ruefully, it hadn't helped that he was fifteen years Jess's senior, or that he had moved her across the country to California, where he headed a successful research and development firm. And then, he preferred chess to tennis. He'd never have gotten within ten yards of Jessica Starbuck if he hadn't been Martin Derick's nephew.

Bless Uncle Martin, Mac thought with a glance at his lovely, adored wife. Ty caught the look and relaxed his grip on his sister. "Where's Pete?" he asked, making the overture by addressing Mac rather than his sister.

Mac acknowledged the gesture with a smile. "With Grandma. They're both pretty pleased with themselves."

Jess gave the bubbling laugh that both men loved. "Hardly more than a year old and he can move like lightning. Mom's thrilled to chase him around for a few weeks. She sends her love," she told Ty. "You know how she feels about long plane flights."

"Yeah." He released his sister to retrieve his bag and racket. "I talked to her just last night; she didn't say anything about your coming."

"We wanted to surprise you." Smug, Jess hooked her hand into Mac's. "Mac thought Paris was the perfect place for a second honeymoon." She sent her husband a brief but intimate look. Their fingers tightened.

"The trick was getting her away from Pete for two weeks." He gave Ty a grin. "You were a bigger incentive than Paris." Bending, he kissed the top of his wife's head. "She dotes on Pete."

"No, I don't," Jess disagreed, then grinned. "Well, I wouldn't if Pete weren't such a smart baby."

Mac began to unpack an old, favored pipe. "She's ready to enroll him in Harvard."

"Next year," Jess responded dryly. "So, you're going in as top seed," she continued, giving her full attention to her brother. Was there some strain around his eyes? she wondered, then quickly discounted it. "Martin's proud enough to bust."

"I was hoping he might make it out for the tournament." Ty glanced toward the empty stands. "Funny, I still have a habit of looking for him before a match."

"He wanted to be here. If there had been any way for him to postpone this trial, but…" Jess trailed off and smiled. "Mac and I will have to represent the family."

Ty slung the bag over his shoulder. "You'll do fine. Where are you staying?"

"At the—" Jess's words came to a stop as she spotted a slender blonde crossing an empty court a short distance away. Reaching up, she brushed at her brow as if pushing aside an errant strand of hair. "Asher," she murmured.

Ty twisted his head. Asher wasn't aware of them, as Chuck was keeping her involved in what appeared to be a long, detailed description of a match. "Yes," Ty said softly. "Asher." He kept his eyes on her, watching the movements of her body beneath the loosely fitting jogging suit. "Didn't you know she was here?"

"Yes, I—" Jess broke off helplessly. How could she explain the flurry of feelings that she experienced in seeing Asher Wolfe again. The years were winked away in an instant. Jess could see the cool blue eyes, hear the firmly controlled voice. At the time there'd been no doubt in her mind about right and wrong. Even the chain reaction that had begun on a hazy September afternoon had only served to cement Jess's certainty. Now there'd been a divorce, and Asher was back. She felt her husband's warm palm against hers. Right and wrong weren't so clearly defined any longer.

A bubble of nausea rose as she turned to her brother. He was still watching Asher. Had he loved her? Did he still? What would he do if he ever learned of his sister's part in what had happened three years before? Jess found the questions trembling on her tongue and was afraid of the answers. "Ty…"

His eyes were dark and stormy, a barometer of emotion. Something in them warned Jess to keep her questions to herself. Surely there would be a better time to bring up the past. She had both a sense of reprieve and a feeling of guilt.

"Beautiful, isn't she?" he asked lightly. "Where did you say you were staying?"

"And because he's eighteen and played like a rocket in the qualifying rounds, they're muttering about an upset." Chuck tossed a tennis ball idly, squeezing it when it returned to his palm. "I wouldn't mind if he weren't such a little twerp."

Asher laughed and snatched the ball as Chuck tossed it again. "And eighteen," she added.

He gave a snort. "He wears designer underwear, for God's sake. His mother has them dry cleaned."

"Down boy," Asher warned good-naturedly. "You'll feel better once you wipe him out in the quarter-finals. Youth versus experience," she added because she couldn't resist. Chuck twisted a lock of her hair around his finger and pulled.

"You meet Rayski," he commented. "I guess we could call that two old pros."

Asher winced. "Your point," she conceded. "So, what's your strategy for this afternoon?"

"To beat the tar out of him," Chuck responded instantly, then grinned as he flexed his racket arm. "But if he gets lucky, I'll leave it up to Ty to smash him in the semis or the finals."

Asher bounced the ball on the clay. Her fingers closed over it, then released it again. "You're so sure Ty will get to the finals?"

"Money in the bank," he claimed. "This is his year. I swear, I've never seen him play better." Pleasure for his friend with the light lacing of envy gave the statement more impact. "He's going to be piling up titles like dominoes."

Asher said nothing, not even nodding in agreement as Chuck sought to prove his point by giving her a replay of Ty's qualifying match. A breeze stirred, sending blossoms drifting to the court at her feet. It was early morning, and the Stade Roland Garros was still drowsily charming and quiet. The thump of balls was hardy noticeable. In a few hours the fourteen thousand seats around the single center court would be jammed with enthusiasts. The noise would be human and emotional, accented by the sounds of traffic and squealing brakes on the highway that separated the stadium from the Bois de Boulogne.

Asher watched the breeze tickle a weeping willow as Chuck continued his rundown. In this first week of the games, tennis would be played for perhaps eleven hours a day so that even the first-round losers used the courts enough to make the trip worthwhile. It was considered by most pros the toughest championship to win. Like Ty, Asher was after her second victory.

Paris. Ty. Was there nowhere she could go that wasn't so firmly tied in with memories of him? In Paris they'd sat in the back of a darkened theater, necking like teenagers while an Ingmar Bergman film had flickered on the screen unnoticed. In Paris he had doctored a strained muscle in her calf, pampering and bullying so that she had won despite the pain. In Paris they had made love, and made love, and made love until they were both weak and exhausted. In Paris Asher had still believed in happy endings.

Fighting off memories, Asher glanced around the stadium. Her eyes locked with Jess's. Separated by a hundred yards, both women endured a jolt of shock and distress. They stared, unable to communicate, unable to look away.

"Hey, it's Jess!" Chuck interrupted himself to make the announcement. He waved, then grabbed Asher's hand to drag her with him. "Let's go say hi."

Panicked, Asher dug in her heels. "No, I—I have to meet..." Her mind was devoid of excuses, but she snatched her hand from Chuck's. "You go ahead, I'll see you later." Over Chuck's protest, she dashed in the opposite direction.

Breathless, Asher found herself in the Jardin des Plantes with its sweet, mingling scents, little plaques and poetry. It seemed an odd setting for jangled nerves. Making an effort to calm herself, she slowed her pace.

Silly to run, she told herself. No, she corrected herself, stupid. But she hadn't been prepared to see Ty's sister, the one person who knew all the reasons. To have confronted Jess then, when her mind was already so crowded with Ty, would have been disastrous. Steadying, Asher told herself she just needed a little time to prepare. And it had been obvious Jess had been just as stunned as she. At the moment, Asher was too busy calming herself to wonder why.

She wouldn't, couldn't, think about the last time she'd seen Jessica Starbuck—that hot, close Indian summer afternoon. It would be too easy to remember each word spoken in the careless disorder of the hotel room Asher had shared with Ty. She would remember the hurt, the frantic packing, then her irrevocable decision to go to Eric.

Oh, Ty had been right, she had run away—but she hadn't escaped. So little had changed in three years, and so much. Her heart had remained constant. With a sigh Asher admitted it had been foolish to believe she could take back what she had given so long ago. Ty Starbuck was her first lover, and the only man she had ever loved.

A child had been conceived, then lost before it could be born. She'd never forgiven herself for the accident that had taken that precious, fragile life from her. Perhaps more than a lack of love and understanding, it had been the loss of Ty's child that had destroyed any hope for her marriage.

And if the child had lived? she asked herself wearily. What then? Could she have kept it from him? Could she have remained the wife of one man while bearing the child of another? Asher shook her head. No, she would no longer dwell on possibilities. She'd lost Ty, his child, and the support of her own father. There could be no greater punishments to face. She would make her own future.

The touch of a hand on her shoulder had her whirling around. Asher stared up at Ty, her mind a blank, her emotions in turmoil. A hush seemed to spread over the garden, so she could hear the whisper of air over leaves and blossoms. The scent that reached her was sweet and heady—like a first kiss. He said nothing, nor did she until his hand slid down her arm to link with hers.

"Worried about the match?"

Almost afraid he would sense them, Asher struggled to push all thoughts of the past aside. "Concerned," she amended, nearly managing a smile. "Rayski's top seed."

"You've beaten her before."

"And she's beaten me." It didn't occur to her to remove her hand from his or to mask her doubts. Slowly the tension seeped out of her. Through the link of hands Ty felt it. They had stood here before, and the memory was sweet.

"Play her like you played Conway," he advised. "Their styles are basically the same."

With a laugh Asher ran her free hand through her hair. "That's supposed to be a comfort?"

"You're better than she is," he said simply, and earned an astonished stare. Smiling, he brushed his fingers carelessly over her cheek. "More consistent," he explained. "She's faster, but you're stronger. That gives you an advantage on clay even though it isn't your best surface."

At a loss, Asher managed a surprised, "Well."

"You've improved," Ty stated as they began to walk. "Your backhand doesn't have the power it should have, but—"

"It worked pretty well on Conway," Asher interrupted testily.

"Could be better."

"It's perfect," she disagreed, rising to the bait before she caught his grin. Her lips curved before she could stop them. "You always knew how to get a rise out of me. You're playing Kilroy," she went on, "I've never heard of him."

"He's been around only two years. Surprised everyone in Melbourne last season." He slipped an arm around her shoulders in a gesture so familiar, neither of them noticed. "What's that flower?"

Asher glanced down. "Lady's slipper."

"Silly name."

"Cynic."

He shrugged. "I like roses."

"That's because it's the only flower you can identify." Without thinking, she leaned her head on his shoulder. "I remember going in to take a bath one night and finding you'd filled the tub with roses. Dozens of them."

The scent of her hair reminded him of much more. "By the time we got around to clearing them out, it took over an hour."

Her sigh was wistful. "It was wonderful. You could always surprise me by doing something absurd."

"A tub of lady's slippers is absurd," he corrected. "A tub of roses is classy."

Her laughter was quick and appreciative. Her head still rested on his shoulders. "We filled everything in the room that could pass for a vase, including a bottle of ginger ale. Sometimes when I—" She cut herself off, abruptly realizing she would say too much.

"When you what?" Ty demanded as he turned her to face him. When she only shook her head, he tightened his grip. "Would you remember sometimes, in the middle of the night? Would you wake up and hurt because you couldn't forget?"

Truth brought tension to the base of her neck. In defense, Asher pressed her palms against his chest. "Ty, please."

"I did." He gave her a frustrated shake that knocked her head back. "Oh, God, I did. I've never stopped wanting you. Even hating you I wanted you. Do you know what it's like to be awake at three o'clock in the morning and need someone, and know she's in another man's bed."

"No, no, don't." She was clinging to him, her cheek pressed against his, her eyes tightly shut. "Ty, don't."

"Don't what?" he demanded as he drew her head back. "Don't hate you? Don't want you? Hell, I can't do anything else."

His eyes blazed into her, dark with fury, hot with passion. She could feel the race of his heart compete with hers. Abandoning pride, she pressed her lips to his.

At the instant of contact he stood still, neither giving nor taking. On a moan she drew him closer, letting her lips have their way. A shudder coursed through him, an oath ripped out, then he was responding, demanding, exciting. Why had he tried to resist? Nothing was clear to him as her lips raced crazily over his face. Wasn't this what he wanted? To have her again, to prove he could, to purge his system of her once and for all. Motives dimmed in desire. There was only Asher—the sweet taste of her, her scent more heady, more seductive than the garden of flowers. He couldn't breathe and not fill himself on her. So he surrendered to the persuading lips and soft body that had haunted his dreams.

Dragging his lips from hers only a moment, Ty pulled her through the fragile branches of a willow. The sun filtered through the curtain of leaves, giving intermittent light. In the cool dimness his mouth sought hers again and found it yielding. The blood pounded in his veins.

He had to know if her body was the same, unchanged during the years he'd been denied her. As his hand took her breast he groaned. She was small and firm and familiar. Through the material of her jacket he felt the nipple harden in quick response. Impatient, he tugged the zipper down, then dove under her shirt until he found the smooth tender flesh that had always made him feel his hands were too rough. Yet she didn't draw away as his calluses met her. She pressed against him. Her moan was not one of discomfort, but of unmistakable pleasure.

Trembling, her fingers reached for his hair. He could feel the urgency in them just as he could taste it on her heated lips. He broke his kiss only to change angles, then deepened it, allowing his tongue to drink up all the dark flavors of her mouth. Against his palm her heart thudded wildly, but only his fingers moved to arouse her.

Slowly his other hand journeyed to her hip to mold the long, slender bone. He was lost somewhere between yesterday and today. The heavy fragrance of flowers still wet with morning dew was more seductive than perfume. Half dreaming, Ty took his mouth to her throat. He heard her sigh float off on the scented air. Was she dreaming too? Was the past overlapping this moment for her as well as for him? The thoughts drifted into his mind, then out again before they could be answered. Nothing mattered but that he was holding her again.

From far off came a ripple of laughter. Ty brought his mouth back to Asher's. A rapid smattering of French drifted to him. Ty drew her closer until their bodies seemed fused. Footsteps and a giggle. Like a dreamer, he sensed the intrusion and swore against it. For another moment he clung, drawing on her lingering passion.

When he released her, Asher was breathless and swaying. Wordlessly he stared down at her with eyes nearly black with emotion. Her lips were parted, swollen from his, and he gave in to need and kissed her one long last time. Gently now, slowly, to store up every dram of sweetness. This time she trembled, her breath coming harsh and fast like a diver's who breaks surface after a long submersion. Disoriented, she gripped his arms.

How long had they been there? she wondered. It could have been seconds or days. All she was sure of was that the longing had intensified almost beyond control. Her blood was racing in her veins, her heart pounding desperately. She was alive. So alive. And no longer certain which path she would take.

"Tonight," Ty murmured, bringing her palm to his lips.

The vibration shot up her arm and into her core. "Ty…" Asher shook her head as she tried to draw her hand away. His fingers tightened.

"Tonight," he repeated.

"I can't." Seeing the temper shoot into his eyes,

Asher covered their joined hands with her free one. "Ty, I'm frightened."

The quiet admission killed his anger. He let out a weary sigh. "Damn you, Asher."

Saying nothing, she wrapped her arms around his waist, pressing her cheek to his chest. Automatically Ty reached to smooth her hair. His eyes closed. "I'm sorry," she whispered. "I was frightened of you once before. It seems to be happening again." And I love you, she told him silently. As much as ever. More, she realized. More, because of the years of famine.

"Asher." He held her away from him. She felt the passion swirling around him. "I won't promise to wait for you to come to me this time. I won't promise to be gentle and patient. Things aren't the same."

She shook her head, but in agreement. "No, things aren't the same. It might be better, much better for both of us if we just stayed away from each other."

Ty laughed shortly. "We won't."

"If we tried," Asher began.

"*I* won't."

She let out a breath of exasperation. "You're pressuring me."

"Damn right." Before she could decide whether to laugh or to scream, she was in his arms again. "Do you think I don't feel pressured too?" he demanded with a sudden intensity that kept Asher from answering. "Every time I look at you I remember the way things were for us and drive myself crazy trying to figure out why you left me. Do you know what that does to me?"

She gripped his upper arms with strong hands. "You have to understand, I won't go back. Whatever happens to us now begins now. No questions, no whys." She saw the anger boiling in his eyes, but kept hers level. "I mean that, Ty. I can't give you explanations. I won't dig up the past."

"You expect me to live with that?"

"I expect nothing," she said quietly. The tone caused him to look deeper for the answers she refused to give. "And I've agreed to nothing. Not yet."

"You ask for too much," he bit off as he released her. "Too damn much."

She wanted to go to him, go back to his arms and beg him to forget the past. Perhaps it was possible to live for the moment if one wanted to badly enough. It might have been pride that stopped her, or the deeply ingrained survival instinct she had developed since that long-ago September afternoon when she had fled from him and the prospect of pain. Asher laced her fingers together and stared down at them. "Yes, I know. I'm sorry, Ty, we'll only hurt each other."

Tense and tormented, he turned back. "I've never wanted to hurt you, Asher. Not even when I thought I did."

The ache spread so quickly, she almost gasped from it. Isn't that what Jess had said that day? *He'd never want to hurt you...never want to hurt you.* Asher could hear the words echoing inside her head. "Neither of us wanted to," she murmured. "Both of us did. Isn't it foolish to do it again?"

"Look at me." The command was quiet and firm. Bracing herself, Asher obeyed. His eyes were locked on hers—those dark, penetrating eyes that conveyed such raw feeling. Gently he touched her cheek. Without hesitation her hand rose to cover his. "Now," he whispered, "ask me again."

A long, shuddering breath escaped. “Oh, Ty, I was so sure I could prevent this. So sure I could resist you this time.”

“And now?”

“Now I’m not sure of anything.” She shook her head before he could speak again. “Don’t ask now. Give us both some time.”

He started to protest, then managed to restrain it. He’d waited three years, a bit longer wouldn’t matter. “Some time,” he agreed, lowering his hand. But as she started to relax, he took her wrist. The grip was neither gentle nor patient. “The next time, Asher, I won’t ask.”

She nodded, accepting. “Then we understand each other.”

His smile was a trifle grim. “That we do. I’ll walk you back.” He drew her through the curtain of leaves.

Chapter 5

Fifth set. Seventh game. At the baseline Ty crouched, ready to spring for Michael's serve. The air was heavy, the sky thick with rain-threatening clouds so that the light was dreary. Ty didn't notice. He didn't notice the stadium full of people, some dangling through the railing, some hanging from the scoreboard. He didn't notice the shouts and whistles that were either for or against him.

Tennis was a game of the individual. That was what had drawn him to it. There was no one to blame for a loss, no one to praise for a win but yourself. It was a game of motion and emotion, both of which he excelled in.

He had looked forward to meeting Michael in the semis. The Australian played a hot, passionate game full of dramatic gestures, furious mutters and pizzazz.

There were perhaps five competitors Ty fully respected, Michael being one of them. Wanting to win was only a step below wanting a challenge. A fight. He'd grown up scrapping. Now the racket was merely an extension of his arm. The match was a bout. The bout was one on one. It had never—would never—be only a game.

The Australian was a set up, with his momentum still flowing. Ty's only thought at the moment was to break his serve and even the match. Thus far he had spotted no weaknesses in his opponent's game. Like a boxer, he watched for the opening.

He heard the sound of the ball hitting the sweet spot of the racket before it rocketed toward him. It landed deep in the corner of the service court, beautifully placed. Ty's mind and body moved as one as he sprang for the return. Defense, offense, strategy all had to be formulated in a fraction of a second. Strength had to be balanced with form. Both men sprinted over the court for the rally, faces glowing with concentration and sweat. The roar of the crowd rose to meet the distant thunder.

Thus far, the ratio had been nearly ten to one in favor of ground strokes. Ty decided to alter the pace and go with power. Using a vicious left-to-right slice, he shook Michael's balance. Ty blasted away at the attempted passing shot, barely shortening his backswing. Michael couldn't reach the backhand volley, let alone return it. Love-fifteen.

Shaking the damp hair back from his face, Ty returned to the baseline. A woman in the crowd called out what could have been a congratulations or a proposition. Ty's French wasn't strong enough to decipher the phrase. Michael's serve sent up a puff of smoke. Before his return was over the net, Ty was at mid-court and waiting. A testing ground stroke, a sharp return. A tricky topspin, a slice. Michael's decision to try to lob over Ty was a mistake. The smoking smash careened off the court and into the grandstands. Love-thirty.

Michael walked a complete circle, cursing himself before he took his position again. Casting off impatience, Ty waited. Crouched, swaying side to side, unblinking, he was ready. Both players exploited angles and depths with ground strokes. There was a long, patient rally as each watched for the chance to smash a winner. It might have been pure showmanship if it hadn't been for the sounds of exertion coming from the two players.

A UPI photographer had his motor drive humming as he recorded the game. He framed Ty, arms extended for balance, legs spread for the stretch, face fierce. It crossed his mind as he continued to snap that he wouldn't want to face that American on any playing field.

Gracefully, with an elegance belied by his expression, Ty executed a backhand with a touch of underspin. Michael's return thudded against the net. Love-forty.

Angry and shaken, Michael punched his first serve into the net. Having no choice at game point, he placed his next serve carefully. Ty went straight for the volley and took the net. The exchange was fast and furious, the players moving on instinct, the crowd screaming in a mixture of languages. Ty's wrist was locked. The ball whipped from racket to racket at terrifying speed. There were bare seconds between contact, making both men anticipate flight rather than see it. Changing tactics in the wink of an instant, Ty brought the racket face under at the moment of impact. With a flick of a wrist he dropped a dump shot over the net. Risky, experts would say. Gutsy, fans would claim. Ty would ignore both. Game and set.

"Oh, Mac!" Jess leaned back and expelled a long breath. "I'd nearly forgotten what it was like to watch Ty play."

"You watched him just a few weeks ago," he pointed out, using a damp handkerchief to wipe his neck. The wish for his air-conditioned office flitted only briefly into his mind.

"On television," Jess returned. "That's different. Being here…can't you feel it?"

"I thought it was the humidity."

Laughing, Jess shook her head. "Always down to earth, Mac. That's why I love you."

Her smile seemed to open just for him. It could still make his blood sing. "Then I intend to stay there," he murmured, kissing her knuckles. Feeling her hand tense, he looked up, puzzled. Her eyes were aimed over his shoulder. Curious, he turned, spotting a few tennis faces he recognized. Among them was Asher Wolfe. It was on her that his wife's gaze was locked.

"That's the former Lady Wickerton, isn't it?" he asked casually. "She's stunning."

"Yes." Jess tore her eyes away, but the tension in her fingers remained. "Yes, she is."

"She won her match this morning. We'll have an American going into the women's finals." Jess said nothing as Mac stuffed the handkerchief back into his pocket. "She was away from the game for a while, wasn't she?"

"Yes."

Intrigued by his wife's flat answer, Mac probed. "Didn't she and Ty have something going a few years back?"

"It was nothing." With a nervous swallow Jess prayed she spoke the truth. "Just a passing thing. She's not Ty's type. Asher's very cool, much more suited to Wickerton than to Ty. He was attracted to that for a while, that's all." She moistened her lips. "And it was obvious she wasn't serious about him, otherwise she'd never have married Wickerton so quickly. She was making Ty unhappy, very unhappy."

"I see," Mac murmured after a moment. Jess had spoken too quickly and too defensively. Studying his wife's profile, he wondered. "I suppose Ty's too involved in his career to be serious about a woman?"

"Yes." The look Jess gave him was almost pleading. "Yes, he'd never have let her go if he'd been in love with her. Ty's too possessive."

"And proud," he reminded her quietly. "I don't think he'd run after any woman, no matter how he felt about her."

Feeling her stomach roll, Jess said nothing. She turned to watch her brother take the position for his first serve.

Instead of the hazy afternoon she saw a brilliant morning. Instead of the clay of Roland Garros she saw the newly empty grass courts of Forest Hills. Ty was leaning over the rail, staring out at center court. She had a fanciful thought that he looked like the captain of a ship with his eyes on the open, endless sea. In her world she loved no one more than him, could conceive of loving no one more. He was brother and father and hero. He'd provided her with a home, clothes and an education, asking nothing in return. As a result, she would have given him anything.

Crossing to him, she slipped her arm around him, nestling her head in the crook of his shoulder.

"Thinking about this afternoon?" she murmured. He was slated to face Chuck Prince in the finals of the U.S. Open.

"Hmm?" Distracted, Ty shrugged. "No, not really."

"It must feel odd to compete against your closest friend."

"You must forget you're friends for a couple hours," Ty returned.

He was brooding; she sensed it. And unhappy. There was no one, including her mother, Jess felt more loyalty to. Her grip around him tightened. "Ty, what is it?"

"Just restless."

"Have you fought with Asher?"

Absently he tousled her hair. "No, I haven't fought with Asher."

He lapsed into silence for so long that Jess began to suspect he wasn't telling the entire truth. She was already worried about him and Asher. The relationship had lasted longer than was habitual for Ty. Jess saw Asher's reserve as coldness, her independence as indifference. She didn't hang on Ty as other women did. She didn't listen raptly to every word he spoke. She didn't adore him.

"Do you ever think back, Jess?" he asked suddenly.

"Think back?"

"To when we were kids." His eyes skimmed over the manicured courts, but didn't see them. "That crummy apartment with the paper walls. The DeMarcos next door screaming at each other in the middle of the night.

The stairwell always smelled of old garbage and stale sweat."

The tone of his voice disturbed her. Seeking comfort as much as to comfort, she turned her face into his chest. "Not often. I guess I don't remember it as well as you. I hadn't turned fifteen when you got us out."

"I wonder sometimes if you can ever escape that, if you can ever really turn your back on it." His eyes were focused on something Jess couldn't see. She strained to share the vision. "Old garbage and stale sweat," he repeated quietly. "I can't forget that. I asked Asher once what smell she remembered most from her childhood. She said the wisteria that hung over her bedroom window."

"Ty, I don't understand."

He swore softly. "Neither do I."

"You left all that behind," she began.

"I left it," he corrected her. "That doesn't mean I left it behind. We were having dinner last night. Wickerton stopped by the table and started a conversation about French Impressionists. After five minutes I didn't know what the hell they were talking about."

Jess bristled. She knew because Ty had sent her to college. She knew because he had provided the opportunity. "You should have told him to get lost."

With a laugh Ty kissed her cheek. "That was my first thought." Abruptly he sobered. "Then I watched them. They understand each other, speak the same language. It made me realize there are some fences you just can't climb."

"You could if you wanted to."

"Maybe. I don't." He let out a long breath. "I don't really give a damn about French Impressionists. I don't give a damn about the mutual friends they have that are distant cousins of the Queen of England, or who won at Ascot last month." Storm warnings were in his eyes, but he shrugged. "Even if I did, I wouldn't fit into that kind of life because I'd always remember the garbage and sweat."

"Asher has no business encouraging that man," Jess stated heatedly. "He's been following her around since Paris."

Ty gave a grim laugh. "She doesn't encourage or discourage. Drawing room conversation," he murmured. "Ingrained manners. She's different from us, Jess, I've known that all along."

"If *she'd* tell him to get lost—"

"She couldn't tell anyone to get lost any more than she could sprout wings and fly."

"She's cold."

"She's different," Ty returned immediately but without heart. He cupped his sister's chin in his hand. "You and me, we're the same. Everything's up front. If we want to shout, we shout. If we want to throw something, we throw it. Some people can't."

"Then they're stupid."

This time his laugh was warm and genuine. "I love you, Jess."

Throwing her arms around him, she hugged him fiercely. "I can't bear to see you unhappy. Why do you let her do this to you?"

Frowning, Ty stroked her hair. "I've been trying to figure that out. Maybe…maybe I just need a shove in the right direction."

Jess held him tighter, searching her mind for the answer.

* * *

Seventh set. Tenth game. The crowd was as vocal, as enthusiastic and as hungry as it had been an hour before. Leaning forward in his seat, his eyes glued to the ball, Chuck sat between Asher and Madge.

"You've got something riding on this one, don't you, cowboy?" Madge commented dryly though her own heart was pumping. Chuck would face the winner in the finals.

"It's the best match I've seen in two years." His own face was damp, his own muscles tense. The ball traveled at such speeds, it was often only a white blur.

Asher spoke to neither of them. Her objectivity had been long since destroyed. Ty enthralled her. Both men possessed the raw athletic ability competitors admired and envied. Both were draining the other's resources without mercy. But it was Ty, always Ty, who ripped the emotion from her.

She could admire Michael, admit his brilliance, but he didn't cause that slow, churning ache in her stomach. Had she not once been Ty's lover, had she not even known him, would she still be so drawn? Controlled rage. How was it a woman raised in such an ordered, sheltered existence would be pulled irresistibly to a man with such turbulent passion? Opposites attract? she wondered. No, that was much too simple.

Sitting in the crowded stadium, Asher felt the thrill of desire as clearly as though she had been naked in his arms. She felt no shame. It was natural. She felt no fear. It was inevitable. Years made up of long, unending days vanished. What a waste of time, she thought suddenly. No, a loss, she corrected herself. A loss of time—nothing's ever wasted. *Tonight.* The decision came to her as effortlessly as it had the first time. Tonight they would be together. And if it was only once—if once was all he wanted—it would have to be enough. The long wait was over. She laughed out loud in relief and joy. Chuck sent her an odd look.

"He's going to win," Asher said on a second laugh. Leaning on the rail, she rested her chin on her folded hands. "Oh, yes, he's going to win."

There was a dull ache in his racket arm that Ty ignored. The muscles in his legs promised to cramp the moment he stopped moving. He wouldn't give in to them any more than he would give in to the man across the net. One thing hadn't changed in twenty years. He still hated to lose.

A point away from the match, he played no less tigerishly than he had in the first game. The rallies had been long and punishing. The ball whistled. Sweat dripped. For the last twenty minutes Ty had forsaken artistry for cunning. It was working.

Power for power, they were in a dead heat, so that Ty chose to outmaneuver the Australian. He worked him over the court, pacing him, some might say stalking him. The game went to deuce three times while the crowd grew frantic. An ace gave him advantage—a screeching bullet that brought Ty the final impetus he needed. Then Ty played him hot-bloodedly. The men drove from side to side, their faces masks of effort and fury. The shot came that he'd been waiting for. Michael's awesome backhand drove crosscourt to his southpaw forehand. The ball came to Ty at waist level. Michael didn't even have to see the return to know it was over.

Game, set and match.

The heat hit him then, and the fatigue. It took an effort not to stagger. Simply to have fallen to his knees would have been a relief. He walked to the net.

Michael took his hand, then draped his free arm around Ty's shoulder. "Damn you, Starbuck," he managed breathlessly. "You nearly killed me."

Ty laughed, using his opponent for balance a moment. "You too."

"I need a bloody drink." Michael straightened, giving Ty a glazed grin. "Let's go get drunk."

"You're on."

Turning, they separated, victor and vanquished, to face the press, the showers and the massage tables. Ty grabbed the towel someone handed him, nodding at the questions and congratulations being hurled at him. Behind the cloth he could hear the click and whir of cameras. He was too weary to curse them. Someone was gathering his rackets. He could hear the clatter of wood on wood. The strength that had flowed freely through him only moments before drained. Exhausted, he let the drenched towel fall. His eyes met Asher's.

So blue, he thought. Her eyes are so blue. And cool, and deep. He could drown in them blissfully. The unbearable heat vanished, as though someone had opened a window to a fresh spring breeze.

"Congratulations." When she smiled, his fatigue slid away. Strangely it wasn't desire that replaced it, but comfort, sweet simple comfort.

"Thanks." He took the racket bag from her. Their hands barely brushed.

"I suppose the press is waiting for you inside."

The short retort Ty made was both agreement and opinion. On a low laugh she stepped closer.

"Can I buy you dinner?"

The quirk of his brow was the only indication of surprise. "Sure."

"I'll meet you at seven in the lobby of the hotel."

"All right."

"Starbuck, what do you feel was the turning point of the match?"

"What strategy will you use playing Prince in the finals?"

Ty didn't answer the reporters, didn't even hear them as he watched Asher weave her way through the crowd. From overhead Jess watched with a small, fluttering sensation of déjà vu.

Ty got under the stream of the shower fully dressed. He let the cool water sluice over him while he stripped. A reporter from *World of Sports* leaned against a tiled wall, scribbling notes and tossing questions. Naked, with his clothes in a soggy heap at his feet, Ty answered. Always, he handled the press naturally because he didn't give a damn what they printed. He knew his mother kept a scrapbook, but he never read the articles or interviews. Lathering the soap over his face with both hands, he washed the sticky sweat away. Someone passed him a plastic jug of fruit juice. With the water streaming over him, he guzzled it down, replacing lost fluid. The weakness was seeping back, and with it the pain. He made his way to the massage table by instinct, then collapsed onto it.

Strong fingers began to work on him. Questions still hammered in his ear, but now he ignored them. Ty simply closed his eyes and shut them out. A line of pain ran up his calf as the muscles were kneaded. He winced and held on, knowing relief would follow. For ten agonizing minutes he lay still while his body was rubbed and pounded. He began to drift. Like a mother's memory of the pain of childbirth, his memory of the pain began to dim. He could remember winning. And he could remember dark blue eyes. With those two visions tangling in his mind, he slept.

The floor of the lobby was marble. White marble veined with pink. Madge had commented that it would be the devil to keep clean. Her husband had dryly commented that she wouldn't know one end of the mop from the other. Asher sat, listening to their comfortable banter while she told herself she wasn't nervous. It was six-fifty.

She'd dressed carefully, choosing a simple crêpe de Chine as pale as the inside of a peach. Her hair fluffed back from her face, exposing the tiny pearl and coral drops at her ears. Her ringless fingers were interlaced.

"Where are you eating?"

Asher brought her attention back to Madge. "A little place on the Left Bank." There was an enthusiastic violinist, she remembered. Ty had once passed him twenty American dollars and cheerfully told him to get lost.

At the bellow of thunder Madge glanced toward the lobby doors. "You're going to play hell getting a cab tonight." She leaned back. "Have you seen Ty since the match?"

"No."

"Chuck said both he and Michael were sleeping on the tables like babies." A chuckle escaped as she crossed strong, short legs. "Some industrious stringer for a French paper got a couple of classic shots."

"Athletes in repose," her husband mused.

"It kind of blows the tough-guy image."

Asher smiled, thinking how young and vulnerable Ty looked in sleep. When the lids closed over those dramatic eyes, he reminded her of an exhausted little boy. It was the only time the frenetic energy stilled. Something stirred in her. If the child had lived… Hurriedly she censored the thought.

"Hey, isn't that Ty's sister?"

Asher turned her head to see Jess and Mac crossing the lobby. "Yes." Their eyes met, leaving no choice. Gripping her husband's hand, Jess walked across the white marble.

"Hello, Asher."

"Jess."

A quick moistening of lips betrayed nerves. "I don't think you know my husband. Mackenzie Derick, Lady Wickerton."

"Asher Wolfe," she replied smoothly, taking Mac's hand. "Are you related to Martin?"

"My uncle," Mac informed her. "Do you know him?"

The smile brought warmth to her eyes. "Very well." She made the rest of the introductions with a natural poise Mac approved of. Cool, yes, he mused, remembering his wife's description. But with an underlying vibrancy perhaps a man would discern more quickly than another woman. He began to wonder if Jess's opinion of Ty's feelings was accurate.

"Are you a tennis fan, Mr. Derick?" Asher asked him.

"Mac," he supplied. "Only by marriage. And no, I don't play, much to Uncle Martin's disgust."

Asher laughed, appreciating the humor in his eyes. A strong man, she thought instantly. His own man.

He wouldn't take second place to Ty in his wife's life. "Martin should be satisfied having cultivated one champion." Her eyes drifted to Jess, who was sitting straight and tense beside Madge. "Is your mother well?"

"Yes, yes, Mom's fine." Though she met the cool, clear gaze, her fingers began to pleat the material of her skirt. "She's at home with Pete."

"Pete?"

"Our son."

Asher's throat constricted. Mac noticed with some surprise that her knuckles whitened briefly on the arm of her chair. "I didn't know you'd had a baby. Ada must be thrilled to have a grandchild." The pressure on her heart was unbearable. Her smile was casual. "How old is he?" she made herself ask.

"Fourteen months." As the tension built in one woman, it flowed out of the other. Jess was already reaching into her purse for her wallet. "I swear he never walked, he started out running. Mom says he's like Ty. He has his coloring too." She was offering a picture. Asher had no choice but to accept it.

There was some of his father in him—the shape of the face. But the Starbuck genes were strong. The baby's hair was dark and thick, like his mother's. Like Ty's. The eyes were large and gray. Asher wondered if she could actually feel the air of perpetual motion around the child, or if she imagined it. Another baby would have had dark hair and gray eyes. Hadn't she pictured the face countless times?

"He's beautiful," she heard herself say in a calm voice. "You must be very proud of him." When she handed the snapshot back her hands were perfectly steady.

"Jess thinks he should wait until he's twelve before he runs for president."

Asher smiled, but this time Mac didn't find the reflected warmth in her eyes. "Has Ty bought him a racket yet?"

"You know him very well," Mac observed.

"Yes." She looked back at Jess steadily. "Tennis and his family come first, always."

"I hate to admit it," Madge put in with a sigh, "but I can remember a dozen years ago when this one was a skinny teenager, chewing her fingernails at every one of Ty's matches. Now you're a mother."

Jess grinned, holding out her hands for inspection. "And I still bite my nails at Ty's matches."

It was Asher who saw him first. But then, her senses were tuned for him. Ty stepped off the elevator dressed in slim black slacks and a smoke-gray shirt. He wouldn't have chosen the shirt because it matched his eyes so perfectly. Asher knew he wore it because it would have been the first thing his hand had grabbed from the closet. He wore clothes with the casual style of one who gave no thought to them and still looked marvelous. A disciplined body and trained grace made it inevitable. His hair had been combed, but defied order. He paused briefly, even in stillness communicating motion. Asher's heartbeat was a dull, quick thud.

"Oh, there's Ty!" Jess sprang up, hurrying across the lobby to meet him. "I didn't get to congratulate you. You were absolutely wonderful."

Though his arm slipped around her, Jess saw that his eyes had drifted over her head. Without turning, she knew who they focused on.

Asher didn't see, nor did she speak.

"Well, Starbuck, you earned your pay today," Madge commented. "The Dean and I are going to the Lido to hold Michael's hand."

"Tell him I lost three pounds on the court today." He spoke to her, lightly enough, but his eyes never left Asher's.

"I don't think that's going to make him feel a hell of a lot better," she returned, giving her husband a nudge as she rose. "Well, we're off to fight for a taxi. Anyone going our way?"

"As a matter of fact," Mac began, picking up the hint easily, "Jess and I were on our way out too."

"Want a lift, Ty?" Madge's husband gave her an offended look as she ground her heel into his foot. But he shut his mouth firmly when Madge shot him a deadly glance.

Even to a man who rarely comprehended subtleties, it became obvious there were things being said without words. The little group had simply ceased to exist for Ty and Asher. After a hard look at the silent couple The Dean straightened his glasses and grinned at his wife.

"I guess not, huh?"

"You're so quick, babe." Madge began shepherding the rest toward the doors. "Anyone know some French obscenities? It's the best way to get a cab in the rain."

Asher rose slowly. From behind her she could hear the ding of a bell on the desk and the whoosh of the storm as the doors were opened then quickly closed. For a moment Ty thought she looked like something that should be enclosed in glass. Not to be touched, not to be soiled. She reached out her hand.

When he took it, it was warm. Flesh and blood.

In unspoken agreement they turned away from the doors and walked to the elevator.

Chapter 6

They didn't speak, but then they didn't need to. With one hand still holding hers, Ty pushed the button for his floor. The elevator began its silent rise. Once, the hand in his trembled lightly. He found it unbearably exciting. The numbers above their heads flashed ponderously until at last the car stopped. When the doors slid open they stepped into the carpeted hall together.

Asher heard the key jingle against loose change as Ty reached into his pocket. She heard the click of the lock before he released her hand. The choice was still hers. She stepped out of the light into the dimness of the room.

It smelled of him. That was her first thought. The air carried Ty's lingering fragrance. Something sharp, something vital. Something she had never forgotten. All at once her nerves began to jump. The poise that had carried her this far fell away. Searching for something to say, she wandered the room. It was untidy, with a shirt thrown here, shoes tossed there. She knew if she opened the closet, she would find a neat stack of rackets, the only semblance of order. Instead, she moved to the window. Rain ran like tears down the glass.

"It's going to storm all night."

As if to accent her words, lightning split the sky. Asher counted to five, then heard the thunder answer. Hundreds of lights spread through the darkness. The city was there, crowded, moving—distant. Staring through the wet glass, she waited for Ty to speak.

Silence. The patter of rain on the window. The distant hum of traffic. Another moan of thunder. Unable to bear it, Asher turned.

He was watching her. The small bedside lamp threw both light and shadow into the room. His stance was neither relaxed nor threatening, and she understood. He had given her a choice before she entered. Now he wouldn't let her go. A bridge had been burned. Asher felt nothing but relief that the decision was already made. But her fingers were numb as she reached to loosen the thin belt at her waist.

Crossing to her, Ty laid his hands over hers, stopping the movement. Asher stared up at him, unsure, as nervous as the first time. Without speaking he took her face in his hands to study her. He wanted to remember her this way—in shadowed light with the fury of a storm at her back. Her eyes were dark with traces of fear, traces of desire. In a gesture of surrender her arms had dropped to her sides. But he didn't want surrender—perhaps she had forgotten.

As he lowered his head Ty watched her lids shut, her

lips part in anticipation. Gently he kissed her temple, then the other, then the delicate curve of an eyebrow. Without haste, his eyes closed. He reacquainted himself with her face through taste and touch. Her lips beckoned, but he nibbled along the line of her jaw, on the hollow of her cheek.

His thumb brushed her bottom lip as he whispered kisses over her face. He remembered every curve. Her breath shuddered out as he kissed the corners of her mouth. He brushed his over it, retreating when Asher sought more pressure. There was only the fleeting promise of more. With a moan she gripped his forearms. He'd waited for the strength. He'd waited for the demands. Again he touched his lips to hers, allowing his tongue a brief taste. Now her arms wrapped possessively around him. Now passion exploded, mouth against mouth. Lightning flashed, illuminating them as one form in the ageless wonder of lovers.

"Undress me," she whispered breathlessly, hardly able to speak as her lips fused again and again with his. "I want you to undress me."

In answer, he lowered the zipper slowly, allowing his fingers to trail along her bare skin. He found more silk, something thin and fragile. The dress slithered down her body to lie at her feet. Growing impatient, Asher worked her hands between them to deal with the buttons of his shirt while her mouth continued to cling to his. She felt the hard muscle, the line of ribs, the mat of hair. A moan wrenched from her out of deep, desperate need.

The thigh-length chemise was too much of a barrier. Longing for the intimacy of flesh against flesh, Asher reached to draw down the strap. Again Ty stopped her.

"Don't rush," he murmured, then tore at her control with a deep, lingering kiss. The pressure was hard and demanding, the lips soft and heated. "Come to bed."

In a haze she let him lead her, felt the mattress give under her weight, then his. Anticipation shivered along her skin. "The light," she whispered.

As he circled her throat with his hand, Ty's eyes met hers. "I need to see you." Thunder exploded as his mouth crushed down on hers.

When she would have hurried, he set the pace. Languorous, sleepy, enervating. It seemed her lips alone would pleasure him enough for a lifetime. She was so soft, so moist. Far from pliant, Asher moved against him, inviting, insisting. Her urgency excited him, but Ty chose to savor. Over the silk his hands roamed to trace her shape from thigh to breast. The peaks strained against the sheer material.

He took his mouth to her shoulder, catching the narrow strap of the silk with his teeth. Inch by inch he lowered it until her flesh was exposed to him. She was firm and creamy-white in contrast to the tan of her arms and shoulders.

"So lovely," he whispered while his fingertip brought down the second strap.

When she was naked to the waist, his mouth ranged down slowly, though with her hands in his hair she urged him down. With lips parted, Ty sought the peak of her breast. Asher arched, pressing him down. She wanted him to be greedy, wanted to feel the rough scrape of his tongue. When she did she could no longer be still. Her body vibrated with the beat of a hundred tiny pulses. Desire, raw and primitive, tore through her with the power to obliterate all but one thought. She was woman; he was man. Seeking pleasure, Asher moved under him, letting her hands roam.

He abandoned gentleness because she wanted none. It had always driven him wild when her passion was unleashed. She had no inhibitions, no shame. When they came together like this she was all fire, and as dangerous as the lightning in the night sky. Ty wasn't even aware of his control slipping away. Hard-palmed hands ran bruisingly over tender skin. Short, manicured nails dug into strong shoulders.

His breathing was ragged when he tore the garment from her. She gave him no time to view her nakedness. Her fingers were busy, struggling to remove the last barrier of his clothing. Their frantic movements took them over the bed, tangling in the sheets. Her skin was damp and trembling, but her hands were so strong, and so certain. There could be no more waiting.

A pain stabbed into him as he entered her. It was sharp, then sweet. He thought he heard her cry out as she had that first night when he had taken her innocence. Then she was wrapped around him—legs, arms. Her mouth fastened on his. The storm crashed directly overhead. They rose with it.

His hand lay lightly on her breast. Asher sighed. Had she ever known such pure contentment? she wondered. No, not even when they had been together before. Then she hadn't known what it would be like to do without him. She shuddered, then moved closer.

"Cold?" Ty drew her to him until her head rested on the curve of his shoulder.

"A little. Where's my chemise?"

"Devoured."

She laughed, flinging her arms around him as though she would never let go. Free, she thought. How wonderful to be free—to love, to laugh. Supporting herself on his chest, she stared down into his face. For once his eyes were calm. A faint smile curved his lips. Beneath her his breathing was even and slow, to match hers. To match, her mind repeated. They had always been like two halves of the same whole.

"Oh, God, I missed you, Ty." On those words she buried her face against his throat. Empty, empty, she thought. It seemed like a lifetime of emptiness had been wiped away with an hour of fulfillment.

"Asher—"

"No, no questions. No questions." Wildly she rained kisses over his face. "Just feel, just be with me. I need to laugh tonight, the way we used to."

He stopped her hurried movements by taking her head in his hands. There was a plea in her eyes and a light trace of desperation. No, he didn't want to see that now. Pushing away the questions that drummed in his head, he smiled at her.

"I thought you were going to buy me dinner."

Relief washed over her before she grinned. "I have no idea what you're talking about."

"You asked me for a date."

Tossing her head back, she arched an elegant brow. "*I* asked you? You've been out in the heat too long, Starbuck."

"Dinner," he repeated, rolling her over until he loomed above her.

"As far as I can tell, you've already eaten a sixty-dollar silk chemise. Are you still hungry?"

For an answer, he lowered his mouth to her neck and

bit, none too gently. Laughing, she tried to twist away. "Food," he muttered. "I have to eat."

Remembering a weakness, she found the spot on his ribs and squeezed. His body jerked, giving her the opportunity to slither away. She was giggling like a girl when he grabbed her and pulled her back. "How many people know the indomitable Starbuck is ticklish?" she demanded when he pinned her arms over her head. "What would the press pay to find out?"

"About the same as they'd pay to find out elegant Asher Wolfe has a heart-shaped birthmark on her very attractive bottom."

Asher considered this a moment. "Even," she decided. Her smile slanted seductively. "Do you really want to go out to eat?"

Desire fluttered lightly in the pit of his stomach as he looked down at her. The light angled across her face, accenting the smooth, glowing skin and darkened eyes. The thunder was a distant rumble now, but he felt it vibrate in his head.

"There's always room service," he murmured, tasting her lips. He kept her arms pinned as he dropped light, teasing kisses over her face. Nestling in the vulnerable curve of her neck, he used his tongue to stir and arouse.

"Ty," she moaned, unable to struggle against the captivity. "Make love to me."

His chuckle was low and he was pleased. "Oh, I am. This time," he whispered into her ear, "we won't hurry. Hours, love." His tongue darted to her ear, making her squirm in agonized delight. "Hours and hours." Then he shifted, bringing her close to his side. Cradling her, he felt her heart pounding against him. When he reached for the phone, Asher glanced up, puzzled. "Food," he reminded her.

She gave a weak laugh. "I should have remembered your stomach comes first."

His hand grazed over her breast. "Not necessarily." Her nipple was already taut. He flicked his thumb over it lazily.

"Ty—" With a kiss he silenced her.

"Champagne," he said into the phone while driving Asher mad with careless strokes and fondling. "Dom Pérignon. Caviar," he went on, sending her a questioning look that she was powerless to answer. "Beluga." He gave her a light kiss, running his hand down to the flat of her stomach. She quivered, turning into him. Legs tangled as he brushed his lips over her shoulder. "Cold shrimp." He bit her tender bottom lip. "Mmm, that'll do. Yes, for two." As he dropped the phone back on its cradle, Asher found his mouth in a desperate, yearning kiss. "Food excites you?" he mumbled against the hungry lips. Struggling not to take her instantly, he ran his hand to her hip, kneading warm flesh.

"I want you." Her voice was low and throaty, her hands questing. "I want you now."

"Shh." Slow, patient, his stroking aroused rather than subdued. "Relax. There's time. I want to see you again." He drew away from her. "Really see you."

She was burning for him. Now she lay naked and vulnerable under his gaze. As she watched, his eyes darkened, grew stormy. Her breathing quickened. When she reached out he took her hand, burying his lips in the palm.

"You're more beautiful than ever," he said huskily.

"It shouldn't be possible. I've looked at you so many times and have been afraid to touch."

"No." Asher pulled him to her until they were heart to heart. "I'm never more alive than when you touch me." With a sigh Ty nestled down until his head rested between her breasts. Asher combed her fingers through his hair as contentment layered over desire. "Today, when I watched you playing Michael, I wanted you. Sitting there, surrounded by thousands of people in the middle of the afternoon, all I could think about was being with you like this." She gave a gurgle of laughter. "Wicked thoughts, such wonderfully wicked thoughts."

"So your invitation to dinner carried an ulterior motive."

"In your weakened condition I knew you'd be a pushover, though I had thought I'd have to take you out and ply you with food and wine first."

"And if I'd refused?"

"I'd have come up with something else."

Grinning, he lifted his head. "What?"

Asher shrugged. "I could have come up here and seduced you before you'd gotten your strength back."

"Hmm…I almost wish I'd said no."

"Too late. I have you now."

"I could get stubborn."

Slowly she smiled. "I know your weaknesses," she whispered, running a fingertip up the nape of his neck. His shudder was quick and uncontrollable. Leaning up, she took his face in her hands. Lazily she rubbed her lips over his, then deepened the touch into a kiss—a long, draining taste that left him weak. Her tongue glided over his, then retreated.

"Asher." On an oath he crushed her beneath him,

savaging her mouth with a need that had risen so quickly, it left him dazed. He didn't hear the discreet knock on the door, nor did he understand her murmurs.

"The door," she managed. "Ty, it's room service."

"What?"

"The door."

Laying his forehead on hers, he struggled to recapture his control. "They're awful damn quick," he muttered. He found he was trembling. How could he have forgotten that she could make him tremble? After letting out a long breath, he rose. Asher pulled the sheets up to her chin and watched him cross to the closet.

A beautiful body, she thought, both proud and admiring. Long and lean, with a network of muscle. She looked her fill as he rummaged through his closet for a robe. Strong shoulders, trim waist, narrow hips and long legs. An athlete's body, or a dancer's. He was made to compete.

He shrugged into the robe, belting it carelessly. Grinning, he turned to her. Asher's heart lodged in her throat. "Ty, you're so beautiful."

His eyes widened in astonishment. Torn between amusement and masculine discomfort, he headed for the door. "Good God," he said, making Asher smother a giggle. She brought her knees up to her chest as he signed the check at the door. In some ways, she mused, he was a little boy. To his way of thinking, the word *beautiful* applied only to a woman—or to an ace. He'd be more insulted than complimented having it applied to himself. Yet she saw him that way—not only physically. He was a man capable of lovely gestures, a man unashamed of his deep love for his mother, unafraid to show tenderness. He had no cruelty in him, though on the court he was unmerciful. His temper was explosive, but he was incapable of holding a grudge. Asher realized that it was his basic capacity for feeling that she had missed most of all. And still he had never, in all their closeness, in all the months of intimacy, told her that he loved her. If he had once said the words, she would never have left him.

"Where have you gone?"

Asher turned her head to see him standing beside a tray, a bottle of champagne in his hands. Quickly she shook her head and smiled again. "Nowhere." She cocked her head at the bottle. "All that just for us?"

He walked to the bed and sat on the edge. "Did you want some too?" The cork came off with a resounding pop as she cuffed his shoulder. With an easy stretch he rolled the tray toward them. "Here, hold the glasses." Without ceremony he poured champagne until it nearly ran over the rims.

"Ty, it'll spill on the bed."

"Better be careful then," he advised as he set the bottle back in the ice. He grinned as she sat cross-legged, balancing two glasses in her hands. The sheet was held in place over her breasts by arms pressed tightly to her sides.

She returned the grin with a glance of exasperation. "Aren't you going to take one?"

"Oh, I don't know." Hooking a finger under the sheet, he nudged it downward, exposing creamy flesh.

"Ty, cut it out, I'll spill it!"

"Better not, we have to sleep here." He urged the sheet a trifle lower. Frustrated, Asher looked from glass to glass. Wine swayed dangerously.

"This is a dirty trick, Starbuck."

"Yeah, I like it."

Asher narrowed her eyes. "I'm going to pour both glasses into your lap."

"Terrible waste," he decided, kissing her. "It's good stuff. I always found it strange," he began, lazily kissing her face as he spoke, "that I was bred for beer and you were bred for champagne, but you haven't any head for it."

"I have a perfectly good head for champagne."

Chuckling, he brushed his lips over her throat. "I remember one very memorable night when we shared a bottle. Three glasses make you crazy. I like you crazy."

"That's absurd." The lift of brow challenged him. Without hesitation Asher brought a glass to her lips, losing the sheet as she drank it. Ty watched the linen pool into her lap before she drained the last drop. "That's one," Asher announced, lifting the second glass. Ty plucked it from her fingers.

"Let's spread it out a little," he advised, amused. He drank, more conservatively, then reached for the tray of caviar. "You like this stuff."

"Mmm." Suddenly hungry, Asher spread a generous amount on a toast point. Ty settled down to the bowl of cold shrimp and spicy sauce. "Here, it's good." Though he allowed her to feed him a bite, he wrinkled his nose.

"Overrated," he stated. "This is better." He popped a shrimp into Asher's mouth.

"'S wonderful," she agreed with a full mouth, then chose another. "I didn't know I was so hungry."

Ty filled her glass again. Could anyone else imagine her, he wondered, sitting naked in bed, licking sauce from her finger? Did anyone else know how totally open she could be? She was talking now, in fits and starts as she ate, replaying her match. Ty let her ramble, pleased just to hear her voice, to see her animation. She was satisfied with her serve, worried about her backhand volley.

Publicly she chose her words with care, and made certain there were few of them. If a reporter could see her now, Ty mused, he'd wear a pencil down to the nub. She was full of joy and doubt, fear and self-congratulation. Words tumbled out without discretion. Her face was animated, her hands gestured. By the time she had slowed down, her second glass was empty. Perhaps she was completely happy, because she wasn't even aware of the sensation. She was simply at ease, completely herself. Comfortably full, she toyed with the last of the caviar.

"Are you worried about playing Chuck in the finals?"

Ty bit into a shrimp. "Why?"

"He was always good," Asher began, frowning a bit. "But he's developed over the past few years."

Grinning, Ty tilted more wine into her glass. "Don't you think I can beat him?"

She sent him a long, considering look. "You were always good too."

"Thanks." After setting the caviar on the tray, he stretched lengthwise on the bed.

"Chuck plays a bit like my father did," Asher mused. "Very clean, very precise. His talent's polished rather than raw."

"Like mine."

"Yes. That raw athletic ability is something every competitor envies. My father used to say that you had more natural talent than any player he'd seen in his career." Over the rim of her glass she smiled down at him. "Yet he always wanted to smooth out your form. Then there were your…antics on the court."

Ty laughed, kissing her knee through the sheet. "It used to drive him crazy."

"I imagine he'd be more pleased if he saw you play now."

"And you?" Ty countered. "How would he feel if he saw you play now?"

Asher shifted her eyes from his to stare into her glass. "He won't."

"Why?"

As if to erase the question, she lifted her hand. "Ty, please."

"Asher," he said quietly, grasping her fingers. "You're hurting."

If she could have held it back, she would have. But the words tumbled out. "I let him down. He won't forgive me."

"He's your father."

"And he was my coach."

Unable to comprehend, Ty shook his head. "What difference does that make?"

"All the difference." The pain slipped out. As if to numb it, she swallowed more wine. "Please, not tonight. I don't want anything to spoil tonight."

Her fingers had tightened on his. One by one Ty kissed them until he felt the tension relax. "Nothing could." Over their joined hands, dark, intense eyes met hers. Spontaneously her pulse began to race. "I never got you completely out of my mind," he confessed. "Too many things reminded me—a phrase, a song. Silence.

There were times alone at night I would have sworn I heard you breathing in the quiet beside me."

The words moved her…hurt her. "Ty, those were yesterdays. We can start now."

"Now," he agreed. "But we'll have to deal with yesterday sooner or later."

Though she opened her mouth to disagree, she knew. "Later then. Right now I don't want to think about anything but being with you."

He grinned, brushing a stray curl from her cheek. "It's difficult to argue with that."

"Don't get cocky," she told him, then tossed off the rest of her champagne. "That was three," Asher said haughtily. "And I'm not the least affected."

Ty had no trouble recognizing the signs—the flushed cheeks, the glowing eyes and misty smile. Whatever she might say, he knew the champagne was swimming in her head. And when they loved again, she would be soft and strong and passionate. He found himself wanting to simply look at her for a few minutes more. Once they touched, the fire would take them.

"Want another?" he offered.

"Sure."

Wisely he filled her glass only halfway before he replaced the bottle. "I caught your interview today," Ty commented. "It was on while I was changing."

"Oh?" Asher shifted to lie on her stomach, propping herself on her elbows. "How'd I do?"

"Hard to say. It was all in French."

She laughed, adjusting her position so that she could take another sip. "I'd forgotten."

"How about a translation?"

"He asked things like—Mademoiselle Wolfe, do you

find any changes in your style after your temporary retirement? And I said something like I feel I've tightened my serve." She chuckled into her wine. "I didn't mention that my muscles beg for me to give them a break after two sets. He asked how I felt about playing the *young* Miss Kingston in the finals and I refrained from punching him in the mouth."

"That was diplomatic," Ty answered, slipping the glass from her fingers.

"I'm a hell of a diplomat," Asher agreed. Rolling over on her back, she looked up at him. He lounged just behind her so that she had to tilt her head at an odd angle to make eye contact. "You stole my glass."

"Yes, I did." After setting it on the tray, Ty gave the wheeled table a slight shove.

"Did we finish dinner?" Reaching up and back, she locked her arms around his neck.

"We've definitely finished dinner." He allowed her to urge him down until his mouth hovered above hers.

"Got any suggestions about what we should do now?" She liked the strangeness of having his face upside down over hers. Playfully she nipped at his lip.

"No. Do you?"

"Got a deck of cards?"

"Uh-uh."

"Then I guess we'll have to make love." She gave a rich, low laugh before she kissed him again. "All night—just to pass the time."

"It's something to do. Rainy nights are so boring."

Eyes dancing, she nodded. "Mmm, yes. Let's make the best of it."

Her lips were curved in a smile as his met them, but they parted eagerly. She found it strangely seductive to have his tongue meet hers this way. On a gurgle of laughter, she closed her teeth gently, capturing him. In response, he trailed his fingers over her breast until her moan freed him.

"I get dizzy kissing you upside down," Asher murmured.

"I like you dizzy." Leaning forward, he trailed moist kisses over her throat. The tip of his tongue picked up her flavor, then lingered over it. He could feel pulse beats both with his hand and his lips. Finding the curve of his neck vulnerable, Asher began to give him the same pleasure he was bringing her.

"I want to touch you," she complained. "I can't touch you this way."

But he continued to explore from where he was, enjoying the freedom his hands had over her body. The scent of the rich sauce still lingering in the air, and the zing of champagne clung to two tongues as they joined. The mattress groaned quietly as she shifted. Then she was on her knees, pressed body to body. In a quick move she had stripped the robe from him so he was as naked as she. With a half laugh, half sigh, she ran her palms up his strong back.

Entwined, enchanted, neither noticed that the rain had ceased. Inside the quiet room, pleasure built. Strong thigh pressed against strong thigh, hungry lips sought hungry lips. Their passion was equal, their needs the same. Together, they lay down.

Soft sighs became moans. Before long, gentle caresses became demanding. Both seemed desperate to touch and be touched, to have their own weaknesses exploited. With instinctive understanding they held back the final gift. The inner fire built, dampening their flesh, but still they lingered over each other. There was so much to make up for, so much time to recapture. Though passion was flaring, this thought hovered in the back of both their minds. Tonight was a fresh beginning. They wanted all of it.

Asher thought her lungs would burst. The combination of wine and passion buzzed in her head. A laugh, smoky with desire, floated from her as he gasped her name. She wanted to tempt him, torment him, give to him. His stomach was hard and flat with muscle, yet the touch of her fingertip could make it quiver. Asher had forgotten this sense of power and exulted in it. Her small hands could make him weak. Her shapely, serious mouth could drive him wild.

The power shifted so abruptly, she was helpless. He found her greatest vulnerability and used his tongue to destroy her last vestige of control. Half wild, she called for him, struggling to have more, desperate to have all. Arching, she pressed him closer, cresting on a wave of delight that had no chance to recede. She thrashed as if in protest, yet arched again in invitation. As she built toward a higher peak, Ty slid up her body. Greedy, she drew him inside of her, hearing his gasp for breath before there was only feeling.

Later, they still clung together, damp, spent, fulfilled. He shifted only to turn out the light. In the midnight darkness they molded to each other, drifting toward sleep.

"You'll move in with me."

The murmur was a statement rather than a question. Asher opened her eyes before she answered. She could just see the outline of his face. "Yes, if you want me."

"I never stopped wanting you."

Without the light he didn't see the flicker of doubt in her eyes before he slept.

Chapter 7

She was afraid of London. Lady Wickerton had lived there—hostessing parties in the elegant three-story house in Grosvenor Square, attending the ballet at the Royal Opera House, the theater in Drury Lane, shopping in the West End. Lady Wickerton had played bridge with members of Parliament and had sipped tea at Buckingham Palace. Lady Wickerton had been a quiet, dutiful wife, a woman of intelligence, breeding and control. She had nearly suffocated in London.

Perhaps if Ty hadn't come between Jim Wolfe's daughter and Eric Wickerton's wife, Asher would have accepted her role with ease. She'd wanted to, had struggled to. Too much passion simmered inside her. It had been there all of her life, but the months with Ty had liberated it. Controlling something dormant was entirely different from harnessing something that pulsed with life. There had not even been her profession as an outlet for the energy that drove her.

Coming back to London was the most difficult step yet. There she would not only have to face memories of Ty, but the ghost of a woman she had pretended to be. It was all so familiar—Westminster Abbey, Trafalgar Square, the smells, the voices. Even the anticipation of Wimbledon couldn't block them out. There would be faces here that would remember the coolly elegant Lady Wickerton. And there would be questions.

Publicly she would remain aloof, distant and uninformative. Asher felt she owed Eric that much. She would simply refuse to discuss her marriage or its demise. Her early training, her years of following her father's rules, would serve her now more than ever.

She would give them tennis. With two straight championships now under her belt, Asher would have been spotlighted in any case. It was up to her to sway the press away from her personal life toward her professional resurgence. What was growing between her and Ty was still too fragile to be shared.

Happiness. She had nearly forgotten how simple and overwhelming the feeling was. Lazy midnight talks, crazy loving, quiet walks. They shared a hotel room and made it home for the days and nights they were there. She felt as much a gypsy as he, and was content to be so. Once she had looked for roots, stability, commitment. She'd learned that they meant nothing without the fullness of love. His spontaneity had always fascinated her. This time Asher would resolve the lingering fear of it and enjoy.

"Aren't you dressed yet?"

At the question Asher stopped tying her tennis shoe

and glanced up. Ty stood in the doorway between the small parlor and bedroom. Fully dressed, impatient, he frowned at her. His hair fell over his forehead as unruly as ever and still slightly damp from his shower. Waves of love radiated through her.

"Nearly," Asher tossed back. "Not everyone can move quickly in the morning, you know—especially on six hours' sleep."

The frown became a grin. "Something keep you up?" He caught the shoe she hurled at him in one hand, his eyes never leaving her face. Apparently the late night hadn't affected him. He looked well rested and full of barely controlled energy. "You can always take a nap after morning practice."

"Awfully pleased with yourself this morning, aren't you?"

"Am I?" Still grinning, he came toward her, tossing her shoe lightly. "It probably has something to do with trouncing that British kid in the quarter-finals yesterday."

"Oh?" Lifting a brow, Asher looked up at him. "Is that all you're pleased about?"

"What else?"

"Let me have my shoe," she demanded. "So I can throw it at you again."

"Did you know you have a poor morning attitude?" he asked, holding the shoe out of reach.

"Did you know you've been insufferable ever since you won the French?" she countered sweetly. "Remember, it's only one quarter of the Grand Slam."

He moved the shoe farther out of reach as she made a grab for it. "For you too, Face," he reminded her.

"The rest's on grass." In an attempt to hold him still, Asher grabbed the waistband of his warm-up pants.

"The woman's insatiable," he sighed. Diving, he pinned her beneath him on the bed.

"Ty! Stop!" Laughing, Asher pushed against him as he nuzzled at her neck. "We'll be late for practice."

"Oh. You're right." Giving her a quick kiss, he rolled away from her.

"Well," Asher muttered as she sat up, "you didn't take much persuading." Even as she started to tidy her hair, she was spun back into his arms. Her startled exclamation was smothered by his lips.

Long, deep, infinitely tender, smolderingly passionate. His arms circled her. Asher felt her bones soften, then dissolve. Her head fell back, inviting him to take more. Cradling her, Ty went on a slow exploration of her mouth. For the moment he enjoyed the sense of total domination. If they continued, he knew she would begin her own demands. Then it would be power for power. The knowledge excited him. Still, he laughed against her lips. There was time. A lifetime.

"You awake yet?" he asked her as he ran a hand lightly over her breast.

"Mmm-hmm."

"Good. Let's go." After setting her on her feet, he gave Asher's bottom a friendly pat.

"I'll get you for that," she promised. Needs stirred inside her, not quite under control.

"I certainly hope so." With an easy smile Ty slipped an arm around her shoulders. "You need to work on your backhand volley," he began as they walked from the room.

Insulted, Asher tossed her head back. "What are you talking about?"

"If you'd shorten your swing a bit more—"

"Shorten your own swing," she retorted. "And while you're at it," she continued, "you weren't exactly Mr. Speed yesterday."

"Gotta save something for the finals."

Asher snorted as she punched the elevator button. "Your conceit never wavers."

"Confidence," Ty contradicted. He liked seeing her this way—relaxed, but ready to laugh or to slap back. Briefly he wondered if she realized she was even more beautiful when she forgot caution. "What about breakfast?"

"What about it?"

"Want to grab some eggs after practice?"

She slid her eyes to his as the doors opened. "Is that your best offer?"

Ty lifted a brow as he followed her into the elevator. Asher exchanged a polite nod with a middle-aged couple in tweed. "Maybe you'd like to take up where we left off last night?" Ty lounged against an elevator wall as Asher gaped at him. "What did you say your name was again?"

Asher could feel two pairs of shocked and interested eyes boring into her back. "Misty," she replied, allowing a trace of cockney to color her voice. "Will you spring for champagne again, Mr. Starbuck? It was ever so good."

He recognized the light of challenge in her eyes and grinned. "So were you, sweetie."

When the doors opened to the lobby, the older couple

moved out reluctantly. Asher punched Ty in the arm before she followed.

In less than an hour they were both concentrating on form and speed and the capricious bounces a ball could take on grass. Was she playing better? Asher wondered as she sprang for Madge's slice. She felt looser, less encumbered. Indeed, she felt as though losing were not even a possibility. At Wimbledon she could forget the city of London.

Instead, she could remember the qualifying games at Roehampton, with their anything-goes attitude. Both bad language and rackets had flown. It was a contrast to the elegance and glamour of Wimbledon. Here both the players and the crowd were steeped in tradition. Hydrangeas against a backdrop of rich green grass, ivy-covered walls, limos and chauffeurs. Colors were soothing, mauve and green, as if time itself had sobered them.

Here spectators would be well-mannered, quiet between points, applauding after them. Even those in standing room would behave, or the chair judge would tell them politely to quiet down. No one hung from the scoreboards at Wimbledon. It was as revered as the changing of the guards, as English as double-decker buses.

There was no doubt, as one gazed around the immaculately tended velvet lawns, the pampered roses, the dollhouse kiosks and the stands that could accommodate more than twenty-five thousand, that Wimbledon *was* tennis. It was here former players migrated to. It was here future players aspired to. Asher remembered Ty telling her about watching the matches one long-ago July Fourth and making a vow. He had kept it, not once, but four times. More than anything she had wanted before, Asher wanted them to both walk away from Centre Court as champions.

Behind the baseline, Asher stood with a racket and a ball, staring off into space.

"Had enough?" Madge called out.

"Hmm…what?" Asher's head snapped around. Seeing Madge standing with her legs spread, hand on hips, had her laughing. "I suppose I have, I was daydreaming."

From opposite ends of the court, they walked toward their bags and jackets. "No sense asking if you're happy," Madge began conversationally. "You look absolutely miserable floating two inches off the ground."

"That obvious, huh?"

"I won't pretend not to be pleased," Madge added smugly. "I've always thought you two made a great team. Going to make it official?"

"I— No, we're just taking it one day at a time." Asher kept her eyes lowered as she packed her racket. "Marriage is just a formality, after all."

"And pigs fly," Madge countered calmly. When Asher glanced up with a cautious smile, she went on. "For some, yes, you're right. Not for you, Face. Why did you stay in an unhappy marriage for three years?" When Asher started to speak, Madge lifted a hand. "Because to you marriage is a promise, and you don't break promises."

"I failed once," she began.

"Oh, all by yourself? Isn't that being a bit self-absorbed?" Impatient, Madge settled her hands on her hips again. "Listen, you aren't going to let one mistake keep you from being happy, are you?"

"I am happy," Asher assured her, punctuating the statement by touching Madge's shoulder. "Ty's all I've ever wanted, Madge. I can't risk losing him again."

Her brow puckered in confusion. "But you left him, Asher, not the other way around."

"I'd already lost him," she said flatly.

"Asher, I don't—"

"It's a new day," she interrupted, then took a deep breath of scented morning air. "A fresh start. I know what mistakes I made and have no intention of repeating them. There was a time in my life that I thought I had to come first, before this." Holding up the small white ball, Asher examined it. "Before anything. I looked on tennis as a competitor, his family as a rival. That was stupid." Dropping the ball into a can, Asher closed it.

"That's funny," Madge mused. "There was a time in my life I thought The Dean's work came first. He thought the same about me. It wasn't true in either case."

With a smile Asher slung her bag over her shoulder. "Ty won't ever forget that tennis took him out of that tenement. Maybe he shouldn't. That's the thing that brings fire to his game."

She knows him so well in some ways, Madge thought, and not at all in others. "And what brings the ice to yours?"

"Fear," Asher answered before she thought. For a moment she gave Madge a blank look, then shrugged. Saying it aloud made it seem rather unimportant. "Fear of failure, or exposure." Laughing, she began to walk. "Thank God you're not a reporter."

The gravel crunched underfoot as they moved down

the path. It was a sound Asher associated with the tidiness of English courts. "Remind me to tell you sometime what goes through my head five minutes before a match."

With a sigh Asher hooked her arm through her old partner's. "Let's hit the showers."

There was no dream. Asher slept as deeply as a child, with no worries, no nagging fears. The curtains were drawn closed so that the afternoon sun filtered through lazily. Traffic sounds muffled through it, coming as a quiet drone. She wore only a short terry robe and lay on top of the spread. Ty would come back to wake her so that they could spend some time sight-seeing before nightfall. Because they were both scheduled to play the following day, they would go to bed early.

The knock on the door wakened her. Sitting up, Asher ran a hand through her tousled hair. He'd forgotten his key, she thought groggily. She stepped from the dim bedroom into the brighter parlor, wincing against the change of light. Absently she wondered what time it was as she opened the door. Shock took a moment to penetrate.

"Eric," she whispered.

"Asher." He gave her what was nearly a bow before he elbowed his way into the room. "Did I wake you?'

"I was napping." She closed the door, trying to recover her scattered wits. He looked the same, she thought. Naturally he would. Eric would see no reason to change. He was tall, slim, with a military carriage. He had a sharp-featured European face, a bit haughty and remote. Dark blond hair was cut and groomed to indicate wealth and conservatism. Light eyes in a pale face—both romantic, yet intelligent and cold. Asher knew that his mouth could twist into a hard line when he was crossed. As a suitor he had been charming, as a lover, meticulous. As a husband he'd been unbearable. She drew herself straight. He was no longer her husband.

"I didn't expect to see you, Eric."

"No?" He smiled. "Did you think I wouldn't drop by while you were in town? Lost a bit of weight, Asher."

"Competition tends to do that." Years of training had her gesturing toward a chair. "Please, sit down. I'll get you a drink."

There was no reason to be upset by him now, she told herself. No need to feel fear or guilt. Divorced couples managed to be civilized more often than not. Eric, Asher thought with a grim smile, was a very civilized man.

"Have you been well?" She poured his scotch neat, then added ice to Perrier for herself.

"Quite well. And you?"

"Yes. Your family?"

"Doing wonderfully." Eric accepted the glass she offered, then eyed her over the rim. "And your father?" He watched for the flash of pain, and was satisfied.

"As far as I know, he's fine." Quite consciously Asher drew on the mask as she sat.

"Still hasn't forgiven you for giving up your career."

Her eyes were level now and expressionless. "I'm sure you're aware he hasn't."

Mindful of the crease in his pants, Eric crossed his legs. "I thought perhaps now that you're competing again…" He allowed the sentence to die.

Asher watched the bubbles rise in her glass, but left

them untasted. “He no longer acknowledges me,” she said flatly. “I’m still paying, Eric.” She lifted her eyes again. “Does that satisfy you?”

He drank leisurely for a moment. “It was your choice, my dear. Your career for my name.”

“For your silence,” Asher corrected. “I already had your name.”

“And another man’s child in your belly.”

Ice clinked against ice as her hands shook. Quickly she controlled the tremor. “One would have thought it would have been enough that I lost the child,” she murmured. “Did you come all this way to remind me?”

“I came,” Eric said as he leaned back, “to see how my ex-wife was adjusting. You’re victorious on the courts, Asher, and as lovely as ever.” She didn’t speak as his eyes roamed the room. “Apparently you didn’t waste too much time picking up with your old lover.”

“My mistake was in leaving him, Eric. We both know that. I’m very, very sorry.”

He sent her an icy look. “Your mistake was in trying to pass his bastard off on me.”

Furious and trembling, Asher sprang to her feet. “I never lied to you. And by God, I’ll never apologize again.”

He remained seated, swirling liquor. “Does he know yet?”

Her color drained dramatically enough to make him smile genuinely. Hate ate at him. “No, I see he doesn’t. How interesting.”

“I kept my word, Eric.” Though her hands were laced tightly together, Asher’s voice was strong. “As long as I was your wife, I did everything you asked of me.”

He acknowledged this with a slight nod. Her honesty

hadn't been enough—nor had her three years of penance. "But you're not my wife any longer."

"We agreed. The marriage was intolerable for both of us."

"What are you afraid he'd do?" Eric mused, frowning up at the ceiling. "He's a very physical man as I remember, with a primitive sort of temper." Lowering his eyes, he smiled again. "Do you think he'd beat you?"

Asher gave a short laugh. "No."

"You're very confident," he murmured. "What exactly are you afraid of?"

Wearily she dropped her hands to her sides. "He wouldn't forgive me, Eric, any more than you have. I lost the child, I lost my father. My self-esteem. I'll never lose the guilt. I hurt nothing but your pride, Eric, haven't I suffered enough for that?"

"Perhaps…perhaps not." Rising, he stepped toward her. She remembered the scent of his crisp, dignified cologne very well. "Perhaps the most perfect punishment might be in never knowing your secret is safe. I'll make you no promises, Asher."

"It astonishes me that I was ever naïve enough to think of you as a kind man, Eric," she said softly.

"Justice," he returned, toasting her.

"Revenge has little to do with justice."

He shrugged an elegant shoulder. "All in your viewpoint, my dear."

She wouldn't give him the satisfaction of breaking down—of weeping, of screaming or begging. Instead, Asher stood perfectly still. "If you've said all you've come to say, I'd like you to go."

"Of course." After finishing off the liquor, he set down the glass. "Sleep well, darling. Don't bother, I'll let myself out." Eric turned the doorknob and found himself face-to-face with Ty. Nothing could have pleased him more.

Ty noted his cold, satisfied smile before his gaze shifted to Asher. Standing in the center of the room, she seemed frozen. There was anguish, and, he thought, fear in her eyes. Her face was dead-white and still. Even as he wondered what it was she feared, Ty took in the rest of her appearance. The tousled hair, the brief robe and exposed skin had rage boiling in him. Asher could feel it from where she stood.

His eyes whipped back to Eric's. There was murder in them. "Get the hell out of here."

"Just on my way," Eric said equably, though he had inched back against the door in instinctive defense. His last thought as he shut it behind him was that Asher would bear the brunt of the fury in Ty's eyes. That alone had made it worth the trip.

The room vibrated with the silent storm. Asher didn't move. It seemed Ty would stare at her for eternity. The trembling was difficult to control, but she forced herself. If she made light of the incident, perhaps so would he.

"What the hell was he doing here?"

"He just dropped by…I suppose to wish me luck." The lie sliced at her.

"Cozy." Crossing to her, Ty caught the lapel of her robe in his hand. "Don't you usually dress for visitors, Asher? Then again, I suppose it isn't necessary for ex-husbands."

"Ty, don't."

"Don't what?" he demanded. Though he struggled against the words, the accusations, the feelings, he knew it was a losing battle. Against the unknown he would always attack. "Wouldn't it be better form to meet him somewhere else? It's a little sticky here, isn't it?"

The cold sarcasm hurt more than his fury would have. With so much to hide, she could only shake her head. "Ty, you know there's nothing between us. You know—"

"What the hell do I know?" he shouted, grasping the other lapel. "Don't ask, don't question. Then I walk in and find you entertaining the bastard you left me for."

"I didn't know he was coming." She gripped his arms for balance as he nearly lifted her off her feet. "If he had called, I would have told him to stay away."

"You let him in." Enraged, he shook her. "Why?"

Despair rather than fear clutched at her. "Would you be happier if I had slammed the door in his face?"

"Yes, damn it."

"I didn't." She pushed at him now, as furious as he. "I let him in, I gave him a drink. Make what you like of it. I can't stop you."

"Did he want you back?" he demanded, ignoring her struggles. "Is that why he came?"

"What does it matter?" Impotently she slammed her fists into his chest. "It's not what *I* want." She threw back her head, her eyes burning.

"Then tell me, tell me now why you married him." When she tried to pull away, he dragged her back. "I'll have that much, Asher, and I'll have it now."

"Because I thought he was what I needed," she cried out. Roaring in her ears was the anger, the fear she had felt for Eric.

"And was he?" To prevent her from striking out, Ty grasped her wrist.

"No!" She jerked but couldn't free herself. Frustration added to an almost unreasonable fury. "No, I was miserable. I was trapped." Her voice was both strong and harsh. "I paid in ways you can't imagine. There wasn't a day I was happy. Does that satisfy you?"

She did something he had never seen her do before. She wept. His grip on her wrists loosened as he watched tears flood her eyes and spill onto her cheeks. Never in all the years he'd known her had he seen that kind of torment on her face. Tearing herself from his grip, Asher fled into the bedroom, slamming the door at her back.

She wanted peace. She wanted privacy. The grief had hit her unexpectedly. If the tears hadn't clogged her throat, she would have told him about the baby. The words had been there, ready to spill out in anger. Then speech had been impossible. Now she needed to weep it out.

Ty stared at the closed door for a long time. The wrenching sound of sobbing came to him. It was a reaction he hadn't expected. His anger was justified, as were his questions. Anger for anger he could have comprehended, but the pain he heard was altogether different. Having come from a family of women, he understood a woman's tears. Over the years he'd done his share of comforting and soothing. But these sobs were hot and bitter—and Asher never wept.

Jess cried easily, quiet, feminine tears. His mother wept with joy or silent sadness. These he could handle. A shoulder could be offered, a few sympathetic words, a teasing comment. Instinctively he knew none of those were the prescription for raw grief.

He still had questions. He still had anger. But the sounds from the bedroom forced him to put them aside. Ty recognized when tears were used as a weapon or a defense. These were being torn from her unwillingly. Dragging a hand through his hair, he wondered if it was Eric or himself who was responsible for them. Or something he knew nothing about. Cursing softly, he went to the door and opened it.

She lay curled on the bed in a ball of misery. Her body shook. When he touched her she jerked away. Saying nothing, Ty lay down beside her, gathering her close. For another moment she fought him. *Alone.* Her tears were not to be observed, not to be shared. *Private.* Ty dealt with her struggles by merely holding her tighter in arms that were both strong and gentle.

"I'm not going anywhere," he murmured.

With no more protest, Asher clung to his comfort and let her grief run its course.

It had grown dark and her body was weak. There were no more tears left in her. Ty's arms were strong around her. Beneath her damp cheek she could hear the steady beat of his heart. Gently, almost absently, his fingers stroked the base of her neck.

She'd nearly told him. Asher closed her eyes, too weary to feel fear or regret. If she could have summoned up the energy, she would have been grateful for the tears that had prevented her confession.

I lost your baby. Would he be holding her now if those words had spilled out? What good would it do to tell him? she asked herself. Why make him grieve for something he had never known? And grieve he would, she knew, after the anger passed. It came to her suddenly that it wasn't only fear that kept the secret locked inside her. She couldn't bear to see Ty hurt as she had hurt.

How could she explain to him about Eric without dragging up old bitterness, opening old wounds? Ty hadn't wanted her any longer—Jess had made that abundantly clear. But Eric had. It had been her pride that had turned to Eric, then her sense of duty that had kept her with him. Perhaps if she had been stronger after the accident she would never have made those promises to him....

Asher had floated to consciousness on a wave of pain. What reason was there to wake up and hurt? she thought groggily. Sleep, sleep was so peaceful.

She remembered the shouting, the fall, the swimming darkness. The baby...Ty's baby. Panic—the panic pierced by lethargy. Her eyelids seemed weighted with lead, but she forced them open even as she reached a protective hand to her stomach. Stern and cold, Eric's face floated in front of her eyes.

"The baby," she managed through dry lips.

"Dead."

Tearing, burning grief replaced the pain. "No." Moaning, she closed her eyes again. "Oh, God, no. My baby, not my baby. Ty—"

"Listen to me, Asher." Eric spoke briskly. For three days he had waited while Asher drifted in and out of consciousness. She had lost the baby and a great deal of blood. Once she had nearly slipped away, but he had willed her to live. The love he had once felt had turned to resentment that bordered on hate. She had deceived him, made a fool of him. Now he would have his payment.

"My baby…"

"The baby's dead," he said flatly, then gripped her hand. "Look at me." She obeyed with eyes glazed with sorrow. "You're in a private clinic. The reason for your being here will never be known beyond the front doors. If you do what I say."

"Eric…" A spark of hope flickered. With what strength she had, Asher tightened her fingers on his. "Are they sure? Couldn't there be a mistake? Please—"

"You miscarried. The servants will be discreet. As far as anyone knows, we've slipped away for a few days."

"I don't understand." She pressed her hand against her stomach as if to make the truth a lie. "The fall…I fell down the stairs. But—"

"An accident," he stated, making the loss of the child sound like a broken glass.

Insidiously the pain slipped through. "Ty," Asher moaned, shutting her eyes.

"You're my wife, and will remain so until I say differently." Eric waited until her eyes focused on him again. "Would you have me call your lover and tell him you married me while carrying his child?"

"No." She could only whisper the word. *Ty.* She ached for him. He was lost to her—as lost as the child they'd made together.

"Then you'll do as I say. You'll retire from professional tennis. I won't have the press speculating about the two of you and dragging my name through the mud. You'll behave as I expect Lady Wickerton to behave. I will not touch you," he continued with a trace of disgust. "Any physical desire I felt for you is gone. We will live in the manner I designate or your lover will hear from me about this game you played. Is this understood?"

What did it matter how she lived? Asher asked herself. She was already dead. "Yes. I'll do whatever you want. Please, leave me alone now."

"As you wish." He rose. "When you're stronger, you'll give an official press release on your retirement. Your reason will be that you have no more time for tennis or any desire for a career that would take you away from your husband and your adopted country."

"Do you think it matters to me?" she whispered. "Just let me alone, let me sleep."

"Your word, Asher."

She gave him a long last look before she wearily closed her eyes. "My word, Eric."

And she had kept it. She had tolerated Eric's pleasure when her father had turned away from her. She had ignored his discreet but frequent affairs. For months she had lived like a zombie, doing as she was bid. When the layers of grief began to peel away, his hold remained through guilt and threats. When she had begun to come to life again, Asher had bargained for her freedom. Nothing was more important to Eric than his reputation. She held his many women in one hand, he held the knowledge of Ty's child in the other. They'd made an uneasy agreement.

Now he was back, Asher mused. Perhaps because she was making a success of her life again. Still, she felt he would keep his silence, if only to ensure a hold over her. Once he spoke, all ties were severed. Or if she spoke…

She remembered the look on Ty's face when he had seen her with Eric. Explanations would never be accepted now. Perhaps the day would come when they fully trusted each other, when the memory of betrayal would be dimmed.

She'd been silent for some time. By the steadiness of her breathing she might have been sleeping. Ty knew she was awake and thinking. What secrets was she holding from him? he wondered. And how long would it be before the air between them was finally cleared? He wanted to demand, but her vulnerability prevented him. More than anything else, he didn't want to risk her slipping behind the wall she could so easily erect.

"Better?" he murmured.

She sighed before he felt the faint movement of her head as she nodded. There was one thing she could settle between them, one thing she could make him understand. "Ty, he means nothing to me. Do you believe that?"

"I want to."

"Believe it." Suddenly intense, she sat up and leaned against his chest. If she could give him nothing else, she could give him this. "I feel nothing for Eric, not even hate. The marriage was a mistake. From the start it was nothing more than a façade."

"Then why—"

"It's always been you," she said before she crushed her mouth to his. "Always you." She pressed her lips to his throat, passion erupting in her as swiftly as the tears. "I stopped living for so long and now..." Her mouth ran wildly over his face. "I need you now, only you."

Her mouth met his fervently, saying more than

words. Her ardor touched off his own. There was no need for questions now, or for answers. She pulled the shirt from him, eager to touch. Pressing her lips to heated flesh, she heard him groan. Though her hands moved swiftly to undress him, her lips loitered, lingering to arouse. With her tongue she left a moist trail of fire.

His body was a pleasure to her—hard muscle, long bones, taut flesh. Delighting in him, she sought new secrets. If she nibbled at his waist, his breathing grew shallow, his fingers gripped her hair. If she moved her palm along his thigh, his moan vibrated with need. Giddy with power, she ran a crazed trail from stomach to chest, her lips hungry and seeking.

He struggled to pull the robe from her as she caught his earlobe between her teeth. Low, sultry laughter drove him wild. Neither heard the seam rip as he tugged the terry cloth from her. Limber and quick, she made it impossible for him to grant them both the final relief. Her lovemaking tormented and thrilled him while her agility held him off.

"Now," he demanded, grasping her hips. "Asher, for God's sake."

"No, no, no," she murmured, then cut off his oath with a searing kiss. She found the torture exquisite. Though her own body begged for fulfillment, she wanted to prolong it. As his hands slid over her damp skin, she arched back, reveling in his touch. She belonged, and always would, to the man who could release her fires.

Neither was in control, each a slave to the other. She wanted nothing more than to be bound to him—here, in a dark room with the sound of her own breathing raging in her ears, in the sunlight with the secrets of the night still humming between them. For always.

Beneath her, his body was hot and moist and moving. The rhythm seduced her. Everything warm, everything giving, flowed through her. Thoughts vanished, memories dimmed. Now—there was only now—the all-powerful, greedy present.

This time when he gripped her hips she made no attempt to stop him. Her head fell back in complete abandonment as they joined. The moan was rich and deep, and from both of them. As one, they were catapulted up, beyond pleasure, into ecstasy.

Chapter 8

Asher had driven in limousines all her life. As a child she'd ridden behind a chauffeur named George in a shiny maroon car with smoked glass and a built-in bar. George had remained the family driver though the cars had changed—an elegant white Rolls, a sturdy blue Mercedes.

Lady Wickerton's driver had been Peter and the car had been an old discreet gray Daimler. Peter had been as silent and as efficient as the car. Asher felt no thrill at being driven in the long black limo toward Wimbledon.

As they passed through Roehampton, she watched the scenery. Tidy, healthy trees, trimmed shrubs, orderly flowers. In a few hours, she would be in Centre Court. Aching, sweating…and winning. This was the big prize. Credibility, prestige, press. They were all at Wimbledon.

Once before she and Ty had taken the championships and led the dancing at the Wimbledon Ball—in that year of her life that had brought complete joy and complete misery. Now she would play her old foe Maria Rayski with all the verve and all the cunning she had at her disposal.

Though she'd thought her life had begun to come to order with her first win, Asher now realized she'd been wrong. The turning point was today, here in the arena that was synonymous with her profession. She would play her best here, on the surface she knew best, in the country in which she had lived like a prisoner. Perhaps true confidence would begin after this match was over.

She thought of Ty, the young boy who had once vowed to play and win. Now, in the lush interior of the limo, Asher made a similar vow. She would have a championship season. Reestablish Asher Wolfe *for* Asher Wolfe. Then she would be ready to face the woman. The woman would face the only man who mattered.

The crowds waited for her and other arriving players. The greetings were enthusiastic. Roaming spectators sipped champagne and nibbled on strawberries and cream. Signing autographs, Asher felt light, confident, ready. Nothing, she thought, could mar such a day. The Fourth of July, the brilliant sunshine, the scent of garden flowers.

She remembered other Wimbledons. So little had changed. Fans mingled with players, chatting, laughing. The atmosphere was one of an informal tea party with the promise of a spectacle. But she could feel the nerves. They were there, just under the bonhomie, in the young players, the veterans, doubles and singles finalists. Mixing among them were rock stars and celebrities, millionaires and landed gentry.

Asher saw faces from the past, players from her father's generation. For them it was a reunion, nostalgia, tradition. There were people she had entertained in Grosvenor Square. For them it was a social event. The dress was summer-garden-party chic—picture hats and pastels. Because yesterdays had to be faced, Asher greeted former acquaintances.

"Asher, how lovely to see you again...." "What a sweet little outfit...." "How strange it is not to see you at the club anymore...." There was speculation, thinly veiled by stretched manners. She dealt with it calmly, as she had during her three years of marriage.

"Where's that old man of yours?"

Turning, Asher clasped two large hands warmly. "Stretch McBride, you haven't changed a bit."

Of course he had. When he'd first tickled Asher's chin, he'd been thirty. His face had been unlined, his hair untouched with gray. He'd won nearly every major championship there was to win twice around. Though he was still tall, and nearly as lean as he had been in his prime, the twenty years showed on his face.

"You always told a lie beautifully." Grinning, he kissed her cheek. "Where's Jim?"

"In the States," she answered, keeping her smile bright. "How have you been, Stretch?"

"Just fine. Got five grandchildren and a nice string of sporting goods stores on the East Coast." He patted her hand. "Don't tell me Jim isn't going to be here? He hasn't missed it in forty years."

It was a struggle not to show the pain, much less not to feel it. "As far as I know, he won't be. I'm awfully glad to see you again. I haven't forgotten that you taught me the dump shot."

Pleased, he laughed. "Use it on Maria today," he advised. "I love to see Americans win at Wimbledon. Tell your old man hello for me."

"Take care, Stretch." Her smile evaded the promise she couldn't give. With a parting kiss, he moved away.

Turning, Asher found herself face-to-face with Lady Daphne Evans. The striking brunette had been one of Eric's more discreet dalliances, and one of Asher's more difficult trials. Her eyes automatically cooled, though her voice was scrupulously polite.

"Daphne, you look exquisite."

"Asher." Daphne skimmed cool eyes over Asher's brief tennis dress, down long bare legs to her court shoes. "You look different. How odd to find you an athlete."

"Odd?" Asher countered. "I've always been an athlete. Tell me, how is your husband?"

The thrust was parried with a quick laugh. "Miles is in Spain on business. As it happens, Eric escorted me today."

Though her stomach churned, her face remained composed. "Eric's here?"

"Yes, of course." Meticulously Daphne adjusted the brim of her rose-pink hat. "You don't think he'd miss this Wimbledon, do you?" Long mink lashes swept down, then up again. "We're all very interested in the results. Will we see you at the ball, darling?"

"Naturally."

"Well, I must let you mingle, mustn't I? That's traditional. Best of luck." With a flash of a smile Daphne swirled her skirts and was gone.

Asher fought the nausea, but began to nudge her way through the crowd. All she wanted was the comparative peace of the A locker rooms. The day ahead promised to be enough of a fight without contending with ghosts. With a few smiles and mechanically gracious greetings, she made her way out of the main throng. A few moments to herself—that was what she needed before the stands began to fill, before her strength and abilities were put to the test.

She knew Eric well enough to be certain he had asked Daphne to seek her out. Yes, he would want to be sure she knew he was there—before the match. As she slipped into the locker room, Asher noticed her hands were shaking. She couldn't allow it. In thirty minutes she would have to be in complete control.

When she walked onto the court Asher was careful not to look into the crowd. It would be easier on her nerves if the people who watched and cheered remained anonymous. As she attempted to empty her mind of all but the first game, Asher watched Maria Rayski.

On her own side of the court, Rayski paced, gesturing occasionally to the crowd, tossing comments. Her nerves were undisguised. It was always so, Asher mused. Rayski chewed her nails, cracked her knuckles and said the first thing that came into her mind. In a wary sort of fashion Asher had always liked her. At five foot ten, she was tall for a woman and rangy, with a deadly stretch. Fatalistically Asher recalled she had a habit of badgering her opponent.

Well, she decided as she chose her game racket, Rayski's histrionics might just keep her mind off who was, and who was not, in the stands. She eyed the television camera dispassionately. With the wonder of technology, the match would be relayed to the States with only a brief delay. Would her father even bother to watch? she wondered. Silently she walked to the baseline for the first serve.

There was no cautious testing in the first games. Rayski went straight for the jugular. Both were fast players, and while Rayski was more aggressive, Asher was a better strategist. A ball could take ungodly bounces on grass, particularly the lush grass of Wimbledon's Centre Court. To defend, to attack, required instinct and timing. It also required complete concentration.

The lead jockeyed back and forth during the first set as the players gave the fourteen thousand spectators the show they'd come to see. Over the elegant, century-old court, they sweated, gritted their teeth and scrambled, not for the enjoyment of those who paid to see, but for the game. Rayski tossed an occasional taunt over the net between rallies. Asher might have been deaf for all the response she gave. She had her rhythm—nothing was going to interfere with it. She placed her ground strokes with deadly precision, charged the net for short angling volleys. Both her form and her energy seemed at perfect peak.

Everything changed when the women took their seats for the towel-off before the third set.

Because she had forgotten about everything but the game, Asher's defenses were lowered. An inadvertent glance up in the stands had her eyes locking with Eric's. A slow, icy smile spread over his face as he lifted a hand in salute—or reminder.

What the devil's wrong with her? Ty asked himself. He shifted closer to the edge of his seat and studied Asher with narrowed eyes. She'd just dropped two games straight, the second one on a double fault. True, Rayski was playing superbly, but so was Asher—until the third set. She was playing mechanically now, as if the life had gone out of her. Too often she was missing basic shots or failing to put anything extra on a return. Rayski's serve was not her strongest weapon, yet she was repeatedly breezing service winners past Asher.

If he didn't know her better, he would have sworn Asher was tanking the match. But Asher wasn't capable of deliberately losing.

Carefully Ty watched for signs of an injury. A strained muscle or twisted ankle would explain the change in her. She gave no sign of favoring a leg. The composure on her face was as perfect as a mask. Too perfect, Ty reflected as the third game went to fifteen-love. Something was definitely wrong, but it wasn't physical. Disturbed, he quickly scanned the crowd.

There were dozens of faces he knew, some by name, some by reputation. There was an award-winning actor he'd once played a celebrity tourney with. Ty had found him an earthy man with a credible forehand. He recognized the ballet star because Asher had once dragged him to see *The Firebird.* Beside the ballerina was a country-western singer with a crossover hit. Ty passed over them, looking for an answer. He found it sitting near the Royal Box.

There was a cool, satisfied smile on Eric's face as he watched his ex-wife. Beside him, a thin, flashy woman in a rose-colored hat looked bored. Rage rose in Ty instantly. His first instinct was to yank Eric up by his five-hundred-dollar lapels and rearrange the expression on his face with his fists.

"Son of a bitch," he muttered, already rising. The hand that grasped his wrist was strong.

"Where are you going?" Madge demanded.

"To do something I should've done three years ago."

Still clinging to his arm, Madge twisted her head to follow the direction of his eyes. "Oh, boy," she said under her breath. Through her fingertips she could feel Ty's temper. Only briefly did she consider the personal satisfaction she would gain from letting Ty do what he wanted. "Hold on," she snapped between her teeth. "Listen to me. Punching him out isn't going to do anything for Asher."

"The hell it won't," he retorted. "You know why he's here."

"To upset her," Madge managed calmly enough. "Obviously he's succeeding. Go talk to her." A strong man might have cringed from the blazing look Ty turned on her. Madge merely arched a brow. "You want to start a fight, Starbuck, do it after the match. I'll referee. Right now, use your head."

His control didn't come easily. Madge watched him struggle for it, lose it, then finally win. Though his eyes were still stormy, the hand under hers relaxed. "If talking doesn't work," he said flatly, "I'm going to break him in half."

"I'll hold your coat," she promised before Ty slipped away.

Knowing he'd have only a moment, Ty decided to use words sparingly—and make them count. After losing the game without making a point, Asher slumped into her chair. She didn't see Ty waiting for her.

"What the hell's wrong with you?"

Her head jerked up at the harsh tone. "Nothing."

She was tired, already defeated as she mopped at the sweat on her face.

"You're handing the match to Rayski on a platter."

"Leave me alone, Ty."

"Going to give him the satisfaction of watching you fall apart in front of fourteen thousand people, Face?" There was sarcasm without a trace of sympathy in his voice. He noted the quick, almost indiscernible flash in her eyes. He'd wanted to see it. Always, she played better if there was anger beneath the ice.

"I never thought I'd see you tank a match."

"Go to hell." Whirling, she stalked back to the baseline. Nobody, she thought as she waited for Rayski to take position, nobody accused Asher Wolfe of tanking. Rayski crouched in her pendulum receiving stance while Asher gave the ball a few testing bounces. Tossing it, she drew back her racket and lunged. The effort of the serve came out in a force of breath. The finely pulverized chalk at the baseline rose on contact. Without giving the ace a thought, Asher took her stance for the next serve.

Her anger had teeth. She could feel it gnawing at her. A photographer zoomed in on her face and captured the contradictory placid expression and frosted eyes. Temper was energy. Asher flew across the court, striking the ball as if it were the enemy. Yet her battle was sternly controlled. No one watching her would realize that she cursed Ty with each stroke. No one but Ty himself. Satisfied, he watched her turn her fury on her opponent.

Oh, she was fabulous to see, he thought. Those long, slim legs, the strong shoulders. Her form was so smooth, so precise, yet beneath was that excitement, that smoldering passion. She was as she played, he mused, and wanted her. No one but he knew just how reckless she could be, just how abandoned. The thought had desire moving through him. She was the woman all men fantasized about—part lady, part wanton. And his, Ty told himself fiercely. Only his.

After watching Asher fire a backhand volley past Rayski, he glanced up. Eric's smile was gone. As if sensing the scrutiny, the Englishman looked down. The two men studied each other as the crowd applauded Asher's game. Ty laughed, softly, insolently, then walked away.

Though the match held close to the last point, the impetus Ty had instilled in her carried Asher to the win. She was polite, even charming as she accepted the Wimbledon plate. Inside she was raging. The joy of victory couldn't penetrate the fury and resentment she was feeling. Ty had turned the tide of her emotions away from Eric and onto himself.

She wanted to shout. She smiled and raised her trophy for the crowd to see. She wanted to scream. Politely she allowed the army of cameras to snap her. Fatigue didn't touch her. The ache in her arm might not have existed.

At last freeing herself from the press and well-wishers, she simmered under the shower and changed. Determination made her remain at Wimbledon to watch Ty's match. Stubbornness made her refuse to admire his game. Eric was forgotten. Asher's only thought was to vent her fury at the first possible moment. It took five hard sets and two and a half hours before Ty could claim his own trophy.

Asher left the stadium before the cheers had died.

* * *

He knew she'd be waiting for him. Even before Ty slipped the key in the lock, he knew what to expect. He looked forward to it. His adrenaline was still flowing. Neither the shower nor the massage had taken it from him. Wimbledon always affected him this way. As long as he played, winning there would be his first goal.

Now, the demanding games behind him, the win still sweet, he felt like a knight returning home victorious from the wars. His woman waited. But she wouldn't throw herself into his arms. She was going to scratch at him. Oh, yes, he was looking forward to it.

Grinning, Ty turned the knob. He had no more than shut the door behind him than Asher stormed out of the bedroom.

"Congratulations, Face," he said amiably. "Looks like I get first dance at the ball."

"How dare you say those things to me in the middle of the match?" she demanded. Eyes glittering, she advanced on him. "How dare you accuse me of tanking?"

Ty set his bag and rackets on a chair. "What do you call what you were doing?"

"Losing."

"Quitting," he corrected her. "You might as well have put up a sign."

"I've never quit!"

He lifted a brow. "Only for three years."

"Don't you dare throw that in my face." Raising both hands, she shoved him. Instead of being offended, he laughed. It pleased him enormously that he could rattle her control.

"You did good," he reminded her. "I couldn't take a

chance on your losing." He gave her cheek an affectionate pinch. "I didn't want to open the ball with Maria."

"You conceited, overconfident louse!" She shoved him again. "Gramaldi almost took you. I wish he had." She shouted the lie at him. "You could use a good kick in the ego." With the intention of storming back into the bedroom, she whirled. Catching her wrist, Ty spun her back around.

"Aren't you going to congratulate me?"

"No."

"Aw, come on, Face." He grinned appealingly. "Give us a kiss."

For an answer Asher balled her hand into a fist. Ducking the blow, Ty gripped her waist and slung her over his shoulder. "I love it when you're violent," he said huskily as she pulled his hair.

To her own surprise—and annoyance—she had to choke back a laugh. "Then you're going to get a real charge out of this," she promised, kicking wildly as he threw her on the bed. Even though her reflexes were quick, Ty had her pinned beneath him in seconds. Breathless, she struggled to bring her knee up to his weakest point.

"Not that violent." Wisely he shifted to safety.

She twisted, squirmed and struggled. "You take your hands off me."

"Soon as I'm finished," he agreed, slipping a hand under the blouse that had come loose from her waistband.

Refusing to acknowledge the sensation of pleasure, Asher glared at him. "Don't you touch me."

"I have to touch you to make love to you." His smile

was reasonable and friendly. "It's the only way I know how."

I will not laugh, she ordered herself as the gurgle rose in her throat. She was angry, furious, she reminded herself.

Ty recognized the weakening and capitalized on it. "Your eyes get purple when you're mad. I like it." He kissed her firmly shut mouth. "Why don't you yell at me some more?"

"I have nothing more to say to you," Asher claimed haughtily. "Please go away."

"But we haven't made love yet." Lightly he rubbed his nose against hers.

Refusing to be charmed, she turned her head away. "We aren't going to."

"Wanna bet?" With one swift move he ripped her blouse from neck to waist.

"Ty!" Shocked, Asher gaped at him, her mouth open.

"I nearly did that when you were on Centre Court today. You should be glad I waited." Before she could react he tore her shorts into ragged pieces. Thinking he might have gone mad, Asher stayed perfectly still. "Something wrong?" he asked as his hand moved to cup her breast.

"Ty, you can't tear my clothes."

"I already did." Soft as a feather, his hand roamed down to her stomach. "Want to tear mine?"

"No." Her skin was beginning to quiver. She tried to shift away and found herself held prisoner.

"I made you angry."

Her head cleared long enough for her to glare at him. "Yes, and—"

"Angry enough to win," he murmured, trailing his

lips along her throat. "And when I watched you I nearly exploded from wanting you. All that passion simmering just under the surface. And only I know what it's like when it escapes."

She gave a little moan as his fingers stroked the point of her breast but tried to cling to reality. "You had no business saying I was tanking."

"I didn't say that, I only planted the idea." When he lifted his head, the look in his eyes had her drawing in a quick breath. "Did you think I'd stand by and watch him get to you like that? No man gets to you, Asher, no man but me."

With a savage kiss he cut off all words, all thoughts.

It always surprised Asher that Ty could project such raw sexuality in black tie. Conservative, formal dress could do nothing to alter his air of primitive masculinity. The material could cover the muscles, but it couldn't disguise the strength. There had been times Asher had wondered if it was his earthiness that had drawn her to him. Glimpsing him in a room filled with elegantly attired men and women, she knew it was more than that. It was all of him, every aspect, from temper to humor, that had made her his.

The Wimbledon Ball was as traditional as the tournament. The music, the lights, the people. It was always an evening to remember for its beauty and tastefulness. Asher counted the hours until it would be over. Scolding herself, she tuned back in to the conversation of her dance partner. She'd always enjoyed a party, always found pleasure in quiet well-run affairs. But now she wished she and Ty could have shared a bottle of wine in their room.

She didn't want the spotlight this evening, but candlelight. Over the heads of the other dancers her eyes met Ty's. It took only one brief glance to know that his thoughts mirrored hers. Love threatened to drown her.

"You're a lovely dancer, Miss Wolfe."

As the music ended, Asher smiled at her partner. "Thank you." Her smile never wavered as it ran through her head that she had completely forgotten the man's name.

"I was a great fan of your father's, you know." The man cupped a hand under her elbow to lead her from the dance floor. "The Golden Boy of Tennis." With a sigh he patted Asher's hand. "Of course, I remember his early days, before you were born."

"Wimbledon has always been his favorite. Dad loved the tradition…and the pomp," Asher added with a smile.

"Seeing the second generation here is good for the soul." In a courtly gesture he lifted her hand to his lips. "My best to you, Miss Wolfe."

"Jerry, how are you?"

A stately woman in silk brocade swept up to them. Lady Mallow, Eric Wickerton's sister, was, as always, elegant. Asher's spine stiffened.

"Lucy, what a pleasure!"

She offered her fingers to be kissed, sending Asher a brief glance as she did so. "Jerry, Brian's been searching for you to say hello. He's just over there."

"Well then, if you ladies will excuse me."

Having dispatched him, Lucy turned to her former sister-in-law. "Asher, you're looking well."

"Thank you, Lucy."

She gave Asher's simple ivory sheath a brief survey,

thinking that if she had worn something so basic, she would have blended in with the wallpaper. On Asher, the muted color and simple lines were stunning. Lucy gave her a candid stare. "And are you well?"

A bit surprised, Asher lifted a brow. "Yes, quite well. And you?"

"I meant that as more than small talk." Lucy's hesitation was brief, as was her glance to determine if they could be overheard. "There's something I've wanted to say to you for a long time." Stiffening, Asher waited. "I love my brother," Lucy began. "I know you didn't. I also know that throughout your marriage you did nothing to disgrace him, though he didn't return the favor."

The unexpected words had Asher staring. "Lucy—"

"Loving him doesn't blind me, Asher," she continued briskly. "My loyalty is with Eric, and always will be."

"Yes, I understand that."

Lucy studied Asher's face a moment, then she seemed to sigh. "I gave you no support when you were my brother's wife and I wanted to offer my apologies."

Touched, Asher took her hand. "There's no need. Eric and I were simply wrong for each other."

"I often wondered why you married him," Lucy mused, still searching Asher's face. "At first I thought it was the title, but that had nothing to do with it. Something seemed to change between you so soon after you were married, hardly two months." Asher's eyes clouded for only a moment under Lucy's direct gaze. "I wondered if you'd taken a lover. But it became very obvious in a short time that it was Eric, not you, who was...dallying. Just as it's become obvious that there's been only one man in your life." Her gaze shifted. Asher didn't have to follow it to know it rested on Ty.

"Knowing that hurt Eric."

"Knowing that, Eric should never have married you." Lucy sighed again, a bit indulgently. "But then, he's always wanted what belonged to someone else. I won't speak of that, but I'll tell you now what I should have told you long before—I wish you happiness."

On impulse, Asher kissed her cheek. "Thank you, Lucy."

Smiling, she glanced over at Ty again. "Your taste, Asher, has always been exquisite. I've envied it, though it's never been right for me. It's time I joined Brian."

As she turned away, Asher touched her hand. "If I wrote you, would you be uncomfortable?"

"I'd be very pleased." Lucy moved away, silks rustling.

Smiling, Asher realized she had been right. Wimbledon was her turning point. Another layer of guilt had been lifted. She was coming closer to discovering who she was, and what she needed. Feeling a hand on her arm, she turned to smile at Ty.

"Who was that?"

"An old friend." Asher lifted a hand to his cheek. "Dance with me? There's no other way I can hold you until we can be alone."

Chapter 9

Asher knew she had made great strides when pressure from the press no longer tightened her nerves. Her habitual terror of saying the wrong thing, or saying too much, faded. She still had secrets. Before coming to Australia she'd promised herself a moratorium. Whatever decisions had to be made would wait. For the moment she wanted to concentrate on happiness. Happiness was Ty—and tennis.

There were good memories in Australia—wins, losses. Good tennis. The people were relaxed, casual. The friendliness was exactly what Asher needed after the tension of England. Aussies remembered The Face, and welcomed her. For the first time since her comeback Asher found the winning taking second place to the enjoying.

The change in her was noticeable even during the

early rounds. Her smiles came more frequently. Though her play was no less intense and concentrated, the air of being driven was fading.

From the first row of the stands Ty watched her in early morning practice. He'd just completed two hours of his own. Now, his legs stretched out, he studied her from behind the protection of tinted glasses. She'd improved, he mused…not only as an athlete. He remembered how important athletic ability was to her. The fact that she was a strategist and a craftsman had never been enough. Always, she had striven to be recognized as a good athlete. And so she would be, he thought, as she raced to the net to slap a return with her two-fisted backhand. Perhaps in some ways the years of retirement had toughened her.

His face clouded a moment. Consciously he smoothed the frown away. This wasn't the time to think of that or to dwell on the questions that still plagued him. Whys—so many whys hammered at him. Yet he recognized that she was grabbing this time to be carefree. He'd give her that. He would wait. But when the season was over, he'd have his answers.

When her laughter floated to him he forgot the doubts. It was a rich, warm sound, heard all too rarely. Leaning back, Ty chugged down cold fruit juice and looked around him.

If Wimbledon was his favorite stadium, the grass of Kooyong was his favorite surface. It was as hard as a roadbed and fast. A ball bounced true here, unlike other grass courts. Even at the end of the season, when the courts were worn and soiled, the surface remained even. Even after a deluge of rain, the Australian grass was resilient. Kooyong was a treasure for the fast, for the aggressive. Ty was ready for just such a match. Through half-closed eyes he watched Asher. She was ready, too, he decided. And ever more ready to enjoy it. A smile touched his mouth. Whatever questions there were, whatever answers, nothing could harm what was between them now.

Noting the practice session was winding up, Ty jumped lightly down to the court. "How about a quick game?"

Madge shot him a look and continued to pack up her rackets. "Forget it, hotshot."

He grabbed a racket from her, bouncing a ball lightly on the strings. "Spot you two points."

With a snort Madge snatched the ball, dropping it into the can. "Take him on, Asher," she suggested. "He needs a lesson."

Catching her tongue between her teeth, Asher studied him. "Head to head," she decided.

"You serve."

Asher waited until he had taken his receiving position. Cupping two balls in her hand, she sent him a smile. "Been a while, hasn't it, Starbuck?"

"Last time we played you never got to game point." He gave Madge a wink. "Sure you don't want that handicap?"

Her ace answered for her. As pleased as he was surprised, Ty sent her a long look. Removing the tinted glasses, he tossed them to Madge. "Not bad, Face." His eyes followed the trail of the next serve. He sent it to the far corner to brush the service line. Ty liked nothing better than to watch Asher run. The range of her backhand was limited, but perfectly placed. He was on it in a flash. The last time they had played he had beaten her handily even while holding back. Now he scented challenge.

Asher lined the ball straight at him, hard and fast. Pivoting, Ty slammed it back. The ball whistled on her return. With a powerful swing Ty sent her to the baseline, then nipped her return so that the ball brushed the net and died in the forecourt.

"Fifteen-all." Ty feigned a yawn as he went back to position.

Narrowing her eyes, Asher served. The rally was a study in speed and footwork. She knew he was playing with her, moving her all over the court. Aware that she was no match for his power, she chose to catch him off guard. The ball thudded. She raced. It soared. She followed. The sounds of rackets cutting air had a steady, almost musical sound. A rhythm was set. Patiently she adhered to it until she sensed Ty relaxing. Abruptly she altered the pacing and slapped the ball past him.

"Getting crafty," he muttered.

"Getting slow, old timer," she retorted sweetly.

Ty slammed her next serve crosscourt. After the bounce, it landed somewhere in the grandstands. Under her breath Asher swore pungently.

"Did you say something?"

"Not a thing." Disgusted, Asher shook her hair back. As she readied to serve, she caught the look in Ty's eyes. They rested not on her ball or racket, but on her mouth.

All's fair, she mused with a secret smile. Slowly and deliberately she moistened her lips with the tip of her tongue. Taking a long, preliminary stretch, she served. Distracted, Ty was slow to meet the ball. Asher had little trouble blowing the return past him.

"Game point," she said softly, sending him an intimate smile. Keeping her back to him, she bent to pick up a fresh ball, taking her time about it. She could almost feel Ty's eyes run up the long length of her legs. Smoothing a hand down her hip, she walked back to the baseline. "Ready?"

He nodded, dragging his eyes away from the subtle sweep of her breasts. When his eyes met hers, he read an invitation that had his pulse racing. His concentration broken, he barely returned her serve. The rally was very short.

Victorious, Asher let out a hoot of laughter before she walked to the net. "Your game seemed to be a bit off, Starbuck."

The gibe and the laughter in her eyes had him wanting to strangle her…and devour her. "Cheat," he murmured as he walked to meet her at the net.

Asher's look was guileless and she was faintly shocked. "I have no idea what you're talking about." The words were hardly out of her mouth when she was pulled against him, her lips crushed under his. Laughter and desire seemed to bubble in her simultaneously. Without being aware of it, she dropped her racket and clung to him.

"You're lucky I don't toss you on the ground here and now," he mumbled against her mouth.

"What's lucky about that?" Enchanted, Asher strained against him. How was it possible for one kiss to make her head swim?

Ty drew back, inches only. His whole body was throbbing for her. "Don't tempt me."

"Do I?" she asked huskily.

"Damn you, Asher. You know just how much."

His voice shook, delighting her. She found she needed him to be as vulnerable as she. "I'm never sure," she whispered, dropping her head to his chest.

His heart was beating too rapidly. Ty tried to fight down the impossible surge of need. Not the time, not the place, his sanity stated. Control was necessary. "You were sure enough to use a few tricks to distract me."

Lifting her head, Asher smiled at him. "Distract you? How?"

"Took your time picking up that ball, didn't you?"

She seemed to consider a moment. "Why, I've seen Chuck do the same thing playing against you. It never seemed to make any difference." She let out a whoop of surprise as he lifted her up and over the net.

"Next time I'll be ready for you, Face." After giving her a brief, bruising kiss, he dropped her to her feet. "You could play naked and I wouldn't blink an eye."

Catching her lip between her teeth, she sent him a teasing glance. "Wanna bet?" Before he could connect his racket with her bottom, she dashed away.

The locker room wasn't empty as Asher walked in, but the crowd was thinning. With the fifth rounds completed, there were fewer contenders, and therefore fewer bodies. She was looking forward to her match that afternoon with a hot newcomer who had hopped up in the rankings from one hundred and twentieth to forty-third in one year. Asher had no intention of strolling into the finals. Even the pressure of Grand Slam potential couldn't mar her mood. If ever there was a year she could win it, Asher felt it was this one.

She greeted a towel-clad Tia Conway as the Australian emerged from the showers. Both women knew they would face each other before the tournament was over. Asher could hear a laughing argument taking place over the sound of running water. As she started to remove her warm-up jacket, she spotted Madge in a corner.

The brunette sat with her head leaning back against the wall, her eyes shut. She was pale despite her tan, and there were beads of perspiration on her brow. Asher rushed over to kneel at her feet.

"Madge."

Opening her eyes slowly, Madge sighed. "Who won?"

For a moment Asher went blank. "Oh, I did. I cheated."

"Smart girl."

"Madge, what's wrong? God, your hands are like ice."

"No, it's nothing." She let out a breath as she leaned forward.

"You're sick, let me—"

"No, I've finished being sick." After a weak smile Madge swiped the sweat from her brow. "I'll be fine in a minute."

"You look terrible. You need a doctor." Asher sprang to her feet. "I'll call someone." Before she could move, Madge had her hand.

"I've seen a doctor."

Every sort of nightmare went through Asher's head. In stark terror she stared at her friend. "Oh, God, Madge, how bad?"

"I've got seven months." As Asher swayed, Madge caught her arm tightly. "Good grief, Asher, I'm pregnant, not dying."

Stunned, Asher sank to the bench. *"Pregnant!"*

"Shh." Quickly Madge glanced around. "I'd like to keep this quiet for a while. Damn morning sickness catches me off guard at the worst times." Letting out a shaky breath, she relaxed against the wall again. "The good news is it's not supposed to last long."

"I don't—Madge, I don't know what to say."

"How about congratulations?"

Shaking her head, Asher gripped both of Madge's hands in hers. "Is this what you want?"

"Are you kidding?" On a half laugh, Madge leaned against Asher's shoulder. "I might not look too happy at the moment, but inside I'm doing cartwheels. I've never wanted anything so badly in my life." She sat silently for a moment, her hand still in Asher's. "You know, during my twenties all I could think about was being number one. It was great being there. The Wrightman Cup, Wimbledon, Dallas—all of it. I was twenty-eight when I met The Dean, and still ambitious as hell. I didn't want to get married, but I couldn't live without him. As for kids, I thought, hell, there's plenty of time for that. Later, always later. Well, I woke up one morning in the hospital with my leg screaming at me and I realized I was thirty-two years old. I'd won just about everything I thought I had to win, and yet something was missing. For the better part of my life I've floated around this old world from court to court. Team tennis, pro-am tourneys, celebrity exhibitions, you name it. Until The Dean there was nothing but tennis for me. Even after him, it was the biggest slice of the pie."

"You're a champion," Asher said softly.

"Yeah." Madge laughed again. "Yeah, by God, I am, and I like it. But you know what? When I looked at the snapshot of Ty's nephew I realized that I wanted a baby,

The Dean's baby, more than I'd ever wanted a Wimbledon plate. Isn't that wild?"

She let the statement hang in silence a moment as both women absorbed it. "This is going to be my last tournament, and even while that's hurting, I keep wishing it was over so I could go home and start knitting booties."

"You don't know how to knit," Asher murmured.

"Well, The Dean can knit them then. I'll just sit around and get fat." Twisting her head to grin at Asher, Madge saw the tears. "Hey, what's this?"

"I'm happy for you," Asher muttered. She could remember her own feelings on learning of her pregnancy—the fear, the joy, the nausea and elation. She'd wanted to learn to sew. Then it had been over so quickly.

"You look overjoyed," Madge commented, brushing a tear away.

"I am really." She caught Madge to her in a viselike hug. "You'll take care of yourself, won't you? Don't overdo or take any chances?"

"Sure." Something in the tone had the seed of a thought germinating. "Asher, did you… Did something happen when you were married to Eric?"

Asher held her tighter for a moment, then released her. "Not now. Maybe someday we'll talk about it. How does The Dean feel about all this?"

Madge gave her a long, measuring look. The nonanswer was answer enough, so she let it lay. "He was all set to take out a full-page ad in *World of Sports,*" she stated. "I've made him wait until I officially retire."

"There's no need to retire, Madge. You can take a year or two off, lots of women do."

"Not this one." Stretching her arms to the ceiling, Madge grinned. "I'm going out a winner, ranked fifth. When I get home, I'm going to learn how to use a vacuum cleaner."

"I'll believe that when I see it."

"You and Ty are invited to my first home-cooked dinner."

"Great." Asher kissed her cheek. "We'll bring the antacid."

"Not nice," Madge mused. "But wise. Hey, Face," she continued before Asher could rise. "I wouldn't want this to get around but—" her eyes were suddenly very young, and she looked very vulnerable "—I'm scared right out of my socks. I'll be almost thirty-four by the time this kid makes an appearance. I've never even changed a diaper."

Firmly Asher took Madge's shoulders and kissed both of her cheeks. "You're a champion, remember?"

"Yeah, but what do I know about chicken pox?" Madge demanded. "Kids get chicken pox, don't they? And braces, and corrective shoes, and—"

"And mothers who worry before there's anything to worry about," Asher finished. "You're already slipping right into the slot."

"Hey, you're right." Rather pleased with herself, Madge rose. "I'm going to be great."

"You're going to be terrific. Let's get a shower. You've got a doubles match this afternoon."

With feelings mixed and uncertain, Asher rode the elevator to her hotel room late that afternoon. She had won her round with the young upstart from Canada in straight sets. Six-two, six-love. There was little doubt that Asher had played some of the finest tennis in her career in court one. But she didn't think of that now. Her mind kept drifting back to her interlude with Madge, and from there back to her thoughts on learning of her own pregnancy.

Would Ty have wanted to take out full-page ads, or would he have cursed her? Like Eric, would he have accused her of deceit, of trickery? Now that they were being given a second chance, would he want marriage and children? What was it Jess had said that day? she wondered. *Ty will always be a gypsy, and no woman should ever expect to hold him.*

Yet Asher had expected to hold him, and, despite all her vows, was beginning to expect it again. Her love was so huge, so consuming, that when she was with him, it was simply impossible to conceive of doing without him. And perhaps because she had once, briefly, carried his child inside her, the need to do so again was overwhelming.

Could a woman tame a comet? she asked herself. Should she? For that's what he was—a star that flew, full of speed and light. He wasn't the prince at the end of the fairy tale who would calmly take up his kingdom and sit on a throne. Ty would always search for the next quest. And the next woman? Asher wondered, recalling Jess's words again.

Shaking her head, she told herself to think of today. Today they were together. Only a woman who had lived through change after change, hurt after hurt, could fully appreciate the perfection of a moment. Others might not recognize it, but Asher did. And the moment was hers.

She unlocked the door to their suite and was immediately disappointed. He wasn't there. Even had he been sleeping in the other room, she would have sensed him.

The air was never still when Ty was around. Tossing her bag aside, she wandered to the window. The light was still full as the sun had only just began to set. Perhaps they would go out and explore Melbourne, find one of the tiny little clubs with loud music and laughter. She'd like to dance.

Twirling in a circle, Asher laughed. Yes, she would like to dance, to celebrate for Madge…and for herself. She was with the man she loved. A bath, she decided. A long, luxurious bath before she changed into something cool and sexy. When she opened the door to the bedroom, Asher stopped and stared in astonishment.

Balloons. Red, yellow, blue, pink and white. They floated throughout the room in a jamboree of color. Helium-filled, they rose to the ceiling, trailing long ribbons. There were dozens of them—round, oval, thin and fat. It was as if a circus had passed hurriedly through, leaving a few souvenirs. Grasping a ribbon, Asher drew one down to her while she continued to stare.

They were three layers deep, she saw in astonishment—at least a hundred of them bumping against one another. Her laughter came out in a quick burst that went on and on.

Who else would think of it? Who else would take the time? Not flowers or jewelry for Ty Starbuck. At that moment she could have floated to the ceiling to join the gift he had given her.

"Hi."

She turned to see him lounging in the doorway. In a flash Asher had launched herself into his arms, the single balloon still grasped in her hand. "Oh, you're crazy!" she cried before she found his lips with hers.

With her arms wrapped around his neck, her legs around his waist, she kissed him again and again. "Absolutely insane."

"Me?" he countered. "You're the one standing here surrounded by balloons."

"It's the best surprise I've ever had."

"Better than roses in the bathtub?"

Tossing her head back, she laughed. "Even better than that."

"I thought about diamonds, but they didn't seem like as much fun." As he spoke he moved toward the bed.

"And they don't float," Asher put in, looking up at the ceiling of colorful shapes.

"Good point," Ty conceded as they fell together onto the bed. "Got any ideas how we should spend the evening?"

"One or two," Asher murmured. The balloon she held drifted up to join the others.

"Let's do both." He stopped her laugh with a soft kiss that became hungry quickly. "Oh, God, I've waited all day to be alone with you. When the season's over we'll find someplace—an island, another planet—anyplace where there's no one but us."

"Anyplace," she whispered in agreement while her hands tugged at his shirt.

Passion soared swiftly. Ty's needs doubled as he sensed hers. She was always soft, always eager for him. If the pounding of his blood would have allowed, he would have revered her. But the force of their joined desire wouldn't permit reverence. Clothes were hastily peeled away—a blouse flung aside, a shirt cast to the floor. Overhead, the balloons danced while they savored each other. The scent of victory seemed to cling to both of them, mixed with the faint fragrance of soap and shampoo from the post-game showers. Her lips tasted warm and moist, and somehow of himself as much as of her.

When there was nothing to separate them, they tangled together, their bodies hot and throbbing. With questing hands he moved over territory only more exciting in its familiarity. He could feel reason spin away into pure sensation. Soft here, firm there, her body was endless delight. The warmth of her breath along his skin could make him tremble. Her moan, as he slipped his fingers into her, made him ache. With open-mouthed kisses he trailed over her, seeking the hot heady flavor of her flesh. It seemed to melt into him, filling him to bursting.

When she arched, offering everything, Ty felt a surge of power so awesome he almost feared to take her. Too strong, he thought hazily. He was too strong and was bound to hurt her. He felt he could have lifted the world without effort. Yet she was drawing him to her with murmuring pleas.

There was no control in madness. She stole his sanity with her smooth skin and soft lips. There were no more pastel colors from frivolous balloons. Now there was gleaming silver and molten reds and pulsing blacks whirling and churning into a wild kaleidoscope that seemed to pull him into its vortex. Gasping her name, Ty thrust into her. The colors shattered, seeming to pierce his skin with a multitude of shards. And in the pain was indescribable pleasure.

When he was spent, nestled between her breasts, Asher gazed up at the darkening ceiling. How could it be, she wondered, that each time they were together it was different? Sometimes they loved in laughter, sometimes in tenderness. At other times with a smoldering passion. This time there had been a taste of madness in their loving. Did other lovers find this infinite variety, this insatiable delight in each other? Perhaps the two of them were unique. The thought was almost frightening.

"What are you thinking?" Ty asked. He knew he should shift his weight from her, but found no energy to do so.

"I was wondering if it should be so special each time I'm with you."

He laughed, kissing the side of her breast. "Of course it should, I'm a special person. Don't you read the sports section?"

She tugged his hair, but tenderly. "Don't let your press go to your head, Starbuck. You have to win a few more matches before you wrap up the Grand Slam."

He massaged the muscles of her thigh. "So do you, Face."

"I'm only thinking as far ahead as the next game," she said. She didn't want to think of Forest Hills, or the States—or the end of the season. "Madge is pregnant," she said half to herself.

"What!" Like a shot, Ty's head came up.

"Madge is pregnant," Asher repeated. "She wants to keep it quiet until the Australian Open is over."

"I'll be damned," he exclaimed. "Old Madge."

"She's only a year older than you," Asher stated defensively, causing him to laugh again.

"It's an expression, love." Absently he twined one of Asher's curls around a finger. "How does she feel about it?"

"She's thrilled—and scared." Her lashes lowered,

shielding her expression a moment. "She's going to retire."

"We're going to have to throw her one hell of a party." Rolling onto his back, he drew Asher close to his side.

After a moment she moistened her lips and spoke casually. "Do you ever think about children? I mean, it would be difficult, wouldn't it, combining a family with a profession like this?"

"It's done all the time, depends on how you go about it."

"Yes, but all the traveling, the pressure."

He started to pass it off, then remembered how she had lived her childhood. Though he had never sensed any resentment in her, he wondered if she felt a family would be a hindrance to her career. Physically a baby would prevent her from playing for some time. And she'd already lost three years, he reflected with an inner sigh. Ty pushed the idea of their children out of his mind. There was time, after all.

"I imagine it's a hassle to worry about kids when you've got a tournament to think of," he said lightly. "A player's got enough trouble keeping track of his rackets."

With a murmured agreement, Asher stared into space.

In the thin light of dawn she shifted, brushing at a tickle on her arm. Something brushed over her cheek. Annoyed, Asher lifted her hand to knock it away. It came back. With a softly uttered complaint she opened her eyes.

In the gray light she could see dozens of shapes.

Some hung halfway to the ceiling, others littered the bed and floor. Sleepy, she stared at them without comprehension. Irritated at having been disturbed, she knocked at the shape that rested on her hip. It floated lazily away.

Balloons, she realized. Turning her head, she saw that Ty was all but buried under them. She chuckled, muffling the sound with her hand as she sat up. He lay flat on his stomach, facedown in the pillow. She plucked a red balloon from the back of his head. He didn't budge. Leaning over, she outlined his ear with kisses. He muttered and stirred and shifted away. Asher lifted a brow. A challenge, she decided.

After brushing the hair from the nape of his neck, she began to nibble on the exposed flesh. "Ty," she whispered. "We have company."

Feeling a prickle of drowsy pleasure, Ty rolled to his side, reaching for her. Asher placed a balloon in his hand. Unfocused, his eyes opened.

"What the hell is this?"

"We're surrounded," Asher told him in a whisper. "They're everywhere."

A half dozen balloons tipped to the floor as he shifted to his back. After rubbing his face with his hands, he stared. "Good God." With that he shut his eyes again.

Not to be discouraged, Asher straddled him. "Ty, it's morning."

"Uh-uh."

"I have that talk show to do at nine."

He yawned and patted her bottom. "Good luck."

She planted a soft, nibbling kiss on his lips. "I have two hours before I have to leave."

"'S okay, you won't bother me."

Wanna bet? she asked silently. Reaching out, she trailed her fingers up his thigh. "Maybe I'll sleep a bit longer."

"Mmm-hmm."

Slowly she lay on top of him, nuzzling her lips at his throat. "I'm not bothering you, am I?"

"Hmm?"

She snuggled closer, feeling her breasts rub against his soft mat of hair. "Cold," she mumbled, and moved her thigh against his.

"Turn down the air-conditioning," Ty suggested.

Brows lowered, Asher lifted her head. Ty's eyes met hers, laughing, and not a bit sleepy. With a toss of her head Asher rolled from him and tugged on the blanket. Though her back was to him, she could all but see his grin.

"How's this?" Wrapping an arm around her waist, he fit his body to hers. She gave him a shrug as an answer. "Warmer?" he asked as he slid his hand up to cup her breast. The point was already taut, her pulse already racing. Ty moved sinuously against her.

"The air-conditioning's too high," she said plaintively. "I'm freezing."

Ty dropped a kiss at the base of her neck. "I'll get it." He rose, moving to the unit. It shut off with a dull mechanical thud. With a teasing remark on the tip of his tongue, he turned.

In the fragile morning light she lay naked in the tumbled bed, surrounded by gay balloons. Her hair rioted around a face dominated by dark, sleepy eyes. The faintest of smiles touched her lips, knowing, inviting, challenging. All thoughts of joking left him. Her skin was so smooth and touched with gold. Like a fist in the solar plexus, desire struck him and stole his breath.

As he went to her, Asher lifted her arms to welcome him.

Chapter 10

"Asher, how does it feel being only three matches away from the Grand Slam?"

"I'm trying not to think about it."

"You've drawn Stacie Kingston in the quarter-finals. She's got an oh-for-five record against you. Does that boost your confidence?"

"Stacie's a strong player, and very tough. I'd never go into a match with her overconfident."

Her hands folded loosely, Asher sat behind the table facing the lights and reporters. The microphone in front of her picked up her calm, steady voice and carried it to the rear of the room. She wore her old team tennis jacket with loose warm-up pants and court shoes. Around her face her hair curled damply. They'd barely given her time to shower after her most recent win at Forest Hills before scheduling the impromptu press conference. The cameras were rolling, taping her every movement, recording every expression. One of the print reporters quickly scribbled down that she wore no jewelry or lipstick.

"Did you expect your comeback to be this successful?"

Asher gave a lightning-fast grin—here then gone—something she would never have done for the press even two months before. "I trained hard," she said simply.

"Do you still lift weights?"

"Every day."

"Have you changed your style this time around?"

"I think I've tightened a few things up." She relaxed, considering. Of all the people in the room, only Asher was aware that her outlook toward the press had changed. There was no tightness in her throat as she spoke. No warning signals to take care flashing in her brain. "Improved my serve particularly," she continued. "My percentage of aces and service winners is much higher than it was three or four years ago."

"How often did you play during your retirement?"

"Not often enough."

"Will your father be coaching you again?"

Her hesitation was almost too brief to be measured. "Not officially," she replied evasively.

"Have you decided to accept the offer of a layout in *Elegance* magazine?"

Asher tucked a lock of hair behind her ear. "News travels fast." Laughter scattered around the room. "I haven't really decided," she continued. "At the moment I'm more concerned with the U.S. Open."

"Who do you pick to be your opponent in the finals?"

"I'd like to get through the quarters and semis first."

"Let's say, who do you think will be your strongest competition?"

"Tia Conway," Asher answered immediately. Their duel in Kooyong was still fresh in her mind. Three exhausting sets—three tie breakers—in two grueling hours. "She's the best all-around woman player today."

"What makes you say that?"

"Tia has court sense, speed, strength and a big serve."

"Yet you've beaten her consistently this season."

"But not easily."

"What about the men's competition? Would you predict the U.S. will have two Grand Slam winners this year?"

Asher fielded the question first with a smile. "I think someone mentioned that there were still three matches to go, but I believe it's safe to say that if Starbuck continues to play as he's played all season, no one will beat him, particularly on grass, as it's his best surface."

"Is your opinion influenced by personal feelings?"

"Statistics don't have any feelings," she countered. "Personal or otherwise." Asher rose, effectively curtailing further questioning. A few more were tossed out at random, but she merely leaned toward the mike and apologized for having to end the meeting. As she started to slip through a rear door, she spotted Chuck.

"Nicely done, Face."

"And over," she breathed. "What are you doing here?"

"Keeping an eye on my best friend's lady," he said glibly as he slipped an arm around her shoulders. "Ty thought it would be less confusing if he kept out of the way during your little tête-à-tête with the members of the working press."

"For heaven's sake," Asher mumbled, "I don't need a keeper."

"Don't tell me." Chuck flashed his boy-next-door smile. "Ty had it in his head the press might badger you."

Tilting her head, Asher studied his deceptively sweet face. "And what were you going to do if they had?"

"Strong-arm 'em," he claimed while flexing his muscle. "Though I might have been tempted to let them take a few bites out of you after that comment about nobody beating Ty. Didn't you hear they were naming a racket after me?"

Asher circled his waist with her arm. "Sorry, friend, I call 'em like I see 'em."

Stopping, he put both hands on Asher's shoulders and studied her. His look remained serious even when she gave him a quizzical smile. "You know, Face, you really look good."

She laughed. "Well, thanks…I think. Did I look bad before?"

"I don't mean you look beautiful, that never changes. I mean you look happy."

Lifting a hand to the one on her shoulder, Asher squeezed. "I am happy."

"It shows. In Ty too." Briefly he hesitated, then plunged ahead. "Listen, I don't know what happened between you two before, but—"

"Chuck…" Asher shook her head to ward off questions.

"But," he continued, "I want you to know I hope you make it this time."

"Oh, Chuck." Shutting her eyes, she went into his arms. "So do I," she sighed. "So do I."

"I asked you to keep an eye on her," Ty said from behind them. "I didn't say anything about touching."

"Oh, hell." Chuck tightened his hold. "Don't be so selfish. Second-seeds need love too." Glancing down at Asher, he grinned. "Can I interest you in lobster tails and champagne?"

"Sorry." She kissed his nose. "Somebody already offered me pizza and cheap wine."

"Outclassed again." With a sigh Chuck released her. "I need somebody to hit with tomorrow," he told Ty.

"Okay."

"Six o'clock, court three."

"You buy the coffee."

"We'll flip for it," Chuck countered before he sauntered away.

Alone, Asher and Ty stood for a moment in awkward silence while an airplane droned by overhead. The awkwardness had cropped up occasionally on their return to the States. It was always brief and never commented on. In the few seconds without words, each of them admitted that full truths would soon be necessary. Neither of them knew how to approach it.

"So," Ty began as the moment passed, "how did it go?"

"Easily," Asher returned, smiling as she stood on tiptoe to kiss him. "I didn't need the bodyguard."

"I know how you feel about press conferences."

"How?"

"Oh..." He combed her hair with his fingers. "*Terrified*'s a good word."

With a laugh she held out her hand as they started to

walk. "*Was* a good word," Asher corrected him. "I'm amazed I ever let it get to me. There was one problem though."

"What?"

"I was afraid I'd faint from starvation." She sent him a pitiful look from under her lashes. "Someone did mention pizza, didn't they?"

"Yeah." He grinned, catching her close. "And cheap wine."

"You really know how to treat a woman, Starbuck," Asher told him in a breathless whisper.

"We'll go Dutch," he added before he pulled her toward the car.

Twenty minutes later they sat together at a tiny round table. There was the scent of rich sauce, spice and melted candles. From the jukebox in the corner poured an endless succession of popular rock tunes at a volume just below blaring. The waitresses wore bib aprons sporting pictures of grinning pizzas. Leaning her elbows on the scarred wooden table, Asher stared soulfully into Ty's eyes.

"You know how to pick a class joint, don't you?"

"Stick with me, Face," he advised. "I've got a hamburger palace picked out for tomorrow. You get your own individual plastic packs of ketchup." Her lips curved up, making him want to taste them. Leaning forward, he did. The table tilted dangerously.

"You two ready to order?" Snapping her wad of gum, the waitress shifted her weight to one hip.

"Pizza and a bottle of Chianti," Ty told her, kissing Asher again.

"Small, medium or large?"

"Small, medium or large what?"

"Pizza," the waitress said with exaggerated patience.

"Medium ought to do it." Twisting his head, Ty sent the waitress a smile that had her pulling back her shoulders. "Thanks."

"Well, that should improve the service," Asher considered as she watched the woman saunter away.

"What's that?"

Asher studied his laughing eyes. "Never mind," she decided. "Your ego doesn't need any oiling."

Ty bent his head closer to hers as a defense against the jukebox. "So what kind of questions did they toss at you?"

"The usual. They mentioned the business from *Elegance.*"

"Are you going to do it?"

She moved her shoulders. "I don't know. It might be fun. And I don't suppose it would hurt the image of women's tennis for one of the players to be in a national fashion magazine."

"It's been done before."

Asher conquered a grin and arched her brows instead. "Do you read fashion magazines, Starbuck?"

"Sure. I like to look at pretty women."

"I always thought jocks tended to favor other sorts of magazines for that."

He gave her an innocent look. "What sorts of magazines?"

Ignoring him, Asher went back to his original question. "They're playing up this Grand Slam business for all it's worth."

"Bother you?" As he laced their fingers together, he studied them. There was an almost stunning difference in size and texture. Often he'd wondered how such an elegant little hand could be so strong…and why it should fit so perfectly with his.

"A bit," Asher admitted, enjoying the rough feel of his skin against hers. "It makes it difficult to go into a match thinking of just that match. What about you? I know you're getting the same kind of pressure."

The waitress brought the wine, giving Ty a slow smile as she set down the glasses. To Asher's amusement, he returned it. He's a devil, she thought. And he knows it.

"I always look at playing a game at a time, one point at a time." He poured a generous amount of wine in both glasses. "Three matches is a hell of a lot of points."

"But you'd like to win the Grand Slam?"

Raising his glass, he grinned. "Damn right." He laughed into her eyes as he drank. "Of course, Martin's already making book on it."

"I'm surprised he's not here," Asher commented, "analyzing every volley."

"He's coming in tomorrow with the rest of the family."

Asher's fingers tightened on the stem of her glass. "The rest of the family?"

"Yeah, Mom and Jess for sure. Mac and Pete if it can be arranged." The Chianti was heavy and mellow. Ty relaxed with it. "You'll like Pete; he's a cute kid."

She mumbled something into her wine before she swallowed. Martin had been there three years ago, along with Ty's mother and sister. Both she and Ty had gone into the U.S. Open as top seeds; both had been hounded by the press. The two of them had shared meals then, too, and a bed. So much was the same—terrifyingly so. But there had been so much in between.

There'd been no small boy with Ty's coloring then. No small boy with that air of perpetual energy to remind her of what was lost. Asher felt the emptiness inside her, then the ache, as she did each time she thought of the child.

Misinterpreting her silence, Ty reached over to take her hand. "Asher, you still haven't spoken to your father?"

"What?" Disoriented, she stared at him a moment. "No, no, not since... Not since I retired."

"Why don't you call him?"

"I can't."

"That's ridiculous. He's your father."

She sighed, wishing it were so simple. "Ty, you know him. He's a very stringent man, very certain of what's right and what's wrong. When I left tennis I did more than disappoint him, I...wasted what he'd given me."

Ty answered with a short, explicit word that made her smile. "From his viewpoint that's the way it was," she went on. "As Jim Wolfe's daughter I had certain responsibilities. In marrying Eric and giving up my career I shirked them. He hasn't forgiven me."

"How do you know that?" he demanded. His voice was low under the insistent music, but rich with annoyance. "If you haven't spoken to him, how can you be sure how he feels now?"

"Ty, if his feelings had changed, wouldn't he be here?" She shrugged, wishing they could have avoided the subject for a while longer. "I thought, at first, that when I started playing again it might make the difference. It hasn't."

"But you miss him."

Even that wasn't so simple. To Ty, family meant

something warm and loving and eternal. He'd never understand that Asher looked not so much now for her father's presence or even his love, but simply his forgiveness. "I'd like him to be here," she said finally. "But I understand his reasons for not coming." Her brow clouded for a moment with a realization that had just come to her. "Before, I played for him, to please him, to justify the time and effort he put into my career. Now I play for myself."

"And you play better," Ty put in. "Perhaps that's one of the reasons."

With a smile she lifted his hand to her lips. "Perhaps that's one of them."

"Here's your pizza." The waitress plopped the steaming pan between them.

They ate amid noise and their own casual chatter. Even the pressure of the upcoming matches had no effect on Asher's mood. The cheese was hot and stringy, making Ty laugh as she struggled against it. The contents of the squat bottle of Chianti lowered as they drank leisurely, content to let the meal drag on. Tennis was forgotten while they spoke of everything and nothing at all. A group of teenagers poured in, laughing and rowdy, to feed another succession of quarters into the jukebox.

Why am I so happy to be in this loud, crowded room? she wondered. The cooling pizza and lukewarm wine were as appealing as the champagne and caviar they had shared in Paris. It was Ty. The place never mattered when she was with him. Abruptly it occurred to Asher that it was herself as well. She was being herself. There weren't any guards, or the need for any. Ty was the only man she'd ever been close to who required none from her.

Her father had wanted her to be perfect—his glass princess. All through her youth she had done everything in her power to please him. With Eric, she had been expected to be the cool, well-mannered Lady Wickerton, a woman who could discuss art and politics intelligently. She was to have been like crystal, many-faceted, elegant and cold.

All Ty had ever expected her to be was Asher. He accepted her flaws, even admired them. Because he had wanted her to be herself, she'd been able to be just that. Not once in all the time she had known him had he ever demanded that she fit a pattern or requested that she conform to any standards but her own. Impulsively she reached over to take his hand, then pressed it to her cheek. There was warmth against warmth, flesh against flesh.

"What's this for?" he asked, allowing his fingers to spread.

"For not wanting glass."

His brows drew together in confusion. "Am I supposed to know what that means?"

"No." Laughing, Asher leaned closer. "Have you drunk enough wine that your resistance is down and you'll be easily seduced?"

A slow smile spread. "More than enough."

"Then come with me," Asher ordered.

It was late when Ty lay sleepless beside Asher. Curled close, her hand caught loosely in his, she slept deeply, drugged with loving and fatigue. Her scent hung in the air so that even in the dark Ty could visualize her. A small alarm clock ticked monotonously at his left, its luminous dial glowing. Twelve twenty-seven.

His mind was far too active for sleep. He sensed, as he knew Asher did, that the idyll was nearly over. They were back where they had once ended, and questions would not be put off too much longer. Impatience gnawed at him. Unlike Asher, Ty looked for the end of the season. Only then would the time be right for answers and explanations. He was not used to biding his time, and the strain was beginning to tell. Even tonight under the laughter he had understood her wordless request that he not probe.

The question of her father, Ty mused, shifting the pillow to brace his back. She was more unhappy about the estrangement than she admitted. It showed in her eyes. It was incomprehensible to him that members of a family could turn away from one another. His thoughts drifted to his mother, to Jess. There was nothing either of them could do he wouldn't forgive. He'd never be able to bear the thought of being responsible for their unhappiness. Could a father feel any different about a daughter? An only daughter, a much-loved daughter, Ty reflected.

He could remember Jim Wolfe's pride in Asher. Ty had often sat beside him during one of Asher's matches in her early days as a pro, then consistently during her last year. Even in such a private man the adoration had showed. It wasn't possible to believe it had been only for the athlete and not for the woman.

Surprisingly Jim had accepted Ty's relationship with his daughter. No, Ty corrected, approved. He'd seemed to enjoy seeing them together. Once, Ty recalled, he had gone as far as outlining his expectations to Ty of their future. At the time Ty had been both amused and annoyed at the fatherly interference. What plans he had had for a future with Asher had still been vague. Then, when they had crystalized in his mind, it had been too late. Frowning, Ty glanced down at her.

In the pale shaft of moonlight her face seemed very fragile. Her hair was a silvery, insubstantial cloud around it. A wave of longing swamped him so that he had to fight the need to wake her and satisfy himself that she was there for him. His feelings for her had always been mixed—wild desire, unbearable tenderness, traces of fear. There had been no other woman who had ever brought him such sharp and conflicting emotions. Watching her sleep, he felt the need to protect. There should be no shadow of unhappiness in her eyes when they opened.

How many obstacles would they have to overcome before they were really together? he wondered. There was one he might remove himself. Perhaps the time had come to take the first step. On impulse, Ty slipped from the bed and into the sitting room.

It took only moments by phone to travel from coast to coast. Dropping into a chair, Ty listened to the faint crackling on the wire before it began to ring.

"Wolfe residence."

In the two words, Ty recognized the trained voice of a servant. "Jim Wolfe please. It's Ty Starbuck."

"One moment please."

Ty sat back, keeping one ear trained on the adjoining bedroom. He heard two distinct clicks as one extension was lifted and the other replaced.

"Starbuck."

The quiet, cautious voice was instantly recognizable. "Jim. How are you?"

"Well." A bit surprised by the late night call, Jim Wolfe settled behind his desk. "I've been reading quite a bit about you."

"It's been a good year. You were missed at Wimbledon."

"That makes five for you there."

"And three for Asher," he returned pointedly.

There was a moment of complete silence. "Your slice volley's cleaner than it once was."

"Jim, I called to talk about Asher."

"Then we have nothing to say."

For a moment the cool, calm statement left Ty speechless. In a flood, fury took over. "Just a damn minute. I have plenty to say. Your daughter's battled her way back to the top. She's done it without you."

"I'm aware of that. Do you have a point?"

"Yes, I have a point," Ty retorted. "I've never seen anyone work as hard as she has these past few months. And it hasn't been easy, dealing with the pressure, the press, the constant questions on why her father isn't in the stands while she wins championship after championship."

"Asher knows my feelings," Jim said flatly. "They're no concern of yours."

"Whatever concerns Asher concerns me."

"So…" Jim picked up a slim gold pen from the desk and carefully examined it. "We're back to that."

"Yes, we are."

"If you've decided to resume your relationship with Asher, it's your business, Ty." He flung the pen back onto the desk. "And it's my business if I don't."

"For God's sake, Jim," Ty began heatedly, "she's your daughter. You can't turn your back on your own child."

"Like father, like daughter," Jim murmured.

"What the hell does that mean?" Frustrated, Ty rose to pace, dragging the phone with him.

"Asher wiped her child out of existence. I've done the same."

All movement stopped. Ty felt something freeze in him as his knuckles turned white on the receiver. "What child?"

"She turned her back on everything I taught her," Jim went on, not hearing Ty's harshly whispered question. "The daughter I knew couldn't have done it." The words, and the anger that accompanied them, had been held in for years. Now they came bursting out. "I tried to understand why she married that pale excuse for a man, even tried to resign myself to her throwing away her career. But some things I won't forgive. If the life she chose to live was worth the price of my grandchild, she's welcome to it."

Enraged at letting his feelings pour out so openly, Jim slammed down the receiver.

Three thousand miles away Ty stood, staring at nothing. With infinite care he placed the phone back on the table. Too many thoughts were whirling in his head, too many questions and half-answers. He had to think, to take his time. Silently he walked back into the bedroom and dressed.

He wanted to shake her awake and demand an explanation; he wanted to wait until he had a grip on himself. Torn, Ty sat on a chair and stared at the still form in the bed. Asher slept so peacefully, her quiet breathing hardly stirred the air.

A child? Asher's child? But there was no child, Ty reasoned. If Lord and Lady Wickerton had produced an offspring, there would have been some mention of it in the press. An heir was never kept secret. Dragging a hand through his hair, Ty shifted. Besides, he reasoned, if Asher had had a child, where was it? Struggling to overcome the jealousy at imagining Asher's bearing another man's child, Ty went over his conversation with Jim Wolfe again.

Asher wiped her child out of existence....

His fingers tightened on the arms of the chair as he stared at her sleeping form. Abortion? Without warning, a storm of emotion took over that he had to systematically fight back until his pulse leveled. All attempts to think of the word with an open mind were futile. He couldn't rationalize it, not when it was Asher, not when the child was part of her. Could the woman he thought he knew have made that kind of choice? For what purpose? Was it possible that the social life she had sought had been more important than…

As bitterness filled him, Ty shook his head. He wouldn't believe it of her. Controlled, yes. There were times Asher could be infuriatingly controlled. But never calculating. Jim had been talking in riddles, he decided. There'd never been a child. There couldn't have been.

He watched Asher stir. With a soft murmur she shifted toward the emptiness beside her where Ty should have been. He sensed the moment she woke.

The moonlight gleamed on her arm as she lifted it, brushing her fingers at the hair that curled around her face. She placed her hand on his pillow, as if testing it for warmth.

"Ty?"

Not trusting himself, he said nothing. If only she would go back to sleep until he had resolved his feelings. He could still taste the bitterness at the back of his throat.

But she wouldn't sleep. Although groggy, Asher sensed tension in the air. Ty's emotions were always volatile enough to be felt tangibly. *Something's wrong, something's wrong,* hammered in her brain.

"Ty?" she called again, and a hint of fear touched the word. Asher had struggled to a sitting position before she saw him. The moonlight was enough to allow her to see that his eyes were dark and fixed on her face. It was also enough to let her see that they were cold. Her pulse began to race. "Couldn't you sleep?" she asked, struggling to convince herself it was all her imagination.

"No."

Asher laced her fingers together as she swallowed. "You should have woke me."

"Why?"

"We—we could have talked."

"Could we?" Cold anger filled him. "We can talk as long as I don't ask any questions you don't want to answer."

She'd been expecting the showdown, but not like this. His resentment was already wrapping around her. Still, he had a right, and she'd put him off too long. "Ty, if it's answers you want, I'll give them to you."

"Just like that?" he snapped, rising. "Just ask and you'll answer. Nothing more to hide, Asher?"

Stung by his tone, she stared up at him. "It wasn't

a matter of hiding, Ty, not really. I needed time—we needed time."

"Why was that, Asher?" he asked in a tone that was uncharacteristically cool. She felt a shudder zip down her spine. "Why was time so important?"

"There were things I wasn't sure you'd understand."

"Like the baby?"

If he had slapped her, Asher couldn't have been more stunned. Even in the moonlight he could see her face go white. Her eyes grew huge and dark and desperate. "How…" The words wouldn't form. Though they raced around in her mind, Asher seemed incapable of forcing any through her lips. How had he found out? Who had told him? How long had he known?

"Eric," she managed, though the name threatened to strangle her. "Eric told you."

Sharp disappointment cut through him. Somehow he had hoped it hadn't been true that she had conceived and rejected another man's child. "So it's true," he exclaimed. Turning from her, Ty stared through the window at the darkness. He found he couldn't be logical or objective. It was one thing to understand the concept of freedom of choice, and another to apply it to Asher.

"Ty, I…" She tried to speak. All of her worst fears were hurtling down on her. The gulf between them was already tangible and threatening to widen. If only she had been able to tell him in her own way, in her own time. "Ty, I wanted to tell you myself. There were reasons why I didn't at first, and then…" Asher shut her eyes. "Then I made excuses."

"I suppose you thought it was none of my business."

Her eyes flew open again. "How can you say that?"

"What you do with your life when you're married

to one man isn't the concern of another, even when he loves you."

Simultaneous flashes of pain and joy rushed through her. "You didn't," she whispered.

"Didn't what?"

"You didn't love me."

He gave a brief laugh, but didn't turn back to her. "No, of course I didn't. That's why I couldn't stay away from you. That's why I thought of you every moment."

Asher pressed the heel of her hand between her eyes. Why now? she thought wildly. Why is it all happening now? "You never told me."

This time he turned. "Yes, I did."

Furiously she shook her head. "You never said it. Not once. Even once would have been enough."

In concentration, his brows drew together. She was right, he decided. He'd never said the words. He'd shown her in every way he knew how, but he'd never said the words. "Neither did you," he blurted, speaking his thoughts.

She let out a breath that was perilously close to a sob. "I was afraid to."

"Damn it, Asher, so was I."

For a long, tense moment they stared at each other. Had she been that blind? Had she needed words so badly that she hadn't seen what he'd been giving her? The words would never have come easily to him because they meant everything. For Ty, a declaration of love wasn't a casual phrase but a declaration of self.

Asher swallowed a tremor, wanting her voice to be strong. "I love you, Ty. I've always loved you. And I'm still afraid." As she held out a hand he glanced down at it, but made no move to accept it. "Don't turn away from me now." She thought of the child she had lost. "Please, don't hate me for what I did."

He couldn't understand, but he could feel. It seemed love for her justified anything. Crossing to her, Ty took the offered hand and brought it to his lips. "It'll be better when we've talked this out. We need to start clean, Asher."

"Yes." She closed her hand over their joined ones. "I want that too. Oh, Ty, I'm so sorry about the baby." Her free arm wrapped around his waist as she dropped her head on his chest. The relief, she thought. The relief of at last being able to share it with him. "I couldn't tell you before, when it happened. I didn't know what to do. I didn't know how you'd feel."

"I don't know either," he answered.

"I felt so guilty." She shut her eyes tight. "When Jess showed me that picture of your nephew, I could almost see how the baby would have looked. I always knew he would have had your hair, your eyes."

"Mine?" For a moment nothing seemed to function. His mind, his heart, his lungs. Then, in a torrent, everything came together. *"Mine?"* Asher gave an involuntary cry as he crushed her fingers in his. Before she could speak he had her by the shoulders, digging into her flesh. His eyes alone brought her ice-cold terror. "The baby was mine?"

Her mouth moved to form words, but nothing came out. Confusion and fear overtook her. But he'd already known, she thought desperately. No, no, he hadn't. Eric's baby, her mind flashed. He'd thought it was Eric's baby.

"Answer me, damn you!" He was shaking her now, violently. Limp as a rag doll, Asher made no protest and sought no defense. Both would have been futile. "Was it my baby? Was it mine?"

She nodded, too numb to feel the pain.

He wanted to strike her. Looking at her face, Ty could almost feel the sensation of his hand stinging against it. And he'd want to keep striking her until rage and grief could no longer be felt. Reading his thoughts in his eyes, Asher made no move to protect herself. For an instant his fingers tightened on her arms. With a violent oath he hurled her away. Hardly daring to breathe, she lay on the bed and waited.

"You bitch. You had my child in you when you married him." He flung the words at her, struggling not to use his fists. "Did he make you get rid of it when he found out? Or did you take care of it so you could play the lady without encumbrances?"

She wasn't aware that her breathing was ragged, or that she was trembling. Her mind was too numb to take in more than half of his words. All she understood was the fury of his feelings. "I didn't know. I didn't know I was pregnant when I married Eric."

"You had no right to keep this from me." Towering over her, he reached down to yank her to her knees. "You had no right to make a decision like that when the child was mine!"

"Ty—"

"Shut up. Damn you!" He shoved her away, knowing neither of them was safe if they remained together. "There's nothing you can say, nothing that could make me even want to look at you again."

He strode from the room without a second glance. The sound of the slamming door echoed over and over in Asher's mind.

Chapter 11

Ty took the quarter-finals in straight sets. Most said he played the finest tennis in his career on that hazy September afternoon. Ty knew he wasn't playing tennis. He was waging war. He'd gone onto the court full of vengeance and fury, almost pummeling his opponent with the ball. His swing was vicious, his aim deadly.

The violence showed in his face, in the grim set of his mouth, in the eyes that were nearly black with emotion. It wasn't the winning or losing that mattered to him, but the release of the physical aspect of the temper that he'd barely controlled the night before. When he struck, he struck brutally, always moving. The motion itself was a threat. He'd often been called a warrior, but the description had never been more true. As if scenting blood, he hounded his opponent, then ground him mercilessly into the ground.

Ty's only disappointment was that the match didn't last longer. There hadn't been enough time to sweat out all of his fury. He wondered if there would ever be enough time.

In the stands there were differing reactions as he stalked off the courts.

"Name of God, Ada, I've never seen the boy play better." Martin Derick beamed like a new father. His voice was hoarse from cheering and cigarettes. A pile of butts lay crushed at his feet. "Did you see how he massacred that Italian?"

"Yes."

"Oh-ho, two matches more and our boy's going to have a Grand Slam." Martin squeezed Ada's workworn hands between his two smooth ones. "Nothing's going to stop him now!"

In her quiet, steady way, Ada stared down at the court. She'd seen more than Ty's victory. There'd been fury in her son's eyes. Outrage, hurt. She recognized the combination too well. She'd seen it in a little boy who'd been teased because his father had deserted him. Then, he'd used his fists to compensate. Today, Ada mused, he'd used a racket. As Martin recounted every serve and smash, Ada sat silently and wondered what had put that look back in her son's eyes.

"Mom." Jess leaned close so that her voice wouldn't carry. "Something's wrong with Ty, isn't it?"

"I'd say something's very wrong with Ty."

Jess rubbed her cheek against Pete's, wishing his powdery scent would calm her. Giggling, he squirmed out of her arms and dove toward his father. "Asher wasn't in the stands today."

Ada lifted her eyes to her daughter's. Jess had mentioned, perhaps too casually, that Ty was seeing Asher Wolfe again. Ada had hardly needed the information. Once she had heard Asher was competing again, she'd known what the results would be.

The only time she had ever seen Ty truly devastated had been when Asher had married the polished British lord. His rage and threats had been expected. But they turned to a brooding that had concerned her a great deal more.

"Yes, I noticed," Ada replied. "Then, she's got a match of her own."

"On the next court, and not for a half hour." Jess cast another worried glance around at the people who filled the stands. "She should have been here."

"Since she wasn't, there must be a reason."

A fresh tremor of unease ran up Jess's back. "Mom, I've got to talk to you—alone. Can we go get a cup of coffee?"

Without question, Ada rose. "You fellas keep Pete entertained," she ordered, tousling her grandson's hair. "Jess and I'll be back in a few minutes."

"You're going to tell her?" Mac spoke softly as he touched his wife's hand.

"Yes. Yes, I need to."

Bouncing his son on his knee, he watched them melt into the crowd.

After they had settled at a table, Ada waited for her daughter to begin. She knew Jess was marking time, ordering coffee, speculating on the chances of rain. Ada let her ramble. An orderly, even-tempered woman, she had learned the best way to deal with her emotional offspring was to ride out the storm. Eventually Jess stopped stirring her coffee and lifted her eyes to her mother's.

"Mom, do you remember when we were here three years ago?"

How could she forget? Ada thought with a sigh. That was the year Ty had won the U.S. Open, then barely had time to savor it before the world had crumbled around his ears. "Yes, I remember."

"Asher left Ty and married Eric Wickerton." When Ada remained silent, Jess lifted her coffee cup and drank as if to fortify herself. "It was my fault," she blurted out.

Ada took the time to taste her own coffee, deciding it wasn't half bad for restaurant brew. "Your fault, Jess? How?"

"I went to see her." In quick jerks Jess began to shred her napkin. She'd thought it would be easier now that she had told Mac everything, but with her mother's gaze steady and patient on hers, she felt like a child again. "I went to her hotel room when I knew Ty wouldn't be there." After pressing her lips together, she let the confession come out in a burst. "I told her Ty was tired of her. I told her he—he was bored."

"I'm surprised she didn't laugh in your face," Ada commented.

Quickly Jess shook her head. "I was convincing," she went on. "Maybe because I was convinced it was the truth. And I—I was sympathetic." Remembering how well she had played the role of reluctant messenger tore at her. "Oh, God, Mom, when I look back and remember the things I told her, how I said them…" Anguished, her eyes met her mother's. "I told her Ty thought she and Eric were suited to each other. There was enough truth in that, but I turned it around to give her the impression that Ty was hoping Eric would take her off his hands. And I defended Ty, telling Asher he'd never want to hurt her, that he was really very concerned that she'd gotten in over her head. I—I made it seem as though Ty had asked my opinion on the best way to untangle himself from an affair he had no more interest in."

"Jess." Ada stopped the movement of her nervous daughter's hands with her own. "Why did you do such a thing?"

"Ty wasn't happy. I'd talked to him just the night before, and he was so down, so unsure of himself. I'd never seen Ty unsure of himself." Her fingers began to move restlessly under her mother's. "It seemed so clear to me that Asher was wrong for him, hurting him. I was convinced I had to save him from being hurt more."

Leaning back, Ada let her gaze drift. The West Side Tennis Club was respectfully dingy, very American. Perhaps that was why she'd always liked it. It was noisy. The Long Island Railroad ran alongside, competing with helicopters, planes and road traffic. Ada had never completely gotten used to the relative quiet of suburbia after a lifetime in the inner city. Now she sat back, absorbing the noise, trying to think of the right words. It occurred to her that parenting didn't stop when children became adults. Perhaps it never stopped at all.

"Ty loved Asher, Jess."

"I know." Jess stared down at the shredded paper napkin. "I didn't think he did. I thought if he'd loved her, he would have been happy. And if she had loved him, she would have…well, she would have acted like all the other women who hung around him."

"Do you think Ty would have loved her if she had been like all the other women?"

Jess flushed, amazing herself and amusing her mother. It was a bit disconcerting to think of the tiny, white-haired Ada Starbuck, mother, grandmother, knowing about passion. "It wasn't until after I met Mac that I realized love doesn't always make you smile and glow," Jess went on, keeping her eyes lowered. "There are times when I was miserable and confused over my feelings for Mac and I began to remember that last talk I had with Ty before I went to see Asher. I realized how alike Ty and I are, how the stronger our feelings are, the more moody we can become."

On a deep breath she met her mother's gaze levelly. "I tried to rationalize that Asher wouldn't have left Ty, that she wouldn't have married Eric if she had really cared. And that if he had, Ty wouldn't have let her go."

"Pride can be just as strong as love. The things you said to Asher made her feel unwanted, and betrayed, I imagine, that Ty would have spoken to you about it."

"If the situation had been reversed, I would have scratched her eyes out and told her to go to hell."

Ada's laugh was a warm, young sound. "Yes, you would. Then you'd have gone to the man you loved and used your claws on him. Asher's different."

"Yes." Miserable, Jess pushed her untouched coffee aside. "Ty always said so. Mom, when they got back together, I was so guilty and frightened. Then I was relieved. And now, I can tell something's gone wrong again." As she had as a child, Jess gave her mother a long, pleading look. "What should I do?"

Strange, Ada mused, that her children wanted to pamper her on one hand, thrusting dishwashers and fancy jewelry on her, while on the other, they still looked to her for all the answers. "You'll have to talk to both of them," Ada said briskly. "Then you'll have to back off and let the two of them work it out. You might be able to heal what you did three years ago, but you can do nothing about what's between them now."

"If they love each other—"

"You made a decision for them once," Ada pointed out. "Don't make the same mistake again."

She hadn't been able to sleep. She hadn't been able to eat. Only the promise she had made to herself never to quit again forced Asher onto the court. Purposely she remained in the dressing room until the last moment to avoid the fans who wandered the walkways and mingled with players. It would take more effort than she could have summoned to smile and make small talk.

When she came outside the humidity hit her like a fist. Shaking off the weakness, Asher went directly to her chair. She heard the applause, but didn't acknowledge it. She couldn't afford to. Even before she began, Asher knew her biggest problem would be concentration.

Her arms ached, her whole body ached and she felt bone-deep exhausted. Pain was something she could ignore once the match was under way, but she wasn't sure she could ignore the jellied weakness inside her, the feeling that someone had punched a yawning hole in the center of her life. Still wearing her warm-up jacket, she took a few experimental swings.

"Asher." Cursing the interruption, she glanced over at Chuck. Concern touched his eyes as he stepped toward her. "Hey, you don't look good. Are you sick?"

"I'm fine."

He studied the shadowed eyes and pale cheeks. "Like hell."

"If I come out on the court, I'm well enough to play," she returned, exchanging one racket for another. "I've got to warm up."

Baffled, Chuck watched her stalk onto the court. It took only a moment of study to see that she wasn't in top form. Chuck moved away to find Ty.

He was in the showers, his eyes closed under the spray. He'd been curt and brief with the press and even briefer with his colleagues. He wasn't in the mood for congratulations. Anger lay curled inside him, undiminished by the physical demands he had placed on himself. He needed more—a sparring match, a marathon run—anything to pump the poison out of his system. Though he heard Chuck call him, Ty remained silent and kept his eyes shut.

"Ty, will you listen to me? Something's wrong with Asher."

Taking his time, Ty stepped back so that the water beat on his chest. Slowly he opened his eyes. "So?"

"So?" Astonished, Chuck gaped at him. "I said something's wrong with Asher."

"I heard you."

"She looks sick," Chuck continued, certain that Ty didn't comprehend. "I just saw her. She shouldn't be playing today. She looks awful."

Ty fought the instinctive need to go to her. He could remember vividly the scene the night before. With a flick of the wrist he shut off the shower. "Asher knows what she's doing. She makes her own decisions."

Too stunned to be angry, Chuck stared at him. He'd

never seen Ty look cold any more than he'd ever seen Asher look furious. Until today. "What the devil's going on here?" he demanded. "I just told you your woman's sick."

Ty felt the tightening in his belly and ignored it. "She's not my woman." Grabbing a towel, he secured it lightly around his waist.

After dragging a hand through his hair, Chuck followed Ty into the locker room. He'd known since that morning when he and Ty had practiced together that something was wrong. Accustomed to his friend's mercurial moods, he had dismissed it, assuming Ty and Asher had had a lover's quarrel. But no lover's quarrel would make Ty indifferent to Asher's health.

"Look, if you two have had a fight, that's no reason—"

"I said she's not my woman." Ty's voice was deadly calm as he pulled on jeans.

"Fine," Chuck snapped. "Then if the field's clear, I might just try my luck." He was slammed back against the lockers, feet dangling as Ty grabbed his shirt in both hands, jerking him up. Coolly, Chuck looked into the stormy eyes. "Not your woman, friend?" he said softly. "Tell that to somebody who doesn't know you."

Breathing hard, Ty struggled against the need to strike back. The hours of violent tennis hadn't drained the anger or the grief. Without a word he dropped Chuck to his feet, then snatched a shirt from his locker.

"Are you going out there?" Chuck demanded. "Somebody should stop her before she makes whatever's wrong with her worse. You know damn well she isn't going to listen to me."

"Don't push me." Ty dragged the shirt over his head

before he slammed the locker door. This time Chuck kept his silence. He heard the tremor in Ty's voice and recognized that the emotion wasn't anger. Only once before had he seen his friend this torn apart. It had been Asher then, as it was obviously Asher now. With warring loyalties, he reached out.

"Okay, you want to talk about it?"

"No." Clenching his fists, Ty fought to regain his control. "No, just go on out…keep an eye on her."

She was fighting, and losing. Asher had used almost all her reserve of energy to take the first set to a tie breaker. The ultimate loss had taken its emotional toll. Kingston was a crafty enough player to sense her opponent's flagging stamina and capitalized on it. Precision was nothing without strength. Asher's strength was ebbing quickly.

The noise played havoc with her concentration. Already playing below par, she needed the sound of the ball hitting the racket. Engines drowned it out, denying her the sense of hearing. On the brittle grass the ball jumped, skidded and stopped. Top speed was necessary, and she didn't have it.

Unable to prevent himself, Ty came to the edge of the tunnel to watch. Immediately he could see that Chuck hadn't exaggerated. She was too pale, too slow. Instinctively he took a step forward. Restraining himself was more difficult than going on, but he stopped, cursing her even as he cursed himself. She'd made her own choice. She herself had cut off any right he had to influence her. From where he stood he could hear her labored breathing, see the strain she fought to keep from her face. At the twinge of fresh pain he turned away from the court.

With a blind determination that was more nerves than power, Asher had taken the second set to three-all. Her face shone with sweat. Weakened, Asher knew that she would have to find a hole in Kingston's game soon, and have the wit and stamina to exploit it. Grit was a weapon, but not weapon enough against power, precision and cunning.

At double break point Asher prepared to serve again. If she could pull this one out, she'd have a chance. If Kingston broke her serve, the match was as good as over. *Concentrate, concentrate,* she ordered herself as she gave the ball a few testing bounces. She counted each one, trying to calm herself. Ty's furious, accusing words hammered in her brain. His face, enraged and stricken, floated in front of her eyes. Tossing the ball, Asher drove at it with her racket.

"Fault."

She shut her eyes and cursed. Control, she ordered herself. If she lost control now, she lost everything. As she took an extra moment, the crowd began to hum in speculation.

"Come on, Face, let's see what you're made of!"

Gritting her teeth, Asher put everything she had left into the serve. The ace brought a roar of approval. She wasn't beaten yet.

But her next serve was soft. Slapping it back to her, Kingston incited a hard, punishing rally. Asher battled by instinct, all reserve depleted. Her eyes, her mind, were fixed on the ball and the ball only. Dodging after a slice, she skidded, barely meeting it with her racket as she stumbled. She went down to her knees, crumbling into a ball of exhaustion and pain.

Someone's hands hooked under her armpits, pulling her to her feet. Asher pushed them away blindly to stagger to her chair.

"Come on, Asher." Chuck toweled off her streaming face, talking to her as she drew in ragged, straining breaths. "Come on, babe, you're not in any shape to be out here today. I'll help you inside."

"No." She shook off his hand. "No, I won't forfeit." Rising, she dropped the towel to the ground. "I'm going to finish."

Helpless, Chuck watched her fight a losing battle.

Asher slept for almost twenty-four hours straight. Her body recharged as she lay motionless in the bed she had shared so recently with Ty. The loss of the match—and the Grand Slam—meant little. She'd finished. Her pride was whole because she had refused to give up, because she had managed to face the reporters after the match and give them a calm accounting. When they had speculated on the state of her health, she'd told them she'd been fit to play. She would give no excuses for losing. If there was blame, it lay within herself. That was the primary rule of the game.

On returning to her room, Asher only took time to strip to her underwear before falling exhausted onto the bed. Sleep came immediately. Hours later she didn't hear the door open or Ty's footsteps as he crossed to the bedroom to look at her.

Asher lay flat on her stomach across the spread—something he knew she did only when absolutely depleted. Her breathing was deep, a heavy sound of fatigue. The hands he had thrust in his pockets balled into fists.

His emotions were pulling in too many directions. She shouldn't be allowed to do this to him, he thought furiously. She shouldn't make him want to hurt and protect at the same time. Walking to the window, he remained silent for a quarter of an hour, listening to her breathe. Before he left her, Ty drew the drapes closed so that the sunlight wouldn't disturb her.

When Asher awoke, a full day had passed. The aches made themselves known.

Keeping her mind a blank, she ran a hot bath. As the water lapped over her, she slipped into a half doze. Asher heard the knock on the door, and ignored it. The phone rang, but she didn't open her eyes.

Disturbed, Jess replaced the receiver after ten full rings. Where could Asher be? she wondered. She knew Asher was still registered at the hotel, but she hadn't answered the phone or the door in more than a day. She'd tried to tell Ty, but he simply wouldn't listen. Any more than he'd listened to her attempts at confession.

Her conscience plagued her. She hadn't tried hard enough, Jess berated herself. She'd been so afraid of losing Ty's love, she had allowed him to brush her off when she tried to talk to him. Well, no more, she determined.

Checking her watch, Jess calculated that Ty would be preparing for the day's match. She cursed, then fretted, then made herself a promise. When it was over, win or lose, she was going to corner her brother and make him listen until she'd told him everything.

Now that the vow had been made, Jess discovered that the waiting wasn't easy. In the stands she marked time. Ty played with the same fierce anger she had observed in his quarter-final match. It was just as effective.

Beneath her pride in him was the constant thought that her brother might turn away from her after he'd heard her out. But Jess sat patiently through the match and through the press conference. She'd left it to her mother to persuade Martin to go back to the hotel instead of dragging Ty off for a replay of the match. Like a tennis groupie, Jess waited for Ty to emerge from the locker room, then pounced.

"Ty, I need to talk to you."

"I'm talked out, Jess." He patted her hand, then removed it from his arm. "I want to get out of here before the next sportswriter latches on to me."

"Fine, I'll drive. You'll listen."

"Look, Jess—"

"Now, Ty."

Annoyed, Ty stalked to the car. For the first time in his life he wished his family hadn't come. He'd managed to avoid them for the most part, using fatigue or practice as excuses. His mother knew him too well, and her silence questioned him constantly. Martin was ecstatic, wanting to analyze every volley and shower praise. And the hardest of all was watching Pete, darting here and there, babbling, laughing, reminding Ty of something that might have been.

"Look, Jess, I'm tired—"

"Just get in," she interrupted tersely. "I've already put this off for too long."

They slammed their doors simultaneously. Not a very auspicious start, she mused as she merged with traffic, but she'd never finish if she didn't begin. "Okay,

I've got some things to tell you, and I'd like you to hear me out before you say anything."

"Unless I want to hitch a damn ride back, I don't have much choice, do I?"

She sent him a worried look. "Don't hate me, Ty."

"Oh, come on, Jess." Ashamed of wishing her away, he gave her hair a quick tousle. "I might be mad at being shanghaied, but I'm not going to hate you."

"Just listen," she started. Staring straight ahead, she began.

At first, Ty paid little attention. She was hopping back to the summer he had first been with Asher. He started once to interrupt, not wanting to be reminded. Jess shook her head fiercely and silenced him. With strained patience Ty sat back and watched the passing scenery.

When Jess told him that she had gone to see Asher, his brows lowered. His concentration focused. Listening to her pouring out the things she had said—*Ty's tired of you.... He doesn't know exactly how to end things without hurting you*—his rage built swiftly. Jess felt the fury swirling, and barely paused for breath.

"She seemed to have no reaction to anything I said. She was very cool, totally in control of herself. It just seemed to reinforce what I thought of her." Stopping for a light, Jess swallowed quickly. "I didn't understand how anyone could have strong feelings and not express them, not then. After I met Mac I realized…" When the light changed she gunned the motor with a jerk of her foot, then stalled the engine. On a frustrated oath she started the car again as Ty remained silent.

"When I look back on it," Jess continued after a shaky breath, "I remember how pale she got, how quiet.

It wasn't indifference, but shock. She listened to everything I said, never raising her voice or shedding a tear. I must have hurt her terribly."

Her voice broke and she waited for him to speak, but there was nothing but thick, vibrant silence. "I had no right, Ty," Jess continued quickly. "I know that. I wanted—I wanted to help, to pay you back somehow for everything you'd done for me. At the time, I thought I was telling her the things you couldn't bring yourself to. I'd convinced myself… Oh, I don't know." Jess made a quick gesture with her hand before she gripped the gear shift. "Maybe I was even jealous, but I didn't think you loved her and I was so sure she didn't love you. Especially when she married so quickly."

Because tears were forming, she pulled over to the side of the road. "Ty, to tell you I'm sorry isn't enough, but I don't have anything else."

The silence in the car vibrated for the space of three heartbeats. "What made you think you could play God with my life?" Ty demanded in a sudden burst that had her jolting. "Who the hell put you in charge?"

Forcing herself to meet his eyes, Jess spoke quietly. "There's nothing you can say to me I haven't said to myself, but you're entitled."

"Do you have any idea what you did to my life?"

She shuddered involuntarily. "Yes."

"I was going to ask Asher to marry me that night, the night I got back and found you in our room. The night you told me she'd gone off with Wickerton."

"Oh, God, Ty." Choking back a sob, Jess laid her head on the steering wheel. "I never thought…I never realized she meant that much to you."

"She was everything I wanted, don't you understand? Everything! I was half crazy because I wasn't sure she'd say yes." He drummed his fist against the dash. "And, God, I'm still not sure. I'll never be sure." The anguish in his voice made Jess straighten.

"Ty, if you'd go see her. If you'd—"

"No." He thought again of the child. His child. "There are other reasons now."

"I'll go," Jess began. "I can—"

"No!" The word whipped out at her, causing Jess to swallow the rest of the sentence. "Stay away from her."

"All right," she agreed unsteadily. "If that's the way you want it."

"That's the way I want it."

"You still love her?" Jess asked.

Ty turned his head so that his eyes met his sister's. "Yes, I love her. That isn't always enough, Jess. I don't think I'd ever be able to forget…"

"Forget?" she prompted when he trailed off. "Forget what?"

"Something she took from me…" Angry energy built up again, grinding at his nerves. "I've got to walk."

"Ty." Jess stopped him with a tentative hand on the arm as he jerked open the door of the car. "Do you want me to go away—back to California? I can make up an excuse, even leave Pete and Mac here for the rest of the tournament. I won't stay for the finals if it upsets you."

"Do what you want," he told her shortly. He started to slam the door of the car when he caught the look in her eyes. He'd protected her all of his life, too long to change now. Love was rooted in him. "It's history, Jess," he said in calmer tones. "Past history. Forget it."

Turning, Ty walked away, hoping he'd be able to believe his own words.

Chapter 12

Asher sat on the bed to watch the men's singles championship. The television commentary barely penetrated as she judged and dissected each stroke and volley for herself. She couldn't go to the stadium, but nothing would prevent her from watching Ty compete.

On the close-ups, she studied his face carefully. Yes, some strain showed, she noted, but his concentration was complete. His energy was as volatile as ever, perhaps more so. For that she could be grateful.

Each time they replayed a shot in slow motion, Asher could fully appreciate the beauty of his form. Muscles rippled as he stretched; feet left the turf in a leap for more power. He was a raw athlete with anger simmering just under the discipline. The graphite racket was no more than an extension of the arm that was whipping the ball harder and harder. As always, his hair flew around the sweatband, dramatic and unruly. His eyes were dark with a rage barely contained. Was it the game that drove him? she wondered. The insatiable thirst to win? Or were there other emotions pushing him this time?

If there were, it was easy to see that they added to the impetus. He was an explosion heating up, a storm rumbling just overhead. Asher knew him well enough to recognize that his control balanced on a very thin edge, but it made his game all the more exciting.

His topspin drove to Chuck's backhand and was returned, power for power. A slice, a lob, an overhead. Turned the wrong way, Chuck pivoted, sprinted, but had no chance to return. The call was late, judging Ty's ball long.

His head whipped around to the judge, his eyes deadly. Asher shuddered when the camera zoomed in so that the undisguised fury seemed aimed directly at her. For a moment they seemed to stare into each other's eyes. Disgust warred with temper before he turned to resume his receiving stance. Crouched like a cat, his eyes intense, he waited. Asher let out an unsteady breath.

Ty was judging the bounce with uncanny accuracy. If it threatened to die, he was under it. When it chose to soar, he got behind it. With unrelenting challenge he charged the net. He baited Chuck, dared him, and, time after time, outwitted him. His game was all aggression and power—Starbuck at his best, she thought with undiminished pride. He could demoralize even a seasoned pro like Chuck with a lightning-fast return that lifted chalk from the service line. With each swing she could hear the grunt of exertion and the swish of air. How she wanted to be there.

He wouldn't want her. She wouldn't soon forget that look of rage and disgust he had turned on her—too much like the one his video image had projected. A man like Starbuck had no ambivalent emotions. It was love or hate; she'd felt them both.

She'd been cut out of his life. She had to accept that. She had to…quit? Asher asked herself. Suddenly her chin rose. Was that what she was doing again? She looked back at the screen as the camera zoomed in on Ty's face. His eyes were opaque and dangerous before he went into a full stretch for his serve. The force of her feelings attacked her. She loved and wanted and needed.

No, damn it! Rising, Asher cursed him. No, if she was going to lose, she was going down fighting, just as she had on the courts. He wouldn't brush her out of his life so easily this time. Briefly she'd forgotten that she no longer aimed her actions at pleasing those around her. Perhaps he didn't want to see her, but that was just too bad. He would see her…and he would listen.

Just as she snapped off the set, a knock sounded on her door. Battling impatience, Asher went to answer. Her expression changed from grim determination to wonder.

"Dad!"

"Asher." Jim met her stunned expression with an unsmiling nod. "May I come in?"

He hadn't changed, she thought wildly. He hadn't changed at all. He was still tall and tanned and silvery-blond. He was still her father. Her eyes filled with love and tears. "Oh, Dad, I'm so glad to see you." Grasping his hand, she drew him into the room. Then the awkwardness set in. "Sit down, please." While gesturing to a chair, Asher sought something to fill the gap. "Shall I order up something to drink? Some coffee?"

"No." He sat as she suggested and looked at his daughter. She was thinner, he noted. And nervous, as nervous as he was himself. Since Ty's phone call, he'd done little but think of her. "Asher," he began, then sighed. "Please sit down." He waited until she settled across from him. "I want to tell you I'm proud of the way you've played this season."

His voice was stiff, but she expected little else. "Thank you."

"I'm most proud of the last match you played."

Asher gave him a small smile. How typical that it was tennis he spoke of first. "I lost."

"You played," he countered. "Right down to the last point, you played. I wonder how many people who watched knew that you were ill."

"I wasn't ill," Asher corrected him automatically. "If I came on court—"

"Then you were fit," he finished, before he shook his head. "I drummed that into you well, didn't I?"

"A matter of pride and sportsmanship," she said quietly, giving him back the words he had given her again and again during her training.

Jim lapsed into silence, frowning at the elegant hands that lay folded in her lap. She'd always been his princess, he thought, his beautiful, golden princess. He'd wanted to give her the world, and he'd wanted her to deserve it.

"I didn't intend to come here to see you."

If the statement hurt, she gave no sign. "What changed your mind?"

"A couple of things, most particularly, your last match."

Rising, Asher walked to the window. "So, I had to lose to have you speak to me again." The words came easily, as did the light trace of bitterness. Though love had remained constant, she found no need to give him unvarnished adulation any longer. "All those years I needed you so badly, I waited, hoping you'd forgive me."

"It was a hard thing to forgive, Asher."

He rose, too, realizing his daughter had grown stronger. He wasn't sure how to approach the woman she had become.

"It was a hard thing to accept," she countered in the calm voice he remembered. "That my father looked at me as athlete first and child second."

"That's not true."

"Isn't it?" Turning, she fixed him with a level stare. "You turned your back on me because I gave up my career. Not once when I was suffering did you hold out a hand to me. I had no one to go to but you, and because you said no, I had no one at all."

"I tried to deal with it. I tried to accept your decision to marry that man, though you knew how I felt about him." The unexpected guilt angered him and chilled his voice. "I tried to understand how you could give up what you were to play at being something else."

"I had no choice," she began furiously.

"No choice?" His derision was sharp as a blade. "You made your own decision, Asher—your career for a title—just as you made it about the child. My grandchild."

"Please." She lifted both hands to her temples as

she turned away. "Please don't. Have you any idea how much and how often I've paid for that moment of carelessness?"

"Carelessness?" Stunned into disbelief, Jim stared at the back of her head. "You call the conception of a child carelessness?"

"No, *no!*" Her voice trembled as it rose. "The loss. If I hadn't let myself get upset, if I had looked where I was going, I never would have fallen. I never would have lost Ty's child."

"What!" As the pain slammed into his stomach, Jim sank into the chair. "Fallen? Ty's child? *Ty's?*" He ran a hand over his eyes as he tried to sort it out. Suddenly he felt old and frail and frightened. "Asher, are you telling me you miscarried Ty's child?"

"Yes." Wearily she turned back to face him. "I wrote you, I told you."

"If you wrote, I never received the letter." Shaken, Jim held out a hand, waiting until she grasped it. "Asher, Eric told me you aborted his child." For an instant, the words, their meaning, failed to penetrate. Her look was blank and vulnerable enough to make him feel every year of his age. "A calculated abortion of your husband's child," he said deliberately. When she swayed he gripped her other hand. "He told me you'd done so without his knowledge or permission. He seemed devastated. I believed him, Asher." As she went limp, he drew her down to her knees in front of him. "I believed him."

"Oh, God." Her eyes were huge and dark with shock.

Her father's fingers trembled in hers. "He phoned me from London. He sounded half mad—I thought with grief. He said that you hadn't told him until after it was done. That you had told him you wanted no children to interfere with the life you intended to build as Lady Wickerton."

Too numb for anger, Asher shook her head. "I didn't know even Eric could be so vindictive, so cruel."

It all began to make horrid sense. Her letters to her father hadn't been answered. Eric had seen that they were never mailed. Then, when she had phoned him, Jim had been cold and brief. He'd told her that he could never resolve himself to her choice. Asher had assumed he meant her rejection of her career.

"He wanted me to pay," she explained as she dropped her head on her father's lap. "He never wanted me to stop paying."

Gently Jim cupped her face in his hands. "Tell me everything. I'll listen, as I should have a long time ago."

She started with Jess, leaving nothing out including her final stormy estrangement from Ty. Jim's mouth tightened at her recounting of the accident and the hospital scene with Eric. Listening, he cursed himself for being a fool.

"And now, Ty…" As realization struck her, she paled. "Ty thinks—Eric must have told him I'd had an abortion."

"No, I told him."

"You?" Confused, Asher pressed her fingers to the headache in her temple. "But how—"

"He called me a few nights ago. He wanted to convince me to see you. I told him enough to make him believe the lie just as I'd believed it."

"That night when I woke up," Asher remembered. "Oh, my God, when he realized it had been his baby…

The things he was saying! I couldn't think at the time." She shut her eyes. "No wonder he hates me."

Color flooded back into her face. "I have to tell him the truth and make him believe it." Scrambling up, she dashed for the door. "I'll go to the club. I have to make him listen. I have to make him understand."

"The match must be nearly over." Jim rose on unsteady legs. His daughter had been through hell, and he had done nothing but add to it. "You'll never catch him there."

Frustrated, Asher looked at her watch. "I don't know where he's staying." Releasing the doorknob, she went to the phone. "I'll just have to find out."

"Asher..." Awkward, unsure, Jim held out his hand. "Forgive me."

Asher stared into his face as she replaced the receiver. Ignoring the hand, she went into his arms.

It was nearly midnight when Ty reached the door of his room. For the past two hours he'd been drinking steadily. Celebrating. It wasn't every day you won the Grand Slam, he reminded himself as he searched for his keys. And it wasn't every day a man had a half dozen women offering to share their beds with him. He gave a snort of laughter as he slid the key into the lock. And why the hell hadn't he taken one of them up on it?

None of them was Asher. He shook away the thought as he struggled to make the doorknob function. No, he simply hadn't wanted a woman, Ty told himself. It was because he was tired and had had too much to drink. Asher was yesterday.

The hotel room was dark as he stumbled inside. If he was right about nothing else, he was right about having too much to drink. Through glass after glass Ty had told himself the liquor was for celebrating, not for forgetting. The kid from the Chicago slum had made it to the top, in spades.

The hell with it, he decided, tossing his keys into the room. With a thud they landed on the carpet. Swaying a bit, he stripped off his shirt and threw it in the same direction. Now if he could just find his way to the bed without turning on a light, he'd sleep. Tonight he'd sleep—with enough liquor in his system to anesthetize him. There'd be no dreams of soft skin or dark blue eyes tonight.

As he fumbled toward the bedroom, a light switched on, blinding him. With a pungent curse Ty covered his eyes, balancing himself with one hand on the wall.

"Turn that damn thing off," he muttered.

"Well, the victor returns triumphant."

The quiet voice had him lowering the hand from his eyes. Asher sat primly in a chair, looking unruffled, soft and utterly tempting. Ty felt desire work its way through the alcohol.

"What the hell are you doing here?"

"And very drunk," she said as if he hadn't spoken. Rising, she went to him. "I suppose you deserve it after the way you played today. Should I add my congratulations to the host of others?"

"Get out." He pushed away from the wall. "I don't want you."

"I'll order up some coffee," she said calmly. "We'll talk."

"I said get out!" Catching her wrist, he whirled her around. "Before I lose my temper and hurt you."

Though her pulse jumped under his fingers, she stood firm. "I'll leave after we talk."

"Do you know what I want to do to you?" he demanded, shoving her back against the wall. "Do you know that I want to beat you senseless?"

"Yes." She didn't cringe as his fury raged down on her. "Ty, if you'll listen—"

"I don't want to listen to you." The image of her lying exhausted on the bed raced through his mind. "Get out while I can still stop myself from hurting you."

"I can't." She lifted a hand to his cheek. "Ty—"

Her words were cut off as he pressed her back into the wall. For an instant she thought he would strike her, then his mouth came down on hers, bruising, savage. He forced her lips apart, thrusting his tongue deep as she struggled. His teeth ground against hers as though to punish them both. There was the faint taste of liquor, reminding her he had drink as well as anger in his system. When she tried to turn her head, he caught her face in his hand—not gently, in the touch she remembered, but viselike.

He could smell her—the soft talc, the lightly sexy perfume. And the fear. She made a small, pleading sound before she stopped fighting him. Without being aware of what he did, he lightened the grip to a caress. His lips gentled on hers, tasting, savoring. Mumbling her name, he trailed kisses over her skin until he felt the essence of her flowing back into him. God, how he'd missed her.

"I can't do without you," he whispered. "I can't." He sank to the floor, drawing her down with him.

He was lost in her—the feel, the taste, the fragrance. His mind was too full of Asher to allow him to think.

Sensation ruled him, trembling along his skin to follow the path of her fingers. It was as if she sought to soothe and arouse him at once. He was helpless to resist her—or his need for her. As if in a trance, he took his lips over her, missing nothing as his hunger seemed insatiable. Her quickening breaths were like music, setting his rhythm.

The air grew steamier as his hands homed in on secrets that made her moan. Her body shuddered into life. No longer gentle, but demanding, she tangled her fingers in his hair and guided him to sweet spaces he'd neglected. Then ever greedy, ever giving, she drew him back to her mouth. Her tongue toyed with his lips, then slid inside to drink up all the flavors. His head swimming, he answered the kiss.

The need for her was unreasonable, but Ty was beyond reason. Without her there'd been an emptiness that even his fury couldn't fill. Now the void was closing. She was in his blood, in his bone, so essential a part of him he had been able to find no place of separation. Now there was no will to do so.

Under him, she was moving, inviting, entreating. He whispered a denial against her mouth, but his pounding blood took control. He was inside her without being aware of it. Then all sensations spiraled together in an intensity that made him cry out. And it was her name he spoke, in both ecstasy and in despair.

Drained, Ty rolled from her to stare at the ceiling. How could he have let that happen? he demanded. How could he have felt such love, found such pleasure in a woman he had vowed to amputate from his life? He wondered now if he'd ever find the strength to stay away from her. Life with her, and life without her, would be two kinds of hell.

"Ty." Reaching over, Asher touched his shoulder.

"Don't." Without looking at her he rose. "Get dressed, for God's sake," he muttered as he tugged on his own jeans with trembling hands. Who had used whom? he wondered. "Do you have a car?"

Sitting up, Asher pushed her hair out of her face. Hair, she remembered, that only moments before he had been kissing. "No."

"I'll call you a cab."

"That won't be necessary." In silence she began to dress. "I realize you're sorry that this happened."

"I'm damned if I'll apologize," he snapped.

"I wasn't asking you to," she told him quietly. "I was going to say that I'm not sorry. I love you, and making love with you is only one way to show it." She managed, after three attempts, to button her blouse. When she looked up, he was at the window, his back to her. "Ty, I came here to tell you some things you must know. When I'm finished, I'll go and give you time to think about them."

"Can't you understand I don't want to think anymore?"

"It's the last thing I'll ask of you."

"All right." In a gesture of fatigue she rarely saw in him, he rubbed both hands over his face. The liquor had burned out of his system—by the anger or the passion, he wasn't sure. But he was cold sober. "Maybe I should tell you first that what Jess said to you three years ago was her own fabrication. I didn't know anything about it until the other day when she told me what she'd done. In her own way, she was trying to protect me."

"I don't understand what you're talking about."

Turning, he gave her a grim smile. "Did you really think I was tired of you? Looking for a way out? Wondering how I could ditch you without raising too much fuss or interfering with my career?"

Asher opened her mouth to speak, then shut it again. How strange that the words still hurt and made her defensive.

"Obviously you did."

"And if I did?" she countered. "Everything she said fit. You'd never made a commitment to me. There'd never been any talk about the future."

"On either side," he reminded her.

Asher pushed away the logic. "If you'd once told me—"

"Or perhaps you were uncertain enough of your own feelings that when Jess dumped that on you, you ran right to Wickerton. Even though you were carrying my baby."

"I didn't know I was pregnant when I married Eric." She saw him shrug her words away. In fury she grabbed both of his arms. "I tell you I didn't know! Perhaps if I had known before I would have simply gone away. I don't know what I would have done. I was already terrified you were growing tired of me before Jess confirmed it."

"And where the hell did you get a stupid idea like that?"

"You'd been so moody, so withdrawn. Everything she said made sense."

"If I was moody and withdrawn, it was because I was trying to work out the best way to ask Asher

Wolfe, Miss Society Tennis, to marry Starbuck, from the wrong side of the tracks."

Asher took an uncertain step toward him. "You would have married me?"

"I still have the ring I bought you," he answered.

"A ring?" she repeated stupidly. "You'd bought me a ring?" For some inexplicable reason the thought of it stunned her more than anything else.

"I'd planned to try a very conventional proposal. And if that didn't work, maybe a kidnapping."

She tried to laugh because tears were entirely too close. "It would have worked."

"If you'd told me you were pregnant—"

"Ty, I didn't know! Damn it!" She pounded once against his chest. "Do you think I would have married Eric if I had known? It was weeks afterward that I found out."

"Why the hell didn't you tell me then?"

"Do you think I wanted to get you back that way?" The old pride lifted her chin. "And I was married to another man. I'd made him a promise."

"A promise that meant more than the life of the child we'd made together," he retorted bitterly. "A promise that let you walk into one of those antiseptic clinics and destroy something innocent and beautiful. And mine."

The image was too ugly, the truth too painful. Flying at him, Asher struck him again and again until he pinned her hands behind her back. *"And mine!"* she shouted at him. "And mine, or doesn't my part matter?"

"You didn't want it." His fingers closed like steel as she tried to pull away. "But you didn't have the decency to ask me if I did. Couldn't you bear the thought of carrying part of me inside you for nine months?"

"Don't ask me what I could bear." She wasn't pale now, but vivid with fury. "I didn't have an abortion," she spat at him. "I miscarried. I miscarried and nearly died in the process. Would you feel better if I had? God knows I tried to."

"Miscarried?" His grip shifted from her wrists to her shoulders. "What are you talking about?"

"Eric hated me too!" she shouted. "When I learned I was pregnant and told him, all he could say was that I'd deceived him. I'd tried to trick him into claiming the baby after you'd refused me. Nothing I said got through to him. We argued and argued. We were near the steps and he was shouting. All I wanted to do was get away." Her hands flew up to cover her face as she remembered again, all too clearly. "I didn't look, I only ran. Then I was falling. I tried to stop, but my head hit the railing, I think. Then I don't remember anything until I woke up and the baby was gone."

Somehow he could see it as vividly as though it were being played on film in front of his eyes. "Oh, God, Asher." When he tried to take her in his arms, she pulled away.

"I wanted you, but I knew you'd never forgive me. It didn't seem to matter anymore, so I did what Eric wanted." To force back the tears, she pressed her fingers to her eyes. "I didn't want you to know, I couldn't have stood it if you had known when you didn't want me." Lowering her hands, she looked at him, dry-eyed. "I paid for losing your baby, Ty. For three years I did without everything that mattered to me, and I grieved alone. I can't mourn any longer."

"No." Going to the window, he flung it up as if he needed air. There was no breeze, nothing to relieve the burning that he felt. "You've had years to deal with it. I've had days." And she'd had no one, he thought. Years with no one. Ty took several long breaths. "How badly were you hurt?"

Puzzled by the question, she shook her head. "What?"

"Were you badly hurt?" The question was rough and turbulent. When she remained silent he turned. "When you fell, how bad was it?"

"I—I lost the baby."

"I asked about you."

She stared without comprehension. No one had asked her that, not even her father. Looking into Ty's ravaged face, she could only shake her head again.

"Damn it, Asher, did you have a concussion, did you break any bones? You said you almost died."

"The baby died," she repeated numbly.

Crossing to her, he grabbed her shoulders. *"You!"* he shouted. "Don't you know that you're the most important thing to me? We can have a dozen babies if you want. I need to know what happened to you."

"I don't remember very much. I was sedated. There were transfusions..." The full impact of his words penetrated slowly. The anguish in his eyes was for her. "Ty." Burying her face against his chest, she clung. "All that's over."

"I should have been with you." He drew her closer. "We should have gone through that together."

"Just tell me you love me. Say the words."

"You know that I do." He cupped her chin to force her head back. "I love you." He saw the first tear fall and kissed it away. "Don't," he pleaded. "No more tears, Face. No more grieving."

She held him close again until the fullness left her chest. “No more grieving,” she repeated, and lifted her face.

He touched it gently, fingertips only. “I hurt you.”

“We let other people hurt us,” she contradicted. “Never again.”

“How could we be stupid enough to almost lose it all twice?” he wondered aloud. “No more secrets, Asher.”

She shook her head. “No more secrets. A third chance, Ty?”

“I work best under pressure.” He brushed his lips over her temple. “Double break point, Face, I’m on a winning streak.”

“You should be celebrating.”

“I did my share.”

“Not with me.” She gave him a light kiss full of promise. “We could go to my place. Pick up a bottle of champagne on the way.”

“We could stay here,” he countered. “And worry about the champagne tomorrow.”

“It is tomorrow,” she reminded him.

“Then we’ve got all day.” He began to pull her toward the bedroom.

“Wait a minute.” Snatching her hand away, she stepped back. “I’d like to hear that conventional proposal now.”

“Come on, Asher.” He made another grab for her hand, but she eluded him.

“I mean it.”

Flustered, he stuck his hands into his pockets. “You know I want you to marry me.”

“That’s not a conventional proposal.” She folded her arms and waited. “Well,” she began when he remained silent, "should I write you a cheat sheet? You say something like, Asher—"

"I know what I'm supposed to say," he muttered. "I'd rather try the kidnapping."

Laughing, she walked over and twined her arms around his neck. "Ask me," she whispered, letting her lips hover an inch from his.

"Will you marry me, Asher?" The lips held tantalizingly near his curved, but she remained silent. His eyes dropped to them, lingered, then rose to hers. "Well?"

"I'm thinking it over," she told him. "I was hoping for something a bit more flowery, maybe some poetry or—" The wind was knocked out of her as he hefted her over his shoulder. "Yes, that's good too," she decided. "I should be able to let you know in a few days."

From the height he dropped her, she bounced twice before she settled on the bed.

"Or sooner," she decided as he began unbuttoning her blouse.

"Shut up."

She cocked a brow. "Don't you want to hear my answer?"

"We'll get the license tomorrow."

"I haven't said—"

"And the blood tests."

"I haven't agreed—"

His mouth silenced her in a long, lingering kiss as his body fit unerringly to hers.

"Of course," Asher sighed, "I could probably be persuaded."

* * * * *

PARTNERS

For Bruce, who changed my plans.

Chapter 1

Bedlam. Phones rang continuously. People shouted, muttered or swore, sitting or on the run. Typewriter keys clattered at varying paces from every direction. There was the scent of old coffee, fresh bread, tobacco smoke and human sweat. An insane asylum? Several of the inmates would have agreed with that description of the city room of the *New Orleans Herald,* especially at deadline.

For most of the staff the chaos went unnoticed, as the inhaling and exhaling of air went unnoticed. There were times when each one of them was too involved with their own daily crises or triumphs to be aware of the dozens of others springing up around them. Not that teamwork was ignored. All were bound, by love for, or obsession with, their jobs, in the exclusive community of journalists. Still each would concentrate on, and greedily guard, his or her own story, own sources and own style. A successful print reporter thrives on pressure and confusion and a hot lead.

Matthew Bates had cut his teeth on newsprint. He'd worked it from every angle from newsboy on the Lower East Side of Manhattan to feature reporter. He'd carried coffee, run copy, written obituaries and covered flower shows.

The ability to scent out a story and draw the meat from it wasn't something he'd learned in his journalism courses; he'd been born with it. His years of structured classes, study and practice had honed the style and technique of a talent that was as inherent as the color of his eyes.

At the age of thirty, Matt was casually cynical but not without humor for life's twists and turns. He liked people without having illusions about them. He understood and accepted that humans were basically ridiculous. How else could he work in a room full of crazy people in a profession that constantly exposed and exploited the human race?

Finishing a story, he called out for a copy boy, then leaned back to let his mind rest for the first time in three hours. A year ago, he'd left New York to accept the position on the *Herald,* wanting, perhaps needing, a change. Restless, he thought now. He'd been restless for...something. And New Orleans was as hard and demanding a town as New York, with more elegant edges.

He worked the police beat and liked it. It was a tough world, and murder and desperation were parts of it that couldn't be ignored. The homicide he'd just covered had been senseless and cruel. It had been life; it had been news. Now, he wiped the death of the eighteen-year-old girl out of his mind. Objectivity came first, unless he wanted to try a new profession. Yet it took a concentrated effort to erase her image and her ending from his mind.

He hadn't the looks of a seasoned, hard-boiled reporter, and he knew it. It had exasperated him in his twenties that he looked more like a carefree surfer than a newsman. Now, it amused him.

He had a lean, subtly muscled body that was more at home in jeans than a three-piece suit, with a height that only added a feeling of ranginess. His dark blond hair curled as it chose, over his ears, down to the collar of his shirt. It merely added to the image of a laid-back, easygoing male who'd rather be sitting on the beach than pounding the pavement. More than one source had talked freely to the façade without fully comprehending the man beneath the image. When and if they did, Matt already had the story.

When he chose, he could be charming, even elegant. But the good-humored blue eyes could turn to fire or, more dangerous, ice. Beneath the easy exterior was a cold, hard determination and a smoldering temper. Matt accepted this with a shrug. He was human, and entitled to be ridiculous.

With a half smile lingering around his mouth, he turned to the woman seated across from him. Laurel Armand—with a face as romantic as her name. She had an aura of delicacy that came from fine bones and an ivory skin that made a man want to touch, and touch gently. Her hair fell in clouds of misty black, swept back from her face, spilling onto her shoulders. Hair made for a man to dive his fingers into, bury his face in. Her eyes were the color of emeralds, dark and rich.

It was the face of a nineteenth-century belle whose life revolved around gracious indolence and quiet gentility. And her voice was just as feminine, Matt mused. It turned vowels into liquid and smoothed consonants. It never flattened, never twanged, but flowed like a leisurely stream.

The voice, he reflected as his smile widened, was just as deceptive as the face. The lady was a sharp, ambitious reporter with a stubborn streak and a flaring temper. One of his favorite pastimes was setting a match to it.

Her brows were drawn together as she finished the last line of her copy. Satisfied, Laurel whipped the sheet from her typewriter, called for a copy boy, then focused on the man across from her. Automatically, her spine straightened. She already knew he was going to bait her, and that—damn it—she would bite.

"Do you have a problem, Matthew?" Her tone was soft and faintly bored.

"No problem, Laurellie." He watched the annoyance flare into her eyes at his use of her full name.

"Don't you have a murder or armed robbery to go play with?"

His mouth curved, charmingly, deepening the creases in his face. "Not at the moment. Off your soapbox for the day?"

She gritted her teeth on a spate of furious words. He never failed to dig for the emotion that seeped into her work, and she never failed to defend it. Not this time, Laurel told herself as she balled her hands into fists under her desk. "I leave the cynicism to you, Matthew," she returned with a sweetness belied by the daggers in her eyes. "You're so good at it."

"Yeah. How about a bet on whose story makes page one?"

She lifted one fragile, arched brow—a gesture he particularly admired. "I wouldn't want to take your money, Matthew."

"I don't mind taking yours." Grinning, he rose to walk around their desk and bend down to her ear. "Five bucks, magnolia blossom. Even though your papa owns the paper, our editors know the difference between reporting and crusading."

He felt the heat rise, heard the soft hiss of breath. It was tempting, very tempting, to crush his mouth onto those soft, pouting lips and taste the fury. Even as the need worked into him, Matt reminded himself that wasn't the way to outwit her.

"You're on, Bates, but make it ten." Laurel stood. It infuriated her that she had to tilt her head back to meet his eyes. It infuriated her more that the eyes were confident, amused and beautiful. Laurel fell back on the habit of imagining him short, rotund and balding. "Unless that's too rich for your blood," she added.

"Anything to oblige, love." He curled the tips of her hair around his finger. "And to prove even Yankees have chivalry, I'll buy you lunch with my winnings."

She smiled at him, leaning a bit closer so that their bodies just brushed. Matt felt the surprising jolt of heat shoot straight through his system. "When hell freezes over," Laurel told him, then shoved him aside.

Matt watched her storm away; then, dipping his hands into his pockets, he laughed. In the confusion of the city room, no one noticed.

* * *

"Damn!" Laurel swore as she maneuvered her car through the choking downtown traffic. Matthew Bates was the most irritating man she'd ever known. Squeezing through on an amber light, she cursed fate. If her brother Curt hadn't met him in college, Matthew would never have accepted the position on the *Herald.* Then he'd be insufferable in New York instead of being insufferable two feet away from her day after day.

Honesty forced her to admit, even when it hurt, that he was the best reporter on the staff. He was thorough and insightful and had the instincts of a bloodhound. But that didn't make him any easier to swallow. Laurel hit the brakes and swerved as a Buick cut her off. She was too annoyed with Matt to be bothered by traffic warfare.

His piece on the homicide had been clean, concise and excellent. She wished she'd stuffed the ten dollars down his throat. That would've made it difficult for him to gloat over it.

In the twelve months she'd known and worked with him, he'd never reacted toward her as other men did. There was no deference in him, no admiration in his eyes. The fact that she despised being deferred to didn't make her resent him any less.

He'd never asked her out—not that she wanted him to, Laurel reminded herself firmly. Except for missing the pure pleasure of turning him down. Even though he'd moved into her apartment building, virtually next door to her, he'd never come knocking at her door on the smallest of pretences. For a year she'd been hoping he would—so she could slam the door in his face.

What he did, she thought as she gritted her teeth,

was make a nuisance of himself in a dozen other ways. He made cute little observations on her dates—all the more irritating because they were invariably true. These days his favorite target was Jerry Cartier, an ultraconservative, somewhat dense city councilman. Laurel saw him because she was too kindhearted not to, and he occasionally gave her a lead. But Matt put her in the intolerable position of having to defend Jerry against her own opinion.

Life would be simpler, she thought, if Matthew Bates were still hustling newsprint in Manhattan. And if he weren't so impossibly attractive. Laurel blocked Matt, and her ten dollars, out of her mind as she left the traffic behind.

Though the sun was hanging low, the sky was still brilliant. Warmth and light filtered through the cypresses and streamed onto the road. Deep in the trees were shadows and the musical sound of insects and birds, creatures of the marsh. She'd always known there were secrets in the marshes. Secrets, shadows, dangers. They only added to the beauty. There was something exciting in knowing another way of life thrived—primitive, predatory—so near civilization.

As she turned into the lane that led to her ancestral home, Laurel felt the familiar mix of pride and tranquility. Cedars guarded each side of the drive, arching overhead to transform the lane into a cool, dim tunnel. The sun filtered through sporadically, throwing patches of light on the ground. Spanish moss dripped from the branches to add that timeless grace so peculiar to the South. As she traveled down the drive of Promesse d'Amour, the clock turned back. Life was easy.

At the end of the drive, Laurel stopped to look at

the house. There were two rambling stories of white-washed brick surrounded by a profusion of azaleas, camellias and magnolias. The colors, vivid and delicate, the scents, exotic and gentle, added to the sense of antebellum style and indolence. With the window down, she could smell the mix of heat and fragrance.

There were twenty-eight Doric columns that added dignity rather than ostentation. Ivy clung to each corner post. The grillwork on the encircling balcony was as delicate as black lace and French doors led to it from every room. The effect of the house was one of durability, security and grace. Laurel saw it as a woman who had coped with the years and emerged with character and gentility. If the house had been flesh and blood, she couldn't have loved it more.

She took the side steps to the porch and entered without knocking. Her childhood had been spent there, her girlhood, her adolescence. A wide hallway split the building in two, running from front door to back. Lingering in the air was the scent of beeswax and lemon, to mix with the fragrance from a bowl of camellia blossoms. The hall would have held the same scent a century before. Laurel paused only briefly in front of a cheval glass to brush the hair away from her face before she walked into the front parlor.

"Hello, Papa." She went to him, rising on her toes to kiss a cheek rough from a day's growth of beard. William Armand was lanky and handsome with dark hair just hinting at gray. While he ran his daily paper with verve, temper and tenacity, he chose an easier pace for his personal life. He smelled of good whiskey and tobacco. In an old habit, he mussed the hair Laurel had just straightened.

"Hello, princess. Good story on the mayor." He lifted a brow in puzzlement as he saw the quick flash of irritation in her eyes.

"Thanks." She smiled so quickly, her father thought he'd imagined that dangerous light. Turning, she studied the woman who sat in a royal-blue tufted chair.

The hair was pure white, but as full and thick as Laurel's. It surrounded a face layered and lined with wrinkles and unashamedly rouged. Olivia Armand wasn't ashamed of anything. Eyes as sharp and green as the emeralds in her ears studied Laurel in turn.

"Grandma." With a sigh, Laurel bent to kiss her. "Will you never grow old?"

"Not if I have anything to say about it." Her voice was raspy with age and stunningly sensual. "You're the same," she continued, taking Laurel's hand in her strong, dry one. "It's good Creole blood." After giving Laurel's hand a quick squeeze, she sat back in her chair. "William, fix the child a drink and top mine off while you're at it. How's your love life these days, Laurellie?"

Grinning, Laurel dropped down on the hassock at her grandmother's feet. "Not as varied as yours." She caught her father's wink as he handed her a glass.

"Hogwash!" Olivia tossed back her bourbon. "I'll tell you what's wrong with the world today, too much business and not enough romance. Your problem, Laurellie—" she paused to jab a finger at her granddaughter "—is wasting time on that spineless Cartier. Not enough blood in him to warm a woman's bed."

"Thank God," Laurel said with a grateful look at the ceiling. "That's the last place I want him."

"Time you had someone there," Olivia retorted.

Laurel lifted a brow while her father tried not to

choke on his drink. "Not all of us," Laurel said smoothly, "have your, shall we say, bawdy turn of mind."

Olivia gave a hoot of laughter and smacked the arm of her chair. "Not everyone admits it, that's the difference."

Unable to resist her grandmother's outrageousness, Laurel grinned. "Curt should be here soon, shouldn't he?"

"Any minute." William eased his tall, angular frame into a chair. "He called just before you came in. He's bringing a friend with him."

"A woman, I hope," Olivia said irrepressibly before she polished off her bourbon. "Boy's got his nose stuck in too many law books. Between the two of you," she added, rounding on Laurel again, "I'll never be a great-grandmother. The pair of you're too wrapped up in law and newspapers to find a lover."

"I'm not ready to get married," Laurel said tranquilly as she held her glass up to the light.

"Who said anything about marriage?" Olivia wanted to know. Heaving a sigh, she looked at her son. "Children nowadays don't know anything."

Laurel was laughing when she heard the sound of the front door closing. "That'll be Curt. I believe I'll warn him about the frame of mind you're in."

"Damned pretty girl," Olivia muttered when Laurel strolled out.

"She's the image of you," her son commented as he lit one of his cigars.

Olivia cackled. "Damned pretty."

The moment she entered the hall, Laurel's smile faded and her jaw tensed. Her eyes flicked over her brother to the man beside him. "Oh, it's you."

Matt took her hand, raising it to his lips before Laurel could jerk it away. "Ah, Southern hospitality." Good God, he thought as his gaze roamed over her, she's beautiful. All that passion, all that fire, under ivory and roses. One day, Laurellie, he promised silently, we're going to set it all loose. My way.

Ignoring the warmth that lingered on her knuckles from his lips, Laurel turned to her brother. He had the angularity and aristocratic features of their father, and the eyes of a dreamer. As Matt watched, the restrained temper on her face softened with affection.

"Hi." She put her hands on her brother's shoulders, leaving them there after she'd kissed him. "How are you?"

"Fine. Busy." He gave her an absent smile, as if he'd just remembered where he was.

"The busy might be an issue tonight," she told him with a chuckle. "Grandma's in one of her moods."

He gave her such a pained look that Laurel laughed and kissed him again. Poor Curt, she thought, so shy and sweet. Turning her head, she looked directly into Matt's eyes. He was watching her coolly, with something undefinable flickering behind the aloof expression. A tremble skidded up her spine, but she kept her eyes level. Who is he really? she wondered, not for the first time. And why, after an entire year, am I still not sure? It always puzzled her how a man with his energy, wit and cynicism should remain such good friends with her gentle, dreamy brother. It puzzled her, too, that she couldn't pin him down to a type. Perhaps that was why he invaded her thoughts so often. Involuntarily, her gaze slipped down to his mouth. It curved. Silently, she swore.

"I guess we'd better go in," Curt said, oblivious to the undercurrents around him. He smiled in a quick, boyish way that animated his soft eyes. "Having Matt along should distract her. Distracting women's one of his best talents."

Laurel gave an unladylike snort. "I'll bet."

As Curt started into the parlor, Matt took Laurel's hand and tucked it into his arm. "Another wager, Laurellie?" he murmured. "Name the stakes."

There was something insolent in the softly spoken words. She tossed her head back in an angry gesture that pleased him enormously. "If you don't let go of my hand, I'm going to—"

"Embarrass yourself," Matt finished as they crossed the threshold into the parlor.

He'd always liked the room—the faded colors and polished old wood. There were times when he was here that Matt forgot the years he'd spent in a cramped third-floor walk-up with a radiator that let off more noise than heat. That part of his life was over; he'd seen to it. Yet snatches of it crept up on him in spite of success. Shoes that were too small, a belly never quite full—an ambition that threatened to outdistance opportunity. No, he'd never take success for granted. He'd spent too many years fighting for it.

"So, you've brought the Yankee, have you?" Olivia sent Matt a sparkling look and prepared to enjoy herself.

Curt greeted his father, dutifully kissed Olivia's cheek, then busied himself mixing drinks. Grandma had that look in her eye.

"Miss Olivia." Matt took the offered hand and lifted it to his lips. "More beautiful than ever."

"Rascal," she accused, but the pleasure came through. "You haven't been to see me for a month—a dangerous amount of time at my age."

Matt kissed her hand again while his eyes laughed into hers. "I only stay away because you won't marry me."

Laurel struggled not to smile as she chose a chair across the room. Did he have to be so damned charming?

Olivia's laugh was a sound of pure, feminine appreciation. "Thirty years ago, you scoundrel, I'd have given you a chase, even if you are a Yankee."

Matt took the offered glass, and the grateful look, Curt gave him before he turned back to Olivia. "Miss Olivia, I wouldn't have run." He perched on the arm of her chair, much, Laurel thought resentfully, like a favored nephew.

"Well, the time's passed for that," she decided with a sigh before she aimed a look at Laurel. "Why haven't you taken up with this devil, Laurellie? He's a man to keep a woman's blood moving."

Color, as much from annoyance as embarrassment, rose in Laurel's cheeks as Matt sent her a wolfish grin. She sat in stony silence, cursing the fairness of her skin.

"Now that's a fine, feminine trick," her grandmother observed, tapping Matt on the thigh. "Good for the complexion, too. Why, I could still call out a blush on demand after I'd had a husband and three lovers under my belt." Pleased with the deadly stare her granddaughter aimed at her, Olivia lifted her face to Matt's. "Good-looking girl, isn't she?"

"Lovely," Matt agreed, enjoying himself almost as much as Olivia was.

"Breed fine sons."

"Have another drink, Mother," William suggested, observing the war signals in his daughter's eyes.

"Fine idea." She handed over her empty glass. "You haven't seen the gardens, Matthew. They're at their peak. Laurellie, take this Yankee out and show him what a proper garden looks like."

Laurel shot her grandmother an icy glare. "I'm sure Matthew—"

"Would love to," he finished for her, rising.

She switched the glare to him without any effort. "I don't—"

"Want to be rude," he supplied quietly as he helped her out of her chair.

Oh, yes, she did, Laurel thought as she swung through the garden doors. She wanted very badly to be rude. But not in front of her family, and he knew it. "You really enjoy this, don't you?" she hissed at him the moment the door closed behind them.

"Enjoy what?" Matt countered.

"Infuriating me."

"It's impossible not to enjoy something one's so good at."

She chuckled, then despised herself. "All right, here's the garden." She made a wide gesture. "And you don't want to see it any more than I want to show it to you."

"Wrong," Matt said simply, and took her hand again.

"Will you stop that!" Exasperated, Laurel shook her hand but failed to free it. "That's a new habit you've picked up."

"I just found out I like it." He drew her off the terrace onto one of the narrow paths that wound through the flowers. "Besides, if you don't make a good showing at this, Olivia'll just think of something else."

Too true, Laurel admitted. She'd tolerate the man beside her. After all, the sun was splashing red on the horizon and the garden smelled like paradise. It'd been too long since she'd taken the time to see it at dusk. They walked under an arched trellis with wisteria dripping like rain. The birds of the sunlight were beginning to quiet, and those of the night had yet to wake.

"I've always loved it best at this time of day," Laurel said without thinking. "You can almost see the women with their hooped skirts swishing along the edges of the paths. There'd have been musicians in the gazebo and strings of colored lanterns."

He'd known she had a streak of romance, a touch of her brother's dreaminess, but she'd been so careful not to show either to him before. Instinctively, he knew she hadn't meant to now, but the garden had weakened her. He wondered, as he trailed his thumb lightly over her knuckles, what other weaknesses she might have.

"It would've smelled the same then as it does tonight," Matt murmured, discovering just how exquisite her skin looked in the golden light of sunset. "Hot and sweet and secret."

"When I was a girl, I'd come out here sometimes at dusk and pretend I was meeting someone." The memory made her smile, a little dreamy, a little wistful. "Sometimes he'd be dark and dashing—or he'd be tall and blond, but always dangerous and unsuitable. The kind of man a young girl's papa would've whisked her away from." She laughed, letting her fingers trail over a waxy, white camellia. "Strange that I would've had those kinds of fancies when my papa knew I was much too ambitious and practical to fall for a…"

Laurel trailed off when she turned her head and found him close—so close it was his scent that aroused her senses rather than the blossom's; his breath she felt on her skin rather than the sultry evening air. The light was touched with gold, blushed with rose. Hazy, magical. In it, he looked too much like someone she might have dreamed of.

Matt let his fingers play lightly with the pulse at her wrist. It wasn't steady, but this time it wasn't anger that unsettled it. "A what?"

"A rogue," Laurel managed after a moment.

They were talking softly, as if they were telling secrets. The sun slipped lower, and the shadows lengthened.

His face was so lean, she thought suddenly. Not predatory, but the face of a man who wouldn't step aside if trouble got in his way. His eyes were guarded, but she'd noticed before how easily he concealed his thoughts. Perhaps that was why he nudged information from people without appearing to nudge at all. And his mouth—how was it she'd never realized how tempting, how sensual his mouth was? Or had she simply pretended not to? It wouldn't be soft, she thought as her gaze lingered on it. It would be hard, and the taste essentially male. She could lean just a bit closer and…

Laurel's eyes widened at the drift of her own thoughts. Beneath Matt's fingers, her pulse scrambled before she yanked her hand away. Good Lord, *what* had gotten into her? He'd tease her for months if he had any idea how close she'd come to making a fool of herself.

"We'd better go back in," she said coolly. "It's nearly time for dinner."

Matt had an urge to grab her and take the kiss she'd very nearly given him. And if he did that, he'd lose whatever inching progress he'd made. He'd wanted her for a long time—too long—and was shrewd enough to know she would have refused ordinary advances from the first. Matt had chosen the out of the ordinary, finding it had its amusements.

Patience, Matt reminded himself, was a crucial element of success—but she deserved one small dig for making him pound with desire and frustration.

"So soon?" His voice was mild, his expression ironic. "If Olivia had sent you out here with Cartier I doubt you'd have cut the tour so short."

"She'd never have sent me out here with Jerry," Laurel said before the meaning of her statement sank in.

"Ah." It was a sound designed to infuriate.

"Don't start on Jerry," Laurel snapped.

Matt gave her an innocent grin. "Was I?"

"He's a very nice man," she began, goaded. "He's well mannered and—and harmless."

Matt threw back his head and roared. "God save me from being labeled harmless."

Her eyes frosted and narrowed. "I'll tell you what you are," she said in a low, vibrating voice. "You're insufferable."

"Much better." Unable to resist, he stepped closer and gathered her hair in one hand. "I have no desire to be nice, well mannered or harmless."

She wished his fingers hadn't brushed her neck. They'd left an odd little trail of shivers. "You've gotten your wish," she said, not quite evenly. "You're annoying, rude and…"

"Dangerous?" he supplied, lowering his head so that their lips were only inches apart.

"Don't put words in my mouth, Bates." Why did she feel as though she were running the last leg of a very long race? Struggling to even her breathing, Laurel took a step back and found herself against the wall of the trellis. She would have sidestepped if he hadn't moved so quickly, blocking her.

"Retreating, Laurellie?" No, it wasn't just temper, he thought, watching the pulse hammer at the base of her throat. Not this time.

Something warm moved through her, like a lazy river. Her spine snapped straight. Her chin jutted up. "I don't have to retreat from you. It's bad enough that I have to tolerate you day after day at the *Herald,* but I'll be damned if I'll stand here and waste my *own* time. I'm going in," she finished on a near shout, "because I'm hungry."

Shoving him out of her way, Laurel stormed back toward the house. Matt stayed where he was a moment, looking after her—the swinging hair, the long, graceful strides, the simmering fury. That, he thought, was one hell of a woman. Making love to her would be a fascinating experience. He intended to have it, and her, very soon.

Chapter 2

Because she was still seething from the night before, Laurel decided to walk to the paper. Half an hour in the warm air, shifting her way through people, pausing by store windows, listening to snatches of casual conversation from other pedestrians would go a long way toward soothing her agitation. The city, like the plantation house outside it, was an old, consistent love. Laurel didn't consider it a contradiction that she could be drawn to the elegant timelessness of Promesse d'Amour and the bustling rush of downtown traffic. For as long as she could remember, she'd straddled both worlds, feeling equally at home in each. She was ambitious—she was romantic. Practicality and dreaminess were both a part of her nature, but she'd never minded the tug-of-war. At the moment, she felt more comfortable with the noise and hustle around her than with the memory of a twilight garden.

What had he been up to? she asked herself again, jamming her hands in her pockets. Laurel felt she knew Matt well enough to understand that he rarely did anything without an underlying purpose. He'd never touched her quite like that before. Scowling into a shop window, Laurel recalled that Matthew Bates had rarely touched her at all in an entire year. And last night…last night, Laurel remembered, there had been something almost casual about the way his fingers had brushed the back of her neck and skimmed over her wrist. *Almost* casual, she repeated. But there'd been nothing casual about her response to it.

Obviously, he had caught her off-balance—intentionally, Laurel added with a deeper scowl. What she'd felt hadn't been excitement or anticipation, but simply surprise. She was fully recovered now. The garden had been moody, romantic. She'd always been susceptible to moods, that was why she'd found herself telling him foolish things. And why, just for a minute, she'd wanted to feel what it would be like to be held against him.

Blossoms and sunsets. A woman might find the devil himself attractive in that kind of a setting. Temporarily. She'd pulled herself back before she'd done anything humiliating, Laurel reminded herself.

Then there was her grandmother. Laurel gritted her teeth and waited for the light to change. Normally, Olivia's outlandish remarks didn't bother her in the least, but she was going too far when she insinuated that Matthew Bates was exactly what her granddaughter needed.

Oh, he'd lapped that up, Laurel remembered, glaring straight ahead. He was easily as impossible as the old girl herself—without her charm, Laurel added loyally. She took a deep breath of the city—exhaust, humanity, heat. Right now, she appreciated it for what it was: genuine. She wasn't going to let an absurd incident in a fantasy world spoil her day. Determined to forget it, and the man who'd caused it, she started to step off the curb.

"Good morning, Laurellie."

Surprised, she nearly stumbled when a hand shot and grabbed her arm. Good God, wasn't there anywhere in New Orleans she could get away from him? Turning her head, she gave Matt a long, cool look. "Car break down?"

Haughtiness suited her, he mused, as well as temper did. "Nice day for a walk," he countered smoothly, keeping her arm as they started to cross the street. He wasn't fool enough to tell her he'd seen her start out on foot and followed the impulse to go after her.

Laurel made a point of disengaging her arm when they reached the sidewalk. Why the hell hadn't she just gotten into her car as she would have any other morning? Short of making a scene on the street, she was stuck with him. When she gave him another glance, she caught the amused look in his eye that meant he'd read her thoughts perfectly. After rejecting the idea of knocking him over the head with her purse, Laurel gave him a cold smile.

"Well, Matthew, you seemed to enjoy yourself last night."

"I like your grandmother, she's beautiful," he said so simply, she stopped short. When her brows drew together, he smiled and ran a finger down her nose. "Isn't that allowed?"

With a shrug, Laurel began to walk again. How was she supposed to detest him when he was being sweet and sincere? Laurel made another stab at it. "You encourage her."

"She doesn't need any encouragement," he stated all too accurately. "But I like to anyway."

Laurel wasn't quite successful in smothering a laugh. The sidewalk was crowded enough to make it necessary for their arms to brush as they walked. "You don't seem to mind that she's setting you up as my…"

"Lover?" he suggested, with the annoying habit of finishing her thoughts. "I think Olivia, for all her, ah, liberated ideas, has something more permanent in mind. She threw in the house for good measure."

Stunned, Laurel gaped at him. He grinned, and her sense of the ridiculous took over. "You'd better be sure she tosses in some cash; it's the devil to maintain."

"I admit, it's tempting." He caught the ends of Laurel's hair in his fingers. "The…house," he said when her gaze lifted to his, "isn't something a man turns down lightly."

She slanted a look at him, one she'd never aimed in his direction before. Under the lashes, sultry, amused and irresistible. "Matthew," Laurel said in a soft drawl, "you'll put me in the position of considering Jerry more seriously."

Then, he thought as desire crawled into his stomach, I'd have to quietly kill him. "Olivia'd disown you."

Laurel laughed and, without thinking, linked her arm through his. "Ah, the choices a woman must make. My inheritance or my sensibilities. I guess it's just too bad for both of us that you're not my type."

Matt put his hand on the glass door of the Herald

Building before Laurel could pull it open. "You put *me* in the position, Laurellie," he said quietly, "of having to change your mind."

She lifted a brow, not quite as sure of herself as she'd been a moment before. Why hadn't she noticed these rapid mood swings in him before? The truth was, she admitted, she'd dedicated herself to noticing as little about him as possible. From the first moment he'd walked into the city room, she had decided that was the safest course. Determined not to lose the upper hand this time, she smiled as she pushed through the door. "Not a chance, Bates."

Matt let her go, but his gaze followed her progress through the crowded lobby. If he hadn't already been attracted to her, her words would have forced his hand. He'd always liked going up against the odds. As far as he was concerned, Laurel had just issued the first challenge. With an odd sort of smile, he moved toward the bank of elevators.

Laurel's entire morning involved interviewing the director of a highway research agency. A story on road repair and detour signs wasn't exactly loaded with fire and flash, she mused, but news was news. Her job was to assimilate the facts, however dry they might be, and report. With luck she could get the story under the fold on page two. Perhaps the afternoon would yield something with a bit more meat.

The hallways, rarely deserted, were quiet in the late-morning lull. Other reporters returned from, or were on their way to, assignments, but most were already in the field or at their desks. Giving a perfunctory wave to a colleague hurrying by with an on-the-run lunch of a candy bar, she began to structure her lead paragraph. Preoccupied, she turned toward the city room and jolted another woman. The contents of the woman's purse scattered onto the floor.

"Damn!" Without glancing over, Laurel crouched down and began to gather things up. "Sorry, I wasn't looking where I was going."

"It's all right."

Laurel saw a very small hand reach out for a plain manila envelope. The hand was shaking badly. Concerned, she looked over at a pale blonde with pretty features and red-rimmed eyes. Her lips were trembling as badly as her hands.

"Did I hurt you?" Laurel took the hands in hers instinctively. A stray, an injured bird, a troubled stranger—she'd never been able to resist anything or anyone with a problem.

The woman opened her mouth, then closed it again to shake her head violently. The fingers Laurel gripped quivered helplessly. When the first tears rolled down the pale face, Laurel forgot the noise and demands of the city room, the notes scrawled in the book in her bag. Helping the woman up, Laurel led her through the maze of desks and into the glass-walled office of the city editor.

"Sit down," she ordered, nudging the blonde into a faded leather chair. "I'll get you some water." Without waiting for an agreement, Laurel strode out again. When she came back, she noted that the woman had swallowed her tears, but her face hadn't lost that wounded, bewildered expression. "Come on, sip this." After offering the paper cup, Laurel sat on the arm of the chair and waited.

Inside the office, she could hear the muted echo of activity from the city room. It was early enough in the day that desperation hadn't struck yet. Deadline panic was hours away. What desperation there was came from the blonde's efforts to steady her breathing. Hundreds of questions buzzed in Laurel's mind, but she gave the woman silence.

"I'm sorry." She crushed the now empty paper cup in her fingers before she looked up at Laurel. "I don't usually fall apart that way."

"It's all right." Laurel noticed the woman was slowly, systematically tearing the paper cup to shreds. "I'm Laurel Armand."

"Susan Fisher." Blankly, she looked down at the scraps of paper in her lap.

"Can I help, Susan?"

That almost started the tears again. Such simple words, Susan thought as she closed her eyes against them. Why should they make her feel all the more hopeless? "I don't know why I came here," she began jerkily. "I just couldn't think of anything else. The police…"

Laurel's reporter's drive rose to tangle with her protective instincts. Both were too natural to her for her to even notice them. She laid a hand on Susan's shoulder. "I work here; you can talk to me. Would you like to start at the beginning?"

Susan stared up at her. She no longer knew whom to trust, or if indeed *trust* was a word to believe in. This woman looked so confident, so sure of herself. She'd never had her life shattered. Why would this poised, vibrant-looking woman listen, or believe?

Susan's eyes were blue, soft and light and vulnerable. Laurel didn't know why they made her think of Matt, a man she thought had no sensitivity at all, yet they did. She put her hand over Susan's. "I'll help you if I can."

"My sister." The words tumbled out, then stopped with a jerk. With an effort, Susan swallowed and began again. "My sister, Anne, met Louis Trulane a year ago."

Louis? The name shot through Laurel's mind so that the hand over Susan's stiffened. Bittersweet memories, loyalties, growing pains. What could this tearful, frightened woman have to do with Louis? "Go on," Laurel managed, making her fingers relax.

"They were married less than a month after they met. Anne was so much in love. We had—we were sharing an apartment at the time, and all she could talk about was Louis, and moving here to live in the fabulous old house he owned. Heritage Oak. Do you know it?"

Laurel nodded, staring off into nothing more than her own memories. "Yes, I know it."

"She sent me pictures of it. I just couldn't imagine Anne living there, being mistress of it. Her letters were full of it, and of Louis, of course." Susan paused as her breath came out in a shudder. "She was so happy. They were already talking about starting a family. I'd finally made arrangements to take some time off. I was coming to visit her when I got Louis's letter."

Laurel turned to take Susan's hand in a firmer grip. "Susan, I know—"

"She was dead." The statement was flat and dull, with shock still lingering around the edges. "Anne was dead. Louis wrote—he wrote that she'd gone out alone, after dark, wandered into the swamp. A copperhead bite, he said. If they'd found her sooner…but it wasn't until the next morning, and it was too late."

Susan pressed her lips together, telling herself she had to get beyond the tears. The time for them was over. "She was only twenty-one, and so lovely."

"Susan, it must've been dreadful for you to hear that way. It was a terrible accident."

"Murder," Susan said in a deadly calm voice. "It was murder."

Laurel stared at her for a full ten seconds. Her first inclination to soothe and comfort vanished, replaced by a whiff of doubt, a tingle of interest. "Anne Trulane died of a snakebite and exposure. Why do you call it murder?"

Susan rose and paced to the window. Laurel hadn't patted her hand, hadn't made inane comments. She was still listening, and Susan felt a faint flicker of hope. "I'll tell you what I told Louis, what I told the police." She took an extra moment to let the air go in and out of her lungs slowly. "Anne and I were very close. She was always gentle, sensitive. She had a childlike sweetness without being childish. I want you to understand that I knew Anne as well as I know myself."

Laurel thought of Curt and nodded. "I do."

Susan responded to this sign of acceptance with a sigh. "Ever since she was little, Anne had a phobia about dark places. If she had to go into a room at night, she'd reach in and hit the light switch first. It was more than just habit, it was one of those small fears some of us never outgrow. Do you know what I mean?"

Thinking of her own phobia, she nodded again. "Yes, I know."

Susan stepped away from the window. "As much as Anne loved that house, having the swamp so near bothered her. She'd written me that it was like a dark closet—something she avoided even in the daytime. She loved Louis, wanted to please him, but she wouldn't go through it with him."

She whirled back to Laurel with eyes no longer calm, but pleading. "You have to understand, she adored him, but she wouldn't, couldn't do that for him. It was like an obsession. Anne believed it was haunted—she'd even worked herself up to the point where she thought she saw lights out there. Anne would never have gone in there alone, at night."

Laurel waited a moment, while facts and ideas raced through her mind. "But she was found there."

"Because someone took her."

In silence, Laurel measured the woman who now stood across from her. Gone was the defenseless look. Though the eyes were still puffy and red-rimmed, there was a determination in them, and a demand to be believed. An older sister's shock and loyalty perhaps, Laurel mused, but she let bits and pieces of the story run through her mind, along with what she knew of Anne Trulane's death.

It had never been clear why the young bride had wandered into the swamp alone. Though Laurel had grown up with swamps and bayous, she knew they could be treacherous places, especially at night, for someone who didn't know them. Insects, bogs…snakes.

She remembered too how Louis Trulane had closed out the press after the tragedy—no interviews, no comment. As soon as the inquest had been over, he'd retreated to Heritage Oak.

Laurel thought of Louis, then looked at Susan. Loyalties tugged. And pulling from both sides was a reporter's instinct she'd been born with. The whys in life always demanded an answer.

"Why did you come to the *Herald,* Susan?"

"I went to see Louis last night as soon as I got into town. He wouldn't listen to me. This morning I went to the police." She lifted her hands in a gesture of futility. "Case closed. Before I had a chance to think about it, I was here. Maybe I should hire a private investigator, but…" Trailing off, she shook her head. "Even if that were the right way to go, I don't have the money. I know the Trulanes are a powerful, respected family, but there has to be a way of getting at the truth. My sister was murdered." This time her voice quivered on the statement and the color that had risen to her cheeks from agitation faded.

Not as strong as she wants to be, Laurel realized as she rose. "Susan, would you trust me to look into this?"

Susan dragged a hand through her hair. She didn't want to fall apart now, not now, when someone was offering the help she needed so badly. "I have to trust someone."

"There're a few things I have to do." Abruptly, Laurel became brisk. If there was a story, and she smelled one, she couldn't think of old ties, old memories. "There's a coffee machine in the lobby. Get a cup and wait for me there. When I've finished, we'll get something to eat—talk some more."

Asking no questions, Susan gathered up her purse, watching the torn bits of the paper cup drift to the floor. "Thank you."

"Don't thank me yet," Laurel advised. "I haven't done anything."

Susan paused at the door to glance over her shoulder. “Yes, you have.”

Mouth pursed in thought, Laurel watched Susan wind her way through the desks in the city room. Anne Trulane, she thought, and let out a sigh. Louis. Good God, what kind of wasp’s nest was she poking into?

Before she could formulate an answer, the city editor came in, his thin face creased into a scowl, his tired eyes annoyed. “Damn it, Laurel, this is a newspaper, not a Miss Lonelyhearts service. When one of your friends has a fight with her boyfriend, find someone else’s office to flood. Now move it.” He flopped down behind his cluttered desk. “You’ve got a story to write.”

Laurel walked over to the desk and perched on the corner. Don Ballinger was her godfather, a man who had often bounced her on his knee. If it came to a toss-up between personal affection and news copy, the copy’d win hands down. Laurel expected no less. “That was Anne Trulane’s sister,” she said mildly when he opened his mouth to swear at her.

“Trulane,” he repeated as his wispy brows drew together. “What’d she want?”

Laurel picked up a hunk of fool’s gold Don used as a paperweight and shifted it from hand to hand. “To prove her sister was murdered.”

He gave a short bark that might have been a laugh or a sound of derision. Don took a cigarette out of the desk drawer and ran it lovingly through his fingers. He stroked it, caressed it, but didn’t light it. He hadn’t lit one in sixteen days, ten hours…twenty-two minutes. “Snakebite,” Don said simply, “and a night’s exposure don’t add up to murder. What about the story on the highway agency?”

"The sister tells me that Anne had a phobia about the dark," Laurel continued. "Anne supposedly mentioned the swamp where she died in her letters. She hadn't set foot in it, and didn't intend to."

"Obviously she changed her mind."

"Or someone changed it for her."

"Laurel—"

"Don, let me do some poking around." Laurel studied the glittering paperweight as she spoke. Things weren't always as they seemed, she mused. Not nearly always. "It couldn't hurt. If nothing else, I could work up a human interest piece."

Don scowled down at his cigarette, running a finger from filter to tip. "Trulane won't like it."

"I can deal with Louis," she said with more confidence than she felt. "There's something in this, Don. There was never any clear reason why Anne Trulane went out there alone. She was already dressed for bed."

They both knew the rumors—that she'd been meeting a lover, that Louis had bracketed her to the house until she'd simply gone out blindly, then lost herself. Don put the cigarette in his mouth and gnawed on the filter. The Trulanes were always good copy. "Nose around," he said at length. "It's still fresh news." Before Laurel could be too pleased that she'd won the first round, he dropped the bomb. "Bates covered the story, work with him."

"Work with Bates?" she repeated. "I don't need him. It's my lead, my story."

"His beat," Don countered, "and no one's story until there is one."

"Damn it, Don, the man's insufferable. I'm not some junior reporter who needs a proctor, and—"

"And he has the contacts, the sources and knows the background." He rose while Laurel simmered. "We don't play personality games on the *Herald,* Laurel. You work together." After shooting her a last look, he stuck his head out the door. "Bates!"

"You can't play personality games with someone who has none," Laurel muttered. "I'm the one who knows the Trulanes. He'll just get in my way."

"Sulking always was a bad habit of yours," Don commented as he rounded his desk again.

"I am not sulking!" she protested as Matt sauntered into the room.

He took one look at Laurel's furious face, lifted a brow and grinned. "Problem?"

Laurel controlled the urge to hiss at him, and sank into a chair. With Matthew Bates around, there was always a problem.

"Cheer up," Matt advised a few minutes later. "Before this is over, you might learn something."

"I don't need to learn anything from you." Laurel swung toward the elevator.

"That," he murmured, enjoying the way her lips formed into a pout, "remains to be seen."

"You're not taking on an apprentice, Bates, but a partner." She jammed her fists into her pockets. "Don insisted on it because you'd covered the investigation and the inquest. You could make it easy on both of us by just giving me your notes."

"The last thing I do," Matt said mildly, "is give anyone my notes."

"And the last thing I need is to have you breathing down my neck on this. It's *my* story."

"That really stuck where it hurts, didn't it?" Casually, he pushed the button on the elevator, then turned to her. "Didn't your papa ever tell you that sharing's good for the soul?"

Fuming, Laurel stepped into the car and pushed for lobby. "Go to hell."

She didn't know he could move quickly. Perhaps this was her first lesson. Before she had an inkling what he was doing, Matt punched a button and stopped the car between floors. Even as her mouth fell open in surprise, he had her backed up against the side wall. "Watch how far you push," he warned softly, "unless you're willing to take a few hard shoves yourself."

Her throat was so dry it hurt. She'd never seen his eyes frost over like this. It was frightening. Fascinating. Odd, she thought she'd convinced herself he didn't have a temper, but now that it was about to grab her by the throat, she wasn't surprised. No, it wasn't surprise that had the chill racing over her skin.

She was frightened, Matt observed. But she wasn't cringing. Common sense told him to back off now that his point had been made. But a year was a very long time. "I think I'll just get this out of my system now, before we get started."

He saw her eyes widen, stunned as he lowered his mouth toward hers. A twist of amusement curved his lips as he allowed them to hover a breath from hers. "Surprised, Laurellie?"

Why wasn't she moving? Her body simply wouldn't respond to the commands of her brain. She was almost certain she was telling her arms to push him away. Good God, he had beautiful eyes. Incredibly beautiful eyes. His breath whispered over her skin, trailing into her mouth through lips that had parted without her knowledge. He smelled of no more than soap—basic, simple. Wonderful.

In an effort to clear her senses, Laurel straightened against the wall. "Don't you dare—"

The words ended with a strangled sound of pleasure as his lips skimmed over hers. It wasn't a kiss. No one would consider such a thing a kiss: a breath of a touch without pressure. It was more of a hint—or a threat. Laurel wondered if someone had cut the cables on the elevator.

She didn't move, not a muscle. Her eyes were wide open, her mind wiped clean as he stepped fractionally closer so that his body made full contact with hers—firm, lean, strong. Even as her system jolted, she didn't move. His mouth was still whispering on hers, so subtly, so impossibly light she might have imagined it. When she felt the moist tip of his tongue trace her lips, then dip inside to touch, just touch, the tip of hers, the breath she'd been holding shuddered out.

It was that quiet, involuntary sound of surrender that nearly broke his control. If she'd spit and snarled at him, he could have dealt with it easily. He'd been angry enough to. He hadn't expected stunned submission, not from her. Over the anger came a tempting sense of power, then an ache—gnawing and sweet—of need. Even as he nipped his teeth into her soft bottom lip he wondered if he'd ever have her at quite such a disadvantage again.

God, he wanted to touch her, to slip that neat little blouse off her shoulders and let his hands mold slowly, very, very slowly, every inch of her. That skin of hers, pale as a magnolia, soft as rainwater, had driven him mad for months. He could have her now, Matt thought as he nibbled ever so gently at her lips. He was skilled enough, she off guard enough that he could take her there on the floor of the elevator before either of them had regained their senses. It would be crazy, wonderfully crazy. Even as she stood still, he could all but taste that passion fighting to overcome her surprise and reach out for him. But he had different plans for the seduction of Laurel Armand.

So he didn't touch her, but lazily backed away. Not once during those shivering two minutes had she taken her eyes off his. Laurel watched that clever, torturous mouth curve as he again pressed the button for the lobby. The elevator started with a rumble and jerk.

"A pity we're pressed for time," Matt commented easily, then gave the elevator car a careless glance. "And space."

Layer by layer the mists that had covered her brain cleared until she could think with perfect clarity. Her eyes were glimmering green slits, her ivory skin flushed with rage as she let out a stream of curses in a fluid, effortless style he had to admire.

"Did you know you completely drop your *R*s when your temper's loose?" Matt asked pleasantly. "It's an education in regional cadence. Truce, Laurel." He held up his hand, palm out as she drew breath to start again. "At least a professional one until we run down this lead. We can take up the private war when we're off duty."

She bit back a retort and smoldered as the elevator came gently to a stop. It wouldn't instill much confidence in Susan Fisher if the two of them were taking potshots at each other. "An armed truce, Bates," she compromised as they stepped into the lobby. "Try anything like that again, and you'll be missing some teeth."

Matt ran his tongue over them experimentally. "Sounds reasonable." He offered his hand, and though she didn't trust that sober expression on his face, Laurel accepted. "Looks like I buy you lunch after all."

Removing her hand, Laurel straightened the purse on her shoulder. "Big talk on an expense account."

Grinning, he swung a friendly arm around her as they moved toward the rear of the lobby. "Don't be cranky, Laurellie, it's our first date."

She snorted, and tossed her head—but she didn't push his arm away.

Chapter 3

Matt chose a noisy restaurant in the French Quarter because he always found it easier to make people talk if they weren't sure they could be heard. He'd sensed, from the introduction, that while Susan Fisher had given her trust to Laurel, she was withholding judgment on him. For the moment, he'd decided to let Laurel lead the way.

He was amiable, sympathetic, as he filed away Susan's every word and gesture. She was a woman, Matt decided, who had buckled under pressure and was fighting her way back up. She still had a long way to go, but on one point she wouldn't be swayed. She'd known her sister. Susan wasn't going to let Anne's death rest until all the facts were laid bare. Perhaps Matt admired her for it all the more because her hands weren't quite steady.

He glanced at Laurel and nearly smiled. She'll take in any stray, he mused, though he didn't doubt she'd bite his head off if he suggested it. She didn't want to be considered soft or vulnerable, particularly by him. They were colleagues or, more accurately, competitors. He'd always enjoyed going head to head with her, reporter to reporter. And after that two minutes between floors on the elevator, he didn't think she'd forget he was a man. He wasn't going to give her the chance to.

Pouring more coffee into Susan's cup, Matt sent Laurel a silent signal that it was his turn. Her slight shrug showed him that the truce was still on. "Your sister died nearly a month ago, Susan." He said it softly, watching her face. "Why did you wait so long before bringing all this up?"

She dropped her gaze to her plate, where she'd been pushing food around for twenty minutes. Over her head, Laurel's eyes met Matt's, brows raised. He could almost hear the question in them. *What the hell's this?* But she knew her job. He felt they were already partners without having stated the ground rules. I question. You soothe.

"Susan." Laurel touched her arm. "We want to help you."

"I know." Setting down her fork, she looked up again, skimming over Matt to settle on Laurel. "It's hard to admit it, but I didn't cope with Anne's death well. The truth is, I just fell apart. I stopped answering my phone—didn't leave my apartment. Lost my job." She pressed her lips together. When she spoke again they had to strain to hear her over the cheerful din in the restaurant. "The worst is, I didn't even come down for the funeral. I suppose I was pretending it wasn't happening. I was the only family she had left, and I wasn't here."

"That isn't important. No, it's not," Laurel insisted when Susan began to speak. "You loved her. In the end, love's all that really matters." Looking over, she saw Matt watching her steadily. For a moment, Laurel forgot Susan, suspicions, the noise and scents of the restaurant. She'd expected to see cynicism in his eyes, perhaps a very faint, very mocking smile. Instead, she saw understanding, and a question she didn't know how to answer. Without speaking, he lifted her hand to his lips, then set it down again.

Oh no, she thought, panicking. *Not him.* That wasn't just impossible, it was ludicrous. Dazed, she picked up her coffee, then set it back down when she saw her hand wasn't quite steady. That one long look had scattered her wits more effectively than the odd kiss that wasn't a kiss, on the elevator. As from a distance, she heard Susan's voice and forced herself to tune in to it.

"It all hit me last week. I guess the first shock had passed and I started to think about her letters. It didn't fit." This time she looked up at Matt, demanding he understand. "Whenever she'd mention that swamp it was with a kind of loathing. If you'd understand just how much she hated the dark, you'd see that she would never have gone into the place alone, at night. Never. Someone took her there, Mr. Bates. Someone made her go."

"Why?" He leaned forward, and while his voice wasn't hard, it was direct. "Why would someone want to kill your sister?"

"I don't know." Her knuckles went white on the edge of the table as she fought the urge to just lay down her head and weep. "I just don't know."

"I covered the inquest." Taking out a cigarette, Matt reached for the pack of restaurant matches. He didn't want to be tough on her, but if she was going to fold it would be better if she did it now, before they got too deep. "Your sister'd been here less than a year and knew almost no one, as she and her husband rarely socialized. According to the servants, she doted on him, there was rarely a cross word between them. The basic motives for murder—jealousy, greed—don't apply. What else is there?"

"That doesn't matter." Susan turned back to Laurel again. "None of that matters."

"Let's take it a step at a time," Laurel suggested. "Do you still have your sister's letters?"

"Yes." Susan let out an unsteady breath. "Back at my hotel."

Matt crushed out his cigarette. "Let's go take a look at them."

When Susan was out of earshot, Laurel brushed close to Matt. "The shock may be over," she murmured, "but she's still not too sturdy. Matthew, I have a feeling about this."

"You've got too many feelings, Laurel."

She frowned at him as they skirted between tables. "Just what does that mean?"

"We have to deal with facts. If you want to play Girl Scout, you're going to cloud the issue."

"I should've known better," she said between her teeth. "For a minute back there, I thought I saw some small spark of sensitivity."

He grinned. "I'm loaded with sensitivity. We can talk about it over drinks later."

"In a pig's eye." Laurel swung out the door behind

Susan and made a point of ignoring Matt through the cab ride to the hotel.

It was seedy—the streets were narrow, the concrete was chipped, the banisters were peeling. Condensation gathered and dripped from the rusting balconies. The paint on the buildings was cracked and coated with layers of grime and moisture from the constant humidity. All the colors seemed to have faded into one—a steamy gray.

The alleyways were shadowed and dank. At night, Laurel knew, the street would be mean—the kind of street you avoided, or walked on quickly while glancing over your shoulder. From the open window across the street the sounds of an argument overpowered a scratchy jazz recording. A bony cat lay over the stoop and made a low, unfriendly sound in his throat when Susan opened the door.

When Laurel cautiously stepped around it, Susan offered an apologetic smile. "This place has its own… atmosphere."

Matt grinned as he cast a look around the dim lobby. "You should've seen the apartment where I grew up in New York."

The strained smile relaxed as Susan turned toward the stairs. "Well, it was here, and it was cheap."

Following them, Laurel frowned at Matt's back. She'd caught another glimpse of sensitivity. Odd. And, though she hated to admit it, the careless comment about his youth piqued her interest. Who had he been? How had he lived? She'd always been very careful not to allow herself to speculate.

The place was so quiet, so empty, that their footsteps echoed on the uncarpeted steps. Cracked paint and graffiti. Laurel studied Susan's profile as she unlocked the door. I'm going to get her out of here, she promised herself, by this afternoon. Catching the amused, knowing look Matt sent her, Laurel glared at him.

"After another merit badge, Laurellie?" he murmured.

"Shut up, Bates." While he chuckled, Laurel stepped into Susan's cramped, shadowy room. It had a narrow bed, a scarred dresser and no charm.

"That's funny, I know I left the shades up." Crossing the room, Susan jerked the cord so that the dusty white shade flapped up and the sun poured into the room. She flicked a switch that had a squeaky ceiling fan stirring the hot air. "I'll get the letters."

Laurel sat on the edge of the bed and looked up at Matt. "What part of New York did you come from?"

His brow lifted, as it did when he was amused—or evasive. "You wouldn't know it." His lips curved as he moved to sit beside her. "Ever been north of the Mason-Dixon line, Laurel?"

"I've been to New York several times," she began testily, then made a sound of frustration when his smile only widened. "Twice," she amended.

"The Empire State Building, Ellis Island, the U.N., tea at the Plaza and a Broadway show."

"You love being smug and superior, don't you?"

He ran a fingertip down her jaw. "Yeah."

She fought back a smile. "Did you know you become even more insufferable with prolonged contact?"

"Be careful," Matt warned. "I've a weakness for flattery."

With his eyes on her laughing ones, Matt lifted her hand, palm up, and pressed his lips to the center. He watched, pleased, when confusion replaced the humor in her eyes. Behind them, Susan began to pull out drawers frantically. They didn't notice.

"They're gone!" Susan swept a handful of clothes onto the floor and stared at the empty drawer. "They're gone, all of them."

"What?" A little dazed, Laurel turned to her. "What's gone?"

"The letters. All of Anne's letters."

Immediately Laurel was on her feet and sorting through Susan's jumbled clothing. "Maybe you put them somewhere else."

"No—there is nowhere else," she said with a dangerous edge of hysteria in her voice. "I put them all in this drawer. There were twelve of them."

"Susan." Matt's voice was cool enough to stiffen her spine. "Are you sure you brought them with you?"

She took long, deep breaths as her gaze shifted from Laurel to Matt. "I had every one of Anne's letters with me when I checked into this hotel. When I unpacked, I put them in that drawer. They were there when I dressed this morning."

Her hands weren't steady, Matt noticed, but her eyes were. He nodded. "I'll go check with the desk clerk."

As the door closed, Susan stared down at the crumpled blouse she held. "Someone was in this room," she said unsteadily. "I know it."

Laurel glanced at the shade Susan had lifted. "Are you missing anything else?"

"No." With a sigh, Susan let the blouse fall. "There isn't anything in here worth stealing. I suppose they realized that. It doesn't make any sense that they'd take Anne's letters."

"Matthew and I'll sort it out," Laurel told her, then was annoyed with herself for linking herself with Matt so easily. "In the meantime…" Bending, she began to gather Susan's clothes. "Can you type?"

Distracted, Susan stared at her. "Well, yes. I work—I worked," she corrected, "as a receptionist in a doctor's office."

"Good. Where's your suitcase?" she asked as she folded Susan's clothes on the bed.

"It's in the closet, but—"

"I have a place for you to stay, and a job—of sorts. Oh, this is lovely." She shook out the blouse Susan had crumpled.

"A job? I don't understand."

"My grandmother lives outside of town. Since my brother and I moved out, she's been lonely." The lie came out too easily to be questioned.

"But I couldn't just stay there."

"You'd pay for it." Laurel grinned as she turned back. "Grandma's been threatening to write her memoirs and I've just about run out of excuses for not typing them up for her. You won't be bored. She's eighty-two and didn't give up men until… Actually, she hasn't given them up at all. If I weren't so busy, I'd love to do it myself. As it is, you'd be doing me quite a favor."

"Why are you doing this for me?" Susan asked. "You don't know me."

"You're in trouble," Laurel said simply. "I can help."

"Just that easy?"

"Does help have to be complicated? Get your suitcase," Laurel ordered before Susan could work out an answer. "You can pack while I see what Matthew's come up with." As she slipped into the hall, Laurel bumped into him. She let the door click shut behind her. "Well?"

"The clerk didn't see anyone." Matt leaned against the wall and lit a cigarette. "But then he's more interested in cheating at solitaire in the back room than covering the desk." He blew out a stream of smoke that rose to the ceiling and hung there. "I spoke to the woman who does the rooms. She didn't pull the shades."

"Then someone was in there."

"Maybe."

Laurel ignored this and stared at the opposite wall. "Susan thinks it was just a break-in. In her state of mind, that's all for the best."

"You're playing mama, Laurel."

"I am not." Angry, she looked back at him. "It'll be a lot easier to sort through this if she doesn't start thinking someone's deliberately trying to stop her."

"There's no reason for her to think that at this point," Matt said dampeningly. "What's she doing?"

"Packing," Laurel muttered.

He nodded. It wasn't wise for her to stay where she was. "Where's she going?"

Laurel angled her chin. "To my grandmother."

Not quite suppressing a smile, Matt studied the tip of his cigarette. "I see."

"You couldn't see through barbed wire. And don't start spouting off about my getting too personally involved, or—"

"All right." He crushed out the cigarette on the dusty, scarred floor. "And I won't comment that you're a very sweet, classy lady. I'll get a cab," he added when Laurel only stared at him.

Just when I think I understand him, she mused, he

throws me a curve. If I'm not careful, Laurel added as his footsteps echoed off the stairs. If I'm not very, very careful, I'm going to start liking him. On that uncomfortable thought, she went back in to hurry Susan along.

In under ten minutes, Laurel was in the back of a cab with Matt, glancing behind her at the taxi that would take Susan to her grandmother.

"Stop worrying about her," Matt ordered. "Olivia'll keep her mind off her sister, and everything else."

With a shrug, Laurel turned back around. "I don't doubt that. But I'm beginning to doubt that Anne Trulane walked into that swamp alone."

"Let's stick with the facts. Motive." Absently, he wound a lock of Laurel's hair around his finger—a habit he'd recently developed and rather enjoyed. "There doesn't seem to be any. Women aren't lured into swamps for no reason."

"Then there was one."

"No sexual assault," Matt continued, half to himself. "She didn't have any money on her own—and her only heir would've been Susan in any case…or her husband. He has a sister, but I can't see any benefit there."

"The last people I'd consider as murder suspects would be Louis or Marion Trulane. And there are other motives for murder than sex and money."

He lifted a brow at her tone but continued to toy with her hair. "True, but those always spring to mind. Most of us are fond of both."

"Some think beyond your scope, Matthew. There's jealousy, if we go back to your two favorites. Louis is rich and attractive. Someone might have pictured herself in Anne's place."

He caught something—the drift of something he

didn't quite understand. And didn't like. "Do you know him well?"

"Louis?" A smile touched her mouth, a gentle one. It reminded him that Laurel had never once looked at him that way. "As well as anyone, I suppose—or I did. He taught me to ride when I was a girl, let me tag along after him when I was ten and he was, oh, twenty-one or -two. He was a beautiful man—and very patient with a girl's infatuation."

When he discovered his fingers were no longer relaxed, Matt released the tendril of hair. "You got over it, I suppose."

Hearing the cynicism in his voice, Laurel turned, the half smile still on her face. "Weren't you ever in love, Matthew?"

The look he gave her was long and guarded while several uncomfortable emotions moved through him. Her eyes were soft; so was her mouth, her skin. If they'd been alone, he might not have answered the question at all, but would simply have taken what he found he needed so badly. "No," he said at length.

"It softens something in you, something that never quite goes away for that particular person." With a sigh, she sat back against the seat. It had been a long time since she'd let herself remember how sweet it had been, and how hurtful. She'd only been a child, and though her dreams had been fairy tales, she'd believed them. "Louis was very important to me. I wanted a knight, and I think he understood that well enough not to laugh at me. And when he married…" She lifted her hands and let them fall. "It broke my heart. Do you know about his first wife?"

Matt was staring down at the hands in her lap; small,

elegant hands with the nails painted in the palest of corals and a smoky emerald in an intricate old setting on her finger. An heirloom, he thought. She would have heirlooms, and genteel ancestors—and memories of riding lessons from a tall young man, dashing enough to be a knight.

"Bits and pieces," Matt mumbled as the cab pulled to the curb. "Fill me in later."

Laurel climbed out of the cab, then meticulously brushed off her skirt. "That's perilously close to an order, Bates. Since Don didn't lay down any ground rules, maybe you and I should take care of that ourselves."

"Fine." He didn't know why he was angry. He studied her with eyes narrowed against the glare of the sun. "This is my beat."

With an effort, Laurel smothered the flare of temper. "And it's my lead."

"If you want to get anywhere with it," he said evenly, "you'll leave certain areas to me. When's the last time you fought your way through the red tape in there?" Matt jerked his head toward the station house beside them.

"I've untangled red tape before."

"Not in there," he countered before he took her arm.

"Just a minute, Bates." Laurel pushed his hand away and faced him. "The one thing you're going to understand, is that I may have no choice but to work with you on this story, but the operative word is *with,* not *for.* For the moment, however much it galls me, we're partners."

This seemed to amuse him as the temper turned into an odd little smile. "A nice ring to that. Partners," he agreed, taking her hand. "It might become a habit."

"The danger of that's slim to none. Would you stop touching me?"

"No," he said amiably as they climbed the steps.

Voices boomed off the walls of the station house. Disgruntled voices, insolent voices, irate voices. It smelled dankly, stalely of humanity. Sweat, coffee, cigarettes, alcohol. Five members of opposing street gangs leaned against a wall and eyed each other. A woman with a badly bruised face huddled in a chair and spoke in undertones to a harassed-looking officer who nodded and typed out her statement with two fingers. A young girl in snug shorts snapped her gum and looked bored.

He'd seen it all before—and more. After a cursory glance around, Matt moved through the people and desks. The officers, the victims, the accused, paid no more attention to him than he to them.

A slim brunette in a wilting uniform cupped a phone on her shoulder and lifted a hand in salute. Matt perched on the corner of her desk. Laurel stood beside him, watching as two elderly men nearly came to blows before they were pulled apart.

"Well, Matt, what brings you to paradise?" The brunette set down the phone and smiled at him.

"How you doing, Sarge?"

The brunette tipped back in her chair to give him a long, thorough look. "I haven't changed my phone number here—or at home."

"The city keeps us both pretty tied up, doesn't it? Been to the Nugget lately?"

She picked up a pen and tapped it lightly against her mouth. "Not since last month. Want to buy me a drink?"

"You read my mind, but I have a little business."

Letting out a quick laugh, the sergeant dropped her pen onto a blotter crisscrossed with scrawled names and numbers. "Sure. What do you want, Matt?"

"A quick glimpse at the file on a case—a closed case," he added. "Need to do a little backtracking on a story I did, maybe a follow-up."

Her eyes narrowed. "What case?"

"Anne Trulane."

"Sensitive ground, Matt." Her eyes drifted past his to Laurel's.

"Laurel Armand, Sergeant Carolyn Baker. Laurel and I are on assignment together," Matt said smoothly. "She's an old family friend of the Trulanes. Thought maybe we'd do something a little more in depth. Case is closed, Sarge, and hell, I covered the thing from start to finish."

"You've already seen the report."

"Then it can't hurt for me to see it again." He gave her a charming smile. "You know I play it straight, Carolyn, no printing privileged information, no hints in a story that messes up an investigation."

"Yeah, you play it straight, Matt." She shot him a look that Laurel thought had more to do with personal feelings than professional ones, then shrugged. "It was all public knowledge at the inquest." Rising, she walked away to disappear into a side room. Beside them, the two old men hurled insults at each other.

"You always work that way, Matthew?"

Matt turned to give Laurel a bland smile. "What way?" When she remained silent and staring, he grinned. "Jealous, love? You've got my heart in your hand."

"I'd rather have it under my foot."

"Vicious," he murmured, then pushed off the desk when Carolyn came back in.

"You can look at the file, take it in the first holding room. It's empty." She gave a quick glance around at the cramped room. "For now," she added dryly. Opening a book, she turned it to face him. "Sign for it."

"I owe you one, Sarge."

She waited until he'd scrawled his signature. "I'll collect."

Chuckling, Matt turned to work his way through to the holding room. An interesting woman, Sergeant Baker. Strange that it was never she who crept into his mind at odd moments. Not her, nor any of the other… interesting women he knew. Just one woman.

"Have a seat," Matt invited, closing the door and shutting out most of the din. The chair he chose scraped over the floor as he pulled it away from a long, battered table.

"Cheerful place," Laurel muttered, glancing around at the dull white walls and dingy linoleum.

"Stick with City Hall if you want tidy offices and white collars." Opening the file, he began to scan it briskly.

He fits here, Laurel realized with a grudging kind of respect. For all his easygoing manner, there was a hard, tough edge underneath she'd only glimpsed briefly. The man on the elevator. Yes, she mused, he'd shown her that ruthless, searing temper there. And more. Laurel didn't want to think of that just yet.

But there was no getting around the fact that there were more facets to him than she'd wanted to believe. It was safer to consider him a shallow, inconsequential man who just happened to be a hell of a reporter.

Seeing him now, completely at ease in the grim little room, made her wonder just how much he'd seen, how much he'd experienced. He dealt with the troubles, the griefs, the viciousness of people day after day, yet he didn't seem hard or cold, or overwhelmed by it. What made Matthew Bates tick? she wondered. And what made her suddenly so sure she had to find out?

"Nothing much here," he muttered, skimming the papers. "Autopsy report...no sexual abuse, contusions, lacerations attributed to her wandering through the swamp. Copperhead got her on the left calf. Cause of death snakebite, complicated by exposure. Time of death between 12:00 and 4:00 a.m." He handed the sheet to Laurel before going on to the investigator's report.

"Trulane was working late in his study. According to him, he thought his wife was upstairs in bed. He went up around two, found the bed empty. He searched the house, then woke his sister and the staff, searched the house again and the grounds."

Absently, he reached for a cigarette, found the pack empty and swore without heat. "None of her clothes were missing, all the cars were there. His call to the station came through at 2:57 a.m." He glanced over at Laurel. "Nearly an hour."

Her fingers were a bit damp on the autopsy report. "It's a big house. A sensible person doesn't call the police until he's sure he needs them."

After a slow nod, Matt looked back down at the report. "The police arrived at 3:15. The house was searched again, the staff questioned..." He mumbled for a moment, skimming the words. "Anne Trulane's body was found at approximately 6:00 a.m., in the southeast section of the swamp."

He'd been there. Matt remembered the gray light, the hot, humid smells, the nasty feel of the swamp even before they'd come across death.

"No one could account for her being out there. According to Marion Trulane, the sister-in-law, Anne had a phobia about the place. That fits with Susan's claim," he murmured. "Trulane stuck with his story about working late, and wouldn't elaborate."

"Have you ever found your wife dead?" Laurel demanded as she took the report from Matt. "It's just possible that he was upset."

He let the scathing words slip off him. "The conclusion is she felt compelled to go in—maybe to face her fears, got lost, bitten, and wandered around until she lost consciousness." He glanced over at Laurel. Her brows were drawn together as she read the report for herself. "You still buddies enough to get us into the house, ask some questions?"

"Hmm? Oh, yes, I suppose so. They'll talk to me. You too," she added, "if you spread some of your charm around."

His mouth twisted into a grin. "I didn't think you'd noticed."

"I noticed that you can pull it out rather successfully when you put your mind to it. It's a bit deliberate for my tastes, but effective enough."

"Please, Laurellie, compliments are so embarrassing."

Ignoring him, Laurel set the investigator's report aside. "Louis hasn't had an easy time. He's closed himself in since his first marriage failed, but I think he'll talk to me."

Idly, Matt twisted the empty pack of cigarettes into a mass of foil and cellophane. "His wife ran off with his brother?"

"It was horrible for Louis." She slipped the next paper from the file as Matt gazed up at the ceiling, lost in thought.

Her skin went to ice, her stomach knotted, but she couldn't look away. The police photo was black and white and grim. She'd seen death before, but not like this. Never like this. Appalled, transfixed, she stared down at Anne Fisher Trulane. Or what she had come to.

Oh, God, Laurel thought as her head went light and her stomach rolled. It's not real. It's a gruesome joke. Just someone's twisted idea of a joke.

"How long ago did—" Matt broke off as he shifted his gaze to Laurel. Her skin was dead white, her eyes full of horror. Even as he swore, he whipped the photo away from her, then pushed her head down between her knees. "Breathe deep," he ordered sharply, but his hand was abruptly gentle on the back of her head. Hearing her breath shudder in and out, he cursed himself more savagely. What the hell had he been thinking of? "Easy, love," he murmured, kneading the tension at the base of her neck.

"I'm all right." But she wasn't so sure. Laurel took an extra moment before she tried to straighten in the chair. When Matt's arms came around her, she let her head rest on his shoulder. "I'm sorry, that was stupid."

"No." He tilted her head back. "I'm sorry." Very slowly, very carefully, he brushed the hair away from her face.

She swallowed, hard. “I guess you’re used to it.”

“God, I hope not.” He drew her close again so that her face was pressed against his neck.

She felt safe there. The chill was passing. Laurel relaxed, letting him stroke her hair, allowing the warm, real scent of him to block out the institutional smell of the waiting room. She could feel the steady beat of his heart against her. Life. When his lips brushed her ear, she didn’t move. It was comfort he offered and comfort she felt. She told herself that was all, as she held on to him as if she’d just discovered him.

“Matthew…”

“Hmmm?”

“Don’t be too nice to me.”

With her eyes closed, her face buried at his throat, she felt the smile. “Why not?”

“Just don’t.” A bit more steady, she drew away because it was much too easy to stay.

He cupped her face in his hand. “You’re beautiful,” he murmured. “Have I told you that before?”

Cautiously she moved out of reach. Treat it light, she warned herself. And think about it later. “No.” She smiled and rose. “I always jot things like that down.”

“Beautiful,” he repeated. “Even if your chin is just a bit pointed.”

“It is not.” Automatically, she tilted it.

“Especially from that angle.”

“I have very delicate features,” Laurel told him decisively as she picked up her purse. No, damn it, her fingers were not steady yet. God, she had to get out of this place, get out and breathe again.

With his back to her, Matt slipped the photo back in the file folder, closing the cover before he turned around. "Except for the chin," he agreed, putting an arm around her shoulders as he started for the door.

With her hand on the knob, Laurel stopped and looked up at him. Her eyes were dark and more aware than they'd been before they'd come into that room. "Matthew." She leaned against him for a moment, just for a moment. "No one deserves to die that way."

He tightened his grip on her for a moment, just for a moment. "No."

Chapter 4

The bar was dim and cool. It was too early for the evening rush, too late for the afternoon regulars. With his mind still on Anne Trulane's file, Matt steered Laurel inside. No, no one deserved to die that way, but then life, and death, didn't always play according to the rules. He'd learned to accept that a long time ago.

Matt had been as quiet as Laurel since they'd walked out of the station house. He was thinking, analyzing. Remembering.

The phone had rung in the early hours of the morning—his source at the station house tipping him on Anne Trulane's disappearance. He'd arrived at Heritage Oak moments after the police. There'd been a mist, he recalled, thinner and nastier than a rain, and an air of silence. He'd sensed Louis Trulane hadn't wanted to call the outside for help. His answers had been clipped, his expression remote. No, he hadn't looked like a harried, concerned husband, but like a man who'd had his evening interrupted.

His sister, and the entourage of servants, had gathered around him a few paces back, in a move that had seemed like a defense before the search had spread into the marsh. It was a winding, humid place with shadows and small, secret sounds. Matt had felt a distaste for it without knowing why. He'd only known he'd rather have been searching the streets and alleyways than that steamy, dripping maze of shadow and bog.

They'd found her, too late, curled on the ground near a sluggish stream when dawn was just breaking. Mist, gray light, wet pungent smells. He'd heard a bird, a lark perhaps, calling in the distance. And he'd heard the crows. Matt remembered Louis Trulane's reaction. He'd been pale, cold and silent. If there'd been anger, grief or despair, he'd closed it inside. His sister had fainted, the servants had wept, but he'd simply stood....

"I'm going to call Louis."

"What?" Matt glanced over to find Laurel watching him.

"I'm going to call Louis, ask if he'll see us."

Slowly, he tore the wrapper from a fresh pack of cigarettes. "All right." He looked after her as she weaved her way through tables to the pay phone in the corner. It wasn't easy for her, Matt thought, and struck a match with more force than necessary. She was too close, too open. Whatever childhood feelings she'd had for Louis Trulane were still too important to her to allow her to see him objectively.

What about you, Bates? he asked himself as he blew out a stream of smoke. You detest him because of the way Laurel says his name. It was time, he told himself, that they both remembered their priorities. The story came first. It had to. If Laurel's relationship with the Trulanes got them in, so much the better. He'd been in the game too long to be under any illusions. People like the Trulanes could toss obstacles in a reporter's way until getting through them was like walking through a minefield.

Not that it would stop him from getting the story—it would only add to the time and the legwork. Either way, Matt mused, either way he was going to poke some holes into that sanctified wall the Trulanes had around themselves and their name.

He saw Laurel coming back, the sadness lingering in her eyes, the color only a hint in her cheeks. She'd get over it, he told himself as something seemed to tear inside him. Because she had to. He waited until she slid into the booth across from him.

"Well?"

"He'll see us at ten tomorrow."

Matt crushed out his cigarette, warning himself not to touch her. "You don't sound too thrilled about it."

"I used the pressure of an old friendship." She looked up then, meeting his eyes with a kind of weary defiance. "I hated it."

"You've got a job to do," he muttered, and found he'd reached for her hand before he could stop himself.

"I know. I haven't forgotten." Instinctively she tightened her fingers on his. "I don't have to like it to do it well." She knew she'd never be able to back off now, not after seeing that picture—not after imagining what Susan Fisher would have felt if she had seen it.

When the waitress stopped beside her, Laurel

glanced up. She had to dull the image. Maybe it was weak, but she had to. "Martini," she said on impulse. "A dry martini with an illusion of vermouth."

"Two," Matt ordered, sending Laurel an off-center smile. "It only helps temporarily, Laurellie."

"That's good enough for now." Resting her elbows on the table, she leaned forward. "Matthew, I'm going to consume great quantities of alcohol. This is totally preplanned and I offer no excuses. I will promise, however, not to get sloppy. Naturally, I'll regret this tomorrow, but I think it'll be a lesson well learned."

He nodded, grinning because he saw she needed it. "Since I'm joining you, I'll try to maintain your high standards. In any case…" He leaned a bit closer. "I've often wondered what it would be like to get you drunk and have my way with you."

She laughed for the first time in hours. "There isn't enough gin in this place for that, Matthew."

"We'll see how you feel in a couple hours." Leaning back, he lit another cigarette. "Why don't you tell me about the Trulanes?"

"What about them?"

"Everything."

She sighed, then, picking up the glass the waitress set in front of her, sipped. "This might just be the only thing in New Orleans completely lacking in humidity."

Matt acknowledged this by tapping the rim of his glass against hers. "The Trulanes, Laurellie."

"All right—and don't call me that. Ancient history first," she began. "Heritage Oak was built in the early nineteenth century. The plantation was vast and rich. The Trulanes still own more land than anyone else in this part of Louisiana. Besides cotton and cattle, they were shipbuilders. The profits from that kept the plantation alive after the war. As far back as anyone would remember, the Trulanes've been an important part of New Orleans, socially, financially and politically. I'm sure Grandma has a large repertoire of stories."

"Undoubtedly," Matt agreed. "Let's just speed up the passage of time a bit. Something in this century."

"Just laying the groundwork." Laurel took a sip from her glass, then toyed with the stem. "Beauregard Trulane—"

"Come on."

"There's always a Beauregard," she said loftily. "Inherited Heritage Oak right after his marriage. He had three children: Marion, Louis and Charles." Her eyes smiled over the rim of her glass. "He was an enormous man, bellowing, dramatic. Grandma loved him. In fact, I've sometimes wondered...well." She grinned and shrugged. "His wife was beautiful, a very quiet, serene sort of woman. Marion looks a great deal like her. Aunt Ellen—I called her that—died less than six months after my mother. I was around six...I've always mixed them a bit in my mind."

With a shrug, she emptied her glass, not noticing that Matt signaled for another round. "In any case, after she died, old Beau went into a steady decline. Louis began to take over the business. Really, he was too young to face those kinds of pressures, but there wasn't much choice. He would've been about eighteen or nineteen at the time, and I suppose I already worshiped him. To me, he was a cross between Prince Charming and Robin Hood. He was kind to me, always laughing and full of fun. That's how I like to remember him," she murmured, and stared into her fresh drink.

"Things change," Matt said briefly. How did a man compete with a childhood memory? he asked himself, frustrated by the look on Laurel's face. Damned if he would. "You're not a child anymore, Laurel."

She shifted her gaze to his and held it steady. "No, but a good deal of my perspective on Louis is that of a child."

He inclined his head and told himself to relax. "Tell me about Marion."

"She's a couple years older than Louis, and as I said, has her mother's looks. When I was young I thought of her as my personal fairy godmother. She was always so poised, and so beautiful."

A picture of dark elegance and flawless skin ran through his mind. "Yes, I noticed."

"She's too old for you," Laurel said without thinking, then looked over with a frown when Matt burst out laughing. "Shut up, Bates, and let me finish."

"I beg your pardon," he said with his tongue in his cheek.

"Marion used to have me over," Laurel continued, rashly finishing off her second martini. "She'd give me tea and cakes in the parlor. She knew I adored Louis and used to tell me to hurry and grow up so Louis could marry me. I adored her too."

"She never married?"

"No. Grandma said she was too choosy, but I think she had a love affair that didn't work out. Once I was there on a gray, gloomy day and she told me if a woman had one great love in her life, it was enough. Of course, at the time I thought she was talking about Louis and me, but when I got older and remembered how she'd looked..." On a sigh, Laurel reached for her glass. "Women like Marion are easily hurt."

He looked at her, the soft skin, soft mouth, soft eyes. "Is that so?"

"Charles was different." Shaking off the mood, Laurel leaned back with her drink. "I suppose he was a bit like Curt, and I thought of him as an extra brother. He was dreamy and abstracted. He was going to be an artist, and when he wasn't sketching, he was studying or hanging around Jackson Square. They'd hung some of his paintings in the main hall—until he left."

"With the first Mrs. Trulane," Matt finished.

"Yes, twelve years ago. It was a nasty scandal, the sort that causes a lot of pain and fabulous headlines." She shook her head over the opposing loyalties and sighed. The martinis were taking the edge off. "Grandma could tell you a great deal more, but from what I remember, Louis came back from a business trip to find Elise and Charles gone. The rumor that buzzed from servants' wing to servants' wing was that there was a note. Most of their clothes and all of Charles's painting gear were gone."

Laurel looked beyond him, unaware that the bar was filling up with people and noise. Someone was playing on the piano in the rear. "That's when Louis changed. He closed himself off from everyone. The few times I did see him, all the laughter was gone. As far as I know, he's never heard from Charles or Elise. About four years ago, he finally filed for divorce. Marion told me he'd done it strictly as a legality, that he was bitter, very bitter. She worried about him. His second marriage was a surprise to everyone."

Idly, she watched the smoke from Matt's cigarette

curl toward the ceiling. The fans spun gently, slicing at the smoke, stirring the air. He hadn't spoken in some time, but she didn't realize it was the quality of his listening that made it so easy to speak. "I called him, first because I really hoped he was happy, and second, because Louis Trulane's remarriage meant a good story. He sounded almost like his old self—older, certainly, but some of the spark was back. He wouldn't give me an interview, he said..." She frowned as she searched back for his words. "He said he'd married a child and he needed to keep spring to himself for a little while."

God, did she know what she did to him when her eyes took on that vulnerable, young look? He wanted to take her away somewhere, anywhere, so that nothing could hurt her. And if he tried, she'd think he was out of his mind. Matt crushed out his cigarette with deliberate care. "What do you know about the first Mrs. Trulane?"

"Nothing really." Looking up again, she smiled wryly. "Except I was horribly jealous of her. She was lovely in that soft, kind of misty style that no one can emulate. I do remember the wedding—pink and white magnolias, a huge, frothy wedding cake and beautiful dresses. Elise wore silk and lace with miles of train. She looked like a porcelain doll—gold and white and tiny. She looked like..." She trailed off, eyes wide, with her glass halfway to her lips. "Oh God, she looked like—"

"Like the second Mrs. Trulane," Matt finished. Leaning back, he signaled the waitress again. "Well, well."

"It doesn't mean anything," she began in a rush. "Only that Louis was attracted to a certain type of woman. The resemblance to his first wife doesn't add up to a motive for murder."

"It's the closest we've got. And we're still a long way from being certain Anne Trulane was murdered." Matt lifted a brow as he studied Laurel's face. "You're quick to rush to his defense, Laurellie. It's going to be difficult for you to think clearly if you don't let go of your childhood infatuation."

"That's ridiculous."

"Is it?" His lips curved without humor.

"Listen, Bates, I always think clearly, and whatever my feelings for Louis, they won't interfere with my work." She looked down at her empty glass. "I finished my drink."

"So I see." This time the amusement leaked through. Indignation was one of her most appealing expressions. She'd had enough of the Trulanes for the day, Matt decided. So had he. Unobtrusively, the waitress replaced empty glasses with fresh ones. "Well, that's for tomorrow. Why don't you bring me up to date on our favorite city councilman? I'm keeping a scrapbook."

"Why don't you leave Jerry alone?" Laurel demanded, starting on the next drink.

"Everyone's entitled to a hobby."

"Don't be so smug and superior," she mumbled into her glass. "Jerry's a very—very…"

"Pompous ass?" Matt suggested blandly, then grinned when she burst into a fit of giggles.

"Damn you, Matthew, if my brain weren't numb, I'd have thought of something." Blowing the hair out of her eyes, she set down her drink and folded her hands. "I find your continually rude comments on Jerry's personality annoying."

"Because I'm right?"

"Yes. I really hate it when you're right."

He grinned, then, tossing a few bills on the table, rose. "I'll walk you home, Laurel. Let's hope the fresh air doesn't clear your brain—you might just be receptive to a few of my baser instincts."

"It'd take more than three martinis to do that." She stood, letting out a long breath when the floor tilted gently under her feet.

"Four," he murmured as he took her arm. "But who's counting?"

"I'm only holding on to you because I have to," Laurel told him as they stepped outside. "After a couple blocks, I'll get my rhythm back."

"Just let me know when you want to go solo."

"How many did you have?"

"The same as you."

Laurel tilted her head back to study him and found the martinis spun not too unpleasantly in her head. "Well, you're taller, and heavier," she added with a smirk. "I have a very delicate build."

"So I've noticed."

She lifted a brow as they passed a sidewalk trumpeter. The sound of jazz was mellow and sad. "Have you really?"

"You could say I've made a study of it—journalistically speaking."

"What's that supposed to mean?"

He paused long enough to touch his lips to hers. "Don't press your luck."

"You have a funny way of kissing," she muttered as her head tilted onto his shoulder. "I don't know if I like it."

To his credit, Matt didn't slip a hand around her throat and squeeze. "We can have a debate on that subject later."

"I really thought you'd have a different technique," she went on. "You know, more…aggressive."

"Been spending time thinking about my technique?" he countered.

"I've given it some thought—journalistically speaking."

"It'd be safer to table this discussion until you can walk a straight line." He turned into the courtyard of the building they shared.

"You know, Matthew…" Laurel gripped the banister as they climbed the stairs. The steps weren't as steady as they'd been that morning. "You're not really so bad after three martinis."

"Four," he mumbled.

"Don't nitpick now that I've decided to tolerate you." Unzipping her purse, she began to fish for her keys. "Here, hold this."

Matt found himself holding a wallet, compact, notebook, broken earrings and several ticket stubs. "Anything else?" he said dryly.

"No, here they are—they always sink to the bottom."

Unceremoniously, he dumped the contents back in her purse and took the keys from her. "Are you going to let me in?" A pot of coffee, he mused as she leaned back against the door. A couple of aspirins and a dark room. He wasn't at all certain she could manage any of the three by herself. "We've been neighbors for nearly a year and I haven't had an invitation."

"What appalling manners." Giving him a misty smile, Laurel gestured him inside.

The room, like the woman, had soft edges, elegance and wit. There was the scent of potpourri with a touch of lavender. The colors were creams and roses. Lace at the curtains, velvet on the sofa. On the wall above a gleaming tea cart was a framed burlesque poster from the 1890s.

"It suits you."

"Really?" Laurel glanced around, unaccountably pleased with herself. "'S funny, even if I'd seen your place I wouldn't know if it suited you." Laurel dragged a hand through her hair as she tried to focus on him. She held it there as she swayed, only a little. "I don't really understand you at all. Framed newsprints or Picassos. In an odd sort of way, you're a fascinating man."

She was smiling at him, only an arm's length away. At the moment, Matt wasn't certain if she was being deliberately provocative or if the martinis were doing it for her. Either way, it wasn't any easier on him. He didn't have many rules, but one of them dealt strictly with making a move on a woman who might not remember it the next morning.

"Coffee," he said briefly and took her arm.

"Oh, did you want some?"

"You do," he said between clenched teeth. "Black."

"Okay." In the kitchen, she stared at the automatic coffee-maker, brows knit. She'd have sworn she knew what to do with it.

"I'll make it," Matt told her, grinning again. "Can you handle the cups?"

"Certainly." Laurel rummaged in a cupboard, and though she rattled them dangerously, managed to set violet-trimmed china cups in their saucers on the counter. "I don't have any beignets."

"Coffee's fine."

"Guess if you *really* wanted some I could make 'em."

"I'll take a rain check."

"You're a good sport, Matthew." Laughing, she turned and tumbled into his arms. With a smile, she curled her arms around his neck. "You've got fabulous eyes," she said on a sigh. "I bet just everyone tells you that."

"Constantly." He put his hands on her waist, intending to draw her away. Somehow, she was pressed against him with his fingers spread over the thin material of her blouse. Desire curled inside him like a fist. "Laurel…"

"Maybe you should kiss me again, so I can figure out why I always think I don't want you to."

"Tomorrow," he murmured as he lowered his mouth toward hers, "if you remember, you're going to hate yourself for saying that."

"Mmmm, I know." Her lashes lowered as his lips brushed over hers. "That's not a kiss." She drew a long sigh as her nerve ends began to tingle. "It's fabulous." Her fingers crept into his hair to tangle and explore. "More…"

The hell with rules, Matt thought savagely. If he had to pay for what he took now, then he'd pay. And by God, it would be worth it. On an oath, he dragged her against him and crushed her mouth with his.

Instant fire. It flared from her into him—or him into her. The source didn't matter, only the results. She moaned. The sound had nothing to do with pain or with wonder, and everything to do with raw desire. Her body strained into his with a certainty. This is right, this had always been right. She found his tongue with hers and let passion and intimacy merge blindingly, then struggled for more.

At that moment, with her head spinning and her body humming, it no longer mattered that it should be he who touched off all the sparks, all the secrets raging in her. No one else ever had. No one else ever could. Again, above all the whirling thoughts in her mind was one simple demand: more.

He was losing. Perhaps he'd been losing since he'd first seen that face. Bits and pieces of himself were being absorbed and he no longer cared. She could have whatever she wanted as long as he could have her like this. Heated, melting, hungry.

Her taste wasn't delicate like her looks, but wild and daring. Her scent was airy, romantic, her mouth ripe with passion. Though he could feel her breasts yield against him, her hands demanded and took. Muttering threats, promises, pleas, he pressed his mouth to her throat and began to please himself.

Her pulse hammered. He could feel it beneath his lips, strong, fast. With a nip of his teeth it scrambled and raced to war with the low sound she made. Then his hands were on her, hard, rushing, urgent until the sound became his name. There was nothing casual about him now, not a trace of the easygoing, faintly amused man who sat across from her day after day. There was the aggression he'd carefully glossed over. The ruthlessness. The excitement.

He wanted her—too much for comfort. Too much for sanity. Perhaps she was all he'd ever wanted, the silkiness, the fire. When she was pressed against him like this, there was no past, no future, only now. Now was enough for a lifetime.

How could her mind be so clouded and her body so alive? Laurel thought she could feel her own blood racing through her veins. Is this what she'd been waiting for? This mindless freedom? It was enough—it was more than she'd ever dreamed of, more than she'd ever understood. She was far from understanding now, but her body was so busy controlling her mind, she didn't care. With a sound of possession and the strength of greed, she dragged Matt's mouth back to hers. It seemed as though her legs dissolved from the knees down.

She heard him swear against her mouth before he clutched her closer. Then he drew her away while she gripped his shoulders in protest, and for support. "Matthew…"

"The door." His voice wasn't any more steady than the rest of him. No, he wasn't steady, Matt realized as he held Laurel away from him. And maybe not quite sane. "Someone's at the door, Laurel. You'd better answer it."

"The door? Whose door?" She stared up at him, aroused, dazed.

"Your door." A faint smile touched his lips.

"Oh." She looked around the sun-washed kitchen as though she'd never seen it before. "I should answer it?"

He nearly dragged her back. Her flushed, bemused expression had his fingers tightening convulsively on her arms. Carefully, he released her. "Yeah." Disoriented, Laurel walked away. He'd come too close, Matt thought, too damn close to yanking her to the kitchen floor and taking her like a maniac. He turned to the hissing coffeepot, not sure whether to be grateful to whoever was banging on the door, or to murder them.

Laurel felt as though she'd been swimming underwater and had come up much too quickly. Drunk? She pressed her fingers to her temple as she reached for the doorknob. Whatever the martinis had started, Matt had finished. She shook her head, hard, and when it didn't clear, gave up and opened the door.

"Laurel, you took so long answering I nearly went away." Jerry Cartier, three-piece-suited and vaguely annoyed, stared at her.

"Oh." Her blood was cooling, but the alcohol still swam in her head. "Hello, Jerry."

Because she stepped back, swinging the door wider, he came in. "What were you up to?"

"Up to?" she repeated…and remembered. Laurel let out a long breath. "Coffee," she murmured. "I was making coffee."

"You drink too much coffee, Laurel." He turned as she closed the door and leaned back on it. "It isn't good for your nerves."

"No." She thought of Matt. She hadn't realized she had so many nerves until a few moments ago. "No, you're probably right about that." She straightened as it occurred to her what Jerry would have to say if he realized just what she'd been drinking, and how much. The last thing she wanted was a twenty-minute lecture on the evils of alcohol. "Sit down, Jerry," she invited, thinking just how much she wanted to lie down—in a dark room—in silence. If she were lucky, very lucky, she could cross the room and get to the sofa without weaving. She took one hesitant step.

"You're not ready."

Laurel stopped dead. He was right, of course, but

crawling wasn't such a good idea. Neither was standing still. "Ready?"

"For dinner," Jerry told her as his brows drew together.

"Hello, Jerry." Carrying a tray of steaming coffee and cups, Matt strolled in.

Jerry crossed one leg over the other. "Matthew."

After setting down the tray, Matt walked casually to where Laurel still stood. "Condemn any good buildings lately?" In an unobtrusive move, he took Laurel's arm and led her to the couch. As she sank down, she shot him a grateful look.

"That's not my jurisdiction," Jerry stated, lacing his fingers together. "The mayor did tell me just the other day about a building on the other side of town. Appalling plumbing."

"Is that so?"

"Coffee?" Laurel interrupted. Martinis or not, she couldn't sit there and let Matt calmly execute an unarmed man. Besides, if she didn't have some coffee, she was going to quietly lay her head on the arm of the sofa and doze off.

"Only a half cup," Jerry told her. "Are you sure you should have any more?"

She made a grab for the handle of the pot and prayed she could pour it. "I haven't had any for hours."

"So, how was your day, Jerry?" Matt asked him as he closed his hand over Laurel's on the handle. Hearing her small sigh of relief, he nearly grinned.

"Busy, busy. There never seems to be enough hours to get everything done."

Matt's gaze slid down to Laurel's, brushing over her mouth. "No, there doesn't."

Jerry reached for the cup Laurel passed him and had to lean to the right when she missed his hand. "Laurel," he began, giving her an oddly intent look. "Have you been…drinking?"

"Drinking?" She set her heel down hard on Matt's foot when he chuckled. "Jerry, I just poured." Lifting the cup to her lips, she drank half the contents. "Why did you say you'd dropped by?"

"Dropped by?" He shook his head as Laurel leaned back, clutching her cup in both hands. "Laurel, we're supposed to go out to dinner."

"Oh." He was probably right, she thought vaguely. If Jerry said they had a dinner date, they had a dinner date. He kept a very precise appointment book.

"Laurel and I are working on a story," Matt put in more for his own amusement than to rescue Laurel. "We've run into some overtime on it. As a matter of fact, we were, ah, covering ground when you knocked on the door." Not by the slightest flicker did he betray the fact that Laurel's heel was digging into his foot. "Reporting really does interfere with a social life."

"Yes, but—"

"You know what it's like to be on deadline, I'm sure." Matt gave him an easy smile. "Laurel and I probably won't have time for anything more than a cold sandwich. We could be tied up on this for…weeks. You'll give Jerry a call when things calm down, won't you, Laurel?"

"What? Yes, yes, of course." She drained her coffee and wished he'd go so that she could pour another. "I'm awfully sorry, Jerry."

"I understand. Business before pleasure." Matt stopped himself before he choked over his coffee. Jerry rose, setting down his cup before he straightened his tie. "Just ring my office when things are clear, Laurel. And try to cut down on that coffee."

"Mmm-hmmm" was the best she could manage as her teeth were digging into her bottom lip. The door closed quietly behind him. "Oh, God!" Not sure whether she wanted to laugh or scream, Laurel covered her face with her hands.

"Tacky, Laurellie," Matt murmured, pouring out more coffee. "Leaving it to me to untangle you."

It would be satisfying to throw the coffee in his face, but she needed it too much. "With everything that happened today—the story," she emphasized firmly when his grin broke out, "I simply forgot about dinner. And I didn't ask you to untangle me."

"That's gratitude." He tugged on her hair until she looked at him. "Not only do I let you break three of my toes, but I help you cover up your…impaired condition from your boyfriend."

"He's not." Laurel drank cup number two without a pause, then set down the cup with a snap.

"You're stringing him along."

"That's not true." She started to rise, found it took too much effort and stayed where she was. "We have a perfect understanding. We're friends. Damn it, he's a very nice man, really, just a little…"

"Don't say harmless again, the poor guy doesn't deserve it. Then again, he doesn't seem to be in danger of having his heart broken."

"Jerry doesn't see me that way," Laurel began.

Looking at her, sulky-mouthed and sleepy-eyed, Matt leaned closer. "In that case, you can leave the pompous off of my earlier description of him."

Laurel put her hand firmly on his chest. She wasn't about to risk letting the room spin around her again. "I'm going to bed."

The corner of his mouth tilted. "I love aggressive women."

"Alone," Laurel told him, fighting back a laugh.

"Terrible waste," he murmured, taking the hand she held against him to his lips. Turning it over, he brushed them over her wrist and felt the wild beat below the skin.

"Matthew, don't."

He looked at her. It would be easy, so very easy. He had only to draw her to him and kiss her once; they both knew it. She wanted, he wanted, yet neither of them was quite sure how it had come to this. "Years from now, I'm going to hate myself for handling it this way," he murmured as he rose. "I'd take some aspirin now, Laurellie. You're going to need all the help you can get with that hangover in the morning."

Cursing himself all the way, Matt walked to the door, then shut it firmly behind him.

Chapter 5

"Damn you, Bates."

Laurel stared at the pale, wan reflection in her bathroom mirror while hammers pounded dully in her head. Why did he have to be right?

Grabbing a bottle of aspirin, she slammed the door of the medicine cabinet closed. This was followed by a pitiful moan as she clutched her head. Laurel knew it wasn't going to fall off; she only wished it would.

She deserved it. Laurel downed the two aspirins and shuddered. Anyone who drank four martinis in an afternoon deserved what she got. She might have accepted it with some grace if he just hadn't been right.

It didn't help her mood that she could remember what had happened after the drinking. She'd practically thrown herself at him. God, what a fool! He wasn't going to let her forget it. Oh, no, he'd tease and torment her for months. Maybe she deserved that, too, but… Oh, Lord, did she have to remember how wonderful it had been, how unique? Did she have to stand here knowing she wanted it to happen again?

Well, it wasn't. Dragging both hands through her hair, she willed the pounding in her head to stop. She wasn't going to fall for Matthew Bates and make an idiot out of herself. She might be stuck with him on the story, but personally it was going to be hands off and keep your distance. She'd chalk up her reaction to him to an excess of liquor. Even if it wasn't true.

With a sigh, Laurel turned toward the shower. She'd do the intelligent thing. She'd soak her head. As she reached for the tap, the pounding started again—at the front door and inside her temples. Whoever it was deserved a slow, torturous death, she decided as she trudged out to answer.

"Good morning, Laurellie." Matt leaned against the doorjamb and grinned at her. His gaze slid down her short, flimsy robe. "I like your dress."

He was casually dressed, as always, but fresh and obviously clearheaded. She felt as though she'd walked through a desert, eating a few acres along the way. "I overslept," she muttered, then folded her arms and waited for him to gloat.

"Had any coffee yet?"

She eyed him warily as he closed the door. Maybe he was just waiting for the perfect moment to gloat. "No."

"I'll fix it," he said easily and strolled into the kitchen.

Laurel stared after him. No smart remark, no smirk? How the hell was she supposed to keep up with him?

she demanded as she dragged herself back to the shower.

She'd been ready to battle, Matt thought as he reached for the glass container of coffee. And all she really wanted to do was crawl back into bed and shut down. A hell of a woman, he thought again. A great deal like her grandmother.

His thoughts traveled back to the evening before. Because he'd known better than to stay in his apartment, one thin wall away from Laurel, Matt had gotten in his car. A little legwork to take his mind off the woman. Olivia Armand would be a fount of information, and her opinion of the Trulanes was bound to be less biased than Laurel's.

Olivia greeted him on her terrace with a look that held both speculation and pleasure. "Well, well, now the evening has possibilities."

"Miss Olivia." Matt took the gnarled, ringed hand in his and kissed it. It smelled of fresh jasmine. "I'm mad about you."

"They all were," she said with a lusty laugh. "Sit down and have a drink, Matthew. Have you softened that granddaughter of mine up yet?"

Matt thought of the fiery woman he'd held only an hour before. "A bit," he murmured.

"You're slow, boy."

"I've always thought a man's more successful if he covers all the angles first." He handed her a drink before he sat down beside her.

"Not joining me?"

"It's hard enough to keep a clear head around you." While she laughed, he sat back and lit a cigarette. "Where's Susan?"

"Upstairs, being shocked by my journals."

"What'd you think of her?"

Olivia took a slow sip. Little fingers of moonlight danced over the diamonds on her hands. Insects buzzed around the hanging lantern by the door, tapping against the glass. The scents from the garden beyond rose up lazily. "Bright girl. Well-bred, a bit shaky and sad, but strong enough."

"She claims her sister was murdered."

The thin white brows rose, more, Matt observed, in thoughtfulness than surprise. "So that's what this is all about. Interesting." She took another sip, then tapped her finger against the glass. "The poor girl was bitten by a snake in the swamps behind Heritage Oak. Tell me why Susan's thinking murder."

In the brisk, concise style he used in his reporting, Matt ran through the entire events of the day. He saw a bat swoop low over the trees, then disappear. The air was full of the sounds of crickets and the occasional croak of a frog. Palm fronds rustled overhead. The breeze carried a teasing scent of magnolia. A long way from New York, he mused.

"Not as cut and dried as the Trulanes like to keep things," Olivia commented. "Well, Matthew, murder and mystery keep the blood moving, but you're not telling me this to keep my arteries from hardening."

He grinned. She could always make him grin. Leaning back, he listened to the sounds of the night. "I know the general background on the Trulanes, and Laurel gave me a few more details—through rose-colored glasses," he added.

"A touch of jealousy's a healthy thing," Olivia decided. "Might get you on your horse."

"The point is," Matthew said dryly, "I'd like you to tell me about them."

"All right. We'll walk in the garden. I get stiff sitting so long."

Matt took the hand she held out and helped her up. She was tiny; it always surprised him. She walked lightly. If there was any pain or discomfort in her joints, she gave no sign of it. He hadn't lied when he'd said he was mad about her. Within five minutes of their first meeting, he'd fallen for her, and had had no trouble understanding why she'd been the most sought-after girl, then woman, then widow, of the parish.

"Marion was finished in France," Olivia began. "There were rumors of an ill-fated love affair, but she'd never talk about it. She's quiet, but she's sharp, always was. For all her good works and elegant airs, she's also a snob. I'm fond enough of the girl, but she's not her mother, as some would like to think."

Matt laughed, patting the hand tucked through his arm. "I knew I could count on you for a straight shot, Miss Olivia."

"Can't stand pussyfooting around. Now Charles was like his mother," she continued. "Good-looking boy, head in the clouds. But he had talent. He was shy about it, but he had talent. One of his watercolors hangs in my sitting room."

Then he was good, Matt mused. Olivia might buy the attempt of a poor neighbor, but she wouldn't hang it in Promesse d'Amour unless it deserved it.

"I was disappointed in him for running off with his brother's wife." Catching the ironic look in Matt's eye, she wagged a finger at him. "I have my standards, Yankee. If Louis's wife and brother wanted each other, they should have been honest about it instead of sneaking off like thieves in the night. Louis would have dealt with it better."

"Tell me about him."

"Laurel's first love." She cackled at Matt's expression. "Simmer down, Matthew, every woman's entitled to one fairy tale. When he was young, he was a vibrant, exciting man. He was devoted to his family, and his family's business, but he wasn't serious or stuffy. I'd never have abided that. I believed he loved his first wife deeply and the betrayal destroyed him. It didn't help when the rumors started that she'd been carrying Charles's baby."

"Did you ever meet Anne Trulane?"

"No, Louis was selfish with her, and I felt he was entitled." She sighed and broke a blossom from an azalea. "They were planning a party in September. Marion told me it was going to be a huge, splashy affair, introducing Anne to New Orleans society. She said the poor child was torn between excitement and terror at the idea. I admit, I was looking forward to getting a close look at her. They said she resembled Elise."

"They?" Matt prompted.

"The servants. Bless them." She turned back toward the house, fleetingly remembering a time when she could have walked and run in the garden for hours. "If I want to know what's going on at Heritage Oak, I ask my cook. She'll tell me what their cook told her." She gave a gusty sigh. "I love espionage."

"You remember what Elise Trulane looked like?"

"My memory's twice as old as you are." She laughed, relishing rather than regretting the years. "More."

Despite the lines time had etched, her face was beautiful in the moonlight. The hand under his was dry with age. And strong. "Miss Olivia, where can I find another like you?"

"You've got one under your nose, you slow-witted Yankee." She settled back in her chair with a little sound of pleasure. "Ah, Susan, come out." She gestured to the woman hesitating at the garden doors. "Poor child," she said to Matt, "she's still blushing. How did you like my journals?"

"They're very—colorful. You've had a..." How did one put it? "A full life, Mrs. Armand."

Olivia gave a hoot of laughter. "Don't water it down, child. I've sinned and loved every minute of it."

"A drink, Susan?" Matt steered her to a chair.

"No, thanks. Laurel's not with you?"

"I don't like to bring her when I'm courting Olivia," he said easily, pleased to see that she could smile. "Since I'm here, I wonder if you can remember any names Anne might have mentioned in her letters, anything unusual or out of place she might have written about."

Susan lifted her hands, then let them fall. "She wrote mostly of Louis and the house...and Marion, of course. She'd grown fond of Marion. The servants...a Binney, a Cajun woman Anne said ran the place." Susan thought back, trying to find the details he wanted. "I got the impression she hadn't really taken over as mistress yet. Anne was a bit overwhelmed by having servants."

"Anyone outside the family?"

"She didn't really know anyone else. Oh, there was one of Louis's accountants, Nathan Brewster. She mentioned him a couple of times. I think he'd come to the house to go over papers with Louis. He made Anne nervous." Susan smiled again, this time with sadness. "Anne was very shy of men. Other than that it was all Louis. He was teaching her to ride…."

"Nathan Brewster," Olivia murmured. "I've heard of him. Sharp boy. Your age, Matthew. Supposed to have a nasty temper, nearly killed a man a couple years back. Seems the man was too friendly with Brewster's sister."

"Anything you don't know, Miss Olivia?"

"Not a damn thing." She grinned and gestured for a fresh drink.

He turned to pour it for her. "Susan, do you have a picture of Anne?"

"Yes, do you want it?"

"I'd like to see it."

When she'd risen to go inside, Matt handed Olivia her drink. "Know anything about the Heritage Oak swamp being haunted?"

"Don't be smug, Matthew," she advised. "We Creoles understand the supernatural more than you Yankees. Most of the swamps are haunted," she said with perfect calm as she swirled her bourbon. "The ghosts in Heritage Oak's date back to before the war."

Matthew settled back down, knowing there was only one war Olivia would feel worth mentioning. He remembered Laurel had done precisely the same thing. "Tell me."

"One of the Trulane women used to meet her lover there. Damned uncomfortable place for adultery," she added practically. When Matthew only laughed, she went on blandly. "When her husband found them, he shot them both—the gun's under glass in their library—and dumped the bodies in quicksand. Since then, occasional lights've been seen or someone'll hear a woman sobbing. Very romantic."

"And terrifying to someone like Anne Trulane," he added thoughtfully.

"It's only a wallet-size," Susan said as she came back out. "But it was taken less than a year ago."

"Thanks." Matt studied the picture. Young, sweet, shy. Those were the words that came to his mind. And alive. He could remember how she'd looked the morning they'd found her. Swearing under his breath, he handed the picture to Olivia.

"I'll be damned," she muttered, tapping the photo against her palm. "She could be Elise Trulane's twin."

The sound of Laurel rummaging in the bedroom brought him back to the present. Matt shifted his thoughts. There was another interview that day. Louis Trulane. He took the coffee out on the gallery and waited for Laurel.

She liked pink begonias, he mused. Pinching off one of the blossoms that trailed over the railing, Matt let the fragrance envelop him. Pink begonias, he thought again. Lace curtains. Where did a man who'd grown up with holes in his shoes fit into that? Strange, he thought more about his beginnings since he'd gotten involved with Laurel than he had in years.

He was staring down into the courtyard when she came out, but Laurel didn't think he was seeing the ferns and flowers. She'd only seen that expression on his face a few times when she'd happen to glance up and see him at his typewriter, immersed in a story. Intense, brooding.

"Matthew?" It was an encompassing question. She

wanted to ask what troubled him, what he was thinking of, or remembering. But the look stayed in his eyes when he turned to her, and she couldn't. Then it cleared, as though it had never been.

"Coffee's hot," he said simply.

She went to it, dressed in a sheer cotton skirt and blouse that made him hope the heat wave continued. "No I-told-you-so?" she asked before she sat on one of the white wrought-iron chairs.

"People in glass houses," he returned, leaning back against the railing. "I've had my share of mornings after. Feeling better?"

"Some. I'm going to call the house before we leave. I want to make sure Susan's settling in all right."

"She's fine." Matt speculated on what a woman like Laurel would wear under a summer dress. Silk—very thin silk, perhaps. "I saw her and your grandmother last night."

The cup paused on its way to Laurel's lips. "You went out there last night?"

"I can't keep away from your grandmother."

"Damn it, Matthew, this is my story."

"Our story," he reminded her mildly.

"Either way, you had no business going out there without me."

Walking over, he helped himself to a cup of coffee. "As I recall, you weren't in the mood to socialize last night. If you had been," he added smoothly, "we wouldn't have found ourselves at your grandmother's."

Her eyes narrowed at that, and she rose. "Just because my mind was fuzzy yesterday, Bates, don't get the idea in your head that you attract me in the least."

Because he only smiled, she plunged on. "*Any* man might look good after four martinis. Even you."

He set down his cup very carefully. "Mind clear this morning, Laurellie?"

"Perfectly, and—" She broke off when he pulled her against him.

"Yes, I'd say your mind was clear." He lowered his mouth to her jawline and nibbled. "You're a woman who knows exactly what she wants, and what she doesn't."

Of course she was, Laurel thought as she melted against him. "I don't want—oh." Her breath shuddered out as he nuzzled her ear.

"What?" Matt moistened the lobe with his tongue, then nipped it. "What don't you want?"

"You to—to confuse me."

She felt the brush of his lashes against her cheek as he made a teasing journey toward her mouth. "Do I?"

"Yes." His lips hovered just above hers. Laurel knew exactly what would happen if they met. She took a step back and waited for her system to level. "You're doing this to take my mind off the story."

"We both know—" he caught her hair in his hand "—this has nothing to do with any story."

"Well, the story's what we have to concentrate on." She spoke quickly, had to speak quickly until she was certain the ground was steady again. "I don't want you digging without me. I found Susan in the first place, and—"

"Damn it, if and when there's a story you'll get your half of the byline."

It was easier to be angry than aroused so she let her temper rise with his. "It has nothing to do with the by-line. I don't like you probing Grandma and Susan for leads without me. If you'd told me what you wanted to do, I'd have had some more coffee, a cold shower and pulled myself together."

"Maybe you could have." Sticking his hands in his pockets, he rocked back gently on his heels. "The point is, I wanted to talk to someone about the Trulanes, someone who has a little objectivity."

She flared at that, then subsided, hating him for being right. "Let's just go," she muttered, whirling away.

"Laurel." Matt took her arm, stopping her at the doorway. "It's not a matter of the story," he said quietly. "I don't want you to be hurt."

She stared at him while her guards began to shift on their foundations. Trouble, she thought. I'm really going to be in trouble. "I asked you before not to be nice to me," she murmured.

"I'll give you a hard time later to make up for it. The way you feel about Louis—"

"Has nothing to do with any of this," she insisted, no longer certain either of them were speaking of the story. "Let me deal with it myself, Matthew. I can."

He wanted to press her, for himself, for what he needed from her. The time would come when he would have to. "Okay," he said simply. "Let's go."

The breeze helped. It whispered soothingly through the windows as they drove out of town. With her head back and her eyes shut, Laurel listened to Matt's accounting of his visit to her grandmother the evening before.

"I take it from that scornful tone in your Yankee voice that you don't believe in the Trulane ghosts?"

"And you do?" Grinning, he sent her a sidelong look. When she didn't answer right away, he slowed down to look at her more carefully. "Laurel?"

She shrugged, then made a business out of smoothing her skirts. "Let's just say I've got Creole blood, Matthew."

He couldn't stop the smile, on his lips or in his voice. "Ghosts, Laurel?"

"Atmosphere," she corrected, goaded into admitting something she'd just as soon have kept to herself. "I've been in that swamp. There're flowers where you least expect them, small patches of prairie, blue herons, quiet water." She turned in her seat so that the breeze caught the tips of her hair and carried them out the window. "There's also quicksand, nasty little insects and snakes. Shadows." Frustrated, she turned to stare through the windshield. "I never liked it there. It's brooding. There're places the sun never reaches."

"Laurel." Matt stopped the car at the entrance to Heritage Oak. "You're going by childhood impressions again. It's a place, that's all."

"I can only tell you how I feel." She turned her head to meet his eyes. "And apparently how Anne Trulane felt."

"All right." Shifting into first, he maneuvered the car between the high brick pillars. "But for now, let's concentrate on human beings."

The oaks lining the drive were tall and old, the Spanish moss draping them gray green and tenacious. It hadn't changed. And, Laurel realized at the first sighting, neither had the house.

The brick had aged before she'd been born. There were subtle marks of time, but they'd been there as long as she could remember. The lines of the house were sharp and clean, not fluid like Promesse d'Amour's, but no less beautiful. The brick was a dusky rose, the balconies were soft black. Their delicacy didn't detract from the arrogance of the house. If Laurel saw her own ancestral home as a woman, she saw Heritage Oak as a man, bold and ageless.

"It's been a long time," she murmured. Emotions raced through her—memories. Knights and tea parties, filmy dresses and pink cakes. She'd been a child the last time she'd seen it, daydreamed in it.

With a sigh, Laurel turned and found her eyes locked with Matt's. There were new emotions now, not so soft, not so tender. This was reality, with all its pain and pleasure. This was real. Too real. Giving in to the panic of the moment, Laurel fumbled with the door handle and got out of the car.

What was happening to her? she asked herself as she took three long, deep breaths. It was getting to the point where she couldn't even look at him without wanting to run—or to reach out. A physical attraction was no problem. She'd managed to submerge that feeling for a year. This was something else again and it promised not to be so easily dealt with. She was going to have to, Laurel told herself, just as she was going to have to deal with her feelings for the Trulanes.

"Matthew, let me handle this." Calmer, she walked with him to the wide, white porch. "I know Louis and Marion."

"Knew," he corrected. He hadn't missed the way she'd looked at the house. Or the way she'd looked at him. "People have the inconsiderate habit of changing.

I won't make you any promises, Laurel, but I won't interfere until I have to."

"You're a hard man, Bates."

"Yeah." He lifted the knocker and let it fall against a door of Honduras mahogany.

A tall, angular woman answered the door. After a brief glance at Matt, her nut-colored eyes fastened on Laurel. "Little Miss Laurel," she murmured, and held out both thin hands.

"Binney. It's so good to see you again."

Josephine Binneford, housekeeper, had weathered the decade since Laurel had last seen her with little change. Her hair was grayer but still worn in the same no-nonsense knot at the back of her neck. Perhaps there were more lines in her face, but Laurel didn't see them.

"Little Miss Laurel," Binney repeated. "Such a fine, beautiful lady now. No more scraped knees?"

"Not lately." With a grin, Laurel leaned over to brush her cheek. She smelled of starch and lilac. "You look the same, Binney."

"You're still too young to know how fast time goes." Stepping back, she gestured them inside before she closed out the brilliant sunshine and heat. "I'll tell Miss Marion you're here." With a gait stiffened by arthritis, she led them to the parlor. *"Revenez bientôt,"* she murmured, turning to Laurel again. *"Cette maison a besoin de jeunesse."* Turning, she headed up the stairs.

"What did she say?" Matt asked as Laurel stared after her.

"Just to come back again." She cradled her elbows in her hands as if suddenly cold. "She says the house needs youth." She crossed into the parlor.

If people change, she thought, this remains constant.

The room could have been transported back a century; it would look the same in the century to come.

The sun gleamed through high windows framed with royal-blue portieres. It shone on mahogany tables, drawing out the rich red tints. It sparkled on a cut-glass vase that a long-dead Trulane bride had received on her wedding day. It lay like a lover on a porcelain woman who'd been captured for eternity in the swirl of a partnerless waltz.

Matt watched Laurel's long, silent survey of the room. The play of emotions on her face had him dealing with frustration, jealousy, need. How could he get her to turn to him, when so much of her life was bound up in what had been, who had been?

"Memories are nice little possessions, Laurel," he said coolly. "As long as you don't ignore the present when you take them out to play."

He'd wanted to make her angry, because her anger was the easier thing for him to deal with. Instead, she turned to him, her eyes soft, her face stunning. "Do you have any, Matthew?" she asked quietly. "Any of those nice little possessions?"

He thought of a roof that leaked and icy floors and a plate that never had enough on it. He remembered a woman hacking, always hacking, in her bed at night, weakening already-weak lungs. And he remembered the promise he'd made to get out, and to take the woman with him. He'd only been able to keep the first part of the promise.

"I have them," he said grimly. "I prefer today."

She'd heard something there, under the bitterness. Vulnerability. Automatically, Laurel reached out to him. "Matthew..."

Not that way, he told himself. He'd be damned if he'd get to her through sympathy. He took the hand she held out, but brought it to his lips. "Life's a ridiculous cycle to be involved in, Laurellie. I've always thought making memories has more going for it than reliving them."

She dropped her hand back to her side. "You're not going to let me in, are you?"

"Today." He ran his fingers through her hair. "Let's concentrate on today."

Unaccountably hurt, she turned from him. "There isn't any without a yesterday."

"Damn it, Laurel—"

"Laurel, I'm sorry to keep you waiting." Marion glided in as only a woman taught to walk can do. She wore filmy dresses in pastels that always seemed to float around her. As Laurel took her hands, soft and small, she wondered how anyone could be so coolly beautiful. Marion was nearing forty, but her complexion was flawless, with a bone structure that spoke of breeding. Her scent was soft, like her hands, like her hair, like her eyes.

"Marion, you look lovely."

"Sweet." Marion squeezed her hands before releasing them. "I haven't seen you since that charity function two months ago. It was odd seeing you there with your pad and pencil. Are you happy with your career?"

"Yes, it's what I've always wanted. This is a colleague of mine, Matthew Bates."

"Nice to meet you, Mr. Bates." Marion held his hand an extra moment, hesitating while her eyes searched his face. "Have we met?"

"Not formally, Miss Trulane. I was here when your sister-in-law was found last month."

"I see." Briefly, her eyes clouded with pain. "I'm afraid I don't remember too much of that day clearly. Please sit down. Binney is seeing to some refreshments. Louis will be along in a moment." She chose a Hepplewhite for herself, straight-backed and dully gleaming. "He's tied up on the phone. Actually, I'm glad to have a moment with you before he comes." Marion folded her hands on her lap. "Laurel, you haven't seen Louis in a very long time."

"Ten years."

"Yes, ten years." Marion gazed out of the window a moment, then sighed. "One loses track of time here. I had to stop having you over after Charles and Elise… went away. Louis wasn't in a proper state for an impressionable young girl."

Ten years, Laurel thought, and it still hurts her. What has it done to him? "I understand that, Marion. I'm not a girl anymore."

"No, you're not." Her gaze shifted back, away from the trim lawn and oaks. "Laurel, you saw only the beginnings of a change in him, but as the months passed, as the years passed, he became bitter," she said briskly. "Given to flashes of temper, of absentmindedness. There were times he wouldn't remember—" She stopped herself again, unlacing her hands. "He didn't forget," she corrected with a wistful smile. "He simply chose not to remember. He and Charles were—well, that's done."

"Marion, I know how difficult it must've been for him." Laurel reached out to lay a hand on hers. "I always knew. The truth is, I didn't stay away because you didn't ask me to come, but because I knew Louis wouldn't want me here."

"You always understood a great deal," Marion murmured. With a sigh, she tried to shake off the mood. "When he brought Anne home, no one was more surprised, more pleased than I. She'd taken that hard edge away."

"I felt that, too." She smiled when Marion sent her a questioning look. "I phoned him a few weeks after he was married."

Nodding, Marion laced her hands again. Her nails were oval, unpainted and buffed. "Perhaps he was overprotective, possessive, but Anne was so young, and he'd been hurt so badly. I'm telling you this now because I want you—" her gaze shifted to Matt "—both of you to understand the state Louis is in now. There's been so much pain in his life. If he seems cold and remote, it's only his way of dealing with grief." She turned her head as Binney wheeled in a tea tray. "Ah, iced tea. Do you still take too many sugars, Laurel?"

She smiled. "Yes. Oh." She glimpsed the tiny pink cakes arranged on the tray. "How sweet of you, Binney."

"I only told the cook Miss Laurel was coming for tea." She gave Laurel a quick wink. "Don't eat more than three, or your grandmother will scold me."

Laughing, Laurel bit into one as the housekeeper left the room. The light, sweet taste brought back a new flood of memories. She heard ice tinkle in the glasses as Marion poured. "Binney hasn't changed. The house, either," she added with a smile for Marion. "I'm so glad."

"The house never changes," Marion told her as she offered Laurel fresh, cold tea in a Waterford glass. "Only the people in it."

Laurel didn't hear him, but sensed him. Carefully, she set down the glass she held. Turning her head, she looked into Louis's eyes.

Chapter 6

Can ten years be so long? she thought with a jolt. She'd thought she was prepared. She'd hoped she was. There was gray in his hair now, near the temples. That she would have accepted. There were lines in his face going deep around his mouth and eyes. She could have accepted them too. But the eyes had none of the warmth, none of the humor she'd loved so much.

He was thin, too thin. It made him look older than thirty-six. She rose, and with a mixture of pain and pity, went to him. "Louis."

He took her hand and the ghost of a smile touched his mouth. "Grown up, Laurel? Why did I expect to find a child?" Very lightly, he touched a fingertip to the underside of her chin. She wanted to weep for him. "You always promised to be a beauty."

Laurel smiled, willing the warmth to come to his

eyes. "I've missed seeing you." But the warmth didn't come, and his hand dropped away. She felt his tension even before she felt her own. "Louis, this is my associate, Matthew Bates."

Louis's eyes flicked over Matt and grew colder. "I believe we've met."

"Some tea, Louis?" Marion reached for the pitcher.

"No." His voice was curt, but Marion made no sign other than a quick compression of lips. Neither man noticed, as their eyes were on Laurel. "We're not here for tea and cakes this time, are we, Laurel?" Louis murmured before he crossed the room to stand in front of the empty hearth. Over it was an oil of his mother. Laurel remembered it well. It had been there for years, except for a brief period when Elise Trulane's portrait had replaced it. "Why don't we get on with this?" Louis suggested. "I agreed to see you and Mr. Bates to put an end to this rumor Susan started." He gave Laurel a long look. "Ask your questions. I used to have all the answers for you."

"Louis..." She wanted to go to him, soothe him somehow, but the look in Matt's eyes stopped her. "I'm sorry to intrude this way. Very sorry."

"It isn't necessary to be sorry." Louis drew out a thin cigar, eyeing it for a moment before lighting it. "Nothing ever remains as it was. Do what you came to do."

She felt her stomach tighten. The power in him was still there, a power she'd recognized even as a child. It had driven him to take up the reins of a multimillion-dollar firm before he'd finished college. It had enabled him to enchant a young girl so that the woman could never forget him. But it was so cold now. Laurel stood where she was in the center of the parlor while the gap between memory and today grew wider.

"Susan is certain that Anne would never have gone out into the swamp alone," she began, knowing she began badly. "Susan claims that Anne had a terror of dark places, and that the letters she'd written expressed a specific fear of the place."

"And she believes Anne was forced to go in there," Louis finished. "I know all of that already, Laurel."

She was a journalist, she had an assignment. She had to remember it. "Was Anne afraid of the swamp, Louis?"

He drew on his cigar and watched her through the cloud of smoke. "Yes. But she went in," he added, "because she died there."

"Why would she have gone in?"

"Perhaps to please me." Carelessly he flicked cigar ash into the scrubbed hearth. "She'd begun to feel foolish about this fear she'd dragged along since childhood. When I was with her," he murmured, "she wouldn't need a light on in the hallway at night." Abruptly, his head lifted again, to the arrogant angle Laurel remembered in a young man. "The story about the ghosts in the swamp had her imagining all sorts of things. I was impatient." He drew on the cigar again, harder. "She had a…need for my approval."

"You think she might have gotten up in the middle of the night and gone out there to please you?" Laurel asked him, taking a step closer.

"It makes more sense than believing someone broke in, dragged her out and left her without myself or any of the servants hearing a sound." He gave her another cool, uncompromising look. "You read the police report, I imagine."

"Yes." She moistened her lips as she remembered the photograph. "Yes, I did."

"Then there's no need for me to go over that."

"Did your wife often have trouble sleeping?" Matt put in, watching as a very small muscle worked in Louis's jaw.

"Occasionally. Particularly when I was working." He glanced over Matt's head, out the long windows. "She thought she'd seen lights in the swamp."

"Did anyone else see them?"

Louis's mouth twisted into something like a smile. "Over the years, dozens of people have claimed to—usually when they've kept company with a bottle of bourbon."

"Mr. Bates," Marion broke in. "Anne was afraid of the swamp, but she was also fascinated with it. It's not unusual for someone to be fascinated by something they fear. She'd become obsessed by the legend. The problem…the blame," she amended slowly, "comes from none of us taking her seriously enough. She was so young. Perhaps if we'd insisted she go in during the daylight, she wouldn't have felt compelled to go in at night."

"Do you think she was capable of going in there alone, at night?" Laurel asked her.

"It's the only explanation. Laurel, we all loved her." She sent Louis a quick, misty look. "She was sweet and soft, but she was also highly strung. I thought her nerves came from the plans we were making for the party."

"What difference does it make now?" Louis demanded and tossed his cigar into the hearth. It bounced, then lay, smoldering. "Anne's gone, and neither Susan nor her letters can change it."

"The letters were stolen from Susan's room," Laurel said quietly.

"That's ridiculous. Who would steal letters? She misplaced them." Louis dismissed them with an angry shrug.

"You were married for nearly a year," Matt said casually. "Yet none of your closest neighbors had met your wife. Why?"

"That's my business."

"Louis, please." Laurel took another step toward him. "If we could just understand."

"Understand?" he repeated, and stopped her with a look. "How can you? She was hardly more than a child, the child you were when I last saw you. But she didn't have your confidence, your boldness. I kept her to myself because I wanted to. I had to. There was a generation between us."

"You didn't trust her," Laurel murmured.

"Trust is for fools."

"Isn't it odd," Matt commented, drawing Louis's fury from Laurel to himself, "how much Anne resembled your first wife?"

The only sound was Marion's sharp intake of breath. Though his hands clenched into fists, Louis stood very still. Without another word, another look, he strode out.

"Please, Louis just isn't himself." Marion fiddled nervously with the glasses. "He's very sensitive about comparisons between Anne and Elise."

"People are bound to make them," Matt returned, "when the physical resemblance is so striking."

"More than physical," Marion murmured, then went on in a rush. "It was a natural observation, Mr. Bates, but Louis won't discuss Elise and Charles. If there's nothing else…?"

"Do you know Nathan Brewster?" Laurel asked abruptly.

Marion's eyes widened before her lashes swept down. "Yes, of course, he's one of Louis's accountants."

Matt's brow lifted before he exchanged a look with Laurel. "His was one of the few names Anne mentioned in her letters."

"Oh, that's natural, I suppose. He came to the house a few times on business. It's true Anne didn't meet many people. Well." She rose, sending them both an apologetic smile. "I'm sorry I couldn't be of more help, but perhaps you can put Susan's doubts to rest now." She held out her hands to Laurel again. "Come back soon, please, just to talk like we used to."

"I will. Tell Louis…" Laurel sighed as she released Marion's hands. "Tell him I'm sorry."

They walked out of the house in silence, drove away in silence. As the frustration, the anger built, Matt swore to himself he'd say nothing. Whatever Laurel was feeling was her own business. If she let her emotions get in the way, let herself grieve, there was nothing he could do about it.

On an oath, he yanked the wheel, skidded to the side of the road and stopped.

"Damn it, Laurel, stop."

She kept her hands very still in her lap and stared straight ahead. "Stop what?"

"Mourning."

She turned her head then, and though her eyes were

dry, they were eloquent. "Oh, Matthew," she whispered, "he looked so lost."

"Laurel—"

"No, you don't have to say it. He's changed. I expected it, but I wasn't ready for it." She drew a deep breath that came out trembling. "I wasn't ready to see him hurting so much."

Cursing Louis Trulane and all he stood for, Matt gathered Laurel close. She didn't protest when he cradled her against him, but held on. The sun streamed into the car. She could hear birds calling and chattering in the trees beyond the car. As he stroked her hair, she closed her eyes, letting herself draw from the comfort he offered.

"I am mourning," she murmured. "I don't know if you can understand just how important Louis was to my childhood, my adolescence. Seeing him like this today..." With a sigh, she kept her head on his shoulder and watched the patterns sun and shade made on the road.

"You're thinking of him as a victim, Laurel. We're all victims of what life deals out. It's how we handle it that's important."

"When you love someone, and you lose them, it kills something in you too."

"No." He let himself breathe in the scent of her hair. "Damages. We all have to deal with being damaged one way or the other."

He was right, of course he was right. But it still hurt. She said nothing, but sat quietly with her cheek on his shoulder while his hand trailed through her hair. His body was so firm, his heartbeat so steady. She could lose herself here, Laurel realized, in the front seat of his car with the sun pouring through and the sound of birds calling lazily from tree to tree.

"I keep telling you not to be nice to me," she murmured.

He tilted his head back to look at her. His eyes were intense again, seeing too much. His fingers spread to cup her face. When her mouth opened, he tightened them. "Shut up," he told her before he pressed his lips to hers.

Not so light this time, not so gentle. She tasted frustration and didn't understand it. But she also tasted desire, simmering, waiting, and couldn't resist it. Her body went fluid, every bone, every muscle, as she surrendered to whatever it was they needed from each other. The need was there, she knew. Had always been there. The more she had resisted it, fought it, ignored it, the stronger it had become, until it threatened to overpower every other. Food, air, warmth, those were insignificant needs compared to this. If she was seduced, it wasn't by soft words or skilled kisses, but by the emotions that had escaped before she'd been able to confine them.

"Matthew." She dropped her head on his shoulder and tried to steady her breathing. "This isn't—I'm not ready for this."

Smoldering with impatience and desire, he forced her head back. "You will be."

"I don't know." She pressed her hands to his chest, wishing he could understand—wishing she could. "I told you that you confuse me. You do. I've never wanted a man before, and I never expected it to be you."

"It is me." He drew her closer. "You'll just have to get used to it." His expression changed slowly from barely restrained temper to intentness. “Never wanted a man,” he repeated. “Any man? You haven’t—been with any man?”

Her chin came up. “I said I never wanted one. I don’t do anything I don’t want to.”

Innocent? Dear God, he thought, shouldn’t he have seen it? Sensed it? Gradually, he loosened his grip until he’d released her. “Changes the rules, doesn’t it?” he said softly. Matt took out a cigarette while she sat frowning at him. “Changes the rules,” he repeated in a whisper. “I’m going to be your lover, Laurellie. Take some time to think about it.”

“Of all the arrogant—”

“Yeah, we’ll get into that in depth later.” He blew out a stream of smoke. She was steadier now, he thought ruefully. He was wired. He’d better give them both some time to think about it. “Let me throw a couple of theories at you on Anne Trulane.”

He started the car again while Laurel struggled to control her temper and to remember priorities. The story, she told herself, and forced her jaw to unclench. They’d deal with this…personal business later. “Go ahead.”

He drove smoothly, ignoring the knot of need in his stomach. “Louis married Anne Fisher because she looked like his first wife.”

“Oh, really, Matthew.”

“Let me finish. Whether he cared for her or not isn’t the issue. Once they were married he brought her back to Heritage Oak and kept her there, away from outsiders. Men. He didn’t trust her.”

“He’d been hurt before, in the cruelest possible way.”

“Exactly.” Matt pitched his cigarette out the window. "He was obsessed with the idea that she might find a younger man. He was possessive, jealous. What if Anne rebelled? What if she gave him a reason to doubt her loyalty?"

"You're suggesting that Louis killed her because he thought she'd violated his trust." She didn't like the chill that brought to her skin, and turned on him. "That's ridiculous. He isn't capable of killing anyone."

"How do you know what he's capable of?" he tossed back. "You didn't know that man in the parlor today."

No, she didn't, and the truth stung. "Your theory's weak," she retorted. "Look at the timetable. Anne died between 12:00 and 4:00 a.m. Louis woke the household sometime between two and three."

"He could've taken her in before two," Matt said mildly. "Maybe he never intended for her to die. He might've wanted to frighten her, taken her in and left her there."

"Then why would he call out a search party?"

Matt turned his head, letting his gaze skim over her face before he shifted it back to the road. "He could've forgotten he'd done it."

Laurel opened her mouth and closed it again. Absentminded, Marion had said. He'd been absentminded, angry, bitter. She didn't like the picture it was drawing in her mind.

Laurel remained silent as he drove through downtown traffic. No man forgot he'd left his wife alone and lost. No sane man. Matt swung over to the curb and stopped. "Where are we going?"

"To see Nathan Brewster."

Laurel glanced up at Trulane's, one of the oldest, most prestigious buildings in the city. Perhaps they'd find something in there that would shift the focus from Louis. "Marion didn't want to talk about Nathan Brewster."

"I noticed." Matt stepped out of the car. "Let's find out why."

"I know what you're thinking," she murmured as they walked toward the front doors.

"Mmmm. That could be embarrassing."

She shot him a look as they walked inside. "Anne was attracted to Nathan Brewster, acted on it and Louis found out. Rather than dealing with it or divorcing her, he drags her into the swamp in the middle of the night and dumps her."

Matt checked the board on the wall and located Accounting. "It crossed my mind," he agreed.

"You've got your own prejudices against Louis."

"You're damned right," he muttered, and took her hand to pull her to the elevator. "Look," Matt began before she could retort. "Let's talk to the man and see what happens. Maybe he's just been embezzling or having an affair with Marion."

"Your ideas get more and more ludicrous." She stepped into the elevator and crossed her arms.

"You're sulking."

"I am not!" Letting out an exasperated breath, she glared at him. "I don't agree with your theory, that's all."

"Give me yours," Matt suggested.

She watched the numbers flash over the elevator door. "After we talk to Brewster."

They stepped out on carpet, thick and plush. Without giving Matt a glance, Laurel crossed to the receptionist. "Laurel Armand, Matthew Bates, with the *Herald,*" she said briskly. "We'd like to see Nathan Brewster."

The receptionist flicked open her book. "Do you have an appointment?"

"No. Tell Mr. Brewster we'd like to speak with him about Anne Trulane."

"If you'll have a seat, I'll see if Mr. Brewster's available."

"Nice touch, Laurellie," Matt told her as they crossed the reception area. "Ever think about the military?"

"It's gotten me into a lot of city officials." She took a seat under a potted palm and crossed her legs.

He grinned down at her. There wasn't a trace of the sad, vulnerable woman who'd rested her head on his shoulder. "You've got style," he decided, then let his gaze sweep down. "And great legs."

Laurel slanted him a look. "Yeah."

"Mr. Brewster will see you now." The receptionist led them down a hallway, past an army of doors. After opening one, she went silently back to her desk.

Laurel's first impression of Nathan Brewster was of sex. He exuded it, ripe, physical. He was dark, and though he wasn't tall, he had a blatant virility no woman could miss. Good looks, though he had them, didn't matter. It was his primitive masculinity that would either draw or repel.

"Ms. Armand, Mr. Bates." He gestured toward two small leather chairs before taking a seat behind his desk. "You wanted to talk to me about Anne Trulane."

"That's right." Laurel settled herself beside Matt as she tried to reason out what kind of reaction a woman like Anne would have had to Nathan Brewster.

"She's dead," Brewster said flatly. "What does the press have to do with it?"

"You met Anne at Heritage Oak," Laurel began. "Not many people did."

"I went there on business." He picked up a pencil and ran it through his fingers.

"Could you give us your impression of her?"

"She was young, shy. My business was with Mr. Trulane; I barely spoke to her."

"Strange." Matt watched Brewster pull the pencil through his fingers again and again. "Yours was one of the few names that came up in Anne's letters." The pencil broke with a quiet snap.

"I don't know what you're talking about."

"Anne wrote to her sister about you." Matt kept his eyes on Brewster's now, waiting, measuring. "Her sister doesn't believe Anne's death was an accident."

Matt watched the little ripple of Brewster's throat as he swallowed. "She died of a snakebite."

"In the swamp," Laurel put in, fascinated by the waves of frustration and passion pouring out of him. "Did you know she was frightened of the swamp, Mr. Brewster?"

He shot Laurel a look, molten, enraged. Matt's muscles tensed. "How would I?" he demanded. "How would I know?"

"Why would you suppose she'd go into a place that terrified her?"

"Maybe she couldn't stand being locked up anymore!" he exploded. "Maybe she had to get out, no matter where, or how."

"Locked up?" Laurel repeated, ignoring the tremor

in her stomach. "Are you saying Louis kept her a prisoner?"

"What else can you call it?" he shot back at her. His hands clenched and unclenched on the two jagged pieces of pencil. "Day after day, month after month, never seeing anyone but servants and a man who watched every move she made. She never did anything without asking him first. She never stepped a foot beyond the gates of that place without him."

"Was she unhappy?" Laurel asked. "Did she tell you she was unhappy?"

"She should've been," Nathan tossed back. "Trulane treated her more like a daughter than a wife. She needed someone who'd treat her like a woman."

"You?" Matt said softly. Laurel swallowed.

Brewster's breathing was labored. The temper Matt had been told of was fighting to get free. He'd have to struggle to control it. And, Matt mused, he wouldn't often win.

"I wanted her," Brewster said roughly. "From the first time I saw her out on the lawn, in the sunlight. She belonged in the sunlight. I wanted her, loved her, in a way Trulane couldn't possibly understand."

"Was she in love with you?"

Matt's quiet question drew the blood to Brewster's cheeks. "She would have left him. She wouldn't have stayed in that—monument forever."

"And come to you?" Laurel murmured.

"Sooner or later." The eyes he turned on Laurel were penetrating, filled with passion and feeling. "I told her she didn't have to stay locked up there, I'd help her get away. I told her she'd be better off dead than—"

"Better off dead than living with Louis," Laurel finished as his harsh breathing filled the room.

"It must've been frustrating," Matt continued when Brewster didn't answer. "Loving your employer's wife, rarely being able to see her or tell her how you felt."

"Anne knew how I felt," Brewster bit off. "What difference does it make now? She's dead. That place killed her. He killed her." Brewster sent them both a heated look. "Print that in your paper."

"You believe Louis Trulane killed his wife?" Matt watched Brewster sweep the remains of the pencil from his desk.

"He might as well have held a gun to her head. She got away," he murmured as he stared down at his empty hands. "She finally got away, but she didn't come to me." The hands curled into fists again. "Now leave me alone."

Laurel's muscles didn't relax until they'd walked out into the sunlight. "That was a sad, bitter man," she murmured.

"And one who takes little trouble to hide it."

She shivered, then leaned against the side of his car. "I can understand why he made Anne nervous."

Matt cupped his hands around a match as he lit a cigarette. "Give me a basic feminine reaction."

"Passion, virility, primitive enough to fascinate." She shook her head as she stared up at the ribbons of windows. "For some women, that would be irresistible simply because it's rather frightening. A woman like Anne Trulane would've seen him as one of her dark closets and stayed away." With a short laugh, she dragged a hand through her hair. "I'm not a psychiatrist, Matthew, but I think a certain kind of woman would be drawn to a man like Brewster. I don't believe Anne Trulane would've been."

Letting out a long breath, she turned to him. "It's my turn to write a scenario."

"Let's hear it."

"Brewster's in love with her—or thinks he is, it wouldn't matter with a man like him. He tells Anne, asks her to leave Louis for him. How would she feel? Frightened, appalled. A little flattered perhaps."

He cocked a brow, intrigued. "Flattered?"

"She was a woman," Laurel said flatly. "Young, unsophisticated." She glanced back up at the windows, thinking of Brewster. "Yes, I believe she might have felt all three emotions. It confuses her, he pressures her. He's very intense, dramatic. She loves her husband, but this is something she doesn't know how to cope with. She can't even write her sister about it."

Matt nodded, watching her. "Go on."

"Suppose Brewster contacts her, demands to see her. Maybe he even threatens to confront Louis. She wouldn't have wanted that. Louis's approval and trust are important to her. Anne had to know about his first wife. So…"

Laurel's eyes narrowed as she tried to picture it. "She agrees to see him, meets him outside, late, while Louis is working. They argue because she won't leave Louis. He's a physical man." She remembered his strong fingers on the pencil. "He's convinced himself she wants him but is afraid to leave. He drags her away from the house, away from the light. She's terrified now, of him, of the dark. She breaks away and runs, but it's dark and she's in the swamp before she realizes it. She's lost. Brewster either can't find her or doesn't try. And then…"

"Interesting," Matt murmured before he flicked his cigarette away. "And, I suppose, as plausible as anything else. I wish we had those damn letters," he said suddenly. "There must be something there or they wouldn't've been taken."

"Whatever it was, we won't find it there now."

Matt nodded, staring past her. "I want to get into that swamp, look around."

Laurel felt the shudder and repressed it. "Tonight?"

"Mmmm."

She supposed she'd known it was bound to come down to this. Resigned, she blew the hair out of her eyes. "Let's go get some mosquito repellent."

He grinned and ran a finger down her nose. "Only one of us has to go. You stay home and keep a light burning in the window."

The brow went up, arrogant, haughty. "My story, Bates. I'm going; you can tag along if you want."

"Our story," he corrected. "God knows if there'll be anything in there but a bunch of filthy insects and soggy ground."

And snakes, Laurel thought. She swallowed, tasting copper. "We'll have to see, won't we? Matthew, we're running out of angles."

They stared at each other, frowning. Dead end—for now.

"Let's get some lunch," Laurel suggested as she swung around to get into the car. "And get back to the paper before we're both out of a job."

Chapter 7

Laurel spent over an hour with Matt in the newspaper morgue, going through files and crosschecking until her neck ached. With luck, the *Herald* would be on computers within the year. Laurel might miss the ambience of the cavernous morgue with the smell of dust and old paper, but she wouldn't miss the inconvenience. Some of the staff might grumble about having to learn the tricks of a terminal, the codes, the ways and means of putting in and taking out information at the punch of a button. She promised herself, as she rubbed at a crick in the back of her neck, she wouldn't be one of them.

"Brewster made page two with his fists," Laurel murmured as she scanned the story. "Two years ago last April." She glanced up briefly. "No one's memory's quite like Grandma's."

"She mentioned a sister."

"That's right. His sister'd been seeing a man who apparently liked his bourbon a bit too well. He'd seen her in a bar with another man and made a scene—tried to drag her out. Brewster was there. It took roughly ten men to pull him off, and before they did, he'd broken a couple of tables, a mirror, three of the guy's ribs, his nose and jaw and his own hand."

Matt lifted a brow at her cool recital of the violence. "Charged?"

"Assault headed the list," Laurel told him. "Ended up paying a fine when his…ah…opponent wouldn't press charges." She scrawled a note on her pad. "Apparently once Brewster's temper is lost, it's lost. I think I'll see if I can trace the sister. He might have talked to her about Anne."

"Mmm-hmm."

She glanced over to see Matt scribbling quickly in his own book. "What've you got?"

"Speculation," he murmured, then rose. "I have a few calls to make myself."

"Matthew," Laurel began as they started down the corridor, "weren't you the one who had all the big talk about sharing?"

He smiled at her, then pushed the button for the elevator. "After I make the calls."

"Make up your own rules as you go along?" she muttered when they stepped inside the car.

He looked down at her, remembering her passion in his arms, the vulnerability in her eyes. Her innocence. "I might just have to."

Laurel felt the quick chill race up her spine and stared straight ahead. "Let's stick with the story, Bates."

"Absolutely." Grinning, he took her arm as the elevator opened. They walked into the city room and separated.

Reporters have to get used to rude replies, no replies, runarounds. Laurel dealt with all three as she dialed number after number in an attempt to trace Kate Brewster. When she finally reached her, Laurel had to deal with all three again.

Brewster's sister flatly refused to discuss the barroom brawl and had little to say about her brother. At the mention of Anne Trulane, Laurel sensed a hesitation and caught a slight inflection—fear?—in Kate's voice as she claimed she didn't know anyone by that name.

Laurel found herself dealing with another hazard reporters face. An abrupt dial tone in the ear. Glancing up, she saw Matt cradling his own phone between his shoulder and ear as he made notes. At least one of us is getting somewhere, she thought in disgust as she rose to perch on the corner of his desk. Though she tried, it wasn't possible to read his peculiar type of shorthand upside down. Idly, she picked up the foam cup that held his cooling coffee and sipped. When she heard him mention the name Elise Trulane, she frowned.

What the hell's he up to? Laurel wondered as he easily ignored her and continued to take notes. Checking up on Elise...he's hung up on the similarity in looks, she decided. What does a runaway first wife have to do with a dead second one? As an uncomfortable thought raced into her mind, Laurel's eyes darted to Matt's. *Revenge?* But that would be madness. Louis wasn't—Louis couldn't... From the way he returned the look, she realized Matt read her thoughts while she wasn't able to penetrate his. Deliberately, she turned away to stare into Don Ballinger's office. The information they'd given their editor might have been sketchy, but it had been enough to give them the go-ahead.

Matt hung up and tapped his pencil on the edge of his desk. "What'd you get?"

"Zero, unless you count the impression that Anne Trulane's name made Brewster's sister very nervous. And another impression that she treads very carefully where her brother's concerned. What're you up to, Matthew?"

He ran the pencil through his hands, but the gesture had none of the nervous passion and energy that Brewster's had. His hands were lean, not elegant like Louis's, she thought, or violent like Brewster's. They were capable and clever and strong—just as he was. Disturbed, she shifted her gaze to his face. It was becoming a habit for thoughts of him to get in the way of what they had to do.

"Matthew?" she repeated as he looked beyond her.

"It seems the two Mrs. Trulanes had one or two things more in common than looks," he began. He dropped the pencil on his desk and drew out a cigarette. "They each had only one relative. In Elise's case, it's an aunt. I just spoke with her."

"Why?"

"Curiosity." He blew out a stream of smoke as a reporter behind them swore and hung up his own phone. "She describes her niece as a shy, quiet girl. Apparently Elise loved Heritage Oak, and unlike Anne, had already begun to take over the position of lady of the manor. She enjoyed the planning, the entertaining, had ideas for redecorating. The aunt was astonished when Elise ran off with Louis's brother—hasn't seen or heard from her since. She thought Elise was devoted to her husband."

"So did everyone else," Laurel commented. "Things like that do happen, Matthew, without anyone on the outside being aware. I don't imagine Elise would've told her aunt or anyone else that she was having an affair with Charles."

"Maybe not. There is something I find interesting," he murmured, keeping his eyes on Laurel's. "Elise inherited fifty thousand dollars on her twenty-first birthday. She turned twenty-one the month after she left Heritage Oak. The money," he said slowly, "was never claimed."

Laurel stared at him while ideas, answers, spun through her mind. "Maybe she—she might've been afraid to claim it thinking Louis could trace her."

"Fifty thousand buys a lot of courage."

"I don't see what digging into Elise's business has to do with Anne."

His eyes were very calm, very direct. "Yes, you do." She looked pale again, drained as she had that morning. Smothering an oath, Matt rose. "It's something to think about," he said briskly. "For now, we'd better concentrate on what we have to do tonight. Let's go home. We can catch a couple of hours' rest before we have to get ready."

"All right." She didn't want to argue, and though it was cowardly, she didn't want to think about what he'd just told her. There'd been enough that day. If she was to win out over her emotions, she needed the time to do it.

Matt didn't press her, but made easy, innocuous conversation on the drive home. He was good at falling back on a relaxed style to conceal his inner thoughts and feelings. It was one of his greatest professional weapons, and personal defenses. If he was furious with Laurel's automatic and unflagging defense of Louis Trulane, it wasn't apparent. If he harbored frustrating, near-violent urges to take her to some dark, private place until she forgot Louis Trulane existed, he didn't show it. His voice was calm, his driving smooth. His muscles were tight.

"A nap," Laurel said as they left his car to cross the courtyard, "sounds like heaven. It's been a long two days."

A long year, he thought as needs crawled in him. "And it's going to be a long night," he said easily.

She smiled at him for the first time since they'd left the *Herald*. "What time do we go on safari?"

"Midnight's the accepted hour, I believe." He touched the tips of her hair, then started up the steps.

"Garlic doesn't work against ghosts, does it?" Laurel mused. "No silver bullets, wooden stakes. What does?"

"Common sense."

She gave a windy sigh. "No romance."

At the top of the steps, he grinned at her. "Wanna bet?"

Laughing, she bent to pick up a wrapped box at the base of her door. "I don't remember ordering anything."

"From Jerry, no doubt—a box of number-two pencils."

She tried to glare at him and failed. "Midnight, Bates." After a brief search, she found her keys and unlocked the door. With a final arch look, she closed the door in his face.

His grin faded as he started down to his own apartment. The woman was driving him crazy. She had to be blind not to see it, he thought as he jabbed his key into the lock. Maybe he'd been too cautious. As he walked into the kitchen, Matt stripped his shirt over his head and tossed it aside. Then again, it had taken him weeks to get used to the fact that he'd been struck by lightning the first time she'd lifted those dark green eyes and looked at him.

At that point, he'd told himself it was impossible, the same way he'd told himself it was impossible for him to lose his head over the neatly framed photograph Curt had put on their shared desk in their college dorm.

"My sister," Curt had said in his abstracted way. "Runs copy at my father's paper during the summer. Guess you'd know about things like that."

The words hadn't registered because Matt had to concentrate on just breathing. There he'd been—a senior in college, a man who'd already seen and worked his way through more than many men do in a lifetime—rooted to the spot with one of the shirts he'd been unpacking dangling from his hand, head swimming over a girl who couldn't have been more than fifteen. Impossible.

Matt grabbed some orange juice from the refrigerator and chugged straight from the bottle. He'd gotten over that first…whatever it had been quickly enough. Or he'd told himself he had. But when William Armand had written him, all those years later, mentioning his relationship to Matt's senior-year college roommate and offering a position on the *Herald,* Matt hadn't hesitated. And he hadn't asked himself why.

It would've helped, he thought as he tossed the empty bottle in the trash, if he'd found a slow brain underneath that fabulous face. Or a bland or too-sweet personality. It would've helped if he hadn't sat next to her for a full year knowing she was everything he'd ever wanted.

He intended to have her, though her innocence urged him toward a traditional courtship—quiet dinners, candlelight, a gentle touch. Matt felt the stir of desire, and swore. He hoped he had the control he was going to need.

He intended to have her, though the difference in their backgrounds sometimes reared up to mock him. He'd already pushed his way through a lot of doors; now he had to make sure his luck held.

He was going to have her.

Matt stuck his hands in his pockets and headed for the shower. And he heard her scream.

Later, he wouldn't remember bursting out of his own apartment and rushing to hers. He'd remember hearing her scream again, and again, but he wouldn't remember beating on her door and finally, in desperation, knocking it in. What he would remember, always, was the way she'd looked, standing frozen with her hands at her own throat, her face like parchment and her eyes terrified.

"Laurel!" He grabbed her, spinning her around and into him where she stood in his arms, rigid as a stone. "What? What is it?"

He could feel the beat of her heart. Was it possible for a heart to beat that fast? Her skin was like ice, dampened by a sheen of sweat, but she didn't tremble. Not yet. "The box," she whispered. "In the box."

With one hand still on her arm, he turned and looked into the box on the table. The oath ripped out under his breath, pungent. "It's all right, Laurel. It's dead, it can't hurt you." His body trembled with fury as he lifted a portion of the copperhead from the box. "It can't hurt you now," he repeated, turning back to see her staring, transfixed at what he held in his hand. Sweat pearled on her forehead. Through her parted lips, her breath came harsh and quick.

"Matthew...please."

Without a word, he covered the box and carried it from the apartment. He returned—twenty, thirty seconds later—to find her leaning, palms down on the table, head lowered, weeping. He still didn't speak as he picked her up to carry her to the sofa and cradle her like a baby. Then the trembling started.

Five minutes...ten, and he said nothing, only holding her as she wept into his bare shoulder and shuddered. She seemed so small. Even when he'd seen those flashes of vulnerability he would never have imagined her like this—totally helpless, without the slimmest defense against anything or anyone. As he held her close, Matt promised himself when he found out who'd sent the box, he'd make them pay for it.

Safe. She knew she was safe now, though the fear kept threatening to bubble up again—that awful, strangling fear that couldn't be described but felt only. She could feel his heartbeat under her hand, and the warm flesh. He was holding her, and the world would settle again.

"I'm sorry," she managed, but continued to cling to him.

"No, don't." He kissed her hair, then stroked it.

"It's always been like that. I was bitten once. I can't remember it, or being sick, but I can't, I just can't handle—"

"It's all right. It's gone now, don't think about it anymore." The trembling had nearly stopped, but he could feel the occasional spasm that passed through her. Her breath still came in hitches. His skin was damp from her tears. He wanted to make her forget—he wanted to get his hands on whoever had done this to her. "Let me get you a brandy."

"No." She said it too quickly, and the hands against his chest balled into fists. "Just hold me," she murmured, hating the weakness, needing his strength.

"As long as you want." He heard her sigh, felt her fingers relax. The minutes passed again, long and silent so that he thought she slept. Her breathing had evened, her heartbeat slowed and she was warm again. He knew if she'd needed it, he could have held her just so for days.

"Matthew..." His name came on a sigh as she tilted her head back to look at his face. Her eyes were still puffy, her skin was still pale. He had to fight the wave of emotion to keep his fingers from tightening on her. "Don't go."

"No." He smiled and traced a finger down her cheek. Her skin was still damp, still warm from her weeping. "I won't go."

Laurel caught his hand in hers and pressed it to her lips. Matt felt something wash over him, warm and sweet, that he didn't yet recognize as tenderness. She saw it move in his eyes.

This was what she'd been waiting for, Laurel realized. This was what she'd needed, wanted, refused to consider. If he would ask her now—but he wouldn't, she knew it. The asking would have to come from her.

"Make love with me," she whispered.

"Laurel..." Her words stirred him, impossibly. How could he take her now, when she was utterly without defense? Another time, oh, God, another time, he'd have given anything to hear her say those words. "You should rest," he said inadequately.

He's not sure of himself, she realized. Strange, she'd thought he was always so sure. Perhaps his feelings for her were as confusing as hers for him. "Matthew, I know what I'm asking." Her voice wasn't strong, but it was clear. "I want you. I've wanted you for a long time." She slipped her hand up over his chest and neck to touch his cheek. "Love me—now." She brought her lips to his as if quietly coming home.

Perhaps he could have resisted his own need. Perhaps. But he couldn't resist hers. He drew her closer with a moan, gathering her against him as his mouth told her everything in silence. She was boneless, so pliant it seemed she might simply melt out of his arms like a mirage he'd traveled to over endless, impossible days and nights only to find it vanished. He deepened the kiss with something like panic, but she remained, warm and real against him.

Her mouth tasted of woman, not of visions, so warm and sweet he had to fight the urge to devour it. Her tastes, that small hand that remained on his cheek, the airy scent, merged together to make his senses swim. He couldn't afford the luxury now, not this first time.

Matt buried his face at her throat, struggling to hold on to some slim thread of control, but his lips wouldn't be still. He had to taste her. His hands roamed up and over subtle curves. He had to touch her.

"Laurel..." He slipped her loosened blouse off one

shoulder so that his lips could wander there. "I want you—I ache with it."

Even as he told himself to move slowly, he was drawing the blouse from her. She shifted to help him, murmuring, then only sighed.

"Not here." He closed his eyes as her lips brushed his throat. "Not here," he said again, and rose with her still in his arms. This time she'd let herself be led. She rested her head on his shoulder as he carried her into the bedroom.

The lights slanted through wooden shutters. It highlighted his eyes, so suddenly intense, as he laid her on the bed. "I won't hurt you."

She smiled and reached for him. "I know."

The mattress sighed as he lay beside her. With her eyes just open, she could see the play of light while his lips traced over her face. It was so easy. She should have known that with him it would be so easy. Running her palms, then her fingertips over his back, she felt the ripple of muscle, the taut skin, the strength. This had attracted her from the beginning, and she had struggled to ignore it. Now, she could take her fill.

He caressed her with his lips. Caressed. She hadn't known such a thing was possible with lips alone. He showed her. Her skin softened, then tingled from it.

Lazily…thoroughly…

His mouth moved over her throat and shoulders while his hands tarried nowhere but in her hair. A gentle nip, a soft flick of tongue and she was floating.

She heard the bluesy sound of a trumpet from outside. The sound drifted into the room to mix in her mind with Matt's murmurs. He nuzzled into her throat so that she turned her head to give him more freedom and breathed in the sweet scent of vanilla from her bedside candle. She made some sound, a long, low sigh, but had no way of knowing that this alone had his pulses hammering.

His lips pressed onto hers with the edge of desperation under the gentleness. She felt it, yielded to it, as she drew him yet closer.

When he touched her, a lean, hard hand over the silk of her camisole, her sigh became a moan. She arched, feeling the aching fullness in her breasts she'd never experienced. Needs sprang up from everywhere, all at once, to pulse under her skin. But he wouldn't be rushed—by her or himself. His fingers trailed, aroused, but stopped just short of demand. He wanted the demand to come from her own needs, not his.

Slowly, inch by inch, he drew the swatch of silk down to her waist, finding her skin no less luxurious. With openmouthed kisses he explored it, listening to the shuddering sound of her breathing that meant the loss of control. He wanted that from her, for her, while he desperately hung on to his own. When his mouth closed over her breast, the muscles in his back relaxed. God, she was sweet.

While Laurel went wild beneath him, he lingered, drawing out their mutual pleasure, drinking in her tastes and textures. He caught her nipple between his teeth, holding it prisoner, tormenting it with the play of his tongue until he knew she was utterly steeped in passion, in the dark, mindless pleasures. Then he went on.

She knew only sensations now—there were no thoughts, no sane thoughts, as flames leaped inside her and fire shivered along her skin. The movements of her body were instinctive, offering, pleading. His lips continued to roam over her as he slipped the rest of her clothes from her. The feel of hot flesh against hot flesh had her gasping. With each trembling breath she took, the scent they made together overwhelmed her. Intimate, earthy. Glorious.

Her body was molten—fluid, fiery—but she was helpless. Whatever he wanted from her he could have taken in whatever way he chose. The choices she had made—first to resist him, then to accept him—no longer applied. There were no choices in this world of dazzling light and radiant heat. Her body craved. Her spirit hungered. She was his.

He knew it. And, knowing, fought to remember her innocence when her passion was tearing at his control. She was agile and slim, and at the moment as abandoned as a sleek young animal. Her hands sought him without hesitation, her lips raced to take whatever he'd allow. With his breath rasping, his blood pounding, he struggled to keep the pace as he'd begun. Easy.

When he touched her, she jolted beneath him, shuddering and shuddering with the first peak. Through his own desire, Matt could feel her stunned, helpless delight. No one else had given her this, no one else had taken this from her. No one.

He buried his face at her throat, groaning. So moist, so warm. So ready. He shifted onto her. "Laurel…"

Suspended on shaft after shaft of sensation, she opened her eyes and looked into his. If her body was fluid, his was tight as a bowstring. Over the waves of passion came one clear certainty. He thought only of her. She couldn't speak, drowned by needs and the sharply sweet newness of love just discovered. Laurel drew his mouth down to hers.

At the touch of her lips, she gave up her innocence as easily, as gently, as sliding down a long, cool bank toward a warm river.

She slept. Matt lay beside her and watched the light through the window slats go from white to rose to gray before the moonlight drifted thinly in. His body was exhausted, from the strain of control, from the ultimate loss of it, but his mind wouldn't rest.

There'd been times over the last months when he'd nearly convinced himself that once he'd had her, the lingering need would pass. Now, as he lay in her bed, with moonlight slanting across her body, with her head nestled against his shoulder, he knew the need would remain as basic and essential as the need for air.

Physically, he knew, she was his. He could touch off her passion, exploit her needs and keep her. It wasn't enough. He wondered if he could draw out her emotions, her love, with the same deliberate care with which he'd drawn out her desire. He wondered if he had the patience he'd need.

Turning his head, he looked down at her as she slept against him. Her skin was like porcelain with the dusky lashes shadowing her cheeks. Delicate… He traced a finger down her cheekbone. Yes, she had delicacy, which at times made him feel like an awkward boy staring at pastries in a bakery window. But she had verve, and energy and ambition. These he understood, as they matched his own.

Partners, he thought, and his eyes glinted with something between amusement and determination. Damn right they were. Bending down, he crushed his mouth to hers.

Head swimming, body throbbing, Laurel came awake on a wave of passion. Her skin leaped under his hands as they raced over her, taking and demanding with a speed that left her giddy. She moaned against his mouth, tossed so quickly from gentle sleep to ruthless desire that she could only cling. He set the pace again, but it was nothing like the first time. She catapulted from peak to peak, swept along, driven, until he took her with all the urgency he'd blocked out before.

Spent, stunned, she waited for her breath to return as he lay over her, his face buried in her hair. Should she have known it would be like this? Could she? More than anything, that quick, desperate loving showed her just how careful he'd been with her the first time.

I love him, she thought as she tightened her arms around him. Wouldn't that knock him off his feet? With a wry smile, she toyed with the hair that curled over his neck. Matthew Bates, I'm going to play a very careful hand with you—and I'm going to win.

She gave a long, luxurious sigh. Did loving make the body feel so wonderfully lazy? "Were you trying to tell me it's time to get up?" she murmured.

Lifting his head, he grinned at her. "I don't think so."

"This wasn't supposed to happen."

"Yes, it was." He kissed her brow lightly, lingeringly. "We're just a little ahead of schedule."

Her brow arched, but the haughty gesture had to compete with the soft, just-loved flush of her skin. "Whose schedule?"

"Ours," he said easily. "Ours, Laurel."

It was difficult to argue with something that seemed so reasonable. Laurel linked her hands at the base of his neck and tilted her head. "You look good, Bates."

Amusement flickered in his eyes. "Yeah?"

"Yeah." She ran her tongue over her teeth. "I guess I'm getting used to those beachboy looks and that Yankee speech pattern. Or maybe—" she caught her bottom lip between her teeth, but the laughter shone in her eyes "—maybe I just like your body. You work out?"

He braced himself comfortably on his elbows. "Now and again."

Experimentally, Laurel pinched his bicep. "Weights?"

"No."

"Well, I've never cared for obvious muscles." She ran a hand down to his wrist, then back again. "You seem to be in good enough shape to handle our plans for the evening."

He nipped at her bottom lip. "Which are?"

"A little hike through the swamp."

He rubbed his lips over hers easily, while his mind did some quick calculations. He could distract her, wait until she slept again, then go without her. "I was thinking we could…postpone that."

"Were you?" Though her body began to soften, her mind was much too sharp. "Until you could sneak out there on your own?"

He should've known better. "Laurel…" He slid a hand up to her breast.

"Oh, no." She shifted quickly until she lay on top of him. "You can forget the idea of going out there without me, Bates. We're a team."

"Listen." He took her firmly by the shoulders while her hair dipped down to brush his. "There isn't any need for you to go. It's just a matter of poking around anyway. It'll be faster and easier with only one of us."

"Then you stay here." She kissed him briskly and sat up.

"Damn it, Laurel. Think."

"About what?" she tossed back as she rose, naked, to rummage through her drawers.

"No one left a nasty little box at my door."

She bit down hard on her lip, then turned with a T-shirt and a pair of panties in her hand. "No, they didn't," she said calmly enough. "They left it at mine, obviously for a reason. We're making someone nervous, Matthew. And that someone is damn well going to have to deal with me."

He looked at her, small and straight with her naked skin glowing in the moonlight. At the moment, she looked perfectly capable of avenging herself. "Okay, tough guy," he drawled as he swung his legs out of bed. "When we find out who it was, you can go a few rounds. In the meantime, you might remember there're snakes in that swamp—and they're not dead in a box."

He knew he'd been deliberately cruel, he'd meant to be. But when he saw her fingers tighten on the shirt she held, he cursed himself.

"I won't look." Jaw set, she wriggled into the panties. "You'd better get dressed."

"Stubborn, hardheaded, obstinate," he began furiously.

"Yeah." Jerking the shirt over her head, Laurel glared at him. "But not stupid. Whoever dropped that thing at my door wanted me to back off. That points to Brewster or—or the Trulanes," she managed after a moment. "If they wanted us to back off, there's a reason, and the reason might just be in that swamp."

"You won't get any argument on that from me," he said evenly. "But it doesn't follow that you have to go."

"If I let that kind of threat steer me away, I'll have to turn in my press badge. Nobody's going to put me in that position." She gave him a long, level look. "Nobody."

Matt's temper struggled toward the surface, then subsided. She was right—that was one point he couldn't get around. In silence, he pulled on his jeans. "I've got to get a shirt, and a flashlight," he said briefly. "Be ready in ten minutes."

"All right." She made a business of searching through her drawers until she was sure he'd gone.

Laurel pressed her fingers to her eyes and let the fear out. It was a sticky, cloying sensation that rolled over her and left her light-headed. As it ebbed, she rested her hands against the dresser and just concentrated on breathing. She had to go—now more than before she'd looked in that box. If a threat wasn't answered, then it was buckled in to. If there was a threat, it meant someone was afraid.

Anne Trulane had been afraid of the swamp. Laurel pulled on worn jeans with hands that were almost steady again. She understood that kind of fear, the kind that has no true explanation but simply is. Laurel didn't believe Anne had voluntarily walked into that dark, secret place any more than she herself would voluntarily walk into a snake exhibit. The full certainty of it hadn't struck until tonight, with the burgeoning of her own fear. And, by God, she was going to prove it.

Matt... Laurel switched on the bedroom light and began to search through the disorder of her closet for boots. He was only being unreasonable because he was concerned for her. While she could appreciate it, she couldn't allow it. Love might urge her to give in to him on this one thing—but then how many other things might she give in to once she started?

However he felt about her, she mused as she located one boot, he felt about her because of the way she was. The best thing she could do for both of them was to stay that way.

Swearing at her own disorganization, Laurel shouldered her way into the closet for the other boot.

When he returned, Matt found her sitting on the floor of her room, fighting with knotted laces. He was wearing an outfit very similar to hers, and his more customary amiable expression. He'd calmed down considerably by rationalizing that she'd be safer with him in any case—and by promising himself he'd watch Laurel like a hawk every moment they were in the swamps of Heritage Oak.

"Having a problem?"

"I don't know how this happened," she muttered, tugging on the laces. "It's like somebody crawled in there, tied these in knots, then buried the boot under a pile of junk."

He glanced at her littered floor. "I'm disillusioned. I always thought you were very precise and organized."

"I am—at work. Damn!" She scowled at a broken nail, then fought with the laces again. "There—now I just need a flashlight." Springing lightly to her feet, she dashed past him and into the kitchen.

"You know, Laurellie," Matt commented as he followed her. "A few more molecules missing and you wouldn't have a seat in those pants."

"It'll be dark."

He patted her bottom. "Not that dark."

Grinning, she pulled a flashlight from the kitchen drawer and tested it. "Then you'll have to walk in front and keep your mind off my anatomy."

"I'd rather watch your back pockets jiggle." Swinging an arm around her, he walked to the door.

"They don't jiggle." She stopped, frowning at the splintered wood. "How did that—"

"You were too busy screaming to open the door," Matt said easily, nudging her outside. "I called the super about it."

"You broke it down?" Laurel turned to stare at him.

He grinned at her expression before he tugged her down the stairs. "Don't make doors like they used to."

He broke it down. The thought of it stunned her, sweetly. At the foot of the stairs she stopped and wrapped her arms around his waist. "You know, Matthew, I've always had a soft spot for knights on white chargers."

He framed her face with his hands before he kissed her. "Even tarnished ones?"

"Especially."

Chapter 8

Matt parked his car in the shadow of the wall that encircled the Trulane estate. The moment he cut the engine, silence fell. He could sense, though she climbed from the car as he did, Laurel's regret over the one thing they'd carefully not talked about. Trespassing, in secret, on what belonged to Louis. He also knew it was something that would continue to remain unsaid. He slipped his flashlight, base first, into his back pocket.

"I'll give you a leg up first."

Nodding, Laurel placed a foot in his cupped hands and reached for the top of the wall. She shinnied up nimbly, then, bracing herself on her stomach, reached a hand down for his. The grip was firm and dry, holding briefly until they lowered themselves on the other side.

"Somehow, I think you've done this sort of thing

before," she murmured, dusting her hands on the back of her jeans.

He grinned. "Let's just say I've had to scale a few walls in my career."

"And not all metaphorical," she concluded.

"You'll force me to mention that you went up and over like a veteran yourself."

Laurel took one brief look around, letting her gaze linger on the shadow of the house in the distance. "I don't suppose you've considered the legal repercussions if we're caught."

It was as close as she'd come, he knew, to speaking of Louis. Matt took her hand, drawing her away from the wall. "Let's not get caught," he said simply.

They moved, as quietly as shadows themselves, over the north lawn. Flashlights weren't needed here. The light of the half-moon was thin, but clear enough to guide the way. The air was still, but far from silent. Night birds rustled in the trees, their whisperings punctuated now and again by the hoot of an owl. Overlaying all was the incessant music of crickets.

Fireflies glimmered with their sporadic gold-toned light. It smelled thickly of summer blossoms and green grass.

Already Laurel could see the gloomy silhouette of the edge of the swamp. The aversion was so ingrained she had to force herself not to hesitate. But her fingers curled tightly around Matt's. His palm was cool and dry against hers.

Doesn't he feel it? she wondered as the chill raced over her skin. Doesn't he feel the *darkness* of the place? It held secrets best left alone—secrets that bred in the soggy grasses. She shuddered as the lawn gave way to it.

"It's a place," Matt said quietly. "It's just a place, Laurel."

"It's evil," she said, so simply he felt a tremor of unease. Then she stepped under the first overhang of trees.

Determination made her force back the fear. Though her fingers remained in his, their grip lightened. "Hard to believe," she began in an easier voice, "even driven by love—or lust—that one of the Trulane women would have picked this place to cheat on her husband. I think her name was Druscilla."

Matt gave a choked laugh as he pulled out his light. "Maybe Druscilla had a thing for humidity and mosquitoes. Now..." He didn't switch the light on, but looked behind him where the outline of the house could just be glimpsed through the trees. "I'd say this is about the most direct spot where someone would enter the swamp if they were coming from the house."

Laurel followed his gaze. "Agreed."

"Then it follows that Anne would most likely have come in somewhere around this point."

"It follows."

"Okay, let's go see what we can find. Stick close."

"An unnecessary warning, Matthew," Laurel said loftily as she unpocketed her flashlight. "If you feel something crawling up your back, it's just me."

They hadn't gone more than three yards when the thick, fat leaves dimmed the moonlight. The shadow of the house was lost behind the tangled hedge of other shadows. Already the wild cane sprang up to block what was within, and what was outside, the swamp.

The twin beams of their flashlights cut a path through the dark.

It was a world of clinging dampness, of shadows and whispering sounds that made the flesh creep. Even the smell was damp, with the ripe odor of rotting vegetation. Matt began to understand why Anne Trulane might have been terrorized in there. He wouldn't care to lose his way, alone, in the dark. But he wondered why she'd only gone deeper rather than turning back. Blind panic? He scowled at the crude, overgrown path. Maybe.

She should've gotten the hell out.

"Doesn't make sense," he muttered.

Laurel shone her light off the path where something rustled. Her fingers closed over Matt's wrist and let the light, steady pulsebeat soothe her. "What doesn't?"

"Why didn't she get out?"

Carefully, Laurel turned her light back to the path. It was probably only a possum, not every sound meant snakes. She remembered, uncomfortably, that black bears had often been seen in the northern, forested part of the swamp. "Whatever theory we go by, Matthew, Anne was frightened in here. She panicked, lost her sense of perspective."

"Are you frightened?" He glanced down to where her fingers dug into his wrist.

"No." Sending him a rueful smile, Laurel loosened her hold. "No, I'm way past fear, closing in on terror."

"Could you get out of here?"

"Well, I—" She broke off, seizing his hand again. There was a time and place for dignity—and this wasn't it. "You're not leaving me in here, Bates."

"What would you do if I did?"

"I'd murder you the minute I got out."

Grinning, he took her arm as they began to walk again. "How?"

"Poison, I imagine, it's the slowest, most painful way."

"No, how would you get out?"

"I'd—" She swallowed on the notion of having to find her way out alone, then turned around. Shadows, rustling, and the cloying smell of wet earth and rotted grass were all around. There was quicksand, she knew, to the east and to the southwest. "I'd head that way in a dead run," she said, pointing, "hang a right at that stump and keep on going."

"And you'd be out in five minutes," he murmured. He turned his face back to hers. The moonlight caught in his eyes, glinting. "Why did she keep going deeper?"

If she tried to think like Anne, Laurel realized, she'd end up losing what courage she had and bolting. Dragging a hand through her hair, she tried to think coolly instead. "She'd been bitten—maybe she was sick, delirious."

"How fast does the poison work, I wonder." He shrugged, making a note to check on it if it became necessary. "It seems she'd've had time to get out, or at least get closer to the edge."

"They found her by the river, didn't they?"

"Yeah." He looked down at her again. "Dead center. When we were searching the place, we'd come across her tracks now and again where the ground was wet enough to hold them. There didn't seem to be any pattern."

Blind panic, he thought again. Yet she hadn't been as frozen as Laurel had been that afternoon. She'd been running, in what had appeared to be a random flight, deeper into what she feared most…or running away from something she found more terrifying.

Laurel jolted as the bushes beside them rustled. Matt aimed his light and sent a raccoon scurrying back into the shadows.

"I hate making an ass of myself," she mumbled as her heart slipped back out of her throat. "Let's go on." Annoyed at the blow to her pride, she started ahead of him.

They moved in silence, going deeper. Laurel kept her flashlight trained on the uneven ground to guide their way while Matt shone his from side to side, searching for something neither of them could have named. But they'd both followed hunches before.

"Don't laugh," Laurel ordered, coming to an abrupt halt.

"Okay," he said amiably.

She hesitated, gnawing at her lip. "I mean it, Bates, don't laugh."

"Cross my heart?" he ventured.

"I feel like—something's watching."

"Another raccoon?"

"Matthew—"

"Relax." He cupped the base of her neck in his hand and rubbed, deliberately treating it lightly because he'd felt that trickle between his shoulder blades, as well. Ghost stories, he told himself. He was letting Laurel's feelings about the place get to him.

If he'd believed such things he'd have said there was something evil in the twisting shadows, something that would shrink from the sunlight. But he didn't believe in such things. Evil, when it came, came from the human element.

"Too many people have died here," she said, and shuddered.

He touched her neck again, and his hand, his voice were gentle. "Do you want to go back?"

Oh, God, yes, she thought, but squared her shoulders. "No, let's go on. You can smell the river now."

As they came near the banks, she could smell the wet leaves, vegetation, but the river made no sound as it flowed slowly. Cypress trees made lumpy shadows. A few slivers of moonlight worked through the overhanging trees and fell palely on the water, but only made it seem darker. A frog plopped into the river as they approached.

There were alligators in there, Laurel thought, wrinkling her nose. Big ones.

"It was here." Matt shone his light on the ground. "Laurel, could you still get out of this place if you had to?"

As she followed the play of his light, she was remembering the picture from the police file. Clamping down on her lip, she forced the image from her mind. "Yes, the way we came's the easiest, I imagine, but almost any direction from here would get you out eventually."

"Yeah." He moved around, playing his light on the ground. "Strange that she picked the core of the swamp to give up." He swore in frustration. Nothing here, he thought, nothing here. What the hell had he expected to find? "I'd like to get my hands on those letters."

"Whoever took them would've destroyed them by now if there was anything in them to work with."

"I wonder if Susan—" He broke off as the beam of

his light picked up a glimmer. Bending, Matt worked a small piece of metal from the ground.

"What is it?"

"Looks like a broken piece of jewelry. Seen better days." Rising, he turned it over in his hands. "Anne's?"

Laurel took it from him, wiping away some of the caked-on dirt. "I don't know, a month in this place..." She shone her light on it as some nagging memory teased the back of her mind. "It looks like the front of a locket—expensive, look how intricate the carving is." The memory lunged toward the front of her mind, then retreated. Laurel shook her head in exasperation. "It's familiar," she murmured. "Maybe it was Aunt Ellen's—Louis could've given it to Anne after they were married."

"We might be able to check it out, for what it's worth." Taking it from her, he slipped it into his pocket. Frustrated, he shone his light to the right and down the bank of the river. "Stay here a minute, I want to get a closer look down there."

"For what?"

"If I knew, I wouldn't feel like I was chasing wild geese."

"I'll go with you."

"Laurel, it's a bog down there. You've been lucky avoiding snakes this far. Don't press your luck."

She remembered the water moccasins that swam in the river. With a gesture of indifference, she shrugged. "You've got two minutes, Bates. Any longer and I'm coming after you."

"Two minutes." He kissed her lightly. "Stay here."

"I'm not moving."

She watched the beam of his light as he walked

away, then made his slippery way down the bank. He didn't know what he was looking for, but she understood his need to do something. All they'd found so far were more questions, and a broken piece of jewelry.

She frowned again, thinking of it. A childhood memory? she wondered, pushing the hair away from her face. Had she seen that locket when it had been bright and clean—against a white dress? Laurel pressed her fingers to her temple as she tried to bring the image into focus. One of Aunt Ellen's lacy party dresses? Frustrated, she dropped her hand.

Another minute, Bates, she told him silently. Why was it the small night noises seemed to grow louder now that he wasn't standing beside her? She shifted uncomfortably as a bead of sweat trickled down her back, leaving a chill in its wake.

It's just this place, she told herself, refusing the urge to look over her shoulder. In an hour we'll be back home and I'll be able to laugh at how I stood here shivering in the heat and imagining goblins at my back. In an hour…

The soft rustle at her back had her stiffening. Damn raccoons, Laurel thought on a wave of self-disgust. She opened her mouth to call for Matt when an arm locked around her throat.

Shock registered first, seconds before her body reacted to it, or the abrupt lack of air. In an instinctive move of self-preservation, Laurel jabbed back with her elbow, only to meet empty space as she was shoved away. Her flashlight spun out of her hand as her body whooshed through wild cane. She landed hard, her head slamming back into the base of a cypress.

At the edge of the river, Matt saw the arch of light, then darkness where he'd left Laurel. He plunged up the bank, cursing the slick grass and shouting her name. When he saw her sprawled, his heart stopped—with the vivid picture of Anne Trulane leaping in his mind's eye. He grabbed her, not gently, and hauled her against him. At her moan, he began to breathe again.

"What the hell're you doing!" he demanded, rolling with the fury fear had given him.

"I'm having a concussion," she managed, and shook her head to clear it—a mistake as the ground tilted under her. "Someone pushed me—came up from behind." She reached gingerly to test the bump at the back of her head, then gripped Matt's shirtfront with sudden strength as he started to rise. "Oh, no, you're not leaving me here again."

Simmering with rage, straining at impotence, he settled beside her again. "All right, just sit a minute." He ran his fingers through her hair to lift her face to his. "Are you hurt?"

She saw the anger, the concern, the frustration in his eyes. "Not really." She smiled—her head was throbbing, but that was all. "Just a bump. It didn't knock me out; I just saw stars—not unlike the ones I saw the first time you kissed me."

That helped, she thought, feeling the grip of his fingers on her arm relax slightly. But that brooding look was still in his eyes as he searched her face.

"I shouldn't have left you alone."

"Matthew, if you're going to start being macho and guilty, I'll get cranky." Leaning forward, she kissed him. "Let's see if I can stand up."

With his hands cupping her armpits, he pulled her gently to her feet. No dizziness, she thought, waiting a moment. The throbbing was subsiding to an ache.

"It's okay, really," she said when he continued to study her face. "I've had worse bumps."

You won't have any more while I'm around, he swore to himself viciously, but smiled. "I won't make any remarks about hard heads. Now, what did you see—besides stars?"

"Nothing." She let out a frustrated breath. "I was so busy telling myself I wasn't going to be a fool that I wouldn't look around when I heard something rustling in the bushes. The next thing I knew someone had an arm around my throat. I hadn't even started defensive move 21-A when they pushed me into that tree. By the time the stars stopped exploding, you were here and they were gone."

Whatever grim thoughts of revenge worked in his mind, his touch was gentle as he felt the back of her head. "You'll have a bump," he said easily as he forced his jaw to unclench, "but the skin's not broken."

"There's good news."

Tilting her head back to his, he gave her one long, hard kiss. His hands were steady again, but his temper wasn't. "Sure you can walk?"

"If you mean as in out of here, absolutely. I lost my flashlight."

"Buy a new one," he advised as he picked up his own. "It went in the river."

"Oh, that's just great. I only bought it a month ago." She scowled over this as they started back the way they'd come. "Well, I guess we found something after all," she murmured.

"Yeah. Someone who knows what we're up to doesn't like it one damn bit. Lovelorn ghosts don't shove people into trees, do they, Laurel?"

"No." And she was thinking, as he was, that the house was close. The people in it knew the swamp.

They walked back in silence, each of them more cautious than before, listening to every sound, second-guessing the shadows. Matt kept Laurel at his side, his hand on hers until they walked into the clear. There wasn't the faintest glimmer of light from the house in the distance.

The lingering distaste for where they'd been clung to him even after they'd dropped on the other side of the wall. He wanted a shower—a long one.

Laurel didn't speak again until Heritage Oak was miles behind them.

"We'll have to talk to Louis and Marion again."

"I know." Matt punched in the car lighter. Maybe if he filled his lungs with smoke he'd stop tasting the air of the swamp. "Tomorrow."

Leaning back, Laurel closed her eyes. And tomorrow was soon enough to think about it. "I don't know about you, but I'm starving."

He turned his head to look at her. She was still a bit pale—but even that could've been the moonlight. Her voice was steady, her breathing calm. He hadn't sensed fear in her, not even when she'd been half-dazed and sprawled on the ground. Frustration, yes, annoyance with herself for being caught unaware. But no fear.

With her head back and the shadows dancing over her face, she reminded him forcibly of Olivia. Unique, indomitable, fascinating. Laughing, Matt grabbed her hand and pressed it to his lips.

"We'll order a pizza and take it back home."

Though she hadn't a clue what had lightened his mood so abruptly, Laurel went with it. "With everything," she demanded.

It was after two when Laurel pushed away from Matt's smoked-glass table, stuffed. She couldn't say his apartment wasn't what she'd expected because she'd had no idea just what to expect. She did know it showed an easy mode of living—deep, plump cushions, thick carpet, soothing colors all mixed together with a flair for style and a penchant for comfort.

There were neither framed newspapers on his walls nor Picassos, but a set of oils done by an artist she didn't recognize. Both were of New York, one a cityscape showing its elegance and glitz, the other a street scene with crumbling buildings and cracked sidewalks. Both were excellent in their way, and the contrasts intrigued her. She supposed, in his career there, he'd have seen both sides.

"I've reached my limit," she said when Matt started to slide another piece onto her plate.

"Big talk about eating it, box and all." Matt bit into the slice he'd offered her.

Picking up her wineglass, Laurel rose to wander the room. Her feet sank into the carpet. "I like your place. You like—" she wiggled her bare toes "—to be comfortable."

"Most people do." He watched as she wandered to his stereo to sort through his album collection.

"Mmmm. But not everyone makes an art out of it." Laurel set a record aside to study the paintings more closely. "These are very good," she commented. "I don't recognize the artist, but I have a feeling I'll be seeing his work again."

"He'd be glad to hear it." Matt picked up his own glass, studying her over the rim. The wine was heavy and sweet. "We grew up in the same neighborhood."

"Really?" Laurel tilted her head, even more interested. "Do you miss it? New York?"

Matt's gaze flicked up to the painting, then back to the wine in his glass. "No."

"But you carry it with you."

"We all carry our baggage around," he murmured, then got up to stick what remained of the pizza in the refrigerator.

Laurel frowned after him. What brought that on? she wondered, then looked back at the paintings. The same neighborhood, she mused, seeing the soiled streets and tired buildings. When he came out of the kitchen, she was still facing them. "You grew up here."

He didn't have to see which painting she was looking at to know what she meant. "Yeah." He pulled his shirt over his head as he walked. "I need a shower."

"Matthew." Laurel went after him, catching his arm outside the bathroom door. She recognized impatience and ignored it. "It was hard, wasn't it?"

"I survived," he said indifferently. "Not everyone does."

Her sympathy was automatic and reflected in her eyes, the touch of her hand on his arm, her voice. "Tell me about it."

"Just leave it."

She stared at him, the hurt unexpected and brutally sharp. Her step back was a retreat from it before she straightened her shoulders. "All right, I'm sorry.

Thanks for the pizza, Bates. I'll see you in the morning."

He took her arm to stop her. "Laurel, you know you can't stay in your place until the door's fixed."

She met his eyes calmly. "Not all of us needs locks and bolts, Matthew."

"Damn it—" He broke off, making a savage effort to keep his temper. He knew he was wound up, still tense from what had happened to her in the swamp, still dazed by what had happened between them in her bed. Emotions were crowding him, and he wasn't dealing with them well. "Listen, I grew up in a tough little neighborhood on the East Side. It has nothing to do with you. Nothing."

A dash of salt for the wound, Laurel thought as she stared up at him. "That's clear enough," she said evenly. "Let's just call it professional curiosity and leave it at that."

"Damn it, Laurel." He grabbed her by the shoulders when she started to leave again. "You're not staying in that place alone tonight."

"Don't you tell me what I'm going to do."

"I *am* telling you," he tossed back. "And for once you're going to *do* what you're told."

She gave him a cold, neutral look. "Take your hands off me."

He started to get angry, but even through his own anger he could see beneath hers to the hurt. On a sigh, he dropped his forehead to hers. "I'm sorry."

"You don't owe me an apology," she said carefully.

"I do." When he lifted his head, his eyes were dark and thoughtful. "I hurt you, I didn't mean to."

"No, it's all right." Without fuel, her temper vanished, leaving only a faint echo of the hurt. "I was prying."

"No, I—" Matt hesitated, then let it go. He wasn't ready to drag it all out and look at it again, not with Laurel. "I don't want to argue with you, Laurel. Look, it's late, we've both had enough to deal with today. I can't dig back there tonight."

Her arms went around him. Even if the anger had still lashed at her, she couldn't have stopped them. "No more questions tonight."

"Laurel…" He covered her offered mouth with his. The tension began to drain, degree by degree, as he filled himself with her. "Stay here," he murmured. "Stay with me."

With a sigh, content, accepting, she rested her head on his shoulder. "Do I get shower privileges?"

She heard his low laugh as he nuzzled at her throat. "Sure. But we have to double up. You've heard about the water shortage."

"No, not a word."

"Really?" He tugged her into the bathroom. "It's at a crisis stage. Let me tell you about it."

She was laughing as he drew her shirt over her head.

When she got out of the shower, Laurel was flushed and tingling. Clutching a towel at her breasts, she looked up at Matt. "I'm so impressed." When his grin tilted, she went on blandly, "With the fact that you're such a conservationist."

"Conservation is my life." He tugged the towel from her, smiling easily when she gasped. "Gotta cut back on the laundry too. You know how many gallons of water a washing machine uses?" His eyes swept down her, then up again. "Better get you into bed, you'll catch a chill."

Regally, she walked away, leaving Matt to admire the view. "I suppose turning on a light would go against your values."

"Civic duty," he corrected, then surprised her by grabbing her around the waist and tumbling onto the bed with her.

Winded, she glared up at him. "Now listen, Bates—"

He silenced her quickly, completely and effectively. He'd meant to tease her, continue the half torturous, half pleasurable game they'd begun under the cool spray of the shower. But her legs were tangled with his, her body yielding, and her mouth…

"Oh, God, Laurel, I need you." His mouth crushed back on hers with a savagery the night seemed to have worked on him.

He forgot patience, and she, the need for it. He forgot gentleness, and she, the need for it. His tongue dived deep into her mouth as if there were some taste, some hint of flavor he might be denied. But she would have denied him nothing. Her passion raced from tingling arousal to raging desire, and her mouth was as greedy, as insistent, as his. She was not to be seduced this time, or to be swept helplessly along, but to take as much as she gave.

She hadn't known passion could strip every remnant of civilization away, but she learned. Glorying in the abandon, she touched and tasted where she would with hands and lips that moved quickly, with no more patience than his. He smelled of the soap she'd lathered on him herself. The sharp, clean scent played with her senses, swam in her head while her needs delved in darker places.

They were only shadows in the bed, tangling, clinging, but their passion had substance and form. Perhaps the whispering threats of the past hours drove them both to take, and take hungrily, all that could be found between man and woman. Damp skin, thundering pulses, breathless moans. For both of them it was the moment, the heady present, that mattered. Yesterday and tomorrow were forgotten.

He knew he was rough, but control had vanished. Heat seemed to pour out of her, drawing him deeper and deeper into his own furious passion. Her body was as it had been when he'd first taken her hours—oh, God, had it only been hours?—before. Sleek and smooth and agile. But the change came from within. There was no pliancy in her now, but an urgency and demand that raced with his.

His lips rushed over her, running low on her stomach with hungry kisses. But his need to taste wasn't any stronger than her need to experience. She wanted all there was to have this time, everything he'd already given her and whatever secrets were left. She wanted to learn whatever desire had left to teach.

She opened for both of them, eager, urging him down until he found her. She arched, stunned and only more desperate at the play of his tongue. He whipped her up and over the first crest, never pausing, relentless, as she shuddered with her nails digging into his shoulders.

Wave after wave of heavy, molten pleasure swept her, but he continued as if he would keep her, keep them both, spinning on the very verge of fulfillment. There couldn't be so much. But even as the thought raced through her mind there was more. And still more. She should have been sated from it, but she pulsed with energy. She should have been overwhelmed, but it was as if, somehow, she'd always known it would be like this. His heart raced with hers, beat matching beat. Passion poured out of her, but as it poured it was replenished.

"Matthew." His name was a moan, a gasp. "I want you."

As his mouth hurried back, skimming over her, she felt his tremors and the hammer-thrust beat of his heart. Each rasping breath seemed to merge with her. She saw his eyes glimmer once in the pale light of the moon, then tasted the mixture of soap and salt on his flesh.

"I need you...." They spoke together. She arched to meet him.

Chapter 9

The sky hung low. Thick pewter clouds trapped the heat and humidity so that rain wouldn't have been a threat, but a blessed relief. The leaves didn't stir, or turn their pale undersides up in anticipation, but hung limply.

Laurel leaned back and let the sticky air coming through the car window do what it could. Along the sides of the road the trees stood, casting shade that could offer only slight relief to the throbbing heat. Glancing at them, she wished she were sitting under one, near a cool river on soft, damp grass.

She was traveling the road to Heritage Oak for the third time in two days. Each time, it was just a bit more difficult to face the kind of answers she might find there.

Louis would be angry, she had no doubt of it. The

man she'd seen yesterday would be furious at being disturbed again—if he spoke to them at all. And Marion… Marion would be hurt, Laurel thought with a flash of guilt. Hurt that she persisted in pursuing something Marion found distasteful and distressing to both herself and her brother.

I won't think about it, Laurel told herself, and turned her head to stare, brooding, out the window. What choice do I have? Questions have to be asked, things have to be said. It's gone too far to turn back now. If anything, it should be easier to have the questions come from me. But it wasn't, she thought miserably. Not for any of us.

She knew why Matt was silent. He was giving her time to pull herself together, sort out her emotions for herself before they arrived at Heritage Oak. Considerate. Strange, she thought with a small smile, a week before she'd have sworn Matthew Bates hadn't a considerate bone in his body. She'd learned quite a bit about him in the last few days. Not quite all, Laurel mused, thinking of the paintings in his apartment. But still, a great many important things—the most important of which was that she loved him.

They'd yet to speak seriously about what had happened between them. In an odd way, she felt they'd both been reluctant to probe the other's emotions. Treat it light—don't press. Those were the words that ran around in her head. She wondered if they ran in his as well.

It had all happened so fast. A year? That's fast? she thought with a faint smile. But it had. Whatever had been building between them over the months had been so cleverly ignored that the sudden blaze of passion had been totally unexpected. And that much more exciting. But was that all it was for him? Laurel wished she had the confidence, or the courage, to ask.

Turning back, she studied his profile. Strong, casually handsome, with an easygoing smile and amused eyes. Yet he wasn't quite all those things. From his writing she'd already known him to be savvy, ironic, insightful. She'd also discovered that he was only laid-back when he chose to be. That wasn't his true nature. He was an impatient, restless man who simply played the game his own way. Over and above the love that had crept up on her, Laurel had discovered to her own amusement, that quite simply she liked his style.

Partners, she thought as her smile widened. You'd better get used to it, Bates, because we're going to stay that way for a long, long time.

"See something you like?" he asked dryly.

Laurel tilted her head and continued to study him. *Play it light.* The words ran through her mind yet again. "As a matter of fact, I do—and it still surprises me."

He chuckled, and with his eyes on the road reached over and tugged on her hair. "I'm crazy about your compliments, Laurellie. A man never knows if he's been pumped up or slapped down."

"Keeps you on your toes, Bates."

"You did tell me once I had fabulous eyes."

Her brow lifted. "I did?"

"Well, you'd had four martinis at the time."

She laughed as he swung between the pillars of Heritage Oak. "Oh, well, who knows what a person might say in that condition? What color are they, anyway?"

He narrowed them as he turned toward her.

"Blue," she said, catching her tongue between her

teeth. "Blond hair, blue eyes—rather an ordinary combination, but you do the best you can with it."

"Yeah. And it is a pity about your chin."

Laurel lifted it automatically. "My chin," she said as he stopped the car, "is not pointed."

"I hardly notice it." Matt jingled the keys in his hand as he stepped from the car. He'd lightened her mood, he noticed, but only temporarily. Already, as she glanced up at the house, he could see the struggle between her emotions and her profession. Laurel being Laurel, the profession won, but not without cost.

"Matthew, Marion will see us because her upbringing wouldn't allow her not to, but..." She hesitated as they climbed the porch. "I doubt if Louis will talk to us."

"We'll have to convince him otherwise," he said flatly, and let the knocker fall heavily on the door.

"I don't want to push him too hard right now. If—"

It was the way his head whipped around, the way his eyes flared, that stopped her. "When?" he demanded.

She opened her mouth, but the annoyance and impatience on his face had her biting back the first reckless words. "All right," she murmured, turning to face the door again. "All right."

Guilt. He felt the sting and wasn't quite sure what to do about it. "Laurel—"

The door opened, cutting off whatever he might have said. Binney glanced at both of them while a flicker of surprise—and something else—came and went in her eyes. "Miss Laurel, we didn't expect to see you again so soon."

"Hello, Binney. I hope it's not inconvenient, but we'd like to speak to Louis and Marion."

Her eyes darted to Matt, then came back to Laurel. "Mr. Louis has a black mood. It's not a good time."

"Black mood?" Laurel repeated. "Is he ill?"

"No." She shook her head, but hesitated as if the denial had come too quickly. "He is…" Binney stopped as if searching for a phrase. "Not well," she finished, lacing her long, bony fingers together.

"I'm sorry." Laurel gave her an easy smile and hated herself. "We won't keep him long. It's important, Binney." Without invitation, she stepped into the hall.

"Very well." Laurel caught the quick, accusing glance before the housekeeper shut the door. "Come into the parlor, I'll tell Miss Marion you're here."

"Thank you, Binney." Laurel caught her hand at the entrance to the parlor. "Is Louis often…not well?"

"It comes and goes."

She closed her other hand over the thin, hard one as if willing Binney to understand. "Did he have these black moods when Anne was—when he was married to Anne?"

Binney's lips compressed until there was nothing but a tight line. In the way of a woman well used to the house she lived in, and the people she lived with, Binney let her gaze sweep down the hall and up the stairs in a gesture so quick it was hardly noticeable. When she spoke, her words were hurried, low and French.

"You knew him, Miss Laurel, but there have been so many changes, so much pain. Nothing as it was when you came for your tea parties and riding lessons."

"I understand that, Binney. I'd like to help him."

Binney's gaze swept the hall again. "Before," she began, "during the time between when Mr. Charles left and when Mr. Louis brought the girl home, he had many…hard moods. He might roam the house and speak to no one, or lock himself in his study for hours. We worried but…" Her shrug was eloquent. "Later, he began to go away on business and it would be better. The years, they weren't easy, but they were…quiet. Then he brought the girl back, his wife."

"And things changed again?" Laurel prompted.

"Only better." The housekeeper hesitated. Laurel thought she understood perfectly the tug-of-war her loyalties were waging. "We were surprised. She had the look of the first one," Binney said so quietly Laurel strained to hear. "It was strange to see her, even her voice…. But Mr. Louis was happy with her, young again. Sometimes, only sometimes, he would brood and lock himself away."

Ignoring the knot in her stomach, Laurel pressed on. "Binney, was Anne afraid when Louis would…brood?"

Her mouth became prim again. "Perhaps she was puzzled."

"Was she happy here?"

The nut-brown eyes clouded. Her mouth worked before her face became still again. "She said the house was like a fairy tale."

"And the swamp?"

"She feared it. She should have stayed away. What's there," she said in a low voice, "is best left alone."

"What's there?" Laurel repeated.

"Spirits," Binney said, so simply Laurel shivered. There was no arguing with old beliefs, old legends. She let it pass.

"Did Anne see Nathan Brewster often?"

"She was a loyal wife." Her tone changed subtly, but enough that Laurel knew the automatic defense of the estate and all in it had been thrown up. Laurel took what she knew might be the final step.

"Did Louis know that Brewster was in love with Anne?"

"It is not my place to say," Binney replied stiffly and with disapproval. *Or yours to ask.* Laurel heard the unspoken words very clearly. "I'll tell Miss Marion you're here." Coolly, she turned her back on them both and walked away.

"Damn," Laurel breathed. "I've lost her, too."

"Sit down," Matt ordered, steering her to a chair. "And tell me what that was all about."

Sitting, Laurel began to speak in the flat tone of recital. "She told me that Louis was prone to black moods and brooding after Charles and Elise left. Understandable enough," she added automatically—too automatically for Matt's liking. "The servants worried about him. Then he apparently pulled out of it a bit when he began to travel on business. They weren't expecting him to bring Anne back and obviously her resemblance to Elise caused some talk, but Binney seemed fond of her. She said Louis was happy, less moody, that Anne was happy too."

She sighed, leaning back in the chair, but her fingers drummed on the arms. "She holds to the local feeling about the swamp."

"Ghosts again?"

"Don't be so literal-minded," Laurel snapped. "It's the…essence of the place," she finished lamely.

As Laurel had with the housekeeper, Matt let it pass. "Didn't I hear Brewster's name mentioned?"

"She'd only say that Anne was a loyal wife. I tried

to press." She lifted her eyes to his. "That's when I lost her."

"Forget your feelings for a minute and use your head." He spoke sharply because he'd rather face her annoyance than her vulnerability. "If the housekeeper knew about Brewster—and from the way she clammed up she must have—who else knew?"

"You don't hide things from servants, Matthew. They'd all know."

"Yet not one of them mentioned his name when they were questioned by the police."

Laurel linked her hands in her lap to stop her fingers from drumming. "To have mentioned it would've cast a shadow on Anne's reputation and therefore Louis's. Remember, too, the investigation led to nothing more than a verdict of accidental death. It would've seemed pointless to stir all that up then."

"And now?"

"The servants are loyal to Louis," she said wearily. "They're not going to gossip to outsiders about something that would bring him more pain."

"I have connections downtown," Matt mused. "I could probably get someone out here to ask a few questions."

"Not yet, Matthew, a few more days." Laurel caught Matt's hand in hers as he stood next to her chair. "I don't want to push the police on Louis until there's no other choice. We don't have enough to justify reopening the investigation in any case. You know it."

"Maybe, maybe not." He frowned down at her and bit back a sigh. "A few days, Laurel. That's all."

"Laurel, Mr. Bates." Marion came in with her hands already extended for Laurel's. "Please, sit down, Mr.

Bates. I'm sorry I've kept you waiting, but we weren't expecting you."

Laurel caught the faint disapproval and acknowledged it. "I'm sorry, Marion, I hope we didn't catch you at a bad time."

"Well, I'm a bit pressed, but…" She squeezed Laurel's hands before choosing the brocade love seat across from her. "Would you like some coffee? A cold drink, perhaps. It's such a dismal day."

"No, thank you, Marion, and we won't keep you long." Party talk, she thought in disgust. How easy it is to cover ugliness with party talk. "It's important that we speak to you and Louis again."

"Oh." Marion's gaze swept from Laurel to Matt and back again. "Louis is out, I'm afraid."

"Will he be back?" Matt asked her, without accepting her invitation to sit.

"I can't say. That is, I can't say when. I'm sorry." Her expression altered subtly, brow creasing as if she were forced to say something unpleasant. "The truth is, Laurel, I'm not sure he'll agree to talk to you again."

That hurt, but she'd expected it. Laurel kept her eyes level. "Marion, Matthew and I went to see Nathan Brewster yesterday."

They both saw, and registered, each flicker of expression on Marion's face. Distress, agitation, annoyance, doubt; all came quickly and were as quickly gone. "Did you? Why?"

"He was in love with Anne," Laurel returned. "And apparently made little secret of it."

Marion's eyes cooled, the only hint of annoyance now. "Laurel, Anne was a lovely child. Any man might be attracted to her."

"I didn't say he was attracted," Laurel corrected. "I said he was in love with her, in his way. He wanted her to leave Louis."

Laurel saw Marion's throat work before she spoke. The thin gold chain she wore around it glittered with the movement. "What Mr. Brewster may have wanted doesn't mean anything. Anne loved Louis."

"You knew about this." Laurel watched Marion's eyes, pale gray like her brother's.

For a moment Marion said nothing, then the only sound she made was a sigh. "Yes," she said at length. "I knew. It would've been impossible not to see by the way the man looked at her. Anne was confused." Her hands lifted, linked, then fell. "She confided in me because she just didn't know how to deal with it. Anne would never have left Louis," she murmured as her fingers unlinked to knead the material of her skirt. As the nervous gesture continued, her eyes remained level and nearly calm, as if her hands were controlled by something else entirely. "She loved him."

"Did Louis know?"

"There was nothing for him to know," Marion said sharply, then struggled to regain her composure. "Anne only spoke to me because the man upset her. She told her sister that he made her nervous. Anne *loved* Louis," Marion repeated. "What difference does it make now?" She looked at both of them with suddenly tormented eyes, her fingers clutching the filmy material of her skirt. "The poor child's dead, and rumors, nasty rumors like this, will only make it more difficult on Louis. Laurel, can't you stop this? You must know what this continued pressure does to Louis."

"If things were just that simple," Matt began, breaking in before Laurel could speak. "Why do you suppose someone sent Laurel a warning?"

"Warning." Marion shook her head as her nervous fingers finally stilled. "What warning?"

"Someone left a box on my doorstep," Laurel said with studied, surface calm. "There was a dead copperhead inside."

"Oh, my God! Oh, Laurel." She stretched her hands out to grip Laurel's. They trembled ever so slightly. "Why would anyone have done something so nasty? When? When did this happen?"

"Late yesterday afternoon. A few hours after we'd left Heritage Oak."

"Oh, my dear, you must have… Anne was bitten by a copperhead," she murmured, as if she'd just remembered. "You think—Laurel, you don't believe that Louis would do such a thing to you. You can't!"

"I can't—I don't want to believe it of Louis," Laurel corrected. "We thought it best if both of you knew about it."

With a steadying breath, Marion released Laurel's hands. "It must have been dreadful for you. My own nerves—Louis's…" She broke off with a shake of her head. "Of course I'll tell him, you know I will, but—"

"Miss Marion?"

Distracted, Marion looked over her shoulder to the doorway. "Yes, Binney."

"Excuse me, but Mrs. Hollister's on the phone, about the hospital charity drive. She's insistent."

"Yes, yes, all right, tell her I'll just be a moment." She turned back, playing with the collar of her dress. "I'm sorry, Laurel, about everything. If you'd like to wait here, I'll take care of this and come back. But I don't know what else I can say."

"It's all right, Marion, go ahead. We'll just let ourselves out."

"Once you put your teeth into it," Matt commented when he was alone with Laurel, "you chomp down nicely."

"Yes, didn't I?" Without looking at him, she picked up her bag and rose. "Professional hazard, I suppose."

"Laurel." Matt took her shoulders until she looked up at him. "Stop doing this to yourself."

"I would if I could," she murmured, then turned away to stare out the window. "I didn't like the way Marion came apart when I mentioned Brewster."

"She knows more than she's saying." He touched her hair, and would have drawn her back against him.

"Louis is outside," Laurel said quietly. "I want to talk to him alone, Matthew."

He took a step back, surprised that such an ordinary request would hurt so much. "All right." When she walked out the French doors, he stuffed his hands in his pockets and moved closer to the window. Without the least compunction, he wished Louis Trulane to hell.

The heat outdoors was only more stifling after the coolness of the parlor. The air tasted of rain, but the rain wouldn't come. What birds bothered to sing, sang gloomily. She smelled the roses as she passed them, and the scent was hot and overripe. As she came closer to him, Laurel could see the damp patches on Louis's shirt.

"Louis."

His head jerked up when she called him, and he stopped. There wasn't any welcome in his face or in his stance, nor was there the cool indifference she'd seen the day before. He was furious. "What're you doing here?"

"I have to talk to you."

"There's nothing to say."

"Louis." She took his arm when he started to go on without her. Though he stopped again, he spun back to her with a look that made her drop the hand.

"Leave us both with a few decent memories, Laurel, and stay away from me."

"I still have the memories, Louis, but I have a job to do." She searched his face, wishing there was something she could do, something she could say, to prevent what she knew could be the final breach between them. "I don't believe Anne went into that swamp freely."

"I don't give a damn what you believe. She's dead." He looked over her head, out to the edge of the north lawn, where the marsh took over. "Anne's dead," he said again, shutting his eyes. "That's the end of it."

"Is it?" she countered, hardening herself. "If there's the slightest possibility that someone lured or frightened her into that place, don't you want to know?"

He broke off a thin branch of crape myrtle. Laurel was reminded forcibly of Brewster's hands on a pencil. "What you're saying's absurd. No one did—no one would have a reason to."

"No?" She heard the quiet snap of wood between his fingers. "Someone doesn't appreciate our probing into it."

"*I* don't appreciate your probing into it," Louis exploded, tossing down the mangled wood and blossoms. "Does it follow that I murdered my wife?" He spun away from her to stare at the edge of the north lawn.

"For God's sake, Laurel. Why do you interfere in this? It's over. Nothing can bring her back."

"Does my interference bother you enough that you'd leave a dead snake on my doorstep?"

"What?" He shook his head as if to clear it. "What did you say?"

"Someone sent me a dead copperhead, all done up nicely in a box."

"A copperhead—the same as..." His words trailed off as he slowly turned back to her. "A nasty joke," he said, tossing the hair back from his face in a gesture she remembered. "I'm afraid I haven't been up to jokes of any kind lately, though I hardly see..." He broke off again, staring down at her. His expression altered into something she couldn't quite read. "I remember. Poor little Laurel, you were always terrified of them. I nearly strangled that cousin of mine the day he stuck a garter snake under your nose at one of Marion's garden parties. What were you? Nine, ten? Do you remember?"

"I remember."

His face softened, just a little. "Have you outgrown it?"

She swallowed. "No."

"I'm sorry." He touched her face in the first gesture of friendship. She found it hurt more than his angry words. "You never liked the swamp because of them."

"I never liked the swamp, Louis."

"Anne hated it." His eyes drifted back. "I used to try to tease her out of it—just as I used to tease you. Oh, God, she was sweet."

"You never let me meet her," Laurel murmured. "Why didn't you let anyone meet her?"

"She looked like Elise." His hand was still on her

face, but she knew he'd forgotten it. "It stunned me the first time I saw her. But she wasn't like Elise." His eyes hardened, as slate gray as the sky. "People would've said differently just by looking at her. I wouldn't tolerate it—the comparisons, the whispers."

"Did you marry her because she reminded you of Elise?"

The fury came back at that, so sudden and fierce Laurel would've backed away if his hand hadn't tightened. "I married her because I loved her—needed her. I married her because she was young and malleable and would depend on me. She wasn't a woman who'd look elsewhere. I stayed with her through the year we had so that she wouldn't grow bored and discontent, as Elise claimed she had in that damned note."

"Louis, I know how you must feel—"

"Do you?" he interrupted softly, so softly the words hung on the stagnant air. "Do you understand loss, Laurel? Betrayal? No," he said before she could speak. "You have to live it first."

"If there had been someone else." Laurel moistened her lips when she found her mouth was dry. "If there'd been another man, Louis, what would you've done?"

He looked back at her, cool again, icy. "I'd have killed him. One Judas is enough for any man." He turned, walking away from her and the house again. Laurel shivered in the sticky heat.

He'd seen enough. Matt crossed to the French doors and, fighting the urge to go after Louis and vent some of his frustration, went to where Laurel still stood, looking after him.

"Let's go," he said briefly.

She nodded. The mood—hers, Louis's, Matt's—

seemed to match the tightness in the air. A storm was brewing in all of them. It wouldn't take much to set it off. In silence, they walked across the neatly trimmed lawn to Matt's car, then drove away from Heritage Oak.

"Well?" Matt touched the car lighter to the tip of a cigarette and waited.

"Binney was right about his mood," Laurel said after a moment. "He's on edge, angry, with nothing to strike out at. He still dismisses Anne's death as an accident. The way he looked out at the swamp..." Laurel glanced up at Matt, seeing the hard, set profile that wasn't so very different from the expression Louis had worn. "Matthew, I'd swear he loved her. He might've gotten involved with her because of her resemblance to Elise, even married her with some sort of idea about having a second chance, but Louis loved Anne."

"Do you think he always kept them separated in his mind?"

"I told you before, I'm not a psychiatrist." Her answer was sharp, and she set her teeth. Nothing would be accomplished if she and Matt started sniping at each other again. "I can only give you my own observations," she said more calmly, "and that is that Louis loved Anne, and he's still grieving for her. Part of the grief might be guilt—that he'd teased her about being afraid of the swamp," she told him when he sent her a quick look. "That he didn't take it seriously enough."

"You told him about the box?"

"Yes." Why doesn't it rain? she thought as she pulled her sticky blouse away from her shoulder blades. Maybe the rain would wash everything clean again. "He didn't put it together at first, then when he did, I'd say he was more disgusted than anything else. Then...then he remembered I'd always been terrified of snakes. For a couple of minutes, he was just like he used to be. Kind, warm." Swallowing, Laurel looked out the side window while Matt swore, silently, savagely.

"I asked him why he hadn't let Anne meet anyone. He said he didn't want the comparisons to Elise he knew would crop up. He kept close to her because he didn't want her to grow bored and—"

"Look elsewhere," Matt finished.

"All right, yes." Laurel's head whipped back around. "Aren't you forgetting about those glass houses now, Matthew? Haven't you any compassion at all? Any understanding as to what it's been like for him?"

He met her heated look briefly. "You've got enough for both of us."

"Damn you, Matthew," she whispered. "You're so smug, so quick to judge. Isn't it lucky you never lost anyone you loved?"

He hurled his cigarette out the window. "We're talking about Trulane, not me. If you're going to start crusading again, Laurel, do it on your own time. Not when you're my partner. I deal in facts."

She felt the rage bubble up and barely, just barely, suppressed it. Her voice was frigid. "All right, then here's another one for you. Louis said he would've killed any man that Anne was involved with. He said it with a cold-bloodedness I'm sure you'd admire. Yet Nathan Brewster still works for him."

"And here's another one." Matt pulled into a parking space at the *Herald* and turned on her. "You're so hung up on Trulane you've made some kind of Brontë hero out of him. You refuse to see him any other way. He's a ruthless, bitter man capable of cold violence. His first wife chose his younger brother. Haven't you ever asked yourself why?"

She jerked her arm out of his hold. "You know nothing about love and loyalty, Matthew."

"And you do?" he tossed back. "If you'd grow up, you'd see that you don't love Trulane, you're obsessed with him."

She paled, and as the blood drained from her face, her eyes grew darker, colder. "I do love him," she said in a low, vibrating voice. "You haven't the capacity to understand that. You want things black-and-white, Matthew. Fine, you stick with that and leave me the hell alone."

She was out of the car quickly, but he had her by the shoulders before she could dash into the building. "Don't you walk away from me." The anger spilled out, with something very close to panic at the edges. "I've had enough of Louis Trulane. I'll be damned if I'm going to have him breathing down my neck every time I touch you."

Laurel stared up at him, eyes dry. "You're a fool. Maybe you'd better take a good look at the facts again, Matthew. Now leave me alone." When her voice broke, they both swore. "Just stay away from me for a while."

This time when she turned from him, Matt didn't stop her. He waited until she'd disappeared inside the building before he leaned against the hood of his car. With the heat shimmering in waves around him, he drew out a cigarette and tried to pull himself together.

What the hell had gotten into him? He'd attacked her. Matt dragged a hand through his hair. An emotional attack wasn't any prettier than a physical one. The heat? He shifted his shoulders beneath his damp, sticky shirt. That might be part of it, it was enough to set anyone's nerves on edge.

Who was he trying to kid—himself? Matt blew out a long breath and watched the smoke hang in the thick, still air. The crux of it was, she'd spent the night with him, giving herself to him, bringing him all the things he'd needed, wanted…then he'd seen Louis put a hand to her cheek.

Idiot. Laurel couldn't have cursed him more accurately than he did himself. He'd let jealousy claw at him until he'd clawed at her. He hadn't been able to stop it. No, he corrected, he hadn't tried to stop it. It'd been easier to be angry than to let the fear take over. The fear that he'd had for her since he'd looked in the box on her table—the fear that he had of her since he'd discovered he was hopelessly in love with her. He didn't want to lose her. He wouldn't survive.

Maybe he'd sniped at her hoping she'd back off and let him take over the investigation. If he'd found a way to prevent her going with him into the swamp, she wouldn't have been hurt.

Maybe he'd used Louis as an obstacle because he'd been afraid to risk telling Laurel how he felt about her. He'd planned things so carefully—he always had. Yet things had gotten out of hand from the moment he'd started to work with Laurel on this story. How was he supposed to tell her that he loved her—perhaps on some level had loved her from the moment he'd seen that picture propped against Curt's books? She'd think he was crazy. Matt crushed the cigarette under his heel. Maybe he was.

But he was still a reporter, and reporters knew how to follow through, step by step. The first thing was to give Laurel the space she'd demanded. He owed her that. In giving it to her, he could do a little digging on his own. The next thing was to find a way to apologize without bringing Trulane into the picture again.

The last thing, Matt thought as he crossed the parking lot, the last thing was to get it into her thick head that he loved her. Whether she liked the idea or not.

Chapter 10

Laurel considered it fortunate that she'd been sent back out on an assignment almost immediately after coming into the city room. She was able to grab a fresh pad, hook up with a photographer and dash out again before Matt was even halfway up on the elevator.

She didn't want to see him, not until the anger and the hurt had faded a bit. The three-car pileup at a main intersection downtown, with all the heat, noise and confusion it would generate, should distract her from her personal problems. Temporarily.

He was being unreasonable, she told herself with gritted teeth while the photographer cruised through a yellow light and joined a stream of traffic. Unreasonable and unyielding. How could anyone be so utterly lacking in compassion or empathy? How could a man who had shown her such unquestioning support and comfort when she'd been frightened feel nothing for someone who'd been through what Louis Trulane had? Didn't he recognize pain? How could she love someone who… That's where she stopped, because no matter how or why, she loved Matt. It was as simple as that.

Because she loved him, his lack of feeling and his words had cut that much deeper. To accuse her of being obsessed by Louis. Oh, that grated. Any rational person would understand that Louis Trulane had been her childhood hero. She'd loved him freely, with a child's heart and in a child's way. In the course of time, the love had changed, not because Louis had changed but because she had.

She still loved Louis, perhaps not quite objectively. She loved Louis the way a woman loves the memory of the first boy who kissed her, the first boy who brought her a bouquet. It was soft and safe and passionless, but it was so very sweet. Matt was asking her to turn her back on that memory. Or to dim it, darken it with suspicion.

To a woman like Laurel, the memory of a young man who'd treated a child and her infatuation gently should have no shadows. But Matt was using it to swipe at her for something she couldn't understand. He'd even implied that she might be thinking of Louis when they were together. How could he possibly believe…

Here, her thoughts broke off again as a new idea crept in. A fascinating one. Matt was plain and simply jealous.

"Ha!" Laurel uttered the syllable out loud and flopped back against the car seat. Her photographer sent her a sidelong look and said nothing.

Jealous…well, that was certainly interesting, even if it was still unreasonable and asinine. But if he was jealous, didn't it follow that his feelings for her were more involved than she'd let herself believe? Maybe. Or maybe he was just being typically insufferable—as she'd almost forgotten in the first heady waves of love that he was. Still, it was something to think about.

They had to stop the car in a thick tangle of traffic and bad-tempered blasting of horns. "I'll get out here and go up on foot," Laurel told her photographer absently. "Pull over as soon as you can." Stepping out, Laurel went to work.

Matt was out on the street as well. The noise in the Vieux Carré might have been a great deal more pleasant than what Laurel was dealing with, but the heat was only slightly less intense. He could smell the river and the flowers, a combination that had come to mean New Orleans to him. At the moment, he hardly thought of them. For the past hour, he'd been very busy.

A trip to the police station and a few carefully placed questions had earned him the information that no official search had ever been issued for Elise or Charles Trulane. A missing-persons report had never been filed on either of them. The note, the missing clothes and painting gear had been enough to satisfy everyone. Matt wasn't satisfied.

When he'd questioned further, he'd hit a blank wall of indifference. What did it matter how they'd left town or if anyone had seen them? They *had* left, and ten years was a long time. There was plenty of other business in New Orleans to keep the force busy other than an adultery that was a decade old. Sure, the lab boys would play with his little chunk of metal when they had the time, and what was he up to?

Matt had evaded and left with fewer answers than

he'd had when he'd gone in. Maybe he'd draw a few out of Curt.

Turning a corner, Matt strolled into a dim little bar where a trio was playing a cool, brassy rendition of "The Entertainer." He spotted Curt immediately, huddled in a corner booth with papers spread all over the table. There was a glass of untouched beer at his elbow. Matt had a quick flashback of seeing Curt exactly the same way during their college days. The smile—the first one in hours—felt good.

"How's it going, Counselor?"

"What?" Distracted, Curt looked up. "Hi." He tipped the papers together in one neat, economical movement and slid them into a folder. "What's up, Matt?"

"The same," he told the waitress, indicating Curt's beer. "A little legal advice," he said when he turned back to Curt.

"Oh-oh." Grinning, Curt stroked his chin, the only resemblance to his sister Matt could see.

"Advice, not representation," Matt countered.

"Oh, well." When the waitress put Matt's beer on the table, Curt remembered his own.

"If I decided to add to my portfolio, would you consider Trulane Shipping a wise investment?"

Curt looked up from his drink, his abstracted expression sharpening. "I'd say that was more a question for your broker than your lawyer. In any case, we both know your portfolio's solid. You're the one who gives me tips, remember?"

"A hypothetical question then," Matt said easily. "If I were interested in speculating with a New Orleans-based company, would Trulane be a wise place to sink my money?"

"All right. Then I'd say that Trulane is one of the most solid companies in the country."

"Okay," Matt muttered. He'd figured that one was a blind alley. "Why do you think no one's touched Elise Trulane's inheritance?"

Curt set down his beer and gave Matt a long, level look. "How do you know about that?"

"You know I can't reveal a source, Curt. Fifty thousand," he mused, running a finger down the condensation on his glass. "A hefty amount. Interest over ten years would be a tidy little sum. I'd think even a man like Trulane would find some use for it."

"He doesn't have any claim on the money. It's a straight inheritance in Elise's name." He shrugged at Matt's unspoken question. "The firm handled it."

"And the lady just lets it sit." Matt's brow rose at his own statement. "Strange. Hasn't your firm tried to track her down?"

"You know I can't get into that," Curt countered.

"Okay, let's take it hypothetically again. When someone inherits a large amount of money and makes no claim, what steps're taken by the executors to locate the beneficiary?"

"Basic steps," Curt began, not sure he liked the drift. "Ads in newspapers. In all likelihood an investigator would be hired."

"Say the beneficiary had a husband she wanted to avoid."

"The investigation, any correspondence pertaining to it, would be confidential."

"Mmm-hmm." Matt toyed with his beer as the piano player did a quick, hot rip over the keys. "Did Elise Trulane have a will?"

"Matt—"

"Off the record, Curt. It may be important."

If it had been anyone else, Curt would have brushed it off and found some handy legal jargon to evade the question. He'd known Matt too long and too well. "No," he said simply. "Both she and Louis had wills drawn up, but Elise took off before they were signed."

"I see. And the beneficiaries?"

"Standard wills for husband and wife without issue. Marion and Charles have their own money."

"Substantial?"

"Putting it mildly. Marion's a very wealthy woman." Then, because he anticipated the question before it was spoken, he added, "Charles's investments and his savings sit collecting interest as Elise's do."

"Interesting."

Curt kept his eyes level—not emerald like his sister's, but sea green and calm. "Are you going to tell me what all this is about?"

"Just covering all the angles."

"It has something to do with what you and Laurel are working on—for Susan."

"Yeah." Matt swirled his beer as he studied his friend. "You've met Susan?"

"I was out at the house." A faint color rose under Curt's skin, bringing Matt a picture of the time, years before, when Curt had fallen hard for a premed student. "She told me about Anne, and the letters." Curt's gaze came back to Matt's, reminding him that Curt wasn't an impressionable college student any longer, but a man with a sharp legal mind and a quiet strength, despite his dreaminess. "Are you going to be able to help her?"

"We're doing what we can on this end. Since you

know her, and she's confided in you, maybe you can keep her calm, and out of it, until something breaks."

"I'd already planned on that," Curt said simply. "You taking care of Laurel?"

Matt grimaced, remembering how they'd parted a few hours before. "Nobody takes care of Laurel," he muttered.

"No, I guess not." Distracted again, Curt slipped his folder into his briefcase. "I've got an appointment, but when there's more time, I'd like a few more details on this."

"Okay. And thanks."

Alone, Matt brooded into his beer. Too many loose ends, he mused. Too many pieces that just don't fit. Two people might turn their backs on friends and relatives, especially in the first impetus of love, but not on more money than most people see in a lifetime. Not for ten years.

Either love made them delirious, he concluded, or they're dead. Dead, to him, made a lot more sense.

Leaning back, he lit a cigarette. If they'd had an accident after leaving Heritage Oak, didn't it follow that they'd have been identified? He shook his head as theories formed and unformed in his mind. It all tied together, somehow, with Anne Trulane. And if one of his theories was right, the one he kept coming back to, then someone had killed not once, but three times.

He studied the thin blue wisp of smoke and swore. It was too late in the day to allow a thorough check of Louis's whereabouts on the day of Elise and Charles's disappearance. And tomorrow was Sunday, which meant he probably couldn't get his hands on the information he needed until after the weekend. Monday then, he thought, and crushed out his cigarette. On Monday, no matter how reluctant Laurel was, they would start digging back, and digging thoroughly.

Rising, he tossed bills on the table and strode out. Maybe it was time they had a talk.

Laurel was totally involved with her story when Matt walked into the city room. He started toward her, glanced at the clock, then went to his own desk. Deadline was sacred. When he sat down across from her, he noticed the expression on her face. Unholy glee was the closest he could come.

Laurel nearly chuckled out loud as she dashed off the story. A three-car pileup, a lot of bent metal. Not normally anything she'd have found amusing, but no one had been hurt. And the mayor's wife had been in the second car.

Better than a sideshow, Laurel thought again as she typed swiftly. The mayor's wife had dropped all dignity and decorum and very nearly belted the hapless driver who'd plowed into her from behind, sandwiching her between him and the car stopped at a light in front of her.

The air, already steaming, had been blue before it was over. Maybe it was the heat, or the pressure she'd been under for the last few days, but Laurel found this a much-needed comic relief. It would've taken a stronger person than she not to be amused watching a prim, nattily dressed woman with a wilted corsage grab a man built like a truck driver by his lapels and threaten to break his nose. And that had been before her radiator had blown, spewing water up like a fountain.

Ah, well, she thought as she finished up the report, it would do everyman good to read that people in high places get their fenders dented and their tempers scraped too. Page one, oh, yes indeed.

"Copy," she shouted, glancing at the clock. Just under deadline. Her smile was smug as she turned back and found her gaze linked with Matt's. A dozen conflicting emotions hit her all at once, with one fighting to push aside all the others. She loved him.

"I didn't see you come in," she said carefully and began to tidy the disorder of her desk.

"Just a few minutes ago. You were working." The bedlam of the city room went on around them with shouts of *"Copy!"* and rushing feet and clicking typewriter keys. "Are you finished?"

"Soon as the copy's approved."

"I need to talk to you. Can we have dinner?"

She hadn't expected that cautious, slightly formal tone from him, and wasn't sure how to deal with it. "All right. Matthew—" The phone on her desk rang. Still thinking about what she would say to him, Laurel answered, "City room, Laurel Armand."

Matt watched her expression change, the color fluctuate before her gaze jerked back to him. "I'm sorry," she began, indicating the phone on his desk a split second after he'd already started to reach for it. "You'll have to speak up, it's very noisy in here." She heard the faint click as Matt picked up her extension.

"You've been warned twice." It was a whisper of a voice, sexless, but Laurel didn't think it was her imagination that she sensed fear in it. "Stop prying into Anne Trulane's death."

"Did you send me the snake?" Laurel watched Matt punch another extension on the phone and dial rapidly.

"A warning. The next one won't be dead."

She couldn't control the silver shot of panic up her spine, but she could control her voice. "Last night, you were in the swamp."

"You have no business there. If you go in again, you won't come out."

Laurel heard someone across the room yell out a request for coffee, no sugar. She wondered if she was dreaming. "What are you afraid I'll find?"

"Anne should've stayed out of the swamp. Remember that."

There was a click, then the drone of the dial tone. Seconds later, Matt swore and hung up his own phone. "Not enough time for the trace. Any impressions on the voice? Anything you recognized?"

"Nothing."

He picked up her pad, where Laurel had automatically recorded the conversation in shorthand. "To the point," he muttered. "We're making someone very nervous." Someone, he thought as his own theory played back in his head, who may have killed three times.

"You're thinking about the police again," Laurel decided.

"You're damn right."

Laurel dragged a hand through her hair as she rose. "Listen, Matthew, I'm not saying you're wrong, I just want some time to think it through. Listen," she repeated when he started to speak. "Whoever that was wants us to back off. Well, for all intents and purposes we will be for the weekend. I want some time to go over my notes, to put them together with yours, hash it out. If we do go to the police, on *Monday,*" she added with emphasis, "we'd better go with all the guns we have."

She was right, but he didn't like it. Several ideas for nudging her out of the investigation ran through his mind. He'd have the weekend to choose the best of them. "All right, check in with Don. I'll get my notes together."

Instead of the rare steak and candlelight Matt had planned on, they ate take-out burgers and chili fries at Laurel's drop-leaf table. Their notes were spread out—Matt's made up of scribbles Laurel thought resembled hieroglyphics while her own were sketched in precise Gregg shorthand. They hadn't taken the time—and both of them separately agreed it was just as well—to touch on their earlier argument or the reasons for it. For now they were professionals covering every angle of a story.

"I'd say it's safe to assume we have enough circumstantial evidence to conclude that Anne Trulane's death was something more than an unfortunate accident." Laurel wrote in a composition notebook, a valiant attempt to organize their snatches of words and phrases into coherency.

"Very good," Matt murmured. "That sounded like something Curt would say to the jury."

"Don't be a smart aleck, Bates," she said mildly. "Pass me that soda." Taking it, she sipped straight from the bottle and frowned. "We have Susan's claim that Anne was afraid of dark places—the swamp in particular—which has since been corroborated by Louis, Marion and Binney. We have the stolen letters from Susan's hotel room, my nasty little box, a hefty shove in the swamp and an anonymous phone call."

Because she was writing, Laurel didn't notice that Matt snapped the filter clean off his cigarette when he crushed it out. "The first interview with Louis and Marion…nothing much to go on there but emotion, which you don't like to deal with."

"It can be useful enough," Matt said evenly, "when you look at it with some objectivity."

She opened her mouth to hurl something back at him, then stopped. "I'm sorry. I didn't mean to snipe. Brewster," she went on briskly. "We know he thought he was in love with Anne, wanted her to leave Louis. No conjecture there, since he said so himself." She underlined Brewster's name heavily and continued. "We also have Marion's corroboration of the first part of that, and Anne's reaction to it. My second interview with Louis leads me to believe that he either didn't know about Brewster's feelings or didn't think they were important enough to worry about, as Brewster's still employed by his company."

Laurel rubbed a hand over the back of her neck, the first and only outward sign that she was tired. "The gist of it is that we agree it seems unlikely Anne would've gone into the swamp without some kind of outside pressure—and that it's less likely she would have continued to head deeper unless she had no choice. In my opinion, Brewster's still the obvious candidate."

Matt flipped over his pad to a new set of notes. "I spoke with Curt today."

"Huh?" Laurel looked up at him, trying to tie his statement with hers.

"I wanted some corroboration on a theory I had."

"What does Curt have to do with this?"

"He's a lawyer." With a shrug, Matt lit a cigarette. "As it turns out, I was luckier than I expected, as he works for the firm that handles Elise Trulane's inheritance."

Laurel put down the bottle she'd lifted. "What does that have to do with any of this?"

"I'm beginning to think quite a lot. Listen." He skimmed through his notes. "Fifty thousand dollars, plus ten years' interest, has never been touched. Charles Trulane's money sits moldering. Untouched. There would've been a very discreet, and I'm sure very thorough investigation on behalf of the bank to locate them." He flipped back a few pages, then lifted his eyes to Laurel's. "No missing-persons report was ever filed on either Elise or Charles Trulane."

"What're you getting at?"

Very carefully, he set down his pad. "You know what I'm getting at, Laurel."

Needing to move, she rose from the table. "You think they're dead," she said flatly. "Maybe they are. They could've had an accident, and—" She broke off, and he knew her thoughts had followed the same train his had. Laurel turned back to him, her eyes very steady. "You think they were dead before they left Heritage Oak."

"It's more than a possibility, isn't it?"

"I don't know." Pressing her fingers to her temples, she tried to think logically. "They could've taken off, changed their names, gone to Europe or the Orient or God knows where."

"Could've," he agreed. "But there's enough room to doubt that, isn't there?"

"All right, yes." She took a deep breath. "And if we go that route, figuring they were tied with Anne's death somehow, it'd put Brewster in the clear. But why?" Laurel demanded. "Who'd have had a motive but Louis, and he was out of town."

"Was he?" Matt rose, knowing they had to tread carefully around Louis Trulane. "He has his own plane, doesn't he? Flies himself— or did. You know what the possibilities are there, Laurel."

She did. An unexpected arrival, the lovers caught, unaware. A moment's madness. In a small private plane the bodies could've been taken anywhere. Pale, she turned back to face Matt. He was expecting her to argue, or to back out. Of course, she could do neither now.

"It won't be easy—maybe impossible," she added in a calm, professional voice, "to check the incoming and outgoing flights on a night ten years ago."

"I'll get started on it Monday."

She nodded. "I'll work on Curt. We might be able to get the name of the firm that looked for Elise and Charles."

"No."

"No?" she repeated blankly. "But it makes sense to try that angle if we're going at it this way."

"I want you to back off." He spaced his words very evenly as he rose. "I don't want you asking any more questions."

"What the hell are you talking about? You don't get a story without asking questions."

"Whatever we get out of this, whatever the outcome as far as the paper is concerned, we'll split down the middle. But from now on I take over."

Laurel tilted her head. "You're out of your mind."

Maybe it was the very calm, very mild way she said it that tripped the last button. Every reasonable argument, every carefully thought-out method of persuasion, deserted him. "I'm out of *my* mind!" he threw back. "That's rich." He paced, deliberately walking away from her so that he wouldn't just grab her by the collar and shake. "It's not a game, damn it. We're not playing who can hit page one."

"I've never considered my profession a game."

"I don't want you in my way."

Her eyes narrowed. "Then I'll stay out of it. You stay out of mine."

"It's dangerous!" he shouted. "Use your head. You're the one who's been threatened, not once, but three times. Whoever's behind Anne's death isn't going to hesitate to kill again."

Her brow lifted—that damned, beautiful, haughty black brow. "Then I'll have to watch my step, won't I?"

"You idiot, no one called me and told me to back off. No one threatened me." There was panic in his voice now, raw panic, but she was too busy fuming to notice.

"You want to know why, Bates?" she hurled out at him. "Because I'm a woman and obviously would buckle under. The same way you figure if you shout enough and throw your weight around I'll do the same thing."

"Don't be any more stupid than you have to."

"But the one thing they forgot," she continued furiously, "the one thing *you* forgot, is that I'm a reporter. And to get a story, to get the truth, a reporter does what's necessary. Most of us deal with being in jeopardy in one form or another. That's the business."

"I'm not in love with most reporters," Matt tossed back. "I'm in love with you!" He stormed right past her as he said it, not stopping until he'd reached the table and his cigarettes.

Laurel stared at him while he pushed aside papers in search of a match. She was winded, as though she'd raced up flight after flight of stairs two at a time. Now that she'd reached the top, she simply forgot why she was in such a hurry in the first place. It wasn't until he'd stopped swearing and muttering to turn to her that she felt the glow, the warmth, the pleasure.

Matt set down the unlit cigarette and stared at her. What the hell had he said? Oh, God, had he just blown everything by laying his cards on the table before he'd covered his bet? And just how was he going to handle this one? He decided to give her a way out if she wanted one.

"Did I…just say what I think I said?"

Laurel didn't smile, but folded her hands neatly in front of her. "Yes, I have a witness."

His brow lifted. "There's no one here."

"I'll bribe someone."

He hooked his hands in his pockets because he wanted so badly to touch her. "Is it what you want?"

She gave him an odd look, then took a step closer. "I wonder why I thought you were insightful and observant. It's a general sort of rule, Matthew, that when a woman's in love with a man she likes it better if he's in love with her too."

His heartbeat was very light and fast. He couldn't remember ever feeling like that before. "Tell me," he murmured. "Don't make me beg you."

"Matthew…" A little dazed that he couldn't see what must have been glowing on her face, she reached for him. "You're the only man I've made love to because you're the only man I've been in love with. Neither of those things is ever going to change."

"Laurel." But he couldn't say more because her mouth was on his, giving, just giving. His arms came around her to draw her closer as thoughts spun in his head. So long—it's been so long. He could hardly remember a time when he hadn't wanted it to be like this. A time when he hadn't wanted to have those words still lingering on the air. "Again," he demanded. "Tell me again."

"I love you. Only you." Her arms curved up his back until she could grip his shoulders. "I thought if I told you before, even an hour ago, you'd think I was crazy. When?" Giddy, she clung to him. "When did it start?"

"You wouldn't believe me." Before she could disagree, his lips were on hers again.

He took her deep, and still deeper, quickly. If he'd thought he'd loved her to the point of madness before, it was nothing compared to what stormed through him now. His love was met, and matched. Everything was washed from his mind but Laurel.

She could lose herself in a kiss from him, lose herself in that soft, velvet-edged darkness he'd first taken her to. To know that he wanted her was exciting. To know that he loved her was glory. Words, there were so many words she wanted to say. But they would wait until this first overriding need was satisfied. As she felt her bones melting, she drew him with her to the floor.

Quickly, quickly. Neither spoke, but each knew the other's mind. Hurry. Just to feel one another's flesh. Clothes tangled, untangled, then were discarded. Oh, the sweetness of it, the sweetness that came from only a touch. She could smell the hot muskiness of the day on him with the lingering scent of soap. She wallowed in it with her lips pressed against his throat. His pulse beat there, fast and light.

He murmured against her ear, only her name, but the sound of it drifted through her softly. The slow, liquefying pleasure made everything she'd ever felt before seem hollow. Then his tongue dipped inside to follow her name.

A long, lingering stroke, a whispering caress. There was no need to hurry now. Passion was filled with wonder. I'm loved, I'm wanted. Spirits are fed on this alone. She could feel it pouring from him—contentment—even as his heartbeat hammered against hers. Desire, when mixed with such emotions, has more power. And at times, more patience. They'd woo each other.

His lips moved over her shoulder, down, lazily down, to linger on the pulse point at the inside of her elbow. She felt the answering beat from a hundred others. Her hand ran through his hair, the curling thickness of it, before she let her fingers stroke beneath to his neck. He lifted his head to look at her and the look held—long, silent—until, smiling, their lips joined again.

The change happened so slowly, perhaps neither of them noticed. Not yet urgent, not yet desperate, but desire grew sharper. Gradually, quiet sighs became quiet moans. With his mouth at her breast he heard her breathing quicken. His senses were clouded—her scent, her taste, the satin that was her skin. Hunger seeped into them, and the excitement that came from knowing the hunger would be satisfied. His hands journeyed down.

The inside of her thighs was as warm and alluring as velvet. He let his fingers linger there, then his mouth. Though she shuddered, the first crest came easily, a gentle lifting up and up, a quiet settling. Her body throbbed with anticipation of the next while her mind was filled with him. Head whirling, she shifted to lie over him, to give to him all the pleasures he'd given to her.

How warm his flesh was, how firm his body. Her hands wandered down to his hips, skimmed over his thighs. She felt the quiver of muscle beneath her.

She was floating, but the air was thick and syrupy. Her limbs were weighted, but her head was light and spinning. She felt him grasp her, heard him hoarsely mutter her name. Then he was inside her and the explosion went on and on and on. She had only enough sanity left to pray it would never stop.

He watched her. He struggled to hold back that seductive darkness so that he would always have this image of her. The light fell over her brilliantly. With her head thrown back, her hair streamed down her back. She knew only pleasure now—his pleasure. He held her there for an instant with perfect clarity. Then the darkness, and all its savage delights, overcame him.

Chapter 11

It was dark. Matt had no idea of the time, and cared less. They were snuggled close in Laurel's bed, naked and warm. Like careless children, they'd left their clothes in heaps in the living room. It was pleasant to imagine they could stay just as they were for the whole weekend—dozing, making love, saturating themselves with each other.

He knew all there was to know about her, what pleased her, what annoyed, what made her laugh. He knew where she'd come from, how she'd grown up, snatches of her childhood that he'd drawn out of Olivia or her father and Curt. She'd broken her ankle when she was nine, and she'd worked on her high school paper. She'd slept with a one-eared stuffed dog until she was seven.

It made him smile to think of it, though he wasn't certain she'd be pleased to learn he knew.

There was so much he hadn't told her. Matt could remember the hurt on her face when he'd pushed her questions away. There was so much he hadn't told her—but she loved him anyway.

Laurel shifted against him, her eyes open and adjusted to the dark, her body quietly content. "What're you thinking?"

He was silent for a moment, then lifted a hand to touch her hair. "I grew up in that painting." Laurel put her hand in his and said nothing. "Old people stayed off the street at night and anyone else traveled in groups. Too many alleys and broken streetlights. Cops patrolled in pairs, in cars. I can't remember a night when I didn't hear the sirens."

She was so warm and soft beside him. The room was so quiet. Why was he bringing it all back? Because it never really goes away, he answered himself. And I need to tell her.

"I worked for a guy who ran a newsstand. One summer we were robbed six times. The last time he was fed up enough to put up a fight. I was out of the hospital in two days, but it took him two weeks. He was sixty-four."

"Oh, Matthew." Laurel pressed her face into his shoulder. "You don't have to talk about it."

"I want you to know where I came from." But he fell silent again as two long minutes passed. "In the apartment where I lived, the halls smelled of old cooking and sweat. It never went away. In the winter it was cold, drafts through the windows, icy floors. In the summer it was a furnace. You could smell the garbage from the alley three floors down. At night you could hear the street—dealers, prostitutes, the kids who looked for both. I stayed away from the dealers because I wanted to stay healthy and used the prostitutes when I could scrape up the extra money."

He waited, wondering if he'd sense her withdrawal. Her hand stayed in his. Laurel was remembering her impression of his apartment. He'd made an art out of comfort. How much he must have hated growing up without the basic rights of warmth and security. And yet...he'd brought the painting with him. He hadn't forgotten his roots, nor was he ignoring the part they'd had in forming him. Neither would she ignore them.

"I lived with my aunt. She took me in when my mother died and my father took off. She didn't have to." He linked his fingers with Laurel's. "She was the most unselfish person I've ever known."

"She loved you," Laurel murmured, grateful.

"Yes. There was never enough money, even though she worked too hard and when I was old enough I brought in more. The rent would go up in that filthy place or..." He broke off and shrugged. "Life," he said simply. "I swore I was going to get us out of there. One way or the other I was going to get us the hell out. I knew what I wanted to do, but it was like pie in the sky. A reporter, a job on one of the big New York papers and a salary that would move her out to some nice little place in Brooklyn Heights or New Rochelle.

"So I ran copy and studied until my eyes hurt. There were other ways," he murmured, "quicker ways, to get the kind of money I wanted, but that would've destroyed her. So when the scholarship came I took it, and I got out. When I'd come back during the summer, it was so hot I'd forget what it was like to live in that place in January. By the middle of my senior year I had nearly enough saved to move her out—not to a house in Brooklyn Heights, but to a decent apartment. By that summer I'd have gotten her out. She died in March."

Laurel turned her head so that her lips could brush over his skin, lightly, easily. "She would've been proud of you."

"If I'd have taken another way, she might still be alive."

"If you'd have taken another way," Laurel said slowly, rising on her elbows to look at him, "you'd have killed her yourself."

His eyes glinted in the filtered light of the moon. "I've told myself that, but other times I think I might've given her even six months of comfort." He caught Laurel's hair in his hand, feeling the fine silk of it. "She used to laugh. Somehow, she'd always find a way to laugh. I owe her just for that."

"Then so do I." Lowering her head, she kissed him. "I love you, Matthew."

"When I've thought of you, and me, I've wondered how the hell I was going to work it." He cupped the back of her neck. "We couldn't have had more different beginnings. There were times I thought I wanted you just because of that."

When she lifted her head, he was surprised to see her smiling. "You ass," she said lovingly.

"So beautiful," Matt murmured. "I'll never forget that picture Curt had of you, the one he kept on his desk in our room."

Surprised, Laurel started to speak, then stopped. He'd said she wouldn't believe it; now, with emotions swamping her, she didn't want to tell him he'd been wrong. She wanted to show him.

"I could see you at one of those long, lazy garden parties in a silk dress and picture hat," Matt said softly. "It made my mouth water. And I could see you with someone bred for the same things."

"I hate to repeat myself," she began, but he didn't smile. "You're thinking of Louis," Laurel said flatly.

"No." He started to draw her back to him. "Not tonight."

"You listen to me." The humor and the softness had fled from her eyes as she pulled away. "The way I feel about you has nothing, *nothing,* to do with the way I feel about Louis. I've loved him since I was a child and in almost exactly the same way. Both he and Marion were an integral, vital part of my childhood. The fairy-tale part. Every girl's entitled to one."

He remembered her grandmother saying essentially the same thing. The muscles in his shoulders began to relax. "I think I understand that, Laurel. It's today that concerns me."

"Today my heart aches for him, for both of them. Today I wish I could help, knowing, at the same time, that what I have to do might hurt them beyond repair. If my feelings had been different, don't you think that sometime over the last ten years, I'd have gone to him? I wonder why," she said heatedly before he could answer, "when I waited all these years to fall in love, I had to fall in love with an idiot."

"The luck of the draw, I guess."

"Well, I'll tell you one thing, Bates, I'm not going to explain myself to you on this again. Take it or leave it."

He let out a deep breath and paused as if weighing

the pros and cons of the ultimatum. In the dim light he could see the angry glare in her eyes, the agitated rise and fall of her shoulders. She might've been molded in a softer manner than he, but no one matched wits or wills so well.

"Will you marry me, Laurel?" he asked simply.

He heard the quick hitch of her breath, saw the surprise rush into her eyes. For a moment, there was quiet. "It took you long enough," she said just as simply, then dived onto him.

Laurel awoke with the sun streaming over her face and Matt nibbling on her ear. She didn't have to open her eyes to know it was a beautiful day. Sometime during the night the rain had come to wash the heaviness from the air. Without opening her eyes, she stretched and sighed. Matt's lips moved to her jawline.

"I love the way you wake up," he murmured. He slid a hand down to cradle her hip.

"Mmmm…what time is it?"

"Morning." His lips finally found hers.

With another lazy stretch, she linked her arms around his neck. "Have I ever told you how much I like you to kiss me just like that?"

"No." Lowering his head, he did so again while she lay boneless beneath him. "Why don't you?"

"If I tell you…mmmm…you'll know how to win every argument."

Laughing, he pressed his lips to the curve of her shoulder. "I'm crazy about you, Laurellie. When're we getting married?"

"Soon," she said definitely. "Although the minute

we tell Grandma she'll—" Laurel broke off, eyes flying open. "Oh, God, *brunch!*"

"I wasn't thinking of food just yet," Matt murmured, going back to nibble on her ear.

"Oh, no, no, you don't understand. What time is it?" Shoving him aside, Laurel grabbed the bedside clock. "Oh, boy, we'd better get moving or we'll be in serious trouble."

Matt grabbed her around the waist as she started to hop out of bed. "If we stay right here," he began, pinning her beneath him again, "we can get into serious trouble by ourselves."

"Matthew." Laurel avoided the kiss, but it landed on the vulnerable hollow of her throat. "Sunday brunch at Promesse d'Amour is sacred," she said unsteadily.

"Can you cook?"

"What? Oh, well, yes, that is, if your stomach's very broad-minded you could almost call it that. Matthew, don't." Breathless, she caught his wandering hand in hers.

"Why don't we have a private brunch here, somewhere around dinnertime?"

"Matthew—" She shook her head to clear it, then put both hands firmly on his shoulders. "Since you're going to join the family, you might as well get used to certain ironclad rules and traditions. Sunday brunch," she continued when he grinned, "is nothing to play around with."

"I'm an iconoclast."

"Bite your tongue," she told him, and struggled with a grin of her own. "Grandma would forgive me if I took up exotic dancing. She'll even overlook the fact that I'm marrying a Yankee, but she'd never, never let me get away with missing Sunday brunch. Even being late clouds the reputation, and we're pushing that."

Matt gave a long, exaggerated sigh. "For Miss Olivia, then," he agreed, and let Laurel wiggle out from under him.

"I'm going to get a shower," she said, dashing toward the bathroom. "If we move fast, we'll make it before deadline."

"Two can shower as quick as one," he commented as he stepped in with her.

"Matthew!" Laughing, Laurel lifted a hand to his chest. "If we're in here together we're definitely going to be late for brunch."

He drew her against him. "I'll risk it."

"Matthew—"

"You forget." He lowered his mouth to nibble on hers. "I know how to win arguments."

"Oh, damn," she sighed, and melted against him.

They were late.

"We're really in for it," Laurel muttered as Matt turned the car under the arched cedars.

Matt sent her a quick wolfish grin. "It was worth it."

"Just get that cat-ate-the-canary look off your face, Matthew," Laurel warned. "Try to look suitably humble."

"We could use the one about the flat tire," he suggested.

"No less than a five-car pileup equals pardon," she said grimly. "And you don't have a dent in this car." She shot him a look.

"No," he said positively, "not even for you."

"It's that practical Yankee streak," she said under her

breath as the house came into view. "Okay, it probably won't work, but we'll go for it. Turn your watch back."

"Do what?"

"Turn your watch back, fifteen minutes." She fussed rapidly with her own. "Go on!"

"What's she going to do?" he demanded as he parked his car beside Curt's. "Take you to the woodshed?"

"You'd be surprised," Laurel muttered. "Oh-oh, here she comes. Listen, I know this might be almost impossible for you, Matthew, but look innocent."

"Maybe I'll just drop you off here and see you back in town."

"You do and I'll break your arm," she promised as she stepped from the car. "Grandma!" Laurel went forward with smiles and open arms. She kissed both lined cheeks and pretended she didn't notice the coolness in the sharp emerald eyes. "You look wonderful."

"You're late," Olivia said flatly.

"Oh, no, minutes to spare. I've brought Matthew with me," she added quickly. With luck, a lot of it, it would be enough to distract Olivia.

"Miss Olivia." He took the haughtily offered hand and lifted it to his lips. "I hope I'm not intruding."

"You're late," she repeated while her gaze raked over both of them.

"Why, how could we be?" Laurel countered, glancing down at her watch. "It's only just eleven now."

"That trick's older than I am." Olivia lifted her chin in the manner her granddaughter had inherited. "*Why* are you late?" she demanded, daring either of them to make an excuse.

Laurel moistened her lips. If she had a few more

minutes, she could probably come up with a great lie. "Well, you see, Grandma—"

"It's my fault, Miss Olivia," Matt put in, earning a grateful glance from Laurel.

"What," Olivia began regally, "does my granddaughter being late have to do with you?"

"I distracted her in the shower," he said easily.

"Matthew!" Laurel cast him a horrified look that altered into one that promised swift and lethal revenge. His name echoed off into silence.

"I see." Olivia nodded. "That's a reasonable excuse," she decreed as Laurel's mouth dropped open. "Close your mouth, girl," she said absently as she continued to study Matt. "Took your own sweet time about it, but that's worked out for the best. You'll be marrying her soon."

It wasn't a question. Matt could only grin as Laurel began to sputter. "Very soon," he told Olivia.

"Welcome to the family—" she grinned and offered her cheek "—Yankee." With a wink for her granddaughter, she held out a hand for Matt to formally escort her around the house to the terrace.

No one's like her, Laurel thought with a fierce flurry of love and pride. Absolutely no one.

With her usual panache, Olivia dominated the table, with her son at the opposite end and the younger generation between them. As always, she'd made the most out of the Sunday tradition. White linen, gleaming silver and crystal, fresh flowers in bowls that had been treasured before the war.

The talk was quiet, general, easy. Laurel could see that Susan was a much different woman from the one who had fallen apart outside the city room. No more trembling fingers. If there was a sadness in her eyes, it was fading. She cast Laurel one look that spoke of complete trust. With it, Laurel felt the burden grow.

Not now, she told herself as she sipped at cool, dry champagne. Tomorrow was soon enough to bring all that back. For today, she needed to absorb the magic and the timelessness. Where else, she wondered, could six people be sitting with the sun gleaming on silver that was more than a century old? There was birdsong and a precious breeze that might only last a moment. It was too rare to crowd with sorrows and suspicions. And she was in love.

She glanced over at Matt, and her eyes told him everything.

"This will be your job one day, Laurellie," Olivia stated, cutting delicately into the crepe on her plate. "Traditions like this are important—more for the children than their parents. You and Matthew are welcome to the west wing when you're married. Permanently or whenever you feel the need to come. The house is big enough so that we won't bump into each other."

"Have some more coffee, Mother," William interrupted, sending her a telling look that expressed his feelings about matchmaking. "I want to talk to both of you." He nodded to his daughter and to Matt. His glance barely skimmed over Susan, but it was enough to tell Laurel he was referring to Anne Trulane. "Monday morning, my office."

"Business is for Monday." Olivia sent her son back a look every bit as stubborn. "I want to talk about the wedding. The garden couldn't be better suited to a summer wedding. You're welcome to have it here on the terrace."

"How about next weekend?" Matt put in, reaching for his coffee.

"Matt, don't encourage her," William advised. "She'll have Curt suing you for breach of promise."

"Damn right!" The thought made Olivia give a hoot of laughter as her hand came down on Laurel's. "We've got him now, Laurellie. William!" She caught him in the act of smothering a laugh with a cough. "Aren't you going to ask this boy all the rude questions a father's supposed to ask? A father can't be too careful when a man wants his daughter—especially a Yankee."

"The truth is," Laurel began before her father could speak, "Matthew's marrying me for the house, and as a cover so he can dangle after Grandma."

Her father's grin altered into blank astonishment. "Are you joking?"

"No," Laurel said lightly as she dipped a strawberry into cream. "Matthew's crazy about Grandma."

"Laurel—" William began with a half laugh, only to break off without any idea what to say.

"She's not joking," Curt murmured, studying his sister. He glanced over at Matt as he remembered his roommate's fascination with a photograph, the questions. "All this time?" he said softly.

"Yes." Matt looked over at Laurel and smiled. "All this time."

"Well, it's been a cleverly kept secret," her father stated. "And from a veteran bloodhound like me."

Smiling, Laurel reached out a hand to him. "Do you mind?"

He gripped her hand. "Nothing could please me more." His gaze shifted to Matt. "Nothing. The point is—" his fingers relaxed with his smile "—I didn't think the two of you even liked each other. You had one particular adjective for Matt, as I recall."

"Insufferable," Laurel supplied. "It still holds."

"That's what adds spice to a relationship," Olivia declared as she pushed back from the table, a signal that meant the formality of the brunch was over. "Susan, be a sweet child and run up to my room. There's a small locket in my jewelry case, gold, encrusted with pearls."

The moment she'd gone, Olivia turned to Curt. "Going to let this Yankee show you up, Curtis?"

Rising, Curt made a great to-do over removing a piece of lint from his jacket. "Ma'am?"

"*He* lollygagged around for a year. I expect you should be able to snatch that girl up in half the time."

"Mother." William strolled over to place a hand on her shoulder. "Be satisfied with one victory."

"After I'm through with Curtis," she continued irrepressibly, "I'm getting started on you."

He acknowledged that with a nod before he turned to his son. "Every man for himself. Ah, Matt, there's something I've been meaning to talk to you about."

"Coward," Olivia murmured as her son drew Matt away.

"Is this it, Miss Olivia?"

"Yes, thank you." She smiled as Susan handed her the locket. "Curtis, why don't you take Susan through the garden. You like the garden, don't you, Susan?"

"Yes." Susan looked down at her hands, then lifted her eyes to Curt's. "Yes, I do."

"There, you see, she likes the garden. Run along. Now then." Without pausing for breath, she turned to Laurel.

"Grandma." Laurel gave her a long, hard hug. "I adore you."

Olivia let herself enjoy the warmth and scent of youth before she drew Laurel away. In her own masterly way, she studied her granddaughter. "You're happy."

"Yes." With a laugh, Laurel tossed back her hair. "If you'd have asked me a month ago—good God, a week ago—how I'd feel about marrying Matthew Bates on the terrace, I'd've said…" She broke off, laughing again. "I'd better not repeat what I'd've said."

"You pretended you weren't attracted to him right from the beginning."

"I did a good job of it."

Olivia gave a hoot. "Ah, but you're like me, child!"

"The highest of compliments."

Olivia dropped the locket into her lap and took Laurel's hands. "When we love, really love, it's with everything we have, so we don't give it easily. Your grandfather…" She looked misty for a moment, young. "God, but I loved that man. Fifteen years with him wasn't enough. When he died, I grieved and grieved hard, but then life—you have to live it as it comes. The others, after him, they were…" She shook her head and smiled again. "They were for fun. I cared about every man I've been with, but only one had all of me. You'd understand that," she murmured. "So would your Yankee."

"Yes." Laurel felt the tears swim into her eyes and blinked them back. "I love you, Grandma."

"You'll lead each other a dance," Olivia said after giving Laurel's hands a quick squeeze. "There's nothing better I could wish for you. This is for you now." Olivia lifted the locket from her lap, cupping it in her hand a moment as if warming it. "Your grandfather gave it to me when we were engaged. I wore it when I married him. It would mean a great deal to me if you wore it when you marry Matthew."

"Oh, Grandma, it's lovely." Laurel took the gold, gleaming dully and still warm from her grandmother's hands. It was studded with tiny pearls that carried just a hint of blue under the white. "I've never seen you wear it."

"I haven't since he died. It's time it was worn again and worn by a bride."

"Thank you." Leaning over, Laurel kissed Olivia's cheek, then with a smile turned the locket over in her palm. So lovely, she thought, and it would look so perfect against a floaty, romantic white dress. Maybe something with lace and…

As memory jarred, she pressed a hand to her temple.

"Laurellie?"

"No." Absently she patted her grandmother's hand. "I'm all right, I've just remembered something. Or think I have. I have to use the phone."

Jumping up, she dashed into the house with the locket clutched in her hand. From memory, she dialed Heritage Oak. With her eyes on the locket in her hand and her mind on another, she barely heard the answering voice.

"Oh, Binney," she said quickly. "It's Laurel Armand." When there was silence, she leaped into it. "Please, Binney, I know you're angry with me for questioning you. I understand. I'm sorry, truly sorry if I pressed too hard."

"It isn't my place to be angry with you, Miss Laurel," she said quietly. "It isn't my place to answer questions."

"Please, there's something I have to know. It could be very important. A locket." She plowed on into the unreceptive silence. "The locket Louis gave Elise before they were married. She wore it on her wedding day, and, I think, always after that. I can remember that I never saw her when she wasn't wearing it. The gold locket with the etching on the front. Do you remember it, Binney? You must," she went on before there could be an answer. "She kept Louis's picture in it."

"I remember the locket."

Something—not excitement, not fear—began to pound in her chest. Laurel recognized it as disillusionment. "She always wore it, didn't she? It was very small and elegant, something she could wear every day and still wear with evening clothes."

"It was her habit to wear it."

Laurel swallowed and fought to keep her voice steady. "Binney, was Elise afraid of the swamp?" She knew the answer herself, but wouldn't go with childhood memories now. It was time for facts, no matter how they hurt.

"It was a long time ago."

"Please, Binney. You knew her, you were there."

"She did not like it," Binney said flatly. "She knew the legend."

"But sometimes—sometimes—she went in there," Laurel whispered.

"Yes, sometimes she went in, but only with Mr. Louis."

"Yes, yes, I know." Laurel let out a long breath. "Only with Louis. Thank you, Binney."

Hanging up, Laurel stared down at the locket in her

hand. She slipped it gently in her pocket and went to find Matt.

He saw her, crossing the lawn. With a brief word to her father, Matt went to meet her. Even from the distance, he'd recognized the look in her eyes. "What is it, Laurel?"

Her arms went around him, her cheek to his chest. For a moment, she just needed that—the strength, the promise. The tug-of-war inside her was almost over. It didn't surprise her that she still loved Louis, or the Louis she'd known. "Matthew, where's the piece of locket you found in the swamp?"

"I took it to the police lab. They're going to run some tests." He drew her away far enough so that he could see her face. "Why?"

Quietly, she drew a breath. Then she straightened and stood on her own. "They're going to find that it was out in the weather, perhaps covered and uncovered by rain and dirt over and over—for ten years."

"Ten—" He broke off as understanding came. "It was Elise's."

"I remembered where I'd seen it. I just called Heritage Oak and spoke to Binney to be sure. Elise wore that locket every day."

Because she was pale, because he loved her, Matt chose to play devil's advocate. "All right, but it's still not proof. She could've lost it in there any time."

"No, it's not proof," Laurel agreed. "But I don't think there's a chance that Elise simply lost it there. First, it was too important to her. And second, she didn't go in there often. She wasn't afraid the same way Anne was, but she had a healthy respect for the legend. The only times she went in, she went in with Louis. Binney just corroborated."

He could see the struggle, the emotion, in her eyes. This time he felt none of the frustration, the jealousy, that had plagued him. Gently, he cupped her face in his hands. "I'm sorry, Laurel."

She caught his wrists in her hands and held tight. "Oh, God, Matthew, so am I."

"I think we should fill in your father before we leave," he said carefully. "But we might want to keep it away from Susan for a while. We still don't have anything solid for the police."

"No." Laurel glanced over as she heard Susan's laugh drift from the garden. "Let's leave her out of it for now. My father can probably put on enough pressure to reopen the investigation on Anne, and stir one up on Elise and Charles."

"We've got enough," Matt agreed, watching the struggle on her face, "to start putting pressure in the right places."

"Oh, God, Matthew, do you realize, if what we're thinking is fact…Louis must be terribly ill. With Charles and Elise it might have been a moment of blind fury, but all these years it would've eaten at him. And then to meet Anne." She pressed her fingers to her eyes. Would she ever be able to separate the emotion from the necessity? "He needs help, Matthew. Can you imagine what a dark place he's been living in all this time?"

"He'll get help. But, Laurel…" He took her shoulders until she dropped her hands and looked at him. "First we have to prove it. I think if we concentrate on the first—on Charles and Elise," he said carefully, "it'll lead to Anne. It's not going to be easy for you."

"No," she agreed, "not easy, but necessary." Watching his eyes, she thought she could almost see the idea forming. "What're you thinking, Matthew?"

"Pressure," he murmured. "The right pressure in the right place." He brought his attention back to her. "Louis must already be on the edge, Laurel, ready to go over. He's warned you off three times. Just what do you think his reaction would be if he saw that piece of locket?"

"I think—" Laurel's hand reached automatically for the one in her pocket "—it would break him."

"So do I." He slipped an arm around her shoulders. "We'll have to make another trip to Heritage Oak tomorrow."

Chapter 12

The clutter of notes was still spread over Laurel's drop-leaf table with the wrappers and cardboard of their take-out meal. Clothes—hers and some of his—were scattered over the floor. Laurel closed the door behind them and jiggled her keys in her palm.

"You're a slob, Matthew."

"Me? It's your place. Besides—" he nudged his shirt out of his way with his foot and sat down "—you were the one who dragged me to the floor, crazy for my body. And," he continued when she snorted, "you were the one who pulled me out of here this morning like the building was on fire."

He was distracting her—she was distracting him—from what hovered around the verges of both their thoughts: Louis Trulane and what to do about him.

"Well, since I've already had your body, and

brunch," she added sweetly, "you can help me clean up this mess."

"Better idea." Rising, he yanked her into his arms. "Let's add to it."

"Matthew!" But his mouth crushed down on hers. His fingers were making quick work of the zipper at the back of her dress. "Stop it!" Half laughing, half in earnest, she struggled against him. "You're crazy. Don't you ever think about anything else?"

"Sometimes I think about eating," he confessed, then nipped, none too gently, at her collarbone.

"Matthew, this is ridiculous." But the quick heating of her blood told her otherwise. "It was only a few hours ago that—oh."

"I'm hungry again," he murmured, then devoured her mouth.

God, he was making her head spin. With her dress already down to her waist, Laurel tried to pull away. "Stop. There's things we have to talk about, and—"

"Mmm, a reluctant woman." He dragged her against him again. "That gets my lust cells moving."

"Your what?" she demanded, choking on a laugh.

"Just watch." Before she realized what he was up to, she was slung over his shoulder.

"Bates! Have you lost your mind?"

"Yeah." He pulled the dress the rest of the way off as he headed for the bedroom. Carelessly, he dropped it at the doorway, sending her shoes to follow. "Blame it on the lust cells."

"I'll tell you what I think about your lust cells," she began, but the wind rushed out of her as she landed on the bed beneath him.

Then he was taking her back to places she'd been,

but so swiftly, so immediately, she couldn't keep up. Relentless, he wouldn't allow her to fall behind. Bright streams of color seemed to burst inside her head while her body was consumed with pleasure, such hot, liquid, throbbing pleasure.

No thought. No words. She could only feel and feel and feel. The rest of her clothes were gone. Had she heard something rip? Did it matter? Her body was wild to be touched, tasted, to experience all the mad things he seemed determined to do.

Emotions exploded in her, poured out of her. Oh, God, she was so free, so wonderfully free. Pleasure was an absence of pain, and she felt only pleasure in his hands, his lips, the taste of his tongue inside her mouth, the feel of his flesh beneath her fingers.

Excitement, heady, steamy excitement. Liberation. Soaring, half crazy with delight. The knowledge that her life would be splashed with moments like this made her laugh aloud. The next moment he had her gasping. She locked her arms around him as her world rocked and spun.

He took her on a roller coaster of sensations, plummeting down, climbing, climbing, only to whip blindly around a turn to fall again. Weightless, helpless, with the air rushing in her lungs and her heart thundering in her ears.

Then he plunged into her, driving her over that last, giddy hill.

When she could breathe again without gasping, when she could think without pooling all her concentration onto one word, Laurel slid a hand across his chest. He was lying on his back, possibly, she thought, just possibly, as enervated as she.

Laurel turned her face into his shoulder. "You did that more for me than yourself."

Matt gave a weak laugh. "I'm a real Samaritan. No lengths I won't go to to serve my fellow man."

"Matthew." Laurel shifted, so that she lay over him, her head supported just under his by her folded arms. "You knew I was tense, trying not to be. You knew I didn't want to think about what's going to happen, even though I have to. I was being a coward."

"No." He brushed the hair back from her face. "You were being human. You needed to wipe it away for a little while, blank it out. I did, too." He smiled, with the touch of irony in the lifted brow. "This was better than an aspirin."

She managed to match the smile. "You'll have to keep yourself available every time I have a headache." She lowered her face to kiss his chest, then lifted it again. "Matthew, I can handle this. I can."

Maybe, he thought. Maybe not. But he'd give her the first test. "Okay. I want to run over to the lab and get the locket back whether it's been tested yet or not. I'd feel better if I had it."

Laurel nodded, accepting. "And in the morning, we take it out to see Louis."

I take it out, he corrected silently, but merely nodded. That was something he'd deal with when the time came. "If he doesn't just fall apart at that, we'll have a lot of legwork to do, but we bring the uniforms in."

"Agreed," she said simply. Her heart was already numb.

He sat up, wondering just where he'd tossed his clothes. "Do you want to come with me now?"

"No." She let out a deep breath. What had her grandmother said? Life—you have to live it. "I'll tell you what I'm going to do for you, Bates, and believe me, you're the first man I've offered this to."

He was standing, pulling on his slacks. The grin tilted. "Fascinating."

"I'm going to cook you dinner."

"Laurel, I'm—overwhelmed."

"You might be a great deal more than that after you eat it," she murmured.

"We could always eat out."

"Don't be a coward," she said absently, wondering just what she had in the freezer that could be used. "Better pick up some wine." Kneeling, she buttoned up the rest of his shirt for him herself. "And some bicarbonate," she added, laughing up at him.

"Bicarbonate," he murmured. "That doesn't inspire confidence."

"No, but it'd be a smart move."

"I shouldn't be long."

"Take my door key in case I'm involved in the kitchen. And, Matthew," she murmured, sliding her arms around his neck, "make sure you control those lust cells until you get back."

He kissed her, then gave her a friendly pat on the bottom. "An hour," he promised before he strolled out.

An hour, Laurel mused, and stretched her arms to the ceiling as she heard the front door close. That should give her time enough to try her hand at being domestic.

It didn't take her long to deal with the disorder of the apartment, or to realize just how smoothly Matt had eased out of helping. She decided that having to eat her cooking would be punishment enough for him. Going to the kitchen, she poked in the refrigerator.

A little juice, less milk, two pounds of butter. *Two* pounds, Laurel mused. How had that happened? Still, there was the makings for a salad in the vegetable bin. A start. Maybe a casserole, she decided. She was almost sure she had a cookbook around somewhere.

Fifteen minutes later, she was elbows deep in the beginnings of a tuna-and-macaroni dish that the cookbook promised was foolproof. With a glance around the now cluttered and disarranged kitchen, she smirked. Whoever wrote the book didn't know Laurel. She was going over the next step when the phone rang.

Matt, she thought, dusting off her hands as she went to answer. He probably wants to know if I'd like him to pick up some take-out Chinese. You're not getting off that easy, Bates. Grinning, she answered.

"Hello."

"Oh, Laurel, thank God you're home."

Tension banded the back of her neck immediately. "Marion? What is it?"

"Laurel, I didn't know what to do. Who else to call. It's Louis."

"Is he hurt?" Laurel asked quickly. "Has he been hurt?"

"No—I don't know. Laurel…" Her voice broke and she began to weep.

"Marion, calm down and tell me what's happened."

Her breathing rasped into the phone. "I've never seen him this bad before. All day, he wouldn't speak to anyone, but that happens sometimes. Oh, God, Laurel," she said on a sudden burst of emotion, "it's been such a strain, worse since Anne… Laurel," she began again, nerves quivering in her voice. "I need help."

"I'm going to help," Laurel said as calmly as she could. "What's happened?"

"Just now, a few minutes ago." Laurel heard her take a steadying breath. "He flew into a rage. He wasn't—wasn't making any sense. He was saying things about Elise, and about Anne. I don't know—it was as though he'd gotten them mixed up in his mind."

Laurel pressed her lips together. She had to be calm, had to think straight. "Where is he now?"

"He's locked himself in his room. He's raging up there, I can hear the furniture… Laurel, he won't let me in."

"Marion, call a doctor."

"Oh, God, Laurel, don't you think I've tried that before? He won't see one, and he's never been as—as out of control as this. Please, come. You were always our friend. Louis was so close to you before—before all of this. You might be able to calm him down, and then if I could just figure out what to do so that he'd—he'd get help," she finished in a whisper. "Laurel, please, I just can't expose him to strangers the way he is now. I don't know who else to trust."

"All right, Marion." She pictured Louis locked in his room, on the edge of madness. "I'll be there as quickly as I can."

"Laurel…as a friend, not as a reporter, please."

"As a friend, Marion." After hanging up the receiver, Laurel pressed the heels of her hands to her eyes.

Matt shifted the bag he carried and slipped Laurel's key into the lock. "I got red and white," he called out.

"You didn't say what we were having." A glance at the living room showed him that Laurel had already tidied up. He was going to hear about that, Matt mused, grinning. "I don't smell anything burning."

He swung into the kitchen and lifted a brow. Whatever she was making, it apparently required every inch of counter space. Matt set the wine in the sink—the only place left for it—and shook his head. This was the woman whose notes were always in perfect order? Whose desk was clear and ordered at the end of each day? Dipping his hand into a bowl he drew out a cold, spongy elbow of macaroni.

"Ah, Laurel," he began, dropping it again. "There's this little place on Canal Street, great seafood. Why don't we..." He paused at the entrance to the bedroom. Empty. He felt the first prickles of unease. "Laurel?" Matt repeated, pushing open the bathroom door. Empty. Fear washed over him; he pushed it back. She'd just gone out for something she was missing for the recipe. She probably left a note.

When he hurried back into the living room, he found it by the phone. But even before he read it, he didn't feel relief, only more fear.

Matthew—Marion phoned, very upset. Louis is losing control, talking about Elise and Anne. He's locked himself in the bedroom. She needs help. I couldn't say no. Laurel.

"Damn it!" Matt tossed down the note and raced for the door. The fear was still with him.

Shadows were lengthening as Laurel turned down the drive toward Heritage Oak. The air was still again in the late-afternoon hush. A bird called out, as if testing the silence, then was quiet again. Even as she stopped the car at the end of the drive, Marion was running down the front steps toward her.

Her hair was loose, her face pale and tear-stained. It ran through Laurel's mind quickly that she'd never seen Marion so totally lacking in composure.

"Oh, God, Laurel." Marion grabbed her as if she were a lifeline. "I couldn't stop him. I couldn't stop him!"

Laurel's head whipped up, her eyes fixing on the window of Louis's room. She had a sickening picture of him lying dead by his own hand. "From what? Marion, what has he done?"

"The swamp. He's gone in the swamp." She covered her face with her hands and sobbed. "I think he's lost his mind. The things he was saying—he pushed me."

Not dead, Laurel told herself. Not dead. You have to be calm. "What did he say?"

Marion lowered her hands. Her eyes were wide, stricken. "He said," she began in a whisper, "he said he was going to find Elise."

"Elise," Laurel repeated, forcing herself not to give in to the horror of it.

"We have to do something!" Marion grabbed her again. "Laurel, we have to do something, go after him—*find* him. He's having a breakdown or—"

"Marion, how can we find him in there? We should call the police."

"*No!* Not the police. It's Louis." She seemed to come to grips with herself as she released Laurel. "I can find him. I know the swamp as well as he does. You don't have to come with me—I asked too much."

Laurel dragged both hands through her hair as Marion started across the lawn. He'd put her up on her first pony, she remembered. Played patient games of chess, listened to her rambling stories. Whatever he'd done, how could she walk away without trying to help?

"Marion, wait. I'm coming with you."

Marion stopped and held out a hand.

They moved quickly toward the swamp. The instant revulsion came as she stood at the edge of it, but she forced it back. It was just a place, she told herself. And Louis was in it.

The shadows were long on the ground now. Daylight was thinning. They'd have an hour, maybe a bit longer, Laurel reassured herself, before it was too dark to see. By then, they'd have found him. She moved into the swamp without hesitation.

"I think he might have gone to the river—to where Anne was found." How much did Marion know or suspect? Laurel wondered. At the moment, she didn't think Marion was in any shape for questions or theories. "Are you going to be all right?" she asked, looking at Marion's flowing pastel skirts and elegant pumps. "It's hard going through here."

"It doesn't matter," Marion said impatiently. "Louis is my brother."

"It's going to work out for the best," Laurel told her, almost believing it herself.

"I know." Marion managed a smile.

They moved slowly, side by side, and then with Laurel just ahead as the path narrowed. The place was alive with noise—birds, insects. Once she saw a blue heron rise up gracefully and glide. They were coming to the river.

"Maybe we should call to him, let him know we're

here," Laurel suggested. "It might frighten him if we're too quiet."

"He won't hear you."

"Not if he's gone the other way, but if he's anywhere near the river, then—" Laurel broke off as she turned around.

Marion held a gleaming old gun in her hand. A sliver of sunlight dashed against the chrome. For a moment, as her gaze rested on it, Laurel's mind went blank. Then, slowly, she looked up into Marion's face. Despite the red-rimmed eyes, the tracks of tears and disordered hair, her expression was calm and composed. There was something buzzing in her ears that Laurel didn't yet recognize as terror. She kept her eyes on Marion's face.

"Marion." The name came out calmly enough. Calmly and very soft. "What are you doing?"

"What I have to do," she said mildly.

Was the gun for Louis? Laurel thought frantically. If it was for Louis, then why was it pointed at her? She wouldn't look at it—not yet—she'd look only into Marion's clear gray eyes. "Where's Louis, Marion? Do you know?"

"Of course, he's working in his study. He's been working all afternoon."

"All afternoon," Laurel repeated, trying to hold back the trickle of fear that was eating at her wall of control. "Why did you call me?"

"I had to." Marion smiled. It was a gentle one. "After I spoke to you this morning about Elise's locket, I knew it had gone too far. You'd gone too far."

"Spoke to me? But I talked to Binney…" She trailed off. "It was you?"

"I'm surprised you didn't remember that Binney

spends her Sundays with her sister. You made it terribly simple, Laurel. You expected Binney, so I was Binney." The smile faded. Marion's brows drew together, delicately, as they did when she was annoyed. "I'm very disappointed in you, Laurel. I warned you to stay out of this. Can you imagine the trouble you'd have caused if it had been Binney? Questioning a servant about family matters." She shook her head as a flicker of irritation darkened her eyes. "You've been raised better than that."

Raised better? Laurel thought giddily. Was she mad? Oh, God, she thought as fear washed over her. Of course she was mad. "Marion, what are you going to do?"

"You'll have to be punished," Marion told her calmly. "Just like the others."

Matt's car skidded to a halt next to Laurel's. He hadn't stopped cursing since he'd tossed her note aside. Cursing helped hold off the fear. If he's hurt her, Matt thought as he sprinted up the steps. By God, if he's touched her… Lifting a fist, he pounded on the door.

"Trulane!" He pounded again, sick with fear. When the door opened, he was through it in seconds, with his hands gripping hard on Louis's shirt. "Where's Laurel?"

"What the hell do you think you're doing?" Louis stood rigid, his eyes burning with fury.

"What have you done with Laurel?" Matt demanded.

"I've done nothing with Laurel. I haven't seen her." He looked down at the hands gripping his shirt. "Get your hands off me, Bates." He'd like a fight, Matt realized. He'd like the simple release of a purely physical explosion—fist against flesh. Matt saw it in his eyes.

"We'll go a few rounds, Trulane," Matt promised grimly. "There's nothing I'd like better—after you tell me what you've done with Laurel."

Louis felt something bubbling inside of him. The emotion, for the first time in weeks, had nothing to do with grief. It was pure fury. Somehow it was cleansing. "I told you I haven't seen her. She isn't here."

"You can do better." Matt flung a hand toward the open door. "Her car's out front."

Louis followed the gesture and frowned. Some of the pent-up anger gave way to puzzlement. "She must've come to see Marion."

"Marion called her." Matt shoved him back against the wall, catching him off-balance. "She told her to come because you were out of control, locked in your room."

"Are you crazy?" Louis pushed him away, and they stood eyeing each other, both tall men, both ready, anxious, for blood. "Marion would hardly call Laurel if I were locked in my room. As it happens, I've been working all afternoon."

Matt stood, breathing fast, trying to hold on. If he hit Trulane, even once, he might never stop. He could feel the violence bubbling up inside him. Not until he saw Laurel, he promised himself. And after that…

"Laurel left me a note that she was coming here after a phone call from Marion concerning your unstable condition."

"I don't know what the hell you're talking about."

"Laurel's car's out front," Matt said between his teeth. "And you're here."

Louis gave him a cold stare. "Perhaps you'd care to search the house."

"I'll do just that," Matt tossed back. "While I'm at it," he continued as he reached in his pocket, "why don't you take a look at this and see what explanation you can come up with?"

Opening his palm, he held out the piece of locket. Louis gripped his wrist, fingers biting into flesh. "Elise—where did you get that?" His eyes whipped up to Matt's, dark, tormented. "Where in hell did you get that?"

"In the swamp." Matt closed his hand over it. "Laurel recognized it too, then confirmed it with your housekeeper on the phone this morning."

"Binney?" Louis stared down at Matt's closed hand. "No, Binney isn't here. The swamp? In the swamp?" Again Louis lifted his head. His face was white. "Elise never went in there without me. She always wore that, always. She had it on the day I left for New York, before she—" He shook his head, color rushing back to his face. "What the hell are you trying to do?"

Matt tried to take it step by step. A new fear was crawling in. "Laurel told me she called here—around noon—and spoke with your housekeeper."

"I tell you Binney isn't here, hasn't been here all day! She goes to her sister's. All the servants are free on Sundays. There's only Marion and I."

"Only Marion?" Matt murmured. Marion who had called—Marion who had, by her nervous distress, sent them after Brewster. And Marion, Matt remembered all at once, who had said Anne had told Susan that Brewster made her nervous. How would she have known that unless—unless she'd seen the letters. "Where is she?" Matt demanded, already halfway down the hall. "Where's your sister?"

"You just wait a damned minute." Louis grabbed Matt by the arm. "What are you getting at? Where did you get that locket?"

"In the swamp!" Matt exploded. "Damn you, don't you understand Marion's got her!" His face became very still and very pale. "In the swamp," he repeated. "She has her in the swamp, just like the others."

"What others?" Louis was on him before Matt could move. *"What others?"*

"Your sister's a murderer," Matt flung back at him. "She's killed three times, and now she has Laurel."

"You're crazy!"

"I'm not crazy." He opened his fist again so that the locket sat dully in the center of his palm. "We were in the swamp the other night—someone attacked her. The same person who sent her the dead snake, and the one who threatened her over the phone yesterday. The same person," he said evenly, "who called her here now. Laurel came here for you," Matt told Louis, watching his eyes. "Are you going to help me?"

Louis stared down at the locket, his breath unsteady. "We'll go in. Wait here."

Turning, he walked into a room across from the parlor. Seconds later, he came back with a small pistol. The color had drained from his face again. In silence, he handed it to Matt. "She's taken the gun." His eyes met Matt's. "The antique we've kept under glass."

Don't panic, don't try to run. Laurel ran the words over and over in her mind as she watched Marion. She looks so calm now, as if any minute she'd smile and offer me tea and cakes. How long has she been mad? Laurel swallowed slowly, careful to make no movement at all. Talk—she wants to talk about it.

"Punish," Laurel repeated. "You punished the others, Marion?"

"I had to."

"Why?"

"You were always a clever child, Laurel, but not clever enough." She smiled again, old friend to old friend. "After all, look how easily I threw your attention onto Brewster, just by telling the truth. Anne would never have left Louis. She adored him."

"Then why did you punish her, Marion?"

"She shouldn't have come back." Marion let out a little, shuddering sigh. "She should never have come back."

"Come back?" Laurel repeated, allowing herself a quick glimpse over Marion's head. If she could distract her, get just a few seconds' head start, could she lose herself in the brush?

"She didn't fool me," Marion said, smiling again. "Oh, she fooled the rest of them—especially Louis—but I knew. Of course, I pretended I didn't. I'm very good at pretending. She was afraid of the swamp," Marion said absently. "I knew why, of course I knew why. She died here before, she had to die here again."

Laurel stared as the horror of what was in Marion's mind washed over her. Keep talking, keep talking, keep talking, she told herself as a thrush began to sing in the cypress behind her. "Why did you kill Elise the first time?"

"She had no right!" Marion exploded so that Laurel gave a quick, involuntary jerk back. "She had no right to the house. It was mine, always it's been mine. Louis was going to will it to her. To *her!* She didn't have Trulane blood, wasn't one of us. *I'm* the oldest," she raged. "By rights, the house was mine. Father was wrong to leave it to Louis."

Her chest began to shudder, but when Laurel looked down, she saw the gun was still steady. "It's always been mine. I love it. All of this." Her eyes skimmed the swamp and softened. "It's the only thing I've ever loved."

"But why Elise?" Laurel interrupted. A house, she thought frantically. Did someone kill for a house, a plot of grass and dirt? It had been done before, she reminded herself. Over and over again, since the caves. "Why didn't you kill Louis, Marion? Then you'd have inherited."

"Laurel." Her voice was soft. "Louis is my brother."

"But—but Charles," she began.

"I never wanted to hurt Charles." Tears sprang and swam in her eyes. "I loved him. But he saw us, he interfered." A single tear drifted down her cheek. "I didn't have a choice. Elise and I went for a walk—she was lonely without Louis. When we were far enough away from the house, I took out the gun. This gun," she said, lifting it higher. "Do you recognize it, Laurel?"

She did. She'd seen it under glass in the library. The same gun another Trulane had used to kill—to punish. "Yes."

"I knew I had to use this." She ran a fingertip down the barrel. "It was as if it was waiting for me, as if someone was telling me that it was right that I punish Elise with this. Do you understand?"

"I'm trying to."

"Poor Laurel," Marion murmured. "Always so understanding, so caring. That's how I knew you'd come today when I called."

Laurel felt her knees start to shake. "You were telling me about Charles."

"Yes, yes. He saw us, you see. Saw me leading Elise into the swamp at gunpoint. At least, he must have—I didn't have time to ask, everything happened so quickly. We were here when he found us. Just here."

She glanced around as if they might not be alone after all. Laurel took a very slow, very small step to the right. "Don't, Laurel," Marion murmured, lifting the gun a fraction higher. Laurel stood still. "Elise went wild—that must be when her locket was broken. I should've been more careful. I had to shoot her. Then Charles was pushing me down. My own brother—shouting at me. The gun seemed to go off again, all by itself. Then he was dead."

Her tears were dry now, her eyes clear. "I didn't know what to do at first, and then, it just came. They'd been lovers, like the other two who'd died here. I'd have to forge another note. This time Elise would tell Louis she'd left him for Charles. It was better," she muttered. "Really, it was better that way. I had to drag them to the quicksand."

"Oh, God." Laurel closed her eyes, but Marion didn't notice.

"I packed some of their clothes. All the servants were gone because it was Sunday. Charles's paints, too—I nearly forgot them. Of course, he'd never have left without his paints. They went in the quicksand too. Then it was done. It was simple. Of course, Louis was hurt. He suffered." Her eyes clouded for a moment. "I know he blamed himself, but I could hardly tell him it was all for the best. The house was mine again, he was busy with his work. But sometimes," she whispered. "Sometimes I'd hear them in here. At night."

Laurel swallowed the metallic taste of horror. "Charles and Elise?"

"I'd hear them—it would wake me up and I'd have to come out, come look. I never saw them—" Again, she looked around as if expecting someone. "But I heard."

It's driven her mad, Laurel thought. How is it no one saw, no one suspected? She remembered Marion at a charity function only months before—delicate, elegant, with a spray of violets pinned to her lapel. She looked down at the gun again.

"Then she came back," Marion said flatly. "She said her name was Anne, and Louis believed her. I knew. She'd look at me with those soft, shy eyes, and she was laughing! I let her think she'd fooled me."

"And you brought her in here again."

"I had to be more careful this time. Louis hardly let her out of his sight, and she'd never, never go near the swamp. That night, he was working late. I heard her in the study with him. He told her he'd probably be a couple hours more, to go up to bed without him. I knew it was time. I went into her room, put a pillow over her face. Oh, I had to be careful, I couldn't kill her then. It had to look like an accident this time. She was very small, and not strong. It only took a minute until she was unconscious. Then I carried her out here."

Marion smiled, remembering. "I had the gun, but she didn't know I couldn't afford to use it. When she came to, she was terrified. Elise knew she was going to die again. She begged me to let her go, but I made her get up. I thought it best if she drowned in the river. When she started to run, I let her. It would be simpler if she exhausted herself first and I kept close. Then I heard her scream. The snake, a young one, Elise had walked right over the nest. You see, it was meant," Marion told her. "It was right. All I needed then was enough time for the poison to work—and a night, a whole night out in that damp air. I waited until she stopped running, until she was unconscious, here, right here where she'd died before. Then I went home." Marion smiled, but now her eyes were blank. "She won't come back this time."

"No," Laurel said quietly. "She won't come back."

"I've always been fond of you, Laurel. If you'd only listened, this wouldn't have happened."

Laurel moistened her lips and prayed her voice would be steady. "If you shoot me, Marion, they'll take you away from Heritage Oak."

"No!" Her hand tightened on the gun, then relaxed. "No, I'm not going to shoot you, unless I have to. If I do, I'll have to place the blame on Louis. I'll have to, you'll be responsible for that."

It was so hard to breathe, Laurel discovered. So hard to make the air come in and go out. If she concentrated on it, she'd keep herself from screaming until Marion made her stop. "I won't walk into the river, or the quicksand for you."

"No," Marion agreed. "You're not like the others, not so easily frightened. But there's one thing..." Holding the gun level, she sidestepped toward the wild cane. "You came in here to snoop around, you couldn't leave it alone. And you met with a tragic accident. Just like Elise—Anne." She drew a wicker hamper out of the bush. "This one," she said quietly, "isn't dead."

She knew, and the fear wrapped around her. Tight. With a long, smooth stick, Marion pushed the hamper closer, then flicked off the lid. Laurel froze, feeling the weightlessness in her head, the ice in her stomach as the snake slithered out. Then another one.

"I didn't want to take any chances," Marion murmured. Setting down the gun, she held the stick with both hands. She looked up at Laurel and smiled. "You've always been terrified of them, haven't you? How well I remember you fainting dead away over a little garter snake. Harmless creatures." She poked her stick at the copperheads until they coiled and hissed. "These aren't."

She wanted to run, to scream. The gun would've been better. But her voice was trapped by the fear, her legs imprisoned by it. As if her consciousness had floated off, she felt her skin spring damp and clammy.

"It won't matter if you don't move," Marion told her easily. "They're angry. I can make them angrier." She prodded them again, nudging them closer to Laurel. One lashed out at the stick, and Marion laughed.

It was the laugh Matt heard. It chilled him to the bone. When he saw them, the snakes were less than a foot away from Laurel, hissing, coiling, enraged, as Marion continued to prod at them. Matt gripped the gun in both hands, prayed, and fired.

"No!" Marion's scream was long and wild as the body of one snake jerked, then lay still. She spun around, stumbling, not even feeling the fangs that sank into her ankle before Matt pulled the trigger again. And she ran, bursting through the wild cane like an animal, hunted.

"Laurel!" Matt had his arms around her, dragging

her against him. "You're all right." Desperate, he closed his mouth over hers. "It's over. I'm getting you out."

"Matthew." The sobs were heaving in her chest and she fought against them. "She's mad. She killed them all—all of them. My God, Matthew. The snakes—"

"Gone," he said quickly, pulling her closer. "They're gone. You're all right."

"For the house," Laurel said into his chest. "Dear God, she killed them for the house. Louis—"

Matt turned his head. Only a few yards away, Louis stood staring at them. There was no color in his face. Only his eyes seemed alive. "She's been bitten," Louis said, so quietly Matt barely heard. "I'll go after her."

"Louis—" Matt looked back at him, finding there was nothing, absolutely nothing, that could be said. "I'm sorry," he murmured.

Nodding, Louis walked into the cane. "Just get Laurel out of here."

"Come on." Matt pressed his lips to her temple. "Can you walk?"

"Yes." The tears were streaming down her face, but she found them a relief. "Yes, I'm all right."

"When I'm sure of that," he said as he held her close by his side, "I'm going to strangle you."

He waited until they were in the clear, then drew Laurel down on the grass. Her head sank to her knees. "I'll be all right in a minute, really. We'll have to call the police."

"Louis took care of it before he left the house. They'll be here any minute. Can you tell me now?"

At first, she kept her head on her knees as she spoke. Gradually, as the horror and the dizziness faded, she lifted it. When she heard the sirens, her hand slipped into Matt's and held tight.

So much confusion—with the police in the swamp, all the questions. A hell of a story, Laurel thought on a bright bubble of hysteria. Though she swallowed it, she gave in to the need to press her face into Matt's shoulder. Just a few more minutes, she told herself. I'll be all right in just a few more minutes. She let Matt lead her back to the house, then drank the brandy he urged on her.

"I'm better," she told him. "Please, stop looking at me as though I were going to dissolve."

He stared at her a minute, then, pulling her into his arms, buried his face in her hair. "Damn you, Laurel." And his voice trembled. "Don't ever do that to me again. I thought I was too late. Another five minutes—"

"No more," she murmured, soothing him. "No more, Matthew. Oh, I love you." She drew his face back. "I love you so much."

She met the aggressive kiss, feeling all the fears drain. He was here, holding her. Nothing else mattered. She lifted a hand to his face as the front door closed. "It's Louis," she said quietly.

He came in slowly. His hair and clothes were streaked and disheveled. His eyes, Laurel saw, were not cold, were not remote, but weary and vulnerable. Without hesitation, she rose and went to him. "Oh, Louis."

He slipped his arms around her, holding on. His face dropped to the top of her head. "We found her. She's—they're taking her to the hospital, but I don't know if... She's delirious," he managed, and drew away. "Did she hurt you, Laurel?"

"No, no, I'm fine."

His gaze shifted to Matt. "I owe you much more than an apology."

"No, you don't."

Louis accepted this with a nod and walked to the brandy. "Are you up to telling me the whole story now?"

He kept his back to them as Laurel related everything Marion had said. Once, when she saw his shoulders shudder, she faltered. He shook his head and gestured for her to finish.

"I need to talk to Susan," he said when Laurel fell silent.

"She's with my grandmother."

Pouring another brandy, Louis nodded. "If she'll see me, I'll go out tomorrow."

"She'll see you, Louis," Laurel murmured. "Please, please, don't take the blame for this."

He turned around slowly. "Do something for me?"

"Of course, you know I will."

"Yes," he said with a faint laugh. "Yes, I know you will. Write your story," he said in a stronger voice. "And make it good. Everything, I want everything out. Maybe then I can live with it."

"Matthew and I'll write it," Laurel told him, and rose to take his hand. "And you'll live with it, Louis. I'm coming back and see that you do." She touched his cheek. "I love you."

With a ghost of a smile, he kissed her. "You're well matched with him, Laurel," he murmured, looking over at Matt. "You're as stubborn as he is. Come back," he agreed, squeezing her hands. "I'm going to need you."

When they walked from the house a few minutes later, Laurel breathed deep. Just the scent of night. The scent of life. "It's beautiful, isn't it?" She threw her face up to the stars. "We'd better call my father, let him know we have one hell of an exclusive on the way."

"Next time you decide to go for one," he said dryly, "remember we're partners. No more solo meets."

"You got it," she agreed. "Let's take your car," she decided, too keyed up to drive. "I can get mine tomorrow. Oh, God, Matthew!" Dropping down inside, she leaned back against the seat. "I never want to go through another night like this, even for a Pulitzer."

"That's what you get for taking off before you fixed dinner." His hands were finally steady, he noted as he turned the key. "Makes a man wonder what kind of wife he's getting."

"A gem," she assured him. "You're getting a gem, Bates." Leaning over, she kissed him. "I haven't thanked you for saving my life."

"No." He smiled, cupping the back of her neck so he could linger over the kiss. "What'd you have in mind?"

"Doing the same for you." She grinned at him. "We're eating out."

* * * * *

#1 *New York Times* bestselling author

LINDA LAEL MILLER

presents the Stone Creek story that started it all…

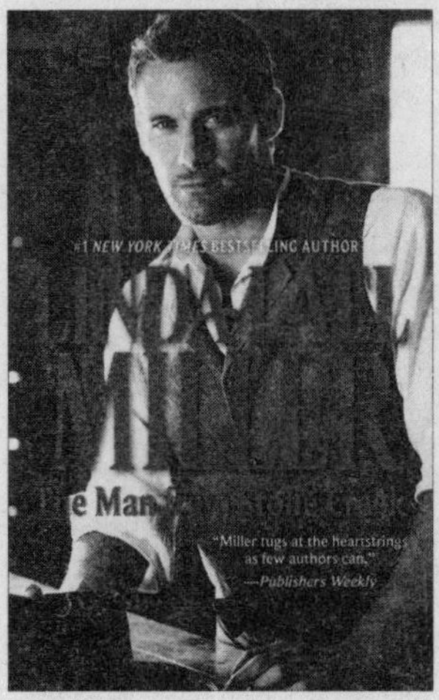

When trouble strikes in Haven, Arizona, Ranger Sam O'Ballivan is determined to sort it out. Badge and gun hidden, he arrives posing as the new schoolteacher, and discovers his first task: bringing the ranchers' children under control. So he starts with a call on Maddie Chancelor, the local postmistress and older sister of a boy in need of discipline.

But far from the spinster Sam expects, Maddie turns out to be a graceful woman whose prim-and-proper demeanor is belied by the fire in her eyes. Working undercover to capture rustlers and train robbers has always kept Sam isolated and his heart firmly in check—until now. But something about the spirited postmistress tempts him to start down a path he swore he'd never travel….

Available wherever books are sold!

Be sure to connect with us at:

Harlequin.com/Newsletters

Facebook.com/HarlequinBooks

Twitter.com/HarlequinBooks

HARLEQUIN® HQN™
www.Harlequin.com

PHLLM721